I0700196

also by fae

SPOOKY BOYS SERIES

Bite Me! (You Know I Like It)

Possess Me! (I Want You To)

Hunt Me! (I Crave the Chase)

There's a Monster in the Woods

King of Hollywood

PNR/OMEGAVERSE

The Devil Takes

CHRISTMAS DADDIES

Let Your Hearts Be Light

You Can Count on Me

If Only in Our Dreams

ALIEN ROMANCE

I'm Not Your Pet!

CONTEMPORARY

Cloudy with a Chance of Bad Decisions

SNOWY SKIES *and* 

puppy eyes

FAE QUIN

SNOWY SKIES
and
puppy eyes

Editing by Angela O'Connell

Cover Art and Interior Artwork by Fae Loves Art

WWW.FAELOVESART.COM

Typography and Interior Formatting by We Got You Covered Book Design

WWW.WEGOTYOUCOVEREDBOOKDESIGN.COM

A full list of content warnings and tropes
is available on my website:

WWW.FAELOVESART.COM

Dedicated to my husband,
for always helping me grow.

For anyone who needs a
little extra Holiday magic.

prologue

JASON

THE FIRST TIME I SAW Joe Milton he was cradling a magpie. *Cradling*, not holding. Hands the size of dinner plates cupped so still, so calmly, he might as well have been a statue. On a sun-drenched Tuesday mid-June, he was the last thing I expected to see when I stepped into the alley behind the grocery store I worked at—and secretly owned. He sat on one of the wooden crates near the dumpsters, all solid muscle and gentility, and I was *full* of questions.

So many questions.

The loudest of which was, *who are you?*

At the time, Joe was nothing but a stranger.

I didn't know his name.

Didn't know where he came from.

Didn't know why he was back here, blocking my way to the trash bins, like it was a totally normal place to be.

But I *burned* with the urge to cross that distance and demand answers from him. I didn't, and I wouldn't—but I *wanted* to. The sudden upsurge of curiosity felt familiar as an old friend.

I'd been the kinda kid who unpicked knots just to see what yarn looked like unravelled. I could always guess, yes. Use my imagination. But nothing was more satisfying than seeing it with my own two eyes.

You'd think I'd have grown out of that, but I hadn't.

My entire life, I'd seen people as lessons. Maybe it was a way to cope with growing up the way I did. Or maybe it was just who I was, broken from the get-go. Internalizing the words my dad had told me once— when I was so little I'd practically been a mirror—and making them my entire personality.

"Your worth is determined by what you give," he'd taught me. "What are *you* worth, Jason?"

I'd asked him why he was leaving. Why he and Mom were going out of town for a charity event when all I'd wanted was for them to stay. Just once. Just once, I wanted to spend Christmas Eve like the families I saw on TV.

Instead, I'd gotten emotionally eviscerated.

You know, classic Dad stuff.

His answer snapped me to attention. Had filled the blank journal of who I was in red ink. I'd decided right then and there that I'd be like him. I wouldn't complain. I'd do what I was meant to. I'd help people, and my life would be worth something. *I* would be *worth* something.

And if I was…if I was useful then maybe, *just maybe,* I wouldn't have to always be alone.

It wasn't until later that I'd realized his and mother's generosity was surface level. They cared about the praise they received more than the people they helped.

I didn't want to be that way.

And yet...Dad's words had altered me.

I was used to cold rooms, cold people. People who wanted me for my money, my connections. People who wanted nothing to do with me because of those same things.

From the day I'd made it home, Belleville had felt like an alternate dimension. People gave because they were kind. Not because they wanted recognition. I'd wanted nothing more than to fit in.

When my marriage ended, rather than being subject to cruel words, my porch was covered in casseroles.

And that changed me, too.

I'd done everything I could to hide that part of myself, terrified my peaceful little paradise wouldn't accept me for who I was, and where I came from.

For decades, I'd made it my mission to be useful. The townies had taught me how to be a "real" person, how to care about people, how to *help* people. What it meant to be part of a community.

And though my love for them had never turned stagnant, I had.

Nothing rocked my foundation.

And the projects that had once meant so much to me didn't fill the silence in my head anymore. I was exhausted. The days dragged on, and I dragged on with them.

I'd sunk into a sort of daze, hibernating in my day-to-day life.

Searching for the spark I'd once had.

For something...*new*.

And here he was.

Right in front of me.

The enigma I'd been waiting for. A man who attracted wildlife like a beefy, manly version of Snow White. Turning boring alleys into fairy tales. Making my dull days bright—even if he didn't know it.

I sucked in a breath, a smile lighting up my face as I hungrily took him in.

Clothing could tell you a lot about a person.

Which was why I was very particular about my own. Why I let my sneakers get ratty. Why I never bought fabric that screamed anything other than "normal". No cashmere or silk for me, no siree. Just the basics. Sweaters, t-shirts, jeans, and khakis that didn't totally clash with my work apron or my hair.

Everything about how I presented myself was carefully constructed.

Other people did that too, even if they didn't realize it.

Clothing would've been the first thing I noticed about my stranger if he hadn't literally been holding a goddamn bird in his hands—seriously. That took the cake, I feel, for obvious reasons. Now that I'd gotten over the bird thing—I mean, *kinda* gotten over the bird thing—I *did* notice what he was wearing.

The stranger had overalls on.

Work boots.

A long-sleeve white t-shirt that clung to every dip and cranny of his impressive build. There were twigs in his hair. A smudge of dirt on his chin. Frown lines at the corners of his mouth. Creases that made him appear world-weary when his youth should've offered him grace.

A working man.

That's what he was.

What occupation? I had no idea. A farm, maybe. The affinity for animals made me think he was used to nature.

Splotches of sunlight crept down the cobblestone street, painting the stranger's knees, his nose, the thick crop of cornsilk blond hair atop his head. Turning him gold where he wasn't golden. Carved from marble like a farm boy Adonis. Gilded to last.

I'd always been good at reading people.

One glance was usually all it took.

As my attention shifted from his clothes to his face, there was no denying that. He wasn't layers so much as he was a brick wall of a man. And his lips, his eyebrows, his *expression* overall told me nothing.

His eyes, though?

Christ.

As the shadows lifted from his brow and I ducked my head to see better, the stranger's gaze came into focus. He was staring down at the bird, barely blinking he was so enraptured.

There was this…*wondrous* sort of light in his eyes.

The kind of light that made me certain—stranger or not—that bird was in safe hands. The door swung shut behind me with a loud thud. I grimaced, guilt filling me as the bird took flight.

White and black feathers cut through dust motes, casting shadows through the air as the bird soared high, high, high and away. The stranger's head tipped back. He watched till the very last second.

Then he turned to regard me.

A shiver coursed through my body, my hands spasming on the boxes I'd brought back here to toss in the recycling bin. For a moment, we simply looked at one another. There was an annoyed tick to the stranger's brow that hadn't been there before.

Those stormy eyes glared into mine, and the rest of the world ceased to exist at all.

"What's your name?" I couldn't help but ask, still juggling the box. He huffed, then turned back to the empty cerulean sky like I wasn't there at all. "You must be new in town!" I tried again, taking a step forward. "I've never seen you before. Where'd you move from? I'm assuming from the twigs in your hair that you've been hard at work. What brings you to my humble alleyway? The bird? I'd assume so. Given the fact I just caught you with it."

Again, he ignored me.

I took another step, acting like I was heading for the recycling bin and not him. Which, technically, could be true—except that it wasn't. And the only thing on my mind was getting an answer to at least one of my questions.

"I'm Jason," I introduced myself, continuing to cross the distance between us. I moved slowly, the same way he had with the bird, worried I'd scare him off. "I work at the grocery store. And I—" A few more steps and I'd be at the bin. He still hadn't looked at me. "Know pretty much everything there is to know about this town and the people in it. So, if you ever need help, just let me kn—"

"*I don't need help,*" the man cut me off.

His voice was quiet, rough—and yet…oddly melodic. It made me trip a little, which was seriously embarrassing. I blamed the uneven pavement. Yep. Totally was not tripping because he sounded like honey spread over warm toast.

"Sure you do!" I chirped, finally reaching the dumpster and tossing my boxes inside. I twisted to look at him. My heart was pounding. He was even bigger up close. And…honest to god, he smelled like sunshine.

Sunshine and apples.

I barely resisted the urge to lean in and sniff.

The look he was giving me was genuinely offended. Even the *suggestion* he might need my help made his eyes blaze.

"Everyone needs help sometimes," I told him, poking the metaphorical bear.

"*Not me. I can take care of myself.*" Tall-blond-and-beefy rose to his full height, looming over me, his shadow casting me in darkness. He didn't say the words like they were a challenge—but hell, I couldn't stop myself from taking them like one.

The gauntlet had just been thrown.

"*When* you do—" I started, maybe a little cockily, this little thrill running through me as his nostrils flared in response. "And you change your mind—" Liquid quick, he side-stepped around me like I was diseased. He was surprisingly agile for a man of his size, and I nearly tripped again turning to watch as he darted toward the mouth of the alley as fast as he could without outright sprinting.

"You know where to find me!" I hollered at his retreating back, both intrigued and amused by the fact that he'd literally sprinted away from me. Quicker than I could blink, the stranger disappeared around the corner like the bird had fled into the sky.

"Tough crowd," I sighed, though there was no one to hear.

For a moment, I waited to see if he'd come back, but he didn't.

I wasn't surprised, given how fast he'd run off. Nor was I disappointed. I had no doubt I'd be seeing more of Belleville's newest addition soon enough.

While I headed back inside the building, I couldn't help but think of feathers, of a square jaw, of thick, gentle, tan hands. Of sunshine and apples. Of the mystery I'd uncovered, the stranger I'd met, and the gauntlet he'd unknowingly thrown my way.

Something told me this man was going to teach me the greatest lesson of all.

I grinned.

one

JASON

IN HINDSIGHT, I PROBABLY SHOULD'VE realized I had a crush, but I didn't. In my defense, I don't think I'd ever *actually* had one before. Never had that flutter in my belly. That warmth in my chest. That overwhelming bubble of need to simply *see* someone—for them to look my way. I was forty-three, for god's sake, I just…assumed crushes were something else. Something less, skin-itchy, dry-mouthy.

I figured this was what it always was, just amplified because of the way we'd met.

At first, I chalked it up to the kinda overall excitement I always felt when I had a new challenge. And boy-oh-boy was Mr. Runs a Lot a challenge.

He was stubborn, I could tell. But he wasn't the only new Bellevillian who had been allergic to my help, and eventually, everyone succumbed to the magic this town held.

I just had to keep pushing, and he'd get there too. He just...had to come into the store first. And then boom—I'd get him.

I always did.

New friend unlocked, just like that.

Newcomers were my favorite.

I lived for the thrill of picking them apart. Using the rumor mill of our small, busy town to discover where they came from, who they were, what they did for a living. Little quirks, bad habits, the lovely puzzle pieces that made up the eclectic mix of townies I called my family.

But more than that, I loved to show people what Belleville had shown me. That this place was special. These *people* were special.

No other newcomer had ever made my belly flip the way it did when my stranger finally walked through the sliding door at the front of the grocery shop for the first time, all golden hair and surly expression. Nor had anyone ever been so...*tricky* to get to know.

Apparently, bird-whisperer-guy was just as determined to avoid me as I was to pursue him.

Case in point: the fact that the moment he had finished shopping, he glanced around the store to locate me, then actively *dodged* me—and used Madison's register instead of mine. Deliberately avoiding me like he was terrified I was going to sniff out all his secrets like a goddamn bloodhound.

He was fun.

Contrary.

I grinned and waved, just to tease him. He pretended like he didn't notice me—badly, because he obviously did. His flush betrayed him. When he paid for his giant pile of TV dinners and bolted out the door, grocery bags thumping against his legs, that flutter in my belly exploded.

Like he thought he was James Bond, I stared through the glass as my newest-future-buddy threw everything he'd purchased into the bed of his faded blue pickup truck. Seconds later, he hauled ass into the front seat and drove away as quickly as possible.

"What did you do?" Madison asked with a put-upon sigh, like Joe bolting was my fault. I resented that—even though it was.

"Nothing," I said, still grinning. "Nothing at all."

"Why do I not believe you?" She popped her cinnamon gum my way. I hated when she did that.

"Gross."

"I need coffee to deal with your bullshit this early in the morning," Madison informed me.

"Ditto," I replied before sticking my tongue out at her like I was fifteen and not pushing forty-three.

I told myself it didn't sting when Joe walked out the door. But even I knew that was a lie.

A week later, after the second episode of farmboy-Adonis's run-and-ride, I came up with a solution. I'd given Madison a little poke and some monetary incentive to "stock the shelves" the third time he came in, determined to get him to actually acknowledge me.

I'll crack him today, I promised myself. Being overly friendly had never steered me wrong before. He needed a little more time for his guard to drop.

He was just shy last time…

And the time before.

And the time before that.

And—

You know what? It didn't matter.

To say Blond-and-Beefy was displeased when the next time he came in he discovered I was the only one manning the registers would be the understatement of the century.

He stood at the end of the bread aisle, eyeing the conveyor belt like it was on fire.

I patted it invitingly, knowing I'd already won.

He had no choice.

We were the only store in town that sold TV dinners. I wasn't judging. I wasn't any better. Ninety percent of what I consumed was takeout of some sort. Or that Weight-Lookers thing I'd subscribed to and kept forgetting to cancel. Or casseroles people gave me after I'd assisted them in one way or another.

Mr. Reluctant dragged his feet as he walked toward me, basket of—you guessed it—more TV dinners clutched to his chest.

The fizzle in my stomach was back. Nervous energy, the strong desire to make him acknowledge me—rely on me—stealing my breath.

He didn't, though. He kept his eyes on the whirring black belt, never once glancing up. Powering through the interaction in the most painful way possible for both of us.

Look at me.

I almost wanted to snap my teeth at him to make him jump.

I didn't, though.

I had a mission today.

Madison knew Beefy-boy's name, apparently, and she was lording that information over me. She would've told me if I asked. But—for some strange reason, I wanted the information to come straight from him. Even if I had to trick it out of him.

"Hey," I said cheerily, the same way I greeted everyone who shopped here. "How are you today?" And then, when he didn't reply, I played my wild card. "How's the orchard?"

He outright dropped the last TV dinner in his grip, but caught it before it could fall to the floor. His eyes snapped to my face, all wide-eyed confusion, like he thought I was a fucking witch.

I grinned.

"How did you—"

"I have my ways." I tapped the side of my nose, wiggling my eyebrows at him. Truth be told, I was a little frustrated I'd learned about the farm he'd bought from someone other than him. Not too annoyed, though, because my comment about it had thrown him off. He didn't think twice about giving me his credit card when I held a hand out for it instead of swiping it through the machine like usual.

With everything bagged, I glanced at his card aaaand *bingo*.

Joe Milton.

It was a nice name.

It suited him.

Strong. Solid. Straight to the point.

A thrill ran through me, my thumb lingering on the raised letters before I handed it back to him.

"Joe Milton," I hummed. Our fingers brushed, and his cheeks went fiery red again as he shoved his card back into his wallet—one of those weird metal things I'd only ever seen outdoorsy people use. "Nice name."

"What?" He said, confused. "How—"

"Your card," I practically purred.

"Oh." Joe's eyes narrowed at his wallet like it'd betrayed him.

Then, liquid-quick, before I could trick anything else out of him, Joe grabbed his groceries and stalked out the door. While he launched himself inside his truck, I performed a victory dance. Unluckily for me, Madison caught the tail-end of said strutting. She paused, hovering in the bread aisle where Joe had been only a few seconds prior.

His departure stung even more this time. I tried to ignore it, but there was this…itch beneath my skin.

"Stop judging me," I complained with a huff.

"Buy me a coffee machine and I will," she retorted.

The next few times I saw Joe, I didn't pull any tricks. Even though I wanted to. I figured poking…possibly wasn't the best way to get him to like me. He was surly when I spoke to him, pale brow furrowed, dark blue eyes guarded. When I waved goodbye and wished him a good day, as friendly as ever, his shoulders climbed all the way to his ears.

He stared at me like he didn't understand me.

It made me feel bare in a way I hadn't since I'd moved here and adopted the persona that'd given my life value.

That should've warned me off. Should've made me take a step back and reevaluate. However, his prickliness where I was concerned simply made me more determined to get him to accept me.

The more he scowled, the more chipper I became.

My friendliness was a weapon, and I knew exactly how to yield it.

At least…I thought I did.

And when that didn't work on its own, I figured maybe proving my usefulness might?

"You know, if you're looking for apple buyers, I know of some interested parties," I offered after a few visits with no incident. I wanted his guard down. At least enough to listen. It was a far-too-hot day in July, and Joe was shuffling an armful of TV dinners onto the conveyor belt like usual.

I'd sent Madison to the back with promises of more toppings for the new "coffee" station we'd just installed in the break room.

So it was just us.

Joe glared at me.

He didn't say anything.

That was fine. I had enough words for both of us, and I'd been practicing this pitch in the mirror for over a week. Okay, and also maybe in front of Madison—and Mary, my ex-wife turned best friend—and her husband, Daniel. Oh, and Marybeth, my god-niece.

"Your harvest is coming up," I began. "Which means you'll be looking for ways to make a profit. I know for a fact that Mr. Peterson at the orchard is looking for a supplier for his fruit wine. The grocery store is always hoping for more local produce to stock. And! Baxter, down at the bakery, would definitely be interested in buying apples from you, too. I could talk to them for you? Set something up. Help you meet them—"

I'd already talked to Mr. Peterson, but he didn't need to know that.

"No thanks," Joe said gruffly. I was surprised he spoke at all.

I frowned at him.

It was probably the first time I'd done that. "Joe—"

"I told you, I don't need your help. And I don't." Joe slapped his card on the counter, glaring at me. "I can do this by myself."

"No one said you couldn't." I took the card, lingering a little as I swiped it through. "Only that it's easier if you don't." Since that day when I'd taken it to read his name, he'd always done that—handed me the card. I liked the way our fingers brushed, so I never complained, even if it did make Madison give me the side-eye every time.

At least when she witnessed it, loitering in the aisles rather than departing to her precious espresso machine.

"Belleville's a special place. You've been here a month max. Maybe you don't know that we…the people here—the Bellevillians—like to look out for one another. And I just want to—"

Joe was stomping toward the door before I could even finish my sentence. His bags of groceries beat against his thick thighs as he moved. The door slid shut after him, and I realized…maybe belatedly…that pushing him was not an effective friendship tactic.

I sighed, dragging my hands up into my hair.

"Maybe you shouldn't have poked him so much earlier," Madison said wisely. She made this godawful slurping sound as she sucked through the straw on her tumbler. I'd gotten it for her for Christmas last year. This red and green atrocity that I'd thought she'd hate-love.

I was right.

Just like she was right.

"I might need a new approach," I admitted. I hadn't been prepared for how much it would hurt to be rejected this time around. The first offer— in the alley—had been one thing. We hadn't talked before. Didn't know each other at all. And now I was genuinely trying to help and…fuck. Well.

Maybe we still didn't know each other.

Maybe that was the problem.

"You think?" Madison sucked on her straw again as she took her spot at the register. She turned around and handed me a list. A fucking list. Of creamers and flavor additives and…marshmallows?

I pulled up a website to purchase them on my phone. We didn't carry the kind of fancy shit she was interested in at the store, so that meant extra work on my end to get it imported.

I didn't mind a little extra work.

two

JASON

"I THINK WE GOT OFF on the wrong foot," I said one day at the beginning of August. Joe had been avoiding me like the plague since I brought up the vineyard contract.

I'd given him time to cool down. And now—maybe, I could convince him to listen.

I'd barely seen him all month—which was a difficult feat to pull off considering how small Belleville was, where I worked, and the fact that he had to eat.

He grunted, slammed his TV dinners onto the conveyor belt, and crossed his arms. The machine whirred, groceries moving almost comically slowly in my direction. I wished I could say I planned that, just to prolong this conversation, but it was simply technology being a dick to me, like it often was.

Beneath the counter, I made a hand signal.

A gaggle of twelve-year-old girls left the bread aisle where I'd had them stationed and stormed toward the front door. Like the tiny professionals they were, they set up their homemade cookie stand in record time, effectively barricading Joe's exit.

Joe's eyes darted over to them, his brow knitting with confusion.

"Kids," I called, just for show. "You're blocking the entrance—"

"Sorry, Mr. Harker," Olivia said, just like we'd rehearsed. She had one canine tooth that was shorter than the other, and freckles across the bridge of her nose. Of the group, she was by far the best actor, which was *why* she had been chosen for the very important role of spokesperson.

"We'll move over," Olivia added. Then, as slowly as physically possible, the girls began to pack up. Buying me time.

"Kids," I sighed conversationally. "Gotta love them. While you're here, I just wanted to say that I'm sorry I—" I started, turning toward him.

He was gone.

I frowned, twisting to see him approaching the cluster of little girls like the big lumbering bear that he was. Oh god. I genuinely had no idea what to expect. Was he going to tell them off? Offer to help?

My plan had gone awry.

I didn't know if they were going to get "grouchy Joe" or "baby bird Joe".

"How much're you selling these for?" he asked, voice so quiet I could barely hear it even though I'd crept behind him for damage control. I paused, eyebrows shooting up. The girls glanced between each other, then at me over his shoulder, then back at him.

"Five bucks," one said, scooting a plastic-covered sheet of pumpkin cookies toward him. Joe nodded and fished a five-dollar bill out of his back pocket. He passed it to Olivia, who looked down at it with a frankly wicked grin. She handed him his plate of cookies.

Like the traitors they were, the twelve-year-olds began to pack up even quicker.

Quick enough that Joe was able to wiggle past them out the front door.

I sighed, half tempted to chase after him, though at that point, I figured it was a lost cause. I'd have to try again another day.

The squirming in my chest expanded tenfold. Finding out Joe was great with kids was not good for my mental health. And I just…god. He was a really nice guy, wasn't he?

He obviously was.

Gentle, kind.

So, why wouldn't he let me in? What was it about me that was so…confusing to him?

"I'm taking this," I told Olivia, snagging a tray of cookies. "For emotional support." The girls giggled. "Tell your Scout leader her kiddos are all sell-outs." They chittered some more. I slapped a twenty-dollar bill on the table, muttering all the way back to my register.

By the time they came through my line, spending the twenty I'd given them on a plethora of snacks, I'd forgiven their treachery.

I wasn't any closer to a solution, and that…well.

That stung even more than Joe's rapid departures did.

I simply couldn't accept that he didn't want to talk to me. That he could dislike me so much, he sabotaged himself. That he could be so kind, so good, and yet…be uncomfortable around me.

Why?

I was a lover, not a fighter. I knew better than to chase things that weren't meant to be. I accepted people as they were. Or…I tried. So what was it about Joe that made me so…so… God.

He was different.

I couldn't let this go, and I didn't know why.

Maybe what I lacked was information.

Over the course of the next month, I gathered a few tidbits of intel from Joe. Like…the fact that he was from Ohio originally.

That'd been hard won.

"Iowa, Montana, Michigan, Minnesota, Maryland—" I listed off as he set his TV dinners down. They whirred toward me slowly. He sighed, brow furrowed.

"What?"

"I'm just guessing where you're from," I told him. "Maine, Georgia, Arkansas, Nebraska, California, Idaho, Washington—"

"Ohio," Joe said, just to get me to stop.

"Columbus?" I perked up. "Or Cleveland?" He huffed in annoyance.

"No."

"What about—"

"You're not going to know the name of where I'm from," Joe informed me. "It's barely on the map." Ah. A small town then. That made…a weird amount of sense.

Just another thing we had in common. Choosing to live in small towns.

The next time I saw Joe, I learned his age.

"Thirty-five."

"What?" Joe blinked at me. This time, when he set his food down on the conveyor belt, he didn't do it quite as angrily.

"Thirty-three. Twenty-nine. Twenty-six. Twenty-two."

"What are you doing this time?" he lamented.

"Thirty-nine," I said as I finished scanning his items.

He figured it out soon enough.

"I'm not thirty-nine," Joe glared at me. "Do I *look* thirty-nine?"

"No."

"Then why did you guess it?" Once more, he was staring at me like he didn't understand me.

I grinned. His nostrils flared. He jabbed his card at me, and I swiped it through the machine. Joe grabbed his bags and stormed toward the door. I conceded defeat for now—at least, until he paused, right as the door opened.

"Twenty-eight," he confessed, shoulders up by his ears again. And then he was gone.

That was about all I learned about Joe directly from him. Which left me breaking my self-imposed rules and hunting for knowledge elsewhere. Hunting for reasons he was refusing my advice, even though it had only been given to help him.

I'd tried to convince the farm laborer who worked with Joe on his orchard—a grizzled older man named Patrick, with white hair and enough wrinkles to form an army—to give me more information, but he'd refused.

Apparently, Joe had been less than pleased when he realized the only reason I'd known about his apple orchard was because of Patrick.

Patrick liked to believe he was separate from Belleville's rumor mill.

In reality, he was the chattiest Cathy there was—at least, when his guard was down. He had a group chat with all the other farmers, and they had their own ecosystem of drama.

"You're gonna get me in trouble again," he chided me with a laugh as I tried to convince him to tell me what Joe was like when he wasn't prickly as all hell.

Patrick's basket of peaches moved gradually down the belt toward us.

"Come on," I whined. "Please? I just—"

"He's as closed-lipped with me as he is with you," Patrick informed me. "Boy's got it in his head, maybe, that he's gotta do everything on his own."

I sighed. I'd gathered that much. It wasn't like it was new information, but at least I now knew I wasn't the only person Joe had his guard up around.

"I just want to help him," I told him. "It's been months since he moved in. The previous farmer had contracts with local businesses. What's he going to do with his harvest if he's not going to sell it? I get being prideful, but this is going to *hurt* him."

"I know." Patrick pulled out his wallet. "He knows. But that doesn't mean he's going to listen." He paid, and I packed up his fruit for him as neatly as I could.

"It's good advice!"

"It is," Patrick nodded. "But he's stubborn as a mule."

I was pushing again, like I'd told myself I wouldn't.

Uneasy at the thought that Joe was going to struggle out of a twisted sense of pride.

There was this weird feeling in my goddamn bones that told me if I could…if I could get Joe to look at me. To…to let me in, it would— God.

I didn't even know what it would be.

Didn't have a name for the feeling thoughts of him inspired. I thought about him all the time. Thought about him when I shouldn't. Couldn't shake the idea that I needed him in my life. That he needed me too.

Call it childhood trauma, but I just…

"Fine," I sighed, scrubbing a hand over my face. "I won't bring it up again."

"Probably a good plan," Patrick said. "He'll come around. He's clever. He'll figure it out on his own."

A week later, when Mr. Peterson, the owner of the vineyard, was in shopping, he informed me that he'd signed a contract with Joe.

I'd been at the bookstore for hours before my shift even started, helping Leanne restock because her part-timer had quit unexpectedly.

I was exhausted.

But…I perked right back up at the mention of my favorite mystery.

Maybe Joe didn't hate me enough to completely ignore my advice?

I couldn't help but feel proud of him then, positively beaming at Mr. Peterson as I nodded along. Baxter had already signed a contract with Joe—which I found out when I was over at the bakery buying my comfort loaf of pumpkin bread before returning to my too quiet, too empty house after a long day of meddling.

Apparently, Joe was Baxter's cousin.

Which…I mean, I probably should've guessed—because of the hair. They shared the same shade of honey blond. The kind of golden you hardly saw out in the wild, it was so rare.

The fact that Joe had been at the bakery, too, meant…he was working his way through the list I'd given him. Or not? I didn't want to assume he was specifically targeting all the people I'd told him about.

That'd be presumptuous.

A secret part of me could only hope that meant the grocery store was next on his list.

My wishes kind of came true the next day when Joe came by, a basket full of apples in his arms, and his eyebrows so low his eyes were shadows.

"Good morning, Joe!" I greeted like I always did. Madison rolled her eyes and wandered into the back without having to be told. Joe watched her go, and for the first time since we'd repeated this little pattern, he looked relieved.

Which was odd.

On top of the apples.

Already, I could feel excitement buzzing beneath my skin as he headed directly toward me for the first time since we'd met. His eyebrows twitched. He set the apples down in front of me. Their glossy red surfaces were lumpy and misshapen, a byproduct of the farm being abandoned for a year or so before he and Patrick had gotten it up and running again, probably.

I didn't know much about farming, but I assumed lack of maintenance was a bad thing.

The apples didn't look bad, though.

In fact, they looked delicious.

"These are for you," Joe said, tone clipped and wary.

I was puzzled but pleased. "For the store?" I said, already eager to get this show on the road.

"What?" Joe blinked. "No."

"No?" I echoed, equally confused. "Sorry—what?"

"These are to thank you. For…" Joe's cheeks went pink. "Putting in a good word for me." My heart skipped a beat. "I was the one who did the heavy lifting," he was quick to reiterate. "But…when I talked to Mr. Peterson, he told me you'd already sold him on me—and that…made it…easier." Joe looked nearly pained, like this sorta social interaction was quite literally bleeding him out.

I was doing victory laps in my head. Strutting around like a goddamn rooster. Celebrating. This was progress. This was *major* progress. Maybe Joe was just a slow-burn kind of guy? Maybe he—

"You're very welcome," I said, putting him out of his misery. I grabbed an apple, tossing it in the air and catching it. The light glinted off its surface, and I couldn't help the little thrill I felt at the thought that this was a gift from Joe. "Like I said before, I love helping, and if you ever need—"

"I'm good." Joe took a step back like he was about to leave.

"Wait—" I held a hand out. "What about…" I bent over, digging around in my drawer for the paperwork I had all the new vendors fill out. "While I appreciate the present, and believe me, I do—these apples are gorgeous." Joe shuffled his big feet, a pleased little twitch to his lips that he quickly schooled into a flat line before it could form a smile. "Why don't you let me sell them? I'm the last one on your list."

Apparently, there *was* a list, because Joe gave me that look again—like he thought I was a fucking wizard. Reading his mind.

He was a list maker. I could relate. I *loved* lists. Ha! See?! We had another thing in common already.

"Let me sell these," I offered. "That's the best way to thank me."

He gave me that baffled look again, like he didn't understand me in the slightest.

And now it was time for me to bullshit again. Though…it didn't really feel like bullshit.

"My goal in life is to help as many of my fellow Bellevillians as possible," I informed him. "I actively hunt out contracts with local vendors, including farmers such as yourself. I would be genuinely so much happier if everything in this store came from someone who lived here. Which…I know is not plausible. But—"

Joe wavered, his hackles falling away. "That's…nice of you." He said this, like it was only now occurring to him that everything I did, I did to be nice.

A little voice in the back of my head reminded me that that wasn't the only reason I did nice things.

You're just like your parents, it warned me.

I shook away the unpleasant thought.

"You'd be doing me a favor," I promised him, pushing the paper toward him. "Then I don't have to buy from some random dude I don't know— and instead, I can upsell 'Joe's Delicious Galas'."

He mulled things over for a moment, but apparently what I'd said worked. Because Joe signed the contract, just like that.

And I was officially one of his vendors.

"Pleasure doing business with you!" I called at his back as he headed out the door and to his pickup truck. It was full of apples. The first of the season, and I had no doubt he was making his rounds dropping them off. Judging by how full it was, I could only assume he'd stopped here first.

That should not have made me as happy as it did.

I was just trying to help him.

And now I had.

Not that he'd outright accepted it, but still.

I hoped that in time, I'd be able to get Joe to *actually* like me. But until then, my bushel of apples and the contract I'd fought tooth and nail for were a pretty good start.

September came with a vengeance. The chill crept up on us, dotted between days of relentless sun. I never knew if it was a jacket day or a tank-top day. Not that I ever wore tank tops. Madison did, though. And any time she predicted the weather wrong, she'd swear up a storm and huff at me like it was my fault.

Joe didn't run from me the way he had before. He was wary, yes. But we'd made some progress. And each week he came by with more apples for me to restock, and I bit my tongue—trying out *actual* patience for once to see if it served me better than pushing had. I wanted another glimpse of that gentle, soft man I'd seen that day in the alley so badly I ached.

Thus far…the closest I'd gotten was Joe with the Scouts and their cookies.

It wasn't enough.

I found myself hungrier with every day that passed. Hunting for glimpses of Joe wherever I went. But he mostly kept to himself. Didn't integrate into our way of life. Didn't participate in the picnic-fair, a delightful pop-up hosted in the town square. Didn't mingle with the townspeople. Stayed for days and days out on his farm, only ever coming into town to drop off apples, or refill his fridge with more cardboard-food.

Always with that serious look on his face.

Still prickly, but slightly less so.

His guard up.

Every time I thought of Joe, this…protective instinct welled up inside me, so strong I could hardly ignore it. I tried. But…to no avail. I asked about him everywhere. I learned nothing. Wore my heart on my sleeve like an idiot. Told everyone it was because I wanted to care for our newest transplant, when in reality I just…

I just *wanted*.

At the end of September, things changed.

The tripping happened.

Tripping over my tongue when Joe walked through the front door. Tripping over my own heartbeat when I realized he was wearing those overalls again, sweaty this time—the ones he'd been wearing that day in the sun when I'd seen a piece of his bare heart without his permission.

They hugged his ass and made his pecs look especially, ah, *nice*.

Nice.

Just like I wanted him to think I was.

Because nice came first.

And as a few more weeks passed, gorgeous.

And a few more days?

Fucking *bitable*.

In a totally platonic, outside perspective kinda way.

Good for him. Being catnip for the ladies like that.

Hell, if I'd been twenty years younger, I would've wished I looked like that. All brawny, sun-soaked muscle. I told myself it was jealousy. Me, looking at a young stud and thinking, *ah if only*.

But as my tripping-fluttering-sputtering continued, the denial in my mind began to ebb. Summer morphed into fall quicker than I could blink. I knew, not because of the changing of the leaves, but because Joe started wearing *flannel*. A dusty pale blue most days, that made his eyes look like oceans.

My eyes lingered on his in a totally-not-at-all-gay-way. Lingered as he headed to the back of the store to the produce stand to restock his apples. Lingered on his shoulders, on his hips, on the way he walked, all quiet confidence.

Lingered on his ass.

Because *damn*.

It was just curiosity.

Just knot unpicking.

Just wanting him to look back at me.

Desperate not to experience another Chauncey. Another person who didn't want to be my friend.

Nothing more.

Definitely not.

"God, you're down bad," Madison said after liberally slurping up another cup of coffee. She was on her third tumbler of the day. That couldn't be healthy—but I didn't say anything. She wouldn't listen, even if I did. Her comment startled me out of yet another Joe Milton-induced space-out session.

Tearing my eyes away from his ass, I eloquently said, "Huh?"

Madison's voice was quiet. Quiet enough, there was no way we'd be overheard. And still, my cheeks went hot as her words actually processed. Hot because *denial*, of course. *What the hell was she talking about? Down bad? For Joe? Ha!*

He was my little duckling. My newest, youngest, cutest little duckling. I was trying to…to guide him. To be his friend. To prove to him that I wasn't the evil gremlin he thought I was. Not—

"You're down bad for Joe," Madison clarified.

"And by *down bad* you mean—" I wheedled, attempting to buy myself time to figure out how to politely tell her that she was way off base. "That I am mentoring the heck out of him? Helping him? Showing him the ways of our tiny little oasis—"

"No." Madison said the word *no* like it was a paragraph, not a word. "By *down bad* I mean that you're down bad." She rolled her eyes at me like I was a total idiot. "Don't pretend you don't know what that means," she pointed out before she stomped off to the stock room to refill her tumbler for a fourth time.

Her coffee station was seriously pimped out now. I'd purchased her everything she'd asked for in exchange for her aid and silence.

Apparently, I hadn't bought her enough.

But…I had to be careful not to expose myself or my true financial situation. Money changed people. That was the lesson my childhood friend, Chauncey, had taught me. It changed people. Its lack, its surplus. It didn't matter.

The last thing I needed was people in town treating me differently because they found out that I was loaded.

I used my secret hoard of wealth to assist where I could, but always anonymously. Always through the guise of charities I'd "discovered." Never as me.

Never.

As much as my dad's words about "worth" had affected me, I didn't want to be like them. Didn't want thank-yous or accolades. I wasn't performing. Didn't help people because I wanted to be praised for it. Maybe I just…maybe I just wanted to matter.

There was a ringing in my ears as I processed what Madison had been implying. Her words should not have made as much sense as they did.

Because they were *wrong*.

She was wrong.

Obviously.

For so many reasons. Number one being: I had never ever ever been interested in a man before. Never once looked at another guy and thought, "hell yeah, that's the ticket."

And yet…

No.

No!

That *wasn't* what this was. Madison was wrong. She *had* to be wrong. I mean? Joe was…*Joe*.

No.

…No.

If I were into men, I would've noticed by now.

Wouldn't I?

A little voice in the back of my mind reminded me that I hadn't ever been interested in anyone before. Not really. So finding Joe's ass interesting was…a bit revolutionary. And even more unlikely.

I glared at the break room where Madison had disappeared, annoyed she'd managed to get into my head. I resolved myself not to spoil her anymore, black mail or not. But even I knew that was bound to last no time at all.

Her dad had walked out on her when she was sixteen. I'd caught her shoplifting a few months later. I offered her a job, and the rest was history.

Ever since, I'd made it my mission to support her and her mother wherever I could. There was no way I was going to deny her anything. Not when I got the feeling she saw me as somewhat of an annoying surrogate father-figure.

Which also meant I wasn't going to freak out on her after what she'd said, no matter how wrong it was.

Still in denial, I tapped my fingers on the counter, mind a million miles away.

Liking a man's biceps did not make a person gay.

Look at all the men who enjoyed watching superhero movies!

Totally straight men.

Muscles were pretty. *Everyone* liked them. Okay, maybe that wasn't true. I backtracked. At least a good portion of people liked muscles. I just so happened to be one of them. That didn't mean I wanted to fuck every person who had them.

Maybe I *did* stare at Joe more than was normal, but—in my defense—Joe was hot!

That was a fact.

I'd have to be blind not to ogle him a *little*. Eye candy was eye candy.

I mean…okay. *Yes.* Maybe I ogled him a bit more than a *little*. I was allowed to ogle people if I wanted to. It wasn't like it was a crime.

And it didn't mean anything deeper than having an appreciation for things that were beautiful.

Screw Madison.

Joe had apparently finished stocking his apples because he came over to the register and interrupted me mid-mental rant. He paused, eyeing me with what I could only describe as wary curiosity. That was a new look on him.

"Are you o—" he started, but I cut him off. Today was not the day for him to exercise empathy. Nope. Not when I was trying to tell myself I'd only been ogling his ass because it was aesthetically pleasing.

"Here's your check," I said—totally normally. I slapped said check onto the register. I didn't even put it in his hand like I wanted to, because then our skin would touch, and even though I usually lived for those little touches, at that moment, I couldn't handle it.

Not because I was into him.

But because…well…*whatever.*

It didn't matter why.

Joe was paid.

Joe could go now.

I was not "down bad" for Joe.

"Bye!" I said, maybe a little less friendly than usual. Joe blinked. He cocked his head to the side, watching me like he always did. Like I was unpredictable, and he didn't know what to do with me.

As if I'd be attracted to that.

And his…many…extremes.

I definitely did *not* find all of said emotions fascinating. Or want to memorize each one of the faces he made. Or desperately want him to drop his guard so I could see *more.* Nope.

I ignored the part of me that thought having a crush on Joe would explain why I couldn't seem to leave him alone.

"See you next week?" Joe asked, surprising me again when he didn't immediately duck out the door like I was bubonic. Of course, today of all days, he decided to look at me. I sighed, pinching the bridge of my nose.

"Same time next week should be great."

He nodded, still hovering, big body held perfectly still. And then he left, like he always did. And this time, I didn't even look at his ass once.

Okay.

Maybe I did.

But Madison wasn't around to shame me for it.

God, this was a nightmare.

three

JOE

GOD, THIS WAS A NIGHTMARE.

Like most horror movies began—I'm guessing, seeing as I'd never watched one—I'd just gotten off the phone with my mother. Mom had been downright gleeful as she'd informed me that she, my dad, my siblings, and their partners were all planning to fly from Ohio to Vermont to visit me for Christmas this year.

"You've had some time to settle," Mom said cheerfully. "We can't wait to see your new home. We're so proud of you, Joe."

Rather than feel all the warm-fuzzies most probably would in this situation, I was full of terror. I could read between the lines. "We're so proud of you, Joe" was something I'd been waiting to hear my whole life. The words sent me flying for all of six seconds before I came crashing down to cold hard reality.

After the way I'd messed up the first time I'd moved out, I seriously hadn't expected to hear that so soon, and over the phone no less. I didn't mean to be pessimistic but…I had no doubt, Mom's visit was a test as much as it was a sign of love.

A test I was bound to fail.

As I studied my skewampus living room floor, the mold stain on my ceiling, the holes in the drywall, and the archway that led into the pretty much useless kitchen, I couldn't help but despair.

Nothing about my life was easy, and this just…took the cake.

Gripping the single mug I'd brought from my childhood home in Ohio tight, I pushed my panicky feelings aside and got to work.

Cataloguing what was wrong with the space was a daunting task.

Just like I'd done when I'd arrived and realized the orchard needed more work than advertised, I decided to make a list. A list was a good starting point. It'd let me know how big the project was going to be and help me plan for what needed to be done first. I didn't even want to think about my practically non-existent budget.

The checks I'd had rolling in from this year's harvest had been only a fraction of what I could expect from later years. I hadn't had many apples to sell, given the state of the farm, but even a small harvest was better than no harvest.

The contracts Jason had helped me—no. No.

The contracts that I had set up helped a lot in the money department, but it was still nowhere near enough to take care of the amount of renovation my house needed to meet…livable standards.

I'd been penny pinching for years to save up for this.

It was my dream.

Everything I'd ever wanted.

And it would mean absolutely nothing if my mom was disappointed in me.

Mom was gonna arrive. She'd take one look at how I'd been living. *One* look. Her eyes would fill with pity.

Her respect—begrudgingly won—would disappear. She'd pat my back and her "I'm so proud of you" would quickly morph into something along the lines of, "Oh…Joe," and an offer to return to living in their basement, where I was "better off."

She'd think I couldn't handle myself.

And she'd be right.

That thought caused me to stumble right into the doorway that led out of the bathroom. I'd been gathering tasks for my list, and luckily for me, it was the least abused space in the house. Mostly just needed a new layer of paint, maybe, and for the pump in the toilet to be replaced.

It also happened to be the last room I was inspecting.

Which meant the next step in my *very important* plan was to scout out what kinda supplies I'd need at the hardware store, get prices, and see what I could believably accomplish. There was a pit in my stomach before I took a single step.

Like I knew something bad was coming.

I dodged one of the floorboards that looked about ready to crumble to dust like I had every day for the last few months. I danced around a rusty nail sticking out of the baseboard in the hallway. And then out the rickety front door I went.

My pulse was racing as I moved across the yawning porch.

Yawning, because that's the sound it made every time I stepped on it.

This horrible almost-sigh.

"I am so screwed," I muttered as I kept moving. "No." No, I wasn't. I could turn this around. I just…I just didn't know how yet.

It wasn't that I didn't care about where I lived. What I'd cared more about was the apples. The apples that'd been sorely neglected.

When I'd arrived in June, the orchard had been overgrown, brambles and wiry grass swallowing the trunks. Some trees had up and quit, wood blackened, not a flower bud or leaf in sight. But most of them? Most of them were thriving, even if a bit wild.

Patrick and I—along with a farmhand named Jordan who was home from college—had broken our backs getting them taken care of before I'd ever thought about taking care of myself.

It was a big project for three people, even with a smaller farm.

There was always something to do.

Always another task that needed to be completed before the day was over.

I had no idea how I would've managed if I didn't have Patrick and Jordan around. The truth? I probably wouldn't've.

Maybe that's why Jason's offers to help me were so goddamn infuriating. Because I'd come here to do this on my own—and there wasn't a single task I'd accomplished without someone else there.

Fixing up the house had been put on the back burner.

To be frank—I didn't really mind the mess. It was just me here. Nobody to impress or concern with the holes in the wall and malfunctioning appliances. And if I never let anyone inside the house, no one was going to see it anyway, so it didn't matter.

Besides, I wasn't home much aside from sleep.

I didn't cook.

Didn't have time for TV.

Didn't have time for anything except work.

During my very few free hours, I'd hike in the woods. Birdwatching. Sent Roderick—my buddy back home—a picture of an acorn, or a tree, whatever cool thing I discovered, and went about my day.

Most of my free time I spent running errands, popping into the town limits—most often to be bombarded with questions I never knew how to answer.

People in Belleville, Vermont, were a lot like the people back home in Chesterton.

Friendly.

Kind.

Nosy.

And the nosiest of all was Jason. Tall and gangly, my first impression of him had been far from positive. He'd been a peeping Tom. Spying on me when I least expected it. When my guard was down.

Scaring off the magpie I'd thought of as a good omen. Then bombarding me with questions—and making me feel like a total idiot. Offering me help like he took one look at me and knew I was hopeless.

Since then, my opinion of him continued to be rocky.

He was pushy. He was too smart for his own good. And no one and *nothing* was safe from Jason and his chatty mouth.

I'd done my best to be closed-lipped around him.

This was my chance.

My one and only chance to get people to take me seriously. Back home, I'd been regarded as a bit of an idiot. I'd caught the tail-end of jokes. Joe the himbo. Baby Milton. Joe the inept. Joe the clumsy, inexperienced—

you get the picture.

No one had ever let me forget homecoming and the fact I'd puked on Olivia. They looked at me and saw a giant toddler. Their pity when I'd returned home after failing as a farmhand was palpable.

I didn't want to be seen that way here.

For the first time in my life, I could be *anybody*. I had one more shot to prove to my family—and myself—that I could do this.

And I didn't need Jason, and his animated hands, or his flashy smiles—didn't need his *help*. I wasn't weak.

I kept my distance as best I could.

I didn't understand him—*couldn't* understand him. His motivations were murky at best. I'd been nothing but cold, and yet he…he wouldn't leave me alone.

He was like a dog with a bone. All I had to do was *breathe* and he thought it was an invitation to offer me the shirt off his back. I'd never accept. Couldn't accept.

Because if I did, I'd be admitting that I couldn't take care of myself, after all.

The hardware store was busy for a Wednesday. Patrick and Jordan were taking care of the farm so that I could focus on the task at hand. I'd managed fifteen or so minutes of wandering the aisles, writing down prices on my paper, before I'd been bombarded with newcomers and the shop had gone from blissfully empty to headache-inducingly full.

The longer I spent in the store, the more sure I was that the cost of renovations on my house was going to be astronomical.

I'd barely gotten halfway down the page and already couldn't breathe.

By the time I got to the end, I was full-on hyperventilating.

Money signs danced in front of my eyes. Making my vision splotchy. Making my heart race. Making my hands clammy and—I dropped my list, only to bend over and pick it back up with clumsy fingers.

"Last year was so cute!" a woman gushed, arms full of tarps as she walked by me. She nodded and smiled my way, but was otherwise too occupied to notice me panicking.

Thank god.

I smoothed out my list, continuing down it as I eavesdropped on her conversation. "Do you think Ms. Daisy is going to be able to pull off *The Grinch*? I mean, it's a bit different, don't you think? When last year, she wrote the whole thing."

"It's easier to use a pre-written play," the man beside her disagreed. "I think she'll do just fine."

"Oh, I just can't *wait* to see what the parents do with the little Who-people's hair!" Another person cooed. "I betcha anything they'll go all out."

There were a half dozen people in line all of a sudden. A whirlwind of activity. All of them were carrying a variety of Christmas lights and lumber. Apparently, the local community theater was going all out with the holiday play this year.

It should've been cool to see the town banding together to get the set built. Instead, the sight of the lights was just another reminder of Mom's visit and the impending doom of the holiday season.

Like a slap to the face.

The last item on my list was the flooring I'd need to replace. I'd need a quote for that—to do some actual math. But…Jesus. Just imagining how much that was going to cost made me feel like I was going to die.

An icy chill ran through me that had nothing to do with the swing of the open door as the other customers filed out, supplies in tow. A wayward flurry of leaves skittered across the floor toward me. I watched them skip across the wood, almost in slow motion.

The store was empty again.

But I still couldn't breathe.

My list crumpled in my grip.

"Joe?" The man behind the desk greeted me. I recognized him briefly from the other occasions I'd come in to purchase tools for the farm, but I didn't know his name. He didn't wear a name tag, and I hadn't known how to ask him what it was, or even if I *should* ask. Everyone in town knew my name because of Jason. Which meant now it was awkward.

"You okay?" he asked.

I steeled my expression, locking everything down as tight as it could go. I supposed it made sense he was concerned. I was kinda just standing there. Unfortunately for me, the drive into town and the hunt for prices had only made the sick pit in my stomach grow.

I had less than two months to get my house livable.

Even if I *had* the money to do it—which I didn't—it felt like an impossible feat.

The task was so daunting for a moment that I couldn't breathe.

I left without a word. In a daze, I swayed back into the street. Driving was a bad idea right now with how fuzzy my head felt, so I bypassed my truck in order to look for somewhere safe to recoup. As I walked, this sluggish feeling weighed my limbs down. Made me feel like I was made of molasses. Everything felt too bright and like too much all at once.

And every breath was more labored than the last.

It didn't matter that it was sunny out. That the air was crisp. That Main Street was as bright and colorful as always. Adorable buildings populated with friendly faces. Personality etched into every brick building and ivy-covered lattice.

I was cold.

So cold.

And the world was nothing but a blur.

The few townies wandering down the sidewalk waved at me like I was an old friend even though I'd never talked to any of them. I waved back, with a jerky arm motion. The list in my left hand felt sweaty now. Cramped. Everywhere I looked there was an audience waiting to ogle me.

Nowhere was safe.

Everything was so bright. Had it always been so bright? So loud? So much?

I just…I just needed a second.

Just a *second* to get my head screwed on straight.

That's it.

Except thinking about "screws" nearly sent me over the deep end again. Because screws reminded me of the project-from-hell. And my mom's face. And the weight of all of that was just…I couldn't—

Everywhere I went there were people.

The bookstore wasn't safe. They were hosting some sort of meet-and-greet with a local author, and a gaggle of elder-ladies in matching "Montgomery Smut Club" shirts were chatting so loudly I didn't even approach the store.

The bakery was no good either.

All I had to do was push the door open to recognize the need for retreat.

My cousin, Baxter—Mom had made sure I knew I had family out here before moving—was chatting away with a sunny smile and a counter full of the most delicious smelling pumpkin bread in the world laid out in front of him. He spotted me and beckoned me closer.

"Joe! Your apples were a hit. Best tarts I've ever made," he said. He was always friendly. Just like everyone else here. And normally, it was nice, even on the days I wanted very little to do with people, too overwhelmed by how much I knew I could mess up each social interaction without even having to try.

But right now, the last thing I needed was to struggle through a conversation.

I just wanted to be alone.

I didn't want to be rude. Mom had taught me better.

Instead of actually entering the bakery, I shook my head. Quickly, I escaped out the door and down the sidewalk out of sight. I'd apologize to Baxter later. When I could get my mouth to work. But for now…for now, the concern on his face was the least of my worries.

Eyes lingered on me as I stumbled to the only other space within walking distance that felt familiar.

The grocery store.

My apple stand.

It was blissfully quiet inside. It seemed the crowds of Belleville had finally offered me a reprieve. I wandered to the back, as far away from the glass at the front and its cheery painted-on sales as I could get. Didn't want anyone to see me. It felt second nature to hunt down my apples. Looking at them made me feel marginally better.

Not enough to get a solid breath in, stiff and shaking as I was.

I didn't do this often.

In fact, I could only recall doing it once.

After we'd visited George in New York for Christmas one year, and I'd suspected his boyfriend at the time—Brendon—was hurting him. We'd gone home and made the "We Hate Brendon Club" after that. All of us were desperate to do something to help George, even if that something was simply being there for him when he ultimately let that relationship go.

The cookies were great too, at the meetings. But even sugar couldn't heal the fear we'd all carried over George. At least until he'd broken up with the bastard himself and moved home for good.

This wasn't nearly as terrible as that.

That's what I tried to tell myself.

Tried to man-up and force these feelings to fade like I had when I'd been able to drive into town earlier. I told myself that freaking out was a waste of precious time. I had so much to do, every minute counted. I needed a battle plan.

But more than that, I needed money.

Money.

I didn't know how I'd get it—but I needed it. I told myself I could figure it out. That I was stubborn as an ox. That I was strong.

But it didn't matter, because the damn feelings kept sinking their claws deeper, deeper, deeper.

And my chest was heaving.

And I still couldn't breathe.

I couldn't breathe—

I couldn't—

"It's fine, it's fine—" I choked quietly, fingers biting hard into the wooden display. Hard enough it rattled and one of my apples nearly came free. "Stop acting like such a—"

"Joe!" Jason's voice was about as startled as I felt. "Hey, buddy. Sorry about the last time you were in. I wasn't at my best—you know how it gets! Changing of the seasons and all that. Can be a real doozy. Is there anything I can help you wi—"

No, no, no.

I jerked around, stiff and awkward. This time, I really did knock an apple off the display. It hit the ground with a thud I felt all the way in my bones.

He was the last person I wanted to see. I'd been an idiot not to anticipate that he would be here.

And there Jason was, having just come out of a door labeled "Staff Only" with a pink coffee tumbler that read *World's Best God Uncle* in hand. He paused, lingering just in front of the doorway, dark eyebrows climbing high.

"I'm fine!" I said way too loud to be anything but fine.

Up, up, up, Jason's eyebrows rose.

No, no, no.

Jason had an expressive face.

The kinda face that told you everything he was about to say before he said it. Handsome too, in a gangly Peter Parker kinda way. Except…middle-aged. And with stubble. Dark circles that made him look perpetually tired. And these pale eyes that reminded me of summer rainstorms, closer to gray than true blue and just as fraught.

His expressions were clear even when his motivations weren't.

And right now, Jason was *concerned.*

Jason was a talker.

And the last person I wanted to see me vulnerable like this. Not when he already thought I was inept. The apple at my foot felt like a bad omen.

"*Hey*," Jason's voice went softer than I'd ever heard it. He sat his tumbler down on the floor. Rising back up, he held both long-fingered hands up in a placating manner. Like I was a spooked animal and he was trying to approach without getting bitten.

He took a careful step forward.

I backed into the stand, sending another apple plummeting to its death. This one rolled farther, past Jason's beat-up sneakers until it hit the vent beneath the other produce stands.

"Hey," he said a third time. Another step. Just as slow. Blue eyes meeting mine, his brow lowered in a serious but kind way. "You're okay," Jason promised.

I wasn't okay.

Of course I wasn't okay.

Everything I'd worked for was falling apart. I was at the bottom of a pit. No ladder. No way out. Stuck. Everywhere everyone was happy and celebrating—and my world…my world was ending, soon enough.

Worst of all, Jason was going to think he'd been right to pity me.

That I was *weak*.

Instead of bolstering my confidence, that thought caused the last of my walls to crumble. A wet noise escaped me. Waterworks I hadn't even known I'd been fighting off spilled free. A tear dashed down my cheek, then another, and another.

And still, I couldn't breathe.

Face hot.

Heart pounding.

"Oh, *Joe.*" Jason's voice remained honey-sweet. He crossed the last of the distance between us, hands hovering uselessly in the air until suddenly they weren't anymore. He was right there. Toe-to-toe with me. Half a head shorter, those blue eyes meeting mine. Not scared. Not patronizing. Not pitying.

Not the way I expected them to be.

Jason looked at me like he *saw* me.

And that was the scariest part.

Because secretly, deep down, I wanted his help. I wanted to give in. Didn't want to do anything on my own ever because it was *so much.*

"Sweet baby, come here." There was a hand at the back of my neck now, yanking me into Jason's shoulder.

I could've resisted.

I didn't.

Shame coursed through me at the show of weakness, a few more tears slipping free and landing on the green of Jason's sweater.

"That's it," he urged, giving my nape another squeeze, tighter this time, collaring me. "I'm here."

Of their own accord, my hands found the hem of Jason's sweater, digging in and pulling till the fabric wheezed along with my lungs. I didn't know how to feel about being called sweet. Didn't know how to feel about the fact that Jason had called me a *baby* of all things. Didn't know how to feel about the horrible, awful thought I'd just had—a thought I already told myself could not be true.

I couldn't want this.

I didn't want this.

I'd been trying so, so hard not to feel this way. To be strong, and serious, and everything I'd never had a chance to be back home.

When Jason was around, it was almost too easy to let go of that. He wanted to carry me.

Especially now.

And I didn't understand *why*.

I was a stranger. I didn't matter to him. Wasn't family. Wasn't his friend. I was just some guy he'd spied on, who'd been dodging him ever since.

He had nice hands. Strong. Lean. And I could admit…as ashamed as I felt about accepting it, the hug was nice too.

Jason was nice. I didn't understand him. Didn't understand him at all. Why he would do this when I'd been so grouchy with him. Why he acted the way he did. Why he wouldn't leave me alone.

I don't know how long I cried—folded into him stiffly, my hands in his shirt, shoulders shaking, lungs threatening to give out on me entirely.

Ten minutes maybe?

The most pitiful, shameful ten minutes of my life.

And Jason held me the whole time.

At some point, his free hand had come up and begun rubbing my back. These steady strokes that made me feel like I was falling apart all over again. When my sobs quieted, he didn't stop rubbing my back. The movement was soothing and the weak part of me didn't want it to end, so I didn't move, even though I'd left a giant puddle on his shoulder and my spine was crunched so that I could fit against him.

"There, there," Jason patted my back. "Get it all out."

I huffed, but didn't complain.

One last sniff, and I felt ready to run again. Ready to leave the grocery store and never come back—ever. Sure, that'd make my apple drop-offs tricky, but I could manage it. Maybe I'd send Jordan? Or Patrick. Maybe

Baxter could drop off my groceries for me from now on? Maybe I'd become a hermit—

Maybe.

I tried to pull back, to escape—but Jason wouldn't let me. As if he could sense my desire to bolt, his hand on the nape of my neck tightened. Heat washed through me, hot and sticky and impossible to ignore. It pooled beneath my legs, made my knees go weak. Made my breaths shallow for a new reason entirely.

More confusing feelings.

"*What happened?*" he asked in that same throaty, gentle voice. "You wanna talk about it?"

"No," I bit out.

He's going to tell everyone.

By this time tomorrow, there won't be a single place in town where people aren't laughing at you.

Just that thought was enough to send a few more hot tears searing down my cheeks. I wanted to be self-sufficient, dammit. And here I was— God.

Fuck.

"I'm not going to tell anyone," Jason promised, reading my mind like a fucking witch. Again.

Weirdly enough, despite the way I'd just been panicking, I wanted to believe him.

Maybe it was the skip of his heart, not nearly as steady as his hands. Or maybe it was his voice, commanding and sure. Maybe it was the fact I still didn't feel like he pitied me—despite what I'd just done, and the puddle I'd left on his shoulder.

Or maybe it was the hot-pink mug staring at me from where he'd left it on the floor next to the two bruised apples I'd sacrificed during my fit. It was the kind of mug only a man who was truly confident in his masculinity would carry around.

I wanted to believe him, and yet I still ran.

I yanked out of his grip in a jerky fashion and pulled away as fast as I could. Jason watched me go like he always did, his hands falling uselessly at his sides, eyes stormy.

"Joe," he said my name quietly. "You don't need to run from me," he repeated. It wasn't a plea so much as it was a promise. A promise to lend an ear if I needed it. A promise to support me if I let him. A promise to help me.

It was too much.

Too much.

I couldn't stomach it.

Not one bit.

four

JASON

JOE CRYING HAD NOT BEEN on my bingo card for this holiday season. And honestly? I had not been emotionally prepared to see him that way. On my third cup of coffee of the day, overrun with tasks in my head I had yet to complete, I'd been caught off guard when I'd spotted him. He was stiff and trembling, hovering over his apple babies like a golden mama bear, and instinct had me snapping to attention immediately.

I knew something was wrong, even if I didn't know exactly what it was.

Not at first.

In my defense, I'd spent the last twenty-four hours in a panic trying to figure out how I felt about him. Had dark circles under my eyes that made me look like produce after it'd been rolling around in the delivery truck.

Suffice to say, I was a mess.

Exhausted.

And not bringing my A-Game.

And yet…my body seemed to know what to do before my brain had caught up. There was no stopping the torrent of protective feelings that inspired my next actions. It was impossible not to react with help-fix-soothe when Joe—the toughest, surliest guy I knew—was hyperventilating, his big shoulders heaving, massive body hunched like he was trying to make himself as small as possible.

I didn't overthink it.

Not the way I'd been overthinking my "supposed crush" on him, and my feelings.

There was no denying that having Joe in my arms felt *right*.

Helped solidify that crush or not, I never *ever* wanted to see him cry like that again. And then, like an idiot, I'd opened my big mouth—I'd pushed, and…

He'd bolted.

He always fucking bolted.

I wasn't surprised, nor was I offended. Joe had just shown me something *vulnerable*. Something that cost far more than simply accepting my "help". He'd cracked open the shell around himself and I'd had my hands all up in his…ah…what do you call the inner part of an egg? Yolk. Yes. I was all up in his yolk.

I had no doubt that rankled.

Especially when over the course of the last few months it'd become more and more apparent that he did not like me. Didn't trust me. Didn't want anything from me if he could help it. Yes, lately, we'd reached a… tentative truce but that was all it was.

Tentative.

I had no doubt this was about to skyrocket us firmly back into hostile territory.

Now he was even less likely to open up to me.

Fuck.

I wasn't sure why that bothered me so much. *Because you have a crush on him*, Madison's voice unhelpfully supplied. Some people had devils on their shoulders. Not me. I had Madison. Pointing out my inconsistencies and trying to set me on the path to the straight-and-narrow.

Only…my path, in her eyes, was far less "straight" than expected.

As Joe had lunged for the door like a clumsy panther, his hip clipped one of the displays he passed, knocking it slightly askew. Nothing fell. Which was good. I had no doubt, based on the fact he was a regular-old-Boy-Scout, that usually he would've paused to fix the mess he'd made.

And he clearly needed space more than anything.

For the second time since we'd met, I waited for Joe to return.

But he didn't.

Sighing, I bent down to retrieve my coffee tumbler and grab the bruised apples that'd dropped on the floor. That was, of course, when I spotted something. Something…new. Out of place.

Huh.

There was a piece of paper on the ground where Joe had previously been standing. It was crumpled and a bit sweat-damp, but there was no denying who had left it there. Coffee mug tucked into my elbow—thank god for proper insulation, so I did not get burnt—I grabbed the paper before I dealt with the apples.

I didn't even question it as I unfolded the thing and curiously read what was on it.

Sure, reading what was clearly a private note was a bit invasive, I'll admit. But I couldn't help myself. I read what was written in spikey all-caps handwriting, as I smoothed out the paper's wrinkles with care. Some of the items were smudged. But most of them were legible enough I could guess what was missing.

It seemed to be a checklist of sorts.

A to-do list?

Along with the items that would be necessary for each job, as well as the prices beside them. Bedroom, living room, bathroom, and kitchen all had their own separate categories. Porch was underlined, like it was a priority. And below that was the word "appliances" with three separate question marks beside it, and no prices.

At the bottom was a simple countdown.

Four weeks, three days.

And then, separately, the flight numbers for what I assumed to be his family traveling in, based on the fact—when I Googled it—the flight numbers said they were coming from Ohio.

It was pretty obvious what I was looking at.

As the prices climbed higher and higher, and the list grew longer and longer, and the countdown and arrival times for his family glared at me from the bottom of the page, I could hazard a guess why Joe had been panicking.

That looked like a lot of renovation, and a lot of money, with very little time to accomplish such a lofty goal. Based on the sheer number of things he'd written down that were broken, I could only assume the state of his home was abysmal.

My stomach clenched.

Thoughts whirring with ideas on how I could help, when Joe had made it pretty clear he wanted nothing to do with me ever, I pocketed the list. Then, I took a fortifying sip of my coffee, and gathered the bruised apples.

How did you help someone who refused to accept your help?

You didn't.

Gah.

What a mess.

A complicated knot-riddled mess.

I didn't go after Joe. I got the feeling that was the last thing he wanted. He'd shown me enough for one day. And I needed time if I was going to do something about this. I'd let Joe lick his wounds in private.

And me?

I would do what I did best.

I'd meddle.

Joe's farmhouse was located at the edge of town. Out past the suburbs and sandwiched between the orchard and the forest. It was a cute house. On the admittedly few occasions I'd been out here—apple picking with Mary back when we'd been freshly married—I'd thought so.

However, as I drove up the gravel driveway, there was no telling how long the space had been abandoned before Joe had come to occupy it.

The driveway was overrun with weeds. Brambles created a blanket of unwalkable foliage for the majority of the drive. Closer to the house, things were somewhat more maintained. Less weeds, at least. Firewood was stacked in a massive pile beside the misshapen front porch. An abandoned axe sat beside it.

Piles and piles and piles of discarded saplings, brambles, and other plants were stacked along the edges of the driveway. The back of Joe's weathered blue truck was full of tools. As I got out of my car and moved to inspect what he'd already purchased, I couldn't help but be glad I'd come all this way. Only a day had passed, and yet, Joe had been hard at work, it seemed.

There was a pizza sitting in my passenger seat, steaming up the windows.

A peace offering.

A pizza-offering.

Ha.

I hoped to break the ice. To…drop his guard a little. An apology for seeing him when he was most vulnerable. Especially when I was here to deliver what I hoped to be good news. Though, knowing Joe and his pride, I doubted he'd see it that way.

As I hopped up the front steps, the porch made a frankly terrifying sound. I paused, grimacing—just waiting for it to cave in. When it didn't, I tested the next step much more slowly. This one also complained, but this time I was prepared for it, so I didn't panic.

With every step I took, I felt my resolve harden.

I'd spent the rest of the previous day and night worrying about Joe. I'd called my mom—to her delight. She *loved* chatting. The only thing she loved more than chatting was charity.

Together we'd hatched up a harebrained scheme.

It felt rather fool-proof.

I'd come to his house—his "territory", so to speak—and I'd offer him pizza. After he'd accepted the cheesy goodness and I'd fallen into his good graces, as much as I was able, anyway, I'd give him my pitch.

I hoped this would go better than the last time I'd tried to help him.

And I hoped…if I offered him money through the fake "charity fund" that Mom was working on legitimizing, he'd be more likely to accept than if I outright offered him cash myself.

Which, again, wasn't something I'd ever do.

Not when I was still trying to keep my financial situation under wraps.

The charity, as a whole, was a fun idea, actually. I was kinda annoyed that I hadn't thought of it sooner. And after I helped Joe, I fully intended on making it a yearly thing. To have a wad of cash I could anonymously offer people. A "Santa Fund" as Mom and I had decided to name it. To help my fellow citizens behind the scenes like I was grocery-store-Batman.

It was actually more straightforward than most of my other endeavors.

Joe would make the perfect guinea pig.

Provided he actually accepted aid.

Which…I was still nervous was not going to happen.

Money was a tricky subject for a lot of people. For good reason. Someone's financial situation was a deeply personal thing. Believe me, I understood that more than anyone. The last thing I wanted to do was accidentally shame Joe for his struggles—presumed struggles, as I still had yet to one-hundred-percent confirm if the panic attack in the grocery store was caused by not being able to pay for the items on that list.

It was a good guess, yes.

But still a guess.

Standing on Joe's porch ruminating wasn't doing anyone, least of all me, any good. So I rapped on the screen door with purpose. The sound chased away the demons in my head. The screen door rattled beneath my fist. Its edges were rusted, the white paint chipped. Behind it, the wooden door was no better. Just as worn.

I didn't hear footsteps and worried I'd just so happened to visit while Joe was out tending to his orchard. The inner wooden door swung open a moment later, revealing Joe's tall, broad form.

His eyes were guarded, brow furrowed as he stared at me.

It was a cute expression.

Perplexed.

Annoyed.

"Hey, buddy!" I said brightly before he could slam the door in my face. "I brought pizza! Peace-za. You know—instead of a white flag."

Joe slammed the door in my face.

A startled laugh escaped me.

That's what you deserve for getting your hopes up, I chided myself. *You should know by now that Joe never makes things easy.* Joe was nothing but contrary when it came to me. The fact that I'd held him while he cried was only bound to make that worse—

To my surprise, the door swung back open.

I moved out of the way as quick as I could, porch wheezing beneath my steps. Joe pushed through both doors with a scowl on his face.

Joe stormed past me and down the steps.

They made even more noise when he was on them, due to his bulk. A frankly hilarious *squeak, whine, squeak, whine* that sounded after every step. I followed behind him dutifully.

Please, dear god, do not crumble beneath us.

The wood held true, thank the lord.

I scurried down the last of the steps as Joe's feet touched gravel, my eyes caught on the width of his shoulders and the rather glorious way they flexed when he walked. Though…walk was maybe not the best word for what he was currently doing.

No.

Stalking was more accurate.

Like a panther.

He had no flannel on today despite the chill. Just a t-shirt. The golden skin of his biceps haunted me. Bounce bounce bouncing. At the last second, right as he'd reached my vehicle, Joe tripped over a twig and nearly face planted into the side of my truck.

"Hey—" I grabbed his shirt on instinct, yanking him back before he could make contact with the metal and get hurt.

Apparently that was a mistake.

Joe growled.

Growled!

"I don't need *your* help!" Joe's voice was sharp. Still quiet, but far closer to a roar than I'd ever heard it. I stepped back, hands up placatingly. Joe jerked around, chest heaving, nostrils flaring as he glared at me. "I can take care of *myself*. I'm not *weak*."

He'd said almost that same thing back in June.

Verbatim.

"*Okay*," I agreed, attempting to sound neutral. My heart was pounding. "Sure, yes. Of course you can! I didn't mean to insinuate that you couldn't."

Backpedal, backpedal.

How was I only realizing what a bad idea this was?

"Why are you always—" Joe made a frustrated noise, hands going up into his hair. He tugged at it harshly, and I couldn't help the way I clucked my tongue at him. Immediately, his grip slackened, following the unspoken command to cease hurting himself. "Why won't you *leave me alone?*"

My heart squeezed.

A balloon with all the air sucked out of it.

I closed down.

Why won't you leave me alone?

I took another step back.

Dropped my hands.

The keys in my pocket jangled.

Suddenly, looking at Joe was too damn hard. Though, admittedly, he was even prettier when he was pissed off than when he was ignoring me. All flashing white teeth, pointy canines, and flexed jaw.

But…I just…I couldn't.

You're an idiot, Jason, I told myself.

What did you think you were doing here?

I opened my mouth to tell him I'd go. That I'd stop pursuing him. That I finally got the hint. That I was sorry, really, genuinely sorry that I'd pushed him to this point.

Because I had, hadn't I?

Always poking.

Meddling.

I opened my mouth, but Joe cut me off.

"I didn't mean that," he said, his tone so defeated I couldn't have stopped myself from looking at him again, even if I'd tried.

His shoulders were slumped, his head dropped down. There was something miserable about the way he held himself. His golden hair fell forward, blocking his forehead from view.

He looked small.

Like he had when I'd held him.

"I'm sorry," he said softly. "I *really* didn't mean that. I know you're just being nice. I just…"

I didn't move. I didn't know what was welcome right now. Wasn't sure where I stood between what he'd just said and the irritation he'd been exhibiting only a few seconds prior.

"I *have* been bothering you," I said, surprised by how even my tone was when I felt like I was at least partially dying. "I know I have."

"Not on purpose."

"*Yes* on purpose." I laughed a little, the sound brittle. That admission made me sound like such a dick. Which…I guess I was. My intentions didn't matter if I'd made him uncomfortable.

"Why?" Joe's hands clenched into fists, released, then clenched again. The veins on the back of them danced.

"Because I think you're interesting," I said. "Because I think you're fun." He clenched again, then released.

It was hard to admit this. Felt like pulling teeth. But I figured after what I'd put him through, the least I could do was tell the truth.

"Because I thought I could make things better for you. *Easier* for you." *Because you're lonely, and old, and wanted his attention,* Madison's voice informed me. "Because I…want to be your friend." Joe was the one who deserved an apology, not me.

I didn't speak again.

Letting Joe process my heartfelt apology and decide for himself what to do with it.

He looked…wild, like a bull ready to charge.

Caught off guard.

And yet…less confused.

There was something almost glassy in his eyes that made it clear that while a day had passed, Joe was definitely *not* more settled than the last time I'd seen him. He looked stressed out. Worn thin. Exhausted.

I itched to fix it.

But now, more than ever, I knew I didn't have the right to.

"You want to be my friend?" Joe repeated, like I was speaking another language. Like no one in his entire life had ever said that to him. In a way I felt like a kindergartner, offering him friendship like that. A friendship he had every right to refuse.

"*Yes*," I confessed. I wanted to be his friend more than anything.

He nodded.

Not acceptance, but acknowledging what I'd said. Mulling it over. I'd never outright asked like that. Not since I was little. Not since I got a taste for how easy rejection could be doled out.

"Why?" Joe asked, voice quiet.

His question caught me off guard. I hadn't anticipated it, so my knee-jerk reaction was to simply admit the truth, even though that wasn't something I often did. "I didn't grow up with a lot of friends," I admitted. "Or any, really."

Joe was quiet for a beat.

"Me neither," he confessed.

And for the first time since we met, it felt like we understood one another.

"Pizza?" I offered, attempting to sound chipper. "I'll go, but don't let the food go to waste. Best piece-a-pie in town, guaranteed."

I wasn't trying to manipulate him this time. The offer to leave was genuine—even though the thought that Joe may not want to share a meal with me made me feel like I was dying.

I'd messed up so badly with him.

So badly I didn't know what to do to fix it.

Didn't know if I was allowed to even try.

But the pizza was innocent. And I wasn't the kind of guy who liked to waste.

Joe's nostrils flared again, and I worried I'd made another mistake, offering him food. But then his stomach gurgled. His eyes darted from me to the house, then to the truck where the pizza box lay tempting him.

The window was cracked, so the scent of cheese and bread filled the air. He exhaled and nodded. Then, just as slow, he took a step to the side so I could reach around him to remove the food.

I did so at a glacial pace, not wanting to push any more buttons than I already had.

"I didn't know what you liked," I hummed, straightening from where I'd bent over the driver's side to reach the pizza. I pulled it out, offering it to him with none of my usual pizazz. "So I got cheese."

"I like cheese," Joe said in the most sullen but adorable voice I'd ever heard. His stomach made another sound. That protective instinct reared up inside me again as I shut the door with my hip.

He eyed the pizza box hungrily.

"Here, take it." Joe wavered, gaze darting between me and the food. "No tricks," I promised. "It's peace-za, remember?"

He nodded again, even more slowly this time. Then, in that same adorable voice, he requested, "Stay?"

Had he really just…?

If I'd been crushed before, this was the absolute opposite.

The balloon inside me expanded so much I felt like it might pop.

"You *want* me to stay and eat with you?" I clarified. "Really? After everything?"

Joe nodded.

The muscle in his jaw jumped, but he looked pretty damn sure of his choice.

"Okay," I agreed easily, sagging in relief. "Awesome. Where do you want to eat?" I asked, waving the box. "Inside? Outside? Hell, we can use my truck bed if you—"

"Porch." A man on a mission, Joe headed toward said porch without a backward glance. I grimaced, shaking off my anxiety over the structural integrity of the thing as I followed after him. I had no idea how I'd managed to luck into this, but I had.

"No one's been in the house," Joe admitted as he reached the top. "Except me."

"Really?" Maybe he was embarrassed. I wasn't going to judge. Nor was I looking to poke a fresh wound by asking him about it.

Joe sat down before I did.

He spread his legs a little, hunching over them as he waited for me to take my seat too. I made sure to keep a respectful distance. He needed space. Even if he'd invited me to stay, he still needed that.

Setting the pizza box down between us, I sprawled wide to stretch out my legs. Once settled, I pulled the lid open and gestured toward the cheesy goodness with a flourish. "Dig in."

Apparently, Joe didn't need any more encouragement, because he immediately grabbed a slice of sweet-sweet pie and began to stuff his face.

Poor baby acted like he hadn't eaten a real meal in months. Which…

maybe was true. I'd only ever seen him buy TV dinners. I'd never spotted him at any of the local cafes or restaurants.

For all I knew this was the first meal he'd eaten since he'd moved to town that hadn't been microwaved before he consumed it.

He'd finished eating half the pizza before he ever paused to breathe.

Like a puppy with no self-control. Perpetually starving. Though in Joe's case, given how big he was, how physical his job was—and how young he was, I had no doubt his appetite was hard to quench.

Truthfully, as much as I liked greasy food—and god, yes, did I like it—my body did not. The pizza I held was more for show than anything, and I was nursing the single slice I'd be eating one delicious bite at a time.

Joe paused his voracious eating, lips shiny, a wayward drop of tomato sauce on his chin. I grabbed a napkin out of the box and offered it to him. He accepted it then rubbed it all over his face—and I mean, allll over, chin to forehead—cleaning himself up.

The next few slices, he ate less ravenously.

Savoring them.

"Good, huh?" I hummed around my last mouthful. "Slice of Heaven is the best!" I'd taken as long as I could consuming my piece so I'd have something to do. I figured sitting there staring at Joe while empty-handed was a recipe for disaster. Even if I personally wouldn't have minded.

He fascinated me now more than ever.

Because you might have a—

No.

No.

Now is not the time.

"Mm," Joe grunted in agreement. His lips turned up a little at the corners—but he quickly squashed the smile. This was the second time I'd seen an almost-smile on his face. It made my heart skip a beat.

"Why did you *actually* bring me pizza?" Joe asked. "Was it supposed to be another trick?"

Ah.

Now that he was full, he was apparently also full of questions.

"No. I mean, yes. Kind of." He waited, surprisingly patient. "It really was supposed to be a white flag." Joe nodded. "I found your list."

I pulled the paper out of my jeans pocket after a little wiggling, and offered it to him.

Joe took it, frowning down at it like he didn't recognize it.

Was it not his? Had I got that wrong? Shit I—

"I thought I dropped it on the way home," he said quietly.

Oh good. At least I wasn't totally off.

"You did. *Technically*. If you count the way you bolted out of the grocery store as part of that journey," I joked. Joe glared at me. Ha. Not on joking terms yet, I should've guessed that. Again, oops.

"Sorry," I apologized. "When I'm uncomfortable I make jokes."

Joe nodded. There was this look in his eyes that said, *that makes a lot of sense*. Sassy. So sassy.

"You're uncomfortable?" he asked.

I winced. "A bit?" The least I could do was be honest. "You're hard to read."

There was a confused tilt to Joe's head as he regarded me for a moment.

His eyes said, *I understand exactly what you mean.*

Apparently, the feeling was mutual.

"You were returning the list?" He filled in the blanks. "Because I dropped it. Because you're trying to be my…friend?"

"Yeah, and—" it was better if I delivered this nice and easy. "After seeing that, I've got a pretty good idea what freaked you out the other day anddddd I think I can help. Scratch that—I *know* I can help. If you let me."

After what he'd said about not needing assistance, I was pretty sure that statement wasn't going to go over well.

I was right.

Joe clammed up again, arms crossing over his chest. It was classic I-don't-want-to-talk-to-you body language. Did not bode well for me and my philanthropy, that was for sure. We'd had a mini heart-to-heart, but that didn't mean anything. Not when I was outright telling him I wanted to do the one thing he'd said he didn't want me to do.

"Before you say no, hear me out—" I cajoled.

"No."

"Joe—"

"*No*, Jason." He rose to his feet. "I can fix my house *by myself.*" He shoved the paper into his own pocket, biceps flexing as he loomed over me, all closed-off walls and stormy blue eyes. "I don't need your pity, or your help."

"I *don't* pity you." Despite the way alarm bells were ringing in my head, I stood too. It felt like we were running in circles. Just…over and over and over. The same problems recycled.

The empty pizza box acted as a barrier between us.

Which was probably good.

"I'm not saying you can't," I promised.

He wavered for a moment.

That was enough.

"Just that…" I had one chance to get him to listen. *One.* I had to make it count. "That list was long and home renovation is *expensive.*" Joe kept glaring. "Look…"

One chance, Jason.

That's it.

Don't fuck this up.

I scrambled to find an analogy that would strike a chord with him.

"Think about your farm." That got his attention. "Your apple trees," I added. "They can produce fruit on their own, can't they? I mean—they do it in the wild." I was grasping at straws here. Apparently, what I said was making sense, though, because Joe's posture relaxed a bit. Begrudgingly he nodded, urging me to keep going.

At least he's hearing me out.

"But…would you not say they thrive so much more when properly cultivated? With someone trimming their ah…branches—" My eyes darted to the piles of brambles around his property. *Quick, what do people with farms do?* "Someone…ah…*fertilizing* them. Someone watching over them. Someone *helping* them?"

"Yes," Joe bit out, like he didn't want to admit what I was saying was true.

"Assisting them is fruitful." I did my very best not to laugh at the pun I'd accidentally just made. If Joe noticed he didn't react. I pushed onward.

"It's like that! Yes, you could definitely accomplish this on your own. I know you can—*you* know you can. But…wouldn't it make more sense— given the timeline at the bottom of that paper, that you…allow me to… fertilize you?"

Joe made a face.

"Not like that." Oh god. Visions of me jerking off onto Joe filled my head. I did *not* need that in there. Not right now. Not ever. Jesus. "But—"

Joe held up a hand to stop me, palm out.

He dropped it by his sides, clenching his fists rhythmically for a moment.

"I get it," he grunted, staring out at his long, winding driveway and the orchard to its left. His lips pressed into a thin, tight line. A bird fluttered through the sky, interrupting our talk as it headed from the forest toward the apple trees. Joe's apple trees.

His expression softened.

I was so close—so fucking close to breaking behind his walls and getting him to say yes.

I could practically taste it.

Which was…amazing considering how full of strife the rest of this little visit to Joe's side of town had been.

"*Hypothetically*," Joe started, just as quiet. "If I were to accept your help, what would that entail?"

I resisted the urge to do a victory dance.

"There's this program that I'm scouting a recipient for called the "Santa Fund". It's its first year. A large amount of money was donated by a local benefactor, who prefers to stay anonymous." This, I hoped Joe would buy, simply based on the fact that I'd told him I knew everything about everyone the very first day we'd met. "This…ah…secret person—"Santa", has asked me to find someone he can help." Joe continued to watch the bird in the sky, though he was listening.

"His goal is to offer financial assistance. He wants to ease the burdens on Belleville's delightful citizens, as a way of giving back to his community." I had not had time to rehearse this, so I seriously hoped I didn't sound like a total idiot, or that Joe realized the "secret benefactor" was in fact me. "He told me to pick someone—so I am. I want that person to be you."

I was nothing if not an excellent bullshitter.

It was a blessing, and a curse.

I picked every word carefully, attempting to side step even more emotional landmines.

"What's the catch?" Joe crossed his arms.

"No catch," I promised. "Just a lonely guy with too much money, and no family, who wants to play Santa."

The look Joe gave me made it pretty clear he was still wary.

I kept my body positioning neutral and my expression friendly as I tried to convince him, "I know it sounds a bit far-fetched, but it's real. I know this guy pretty personally—and he's only after one thing."

"Helping people," Joe filled in.

"Yep! Helping people." There wasn't anything I loved more than taking care of my town and the people inside it. They were my family. The family I'd always craved. The friends I'd always wanted.

"If this…secret millionaire guy is Santa what does that make you?" Joe asked, still perplexed, still wary.

"Think of me as his elf," I replied.

I didn't need the credit. In fact, I didn't *want* it.

Didn't want anything from Joe except to make his life better.

And also…yes, his friendship would be pretty nice, too.

Though I wasn't about to buy that from him, even if I had just bribed him with pizza, and that's what this would feel like if he knew I was the one providing the cash.

Joe narrowed his eyes, waiting for me to yell *psych*! If the expression on his face could be believed.

His eyes said, *I don't know if I can let go.*

My heart skipped a beat.

"It's free money," I said, even more calmly. "Free money that's yours if you want it." My voice dropped a little, turning slow and steady the same way it had when I'd held him at the grocery store. "You should take it. There's no shame in taking it. Accepting help doesn't make you weak. In fact, sometimes it's the bravest thing you can do. Life is about choices, Joe. This is a good choice."

He regarded me for what felt like a lifetime, gauging my expression, his own face as unreadable as ever. A goddamn enigma. I never knew what he was thinking.

"I'll…think about it." Joe finally said, then paused. "How long until the offer expires?"

I hadn't thought that through.

Fuck.

"A week," I decided, because that seemed like a good amount. "Then he'll have me pick someone new." I really would, too. I had every intention of using the money I had put aside for it to help someone. I could only hope that person was Joe.

I could practically see him counting down the weeks until Christmas in his head. We both knew time was not a luxury he had. He couldn't sit on this for a whole week. He needed to decide far sooner than that.

"Think about it," I smiled, figuring now was the perfect time for a tactical retreat. I headed back down the porch steps, maintaining that same friendly air. "Mull it over. And if you're interested, you know where to find me."

Joe nodded, expression still guarded.

This had gone…way better than I'd expected.

I hardly knew what to do with myself.

I kind of wanted to perform a victory dance—but that would have to wait till I got home.

It took everything in me not to try and convince Joe to accept immediately with the timer ticking over our heads. I could feel it as strongly as he probably could. The countdown to Christmas was daunting.

I'd just have to bite back my instincts and see what he chose.

Joe would need to decide to accept my help.

As I pulled out of his driveway and headed back into town I couldn't help but wonder if what I was doing was totally unhinged.

Probably.

But…I was too stubborn to back out now. And for the first time since we'd met, Joe didn't seem to dislike me. I had to count that as a win.

five

JOE

"HAVE YOU EVER HEARD OF charities doing stuff for the holidays?" The moment the question was out, I realized how stupid it sounded. It was too late to take it back, though.

My older brother, George, to his credit, didn't say anything derogatory, nor did he make me feel like an idiot when he replied, "I think that's pretty common actually."

All of the Milton siblings teased one another. That was a fact. I was lucky he hadn't taken the bait I'd accidentally dangled in front of him. I was too raw and conflicted right now to handle even good-natured ribbing.

The last time I'd lived on my own—the first time—and the reason I'd been dead set on doing everything myself was heavy on my mind. I'd failed then. Been a farm laborer for all of six weeks before I'd been forced back home, broke and humiliated. The worst part? I'd lost my backbone.

I hadn't known how to exist on my own, and that had led to my ultimate failure. And no one in town had ever let me forget it.

I didn't want to do that again.

Couldn't do that again.

I couldn't let myself down like that.

And yet…Jason's words wouldn't leave me.

"Are you talking about fundraising?" George inquired. He'd been speaking, and I'd missed a lot of it. Oops.

"No," I frowned down at my phone, and the little image of his kitchen ceiling inside it. "I'm talking about a charity that has a Christmas fund that they offer to people in need around the holidays. It's called the Santa Fund."

"Cute name."

Accepting help was the hardest thing I would ever do.

If I decided I would—which I still wasn't sure about.

Jason had said he wanted to be my friend. And I…didn't know how to feel about that. I'd chewed over it, processed it, then chewed it up again. All to come to the conclusion that it made sense.

For months he'd hounded me, hunted me like a goddamn predator. I'd wondered why. Been confused, frustrated. Just wanted an answer. Wanted to understand what it was that he was after.

And now that I knew…

I…well.

Jason reminded me of a wolf.

Wolves were pack animals. Meant to be surrounded. He'd said he hadn't had a lot of friends as a kid. We were kindred spirits in that way. Maybe that was why he collected friends now.

I could…understand that.

It was a weird thought. The only friend I'd ever really had was Roderick, my hiking buddy. And that was only because he'd lived across the street from us growing up and been George's boyfriend in high school. I'd never made a friend of my own, nor had I ever been *pursued* by someone else.

It made me feel…happy in a way.

I hadn't realized anyone would *want* to be close to me.

I didn't know what to do with that, just like I didn't know what to do with the money Jason had dangled in front of me—no strings attached.

George was cooking, but had video chatted me anyway, even though for ninety percent of the conversation, he'd given me a whole lot of nothing. Just his walls, or his elbow, and now—his ceiling.

The thunk of his knife hitting the cutting board was methodical and practiced. Somewhere in the distance, the buzz of theater music was in the air, and even farther away, Alex—George's husband's—voice could be heard singing along rather horribly. He kept making George laugh, but he'd cover it up with a cough, pretending like he wasn't amused as hell by his antics.

They were cute together.

The true definition of the word soulmate. I'd asked George once, at his wedding, how he'd known Alex was the one for him. He'd been mid-bridezilla moment, panicking over something about…flowers and the shade of blue—something silly.

And he'd turned to me, softened immediately, all that angry energy gone, and said he just…knew.

"It's a feeling," he'd said. "I don't know how to explain it. Sometimes you meet someone and they just feel…right." It made sense, though, in a cosmic sort of way. When you loved someone, maybe that wasn't something that could be explained. Maybe…it was straight-forward that way. A feeling. Undeniable. Words could be discounted, argued, denied.

But a feeling?

A feeling was just a feeling.

It was immensely satisfying to know that my family had been the ones to instigate their matchmaking.

When he'd picked up the phone, George had informed me he was cooking something special for dinner to celebrate Alex winning one of his hockey games earlier that week. He played recreationally and had convinced my very neurotic, anxiety-riddled older brother to try the ice himself.

George favored the figure skating side of things and often sent the family's group chat videos of him attempting spins. Attempting, yes, because George was absolutely horrible and fell on his ass more often than not.

"Why do you ask?" George hummed, some more thunks of the knife echoing in the background. "Are you thinking of donating to it?"

It was a testament to how well I'd kept my financial woes a secret that George even asked that question. He—and everyone else in my nosy family— had no idea how much I'd been struggling. I wanted to keep it that way.

Which meant I needed to be careful with my next words.

"Maybe." I clammed up immediately. "I saw something about it online and was curious if it was legitimate." I'd never been the best liar so I hoped he bought it. "Figured I'd ask."

"I could look into it for you."

"No thanks," I cut him off quickly. "I'm good."

George paused, even his knife stilled. I held my breath, worried he'd figured me out. A moment later, I realized why he'd stalled. Just gathering his thoughts, I guess.

Thank god.

"Have you thought about my offer?" George asked, taking some of the pressure off of me without even realizing it. "I've got some time off prior to visiting you and figured I could start on the website. Grab pictures while I'm there. Set you up an online presence." Before I could awkwardly tell him I didn't have the money to pay him, he added, "Pro-bono."

"I can pa—"

"You will do no such thing. That would be like taking candy from a baby. No thank you."

I made a sound, and George laughed.

As the youngest sibling, I got those kinds of comments a lot.

It didn't matter that I'd been the one to practically raise my niece, Mavis, for the last few years—and Dad'd trusted me to fix more and more around the house as I'd gotten older. Didn't matter that I owned my own farm now, or that I was nearly thirty fucking years old.

I was still Joe.

Their baby brother.

All I wanted was for someone in my family to finally respect me.

To see me as capable.

George was my primary motivator.

He was my only brother and god…I'd always thought he was so fucking cool. He'd moved away from home and made a life for himself in one of the most cutthroat cities in the world. Even more brave? He'd given up that life and moved back home to start over when he realized how unhappy he'd been. Never afraid of anything, George. Unless you counted bugs. And—well, snakes? And also—

Anyway.

Didn't matter.

Point is, I wanted to prove that I could be like him. Even though I'd never had the chance to show it, deep down, I hoped I was every bit as strong as George. I wanted Mom to think I was independent.

I refused to fail again.

And I certainly wasn't going to spill the beans about the house.

I had an out now.

That's what I'd been looking for, hadn't it? A way up.

I just…didn't know how I felt about the fact that Jason, of all people, was offering it. I'd decided to forgive him after his rather heartfelt apology. He'd been sincere. I could see that. His offer of friendship still perplexed me, but it wasn't like I was drowning in those.

And…he was a pretty good hugger. And generous. And as abrasive as he could be, so far, there was no denying the fact that he was kind.

But…to accept help outright? After telling Jason for months I wanted nothing of the sort? That was going to take some time to chew over.

It was hard to trust that the Santa Fund was real.

Hard to believe that it could be mine.

That he was offering it to me because he liked me, not because he pitied me. I'd thought that was the case. That he'd taken one look at me in that alleyway the first day we'd met and somehow seen beneath my skin.

Seen that I was struggling—that I was scared.

Seen that I was weaker than I projected.

Seen my contradictions.

And thought I couldn't handle myself.

But maybe that wasn't the case.

I was one "yes" away from having the money to solve all my woes. I wanted to believe it, though. Wanted to believe that there was some sort of kindhearted millionaire looking out for me somewhere.

A secret Santa.

I'd been so bound and determined to do all of this on my own, but maybe Jason had a point. Maybe a little financial help wasn't the end of the world. Like he'd said, even trees that could exist in the wild on their own thrived with a little cultivation.

Maybe Jason was correct.

It didn't *have* to mean that I was weak. Maybe in this case…it might even be brave.

Right?

JASON

"HAVE YOU EVER HAD A crush on a man?" I asked my ex-wife, Mary, over coffee. The air was brisk, and the crowds outside the cafe were sparse. That served me just fine, as it wasn't like I wanted the whole town to hear this particular conversation.

Not that I had a thing against gossip.

Hell, I was the *king* of gossip.

I was just gathering intel, that's all. I'd run myself ragged the previous night trying to convince myself that I'd been wrong about Joe. That I didn't have a crush. That I'd been overwhelmed when he'd yelled at me— god, did I have a thing for when he yelled. That Madison was incorrect. That the fizzle in my stomach when I'd held him was a figment of my imagination.

But I couldn't escape the fear that I was firmly in denial.

One didn't just…totally shake up the foundation of their life and have a sexual awakening in their forties. That was not a thing. Was it? And if it was…how did I confirm it? I hadn't been lying when I told Joe I wanted to be his friend.

I could think of nothing in this world I wanted more than that.

But…did I want more?

And if I did…how would I *know* that?

Hence why talking to Mary before I picked up Marybeth from school was a good idea. Mary had to head into the city for a meeting and she wouldn't be back till later that night. Because I was the best not-uncle ever, me and the kiddo were going to have a grand ole time after my half-shift at the grocery store. A Christmas movie. Dinner. The whole shebang.

I was looking forward to it.

It was the perfect distraction after this conversation.

"Can you repeat that?" The look Mary gave me in response to my question was so sour it could've curdled milk.

"I asked if you'd ever had a crush on a man," I said again.

"Yep. That's what I thought you said the first time." Mary arched a brow. "Jason…" She dragged every syllable of my name out for maximum effect. "You do realize I *married* you, right?" A lock of soft brown hair drifted across her brow as a breeze blew through the umbrella-covered tables.

She raised her coffee to her lips with a little head shake that conveyed just how fed-up she already was with my shit. Her eyes danced with amusement, proving she still enjoyed me even if I annoyed her.

"*Right*," I nodded, once again attempting to cut to the chase, "true."

"I am *also* remarried," she added, sipping again. "In case you've forgotten."

"How could I ever forget Daniel?" I sighed dreamily, just to make her laugh. "Hunky sweetheart that he is."

"That's two crushes at least," she informed me.

"We'd hope," I agreed.

"We'd hope," she echoed. She knew I hadn't felt the same way about her. We'd talked about it. In depth. Especially during the divorce. So those words nearly made me laugh. I knew she'd intended them as a joke, a gentle poke. A secret that was ours and ours alone.

Both of us had theorized, over wine on more than one occasion, that I might be on the aromantic spectrum. Greyromantic, possibly. Or demiromantic? I could have sex. I *enjoyed* sex. The release, the physicality. In fact, before we'd been together, I'd had a lot of it, chasing away my perpetual loneliness in whatever way I could.

It scratched a physical itch, but the emotional aspect had always been lacking. Even with Mary. Besides that, there were a lot of ways we were incompatible. We were both too bossy for our own good.

Sex had never equaled feelings for me. It'd just…taken me a long time to realize that. That the endorphins I felt weren't the warm-fuzzies everyone else talked about when they were physical with the person they loved.

Even when I'd been in my college-slut-phase, though, I'd never been interested in having sex with men. Which made my current set of warm-fuzzies and the fact my eyes kept straying to Joe's ass (or chest) even more confusing.

"You're kind of a crush expert then," I started again. This time, Mary outright laughed. Which had been the goal, so I felt pretty accomplished. I grinned. "So…how did you *know* you had a crush?" I asked her. "Definitively."

"Hmm." She took another sip, mulling over the question. "Definitively?

Because I wanted to jump into bed with my crushes."

I wrinkled my nose, even though she was talking about me. Which—just felt weird. At this point, she was more my sister than an ex. "Mary—" I complained. "Be serious."

"I *am* serious." She set her coffee down for a moment. "Everyone is different. For me, the first thing I noticed was my sexual interest. I'm not saying *you'd* be the same if you had one—"

Abort abort!

"Ah," I cut her off before she could continue. "I can see why you'd think I'm talking about *me*—"

"Are you?"

"But I'm not." I walked my fingers across the table and snagged one of the pastries off her plate. "I am only asking out of the goodness of my heart on…behalf of…" Lies, lies. "A friend. Yes. A friend. Not me. *Someone else.* A man. In his…mid…life years. Who has maybe, *possibly*, developed a thing for another man for the very first time. For backstory: he has never had a thing for another guy before. Never. *Is that…weird?*" Mary blinked, and to cover my tracks I added, "I said it wasn't."

At this point I had no idea what was coming out of my mouth.

It wasn't very convincing, probably.

I squinted at her, trying to gauge her reaction. My heart was about ready to leap out of my chest.

"Is that…*possible?*" I asked.

Truthfully, it wasn't Joe's gender that was throwing me for a loop, but the fact that I was interested in anyone in general.

There was no way Mary believed this lie, but she let me bullshit anyway—charitable as she was.

"Of course it's possible," Mary said. "Humans are ever evolving. You and I know that better than anyone." She was a lawyer. She saw a lot of different kinds of people in her line of work. I did too—manning the only grocery store in town—but in a totally different way.

I was constantly surprised by the best in people, and Mary? Well. Mary was constantly surprised by the worst.

"But…" I started. "What about if…the…ah…man? The object-of-affections man, not the crusher-in-his-forties man, was *young*."

"How young?"

"Late twenties." I waited for judgment. "Would *that* be weird? To be interested in someone…younger?"

"Not necessarily, no," Mary shook her head. "So long as the arrangement was mutual and both parties are adults, I don't see why a relationship with a ten-plus-year age gap would be that odd. It happens more often than you'd think. Compatibility transcends numbers."

"Huh." That was enlightening. I nodded along. "How could my friend confirm he has *feelings*? I think…his biggest concern is that because it's a first-time experience, he worries he'll shake up his life and find out that he was simply misunderstanding himself. It wouldn't be the first time he's done that."

"The only way to gather more data is to…gather more data," Mary said. "Tell your friend to spend more time with his crush. Time can be enlightening. Get to know one another. Try not to overthink things."

"I'll tell my guy. My friend-guy. Person. So he knows. That's pretty sound advice."

"I'm surprised your friend-guy-person cares what I think." She had a point there.

"Why wouldn't he?" I huffed, cheeks going hot. "You're very intelligent."

"And this…totally random person we're talking about *knows* that I'm intelligent? Knows *of* me? Enough to value my opinion on the matter?" God, she was pushy.

"I was just consulting you," I admonished. "No need to read between the lines." I took a long sip of my drink to stall.

"I see," Mary said, cocking her head to the side. "Because for a moment there, I thought you were alluding to the massive crush you have on Joe Milton."

I choked.

Then dodged the conversation as quickly as I possibly could.

"Ha! No." I stole the pastry again and shoved it into my mouth, munching through the buttery flaky bread and not tasting a damn thing. When I swallowed, my throat felt like sandpaper. "Why would you think that?" If my voice was a little shrill, that was totally intentional.

"No one, least of all me, would be surprised you have feelings for Joe."

"Except that I *don't*," I glared at her. "And my questions were obviously asked to help someone else. Not me."

"Mhm," Mary's eyes glittered with mischief.

"Stop looking at me like that," I huffed, crumbs spraying across the table.

"Like what?" Mary's lips curled upward.

"Like you know something I don't."

She cocked her head to the side, smug as hell.

I added her to my shit list along with Madison.

And then I headed to work.

seven

JOE

JASON WASN'T AT WORK WHEN I went looking for him. Which was incredibly frustrating. It'd taken me so long to work up the nerve to hunt him down—and here he was, missing. Where the hell was he?

Every other time I'd gone to the grocery store he'd been there.

Like my own personal demon.

And the one time I was actually seeking him out—okay, yes, I'd done that once before—he was gone. Which meant I had no choice but to talk to people. It wasn't like I had his number and could call him, after all.

And it also gave me more time to stew over my decision about the Santa Fund.

Late last night, after talking to George, I had lain in bed, ruminating.

The wind had whistled, rattling the windows, my small space heater on full blast because the wood-burning stove in the living room wasn't doing much to heat the rest of the house. The house had been so quiet after Jason left.

Still.

Normally, that didn't bother me.

But it did right then. Bothered me more than the holes in the walls ever had. More than the horrible flooring, and the decimated door frames—it seriously looked like a raccoon had clawed the shit out of them. Bothered me more than the mold on the ceiling, and the way the toilet was never actually silent.

Bothered me more than the list of things I'd need to accomplish on the farm. Things that took me away from working on the house—even if they did create income to pay for said house.

Bothered me more than the knowing look Patrick had given me when I'd popped down to the orchard to stew. He was a busybody. Worse than Jason. Apparently, he'd seen Jason's car going up the road, and since my house was practically the only place out this far, he'd connected the dots.

Not about the charity.

Obviously.

"Glad to see you're making friends," he'd said, clapping me on the back with one weathered hand. He loved the work as much as I did. More, maybe. Said it was in his blood. That he'd been working this land for his whole life and never planned on changing, even if his wife thought it was high time he truly retire.

Jordan wasn't around, which was probably good. I didn't think I could've handled another person looking at me like that.

"I'm not sure Jason is my friend," I'd bit out, because I was still confused.

"Why not?" Patrick replied. "He's a good kid. Means well, even if he can get caught up in his own web sometimes. There are worse friends to have."

He was right.

Of course he was.

In search of clarity, I'd wandered deeper into the orchard. I moved away from Patrick's knowing eyes. Away from my house and the stresses just looking at it brought to mind. I ran. I ran and ran and ran—until I reached the wooden fence that marked the edge of the property line. Sweat clung to my body in rivulets. My chest heaved.

I'd gone as far as I could go, and yet…thoughts of Jason remained. Clinging to me just like the sweat did. His dorky smile lingering in the back of my mind. Making a place for itself beside the to-do lists I had memorized and my worries, so commonly sifted through they were practically alphabetized at that point.

I thought about what Jason's reaction would be if I said yes to the money and his friendship.

I thought about the way it'd felt to be tucked in his arms. How warm his hand was as it'd squeezed my nape with authority. The flicker of his breath on the shell of my ear. How being with him didn't make me feel scared, even when it should.

I'd felt small.

I'd never felt small before.

Jason was as patient with me as I was with my apple trees.

Coaxing, the way I was with animals.

Like that's what he thought I was.

A wild creature, looking to be appreciated—not tamed. I didn't get the feeling Jason wanted that. In fact, when I'd panicked, when I'd gotten angry, he'd never once given me the impression that he'd been cowed. No.

Instead, he'd been just as sure as he always was.

Not afraid of me.

Maybe it was that thought, the one that kept me up at night. The one that made my house feel so empty and cold when it'd never felt that way before.

Maybe it was that thought that led to *now*.

To me hunting Jason down.

To me…planning to say yes to his hair-brained, generous scheme.

To me standing awkwardly in the grocery store, like an idiot as I searched for a man who simply wasn't there. Stumbling over my words, I managed to inquire about Jason's whereabouts from the other cashier.

Her name tag read Madison. She was a dark-haired waif of a girl with a permanent frown, and for some ungodly reason, every time I'd come in since June she'd headed straight into the back room like she thought I had the plague.

"Jason's going to the theater," Madison said, slurping out of a frankly heinous-looking Christmas cup. I had to assume that Jason had bought for her. It seemed like something he'd purchase. A way to tease her. The way he teased me.

He teased his friends.

It was kind of relieving to understand that now.

"If he's not late, he'll get there in the next few minutes," Madison tacked that last bit on after checking the time on her phone. It was a testament to how much Jason ran his mouth that she knew his exact location and schedule for the day.

When I arrived at the theater I didn't see Jason's truck.

Most people in Belleville drove trucks.

It had to do with the nature of the town and its businesses, but even more so with the sheer amount of snow that hit come winter. Vermont was a different beast entirely. When snow came, it came down hard—and fast.

I'd yet to see a winter in Vermont, but I'd been told as much at least a dozen different times when I'd been purchasing my own truck. It was used. Run-down. But it suited my needs just fine. Reliable. Big. Blue.

I loved blue.

Jason's truck was green.

A glossy, new, monstrous-looking thing. He'd had a booster seat in the back. A fact I'd noticed when he'd brought over pizza, but hadn't really mulled over until now. If I hadn't seen it when he'd come to my house I never would've known what to keep an eye out for.

I sat stewing in the parking lot for a solid ten minutes before I figured waiting inside the theater was a better plan. Then, at least, I wouldn't be wasting gas. It was chilly again, the skitter of leaves on the pavement setting me on edge as I pulled my flannel snug around myself and strode across the asphalt and into the cinema.

Why the hell was Jason late for his own damn movie?

That was just poor planning.

Also…who goes to the movies by themselves?

I stalked through the dark interior of the building all the way to the benches at the back wall. They sat beneath an array of movie posters. All stuff that I was genuinely interested in but didn't have the money or the time to watch.

And yet—here I was.

Wasting time.

For Jason.

Groaning, I dragged my hands over my face and into my hair. Maybe this was a bad idea. Maybe Jason's being late was a sign of that. Maybe I should go. Maybe I should—

"Joe!" Jason's voice interrupted my thoughts. I couldn't help the way I perked up, dropping my hands back into my lap, eyes hunting for him.

He wasn't difficult to spot.

There were only a handful of people in the lobby since it was midday. My stomach growled, the scent of popcorn only truly hitting now that I was no longer stewing in my own head. It was good I'd gotten what I needed to at the farm done earlier that morning, so no one was waiting on me.

But I'd hoped for this to only last an hour at most so I could head back to the house and get started on what I could.

"Hey!" Jason was wearing a sweater today. Plush looking. Green. The same color as his truck. He wore skinny jeans that hugged the shape of his legs. They were bowed slightly, making his walk more of a swagger than anything else as he approached.

That was when I noticed her.

There was a little girl holding his hand, probably six years old? Maybe seven. Tiny. Brown hair. Big dark eyes so clever they bore right into my soul. Staring at me curiously, like she didn't understand who I was—or why Jason was heading straight for me when he was at the movies with her.

It was only then that I realized what an ass I was being.

I hadn't even considered the fact he might have company.

I'd come all the way across town to…to take his—well, his buddy's—money? Without thinking of or considering him at all. My cheeks flushed bright red, shame and mortification burning through me like wildfire.

I needed to get out of here.

I prided myself on being polite. Hell, even when I hadn't liked him I'd still brought him apples as a thank you. And here I was, being rude as hell.

"Are you here to see the movie too?" Jason asked curiously, pausing right in front of me, blocking my exit.

I nodded, even though I had no idea what movie he was talking about. It was easier than admitting that I was a total dick. I couldn't ask him for the money *now*. This whole thing was a lost cause.

"That's good," Jason said. "I was starting to worry you never did anything to relax." And then, "We haven't bought our tickets yet," Jason said, just as chipper as ever. "Maybe my niece and I can sit by you?" His smile was easy, his eyes glittering. He looked pleased to have run into me. Which…only made me feel more like a total ass.

He wanted to be my friend.

He was happy to see me.

God, I was a jerk.

"I haven't bought mine yet either," I bit out sullenly, resigning myself to spending money that I did not have.

"Great." Jason turned to his niece, folding his body low and giving her a playful little shake. "Miss Marybeth," Jason started.

She snapped to attention, saluting him like he was her drill sergeant. "Yes, sir?!"

"I have an important mission for you."

She giggled, still holding her salute. "Okey dokey, sir!"

"Can you babysit Joe for me while I buy tickets for the three of us, please?" She nodded very seriously. His words had been very intentional there. A cautious poke so that I knew not to worry about my own ticket.

Warmth flooded my chest.

Jason kissed Marybeth's cheek. She chortled, dropping her salute so she could tip into the kisses. He kissed it again. Another giggle. Then he was off, leaving Marybeth behind to "babysit me" as he headed to the counter to pay.

Marybeth regarded me, her smile fading a smidge.

I was no stranger to interacting with kids. Which was why I knew I could be intimidating, especially to little folk. And why I knew how to talk to them so they wouldn't be scared.

"Hi," I said, keeping my voice gentle.

"Hi," Marybeth said back, smiling at me shyly.

"I'm Joe." I didn't stand up, worried my height would freak her out. Jason was tall but not as tall as I was. And besides, he wasn't solid muscle like me.

"I know," she said, a clever little smirk on her face. "Uncle Jason said so."

"Okay, sassy." I grinned, digging around in my pockets for something to give her. "You like apples?" I'd picked a small one up on my run last night. A late bloomer. It'd sat forgotten in my pocket. Forgotten until now, anyway, as my fingers bumped against its smooth surface.

Marybeth perked up.

Kids were so much easier to talk to than adults.

I pulled the apple out, amused and delighted when Marybeth's eyes lit up.

"That's the littlest apple I've ever seen!" she said, obviously amazed. She cupped her small hands beneath it. I dropped it into them, unable to hide my grin. "Thanks, Joe!"

"No problem."

Jason returned a second later.

His eyes drank me in, settling on my mouth in particular.

I dropped my grin quickly, but the heat of Jason's knowing blue eyes lingered even with it gone. He had a giant bucket of popcorn in his grip, as well as a stack of colorful candy boxes, and three empty cups.

Jason offered the cups to me with a pointed waggle.

"Diet Coke, please," he said. "I've gotta watch my figure. And for Miss Marybeth—"

"Sprite!" Marybeth finished for him.

I was on my feet a second later, moving slower than usual—again, because I didn't want to freak the kid out. Jason's fingers brushed mine when he passed the cups to me. I shivered.

Had Jason always been this way? This…kind? This sure of himself? I wasn't certain I'd ever seen him without a manic grin on his face.

Patrick's words came back to me, unbidden.

There are worse friends to have.

Jason and Marybeth observed as I headed to the drink fountain and filled our cups. I spilled a bit. I tended to do that. Spill. With liquids. I cleaned up the mess with one of the napkins, just grateful it hadn't been wine, and I hadn't leaked all over myself like I had at my buddy Roderick's wedding.

God, that sounded bad.

I meant leaked—as in the wine. Not…ugh.

Jason didn't comment on my clumsiness as I returned to the little group, this time juggling the full drinks. I was surprised. Considering his penchant for teasing, I would've expected at least a little ribbing.

But nope.

Nothing.

He was friendly and sass-less as he led us toward the ticket booth.

As we walked, Marybeth showed Jason her tiny apple. I puffed up with pride as she gushed about how it was, "the ittiest bittiest, cutest little apple in the whole wide world!"

"That thing is absolutely adorable," Jason agreed. "Just like you." He blew her a kiss, and she grinned, ducking her head shyly though she was clearly pleased.

"Oh hey, Jason!" the attendant said when we arrived at the booth. She barely looked at our tickets before handing them back. Her smile was sunny. Jason's magnetic pull was hard at work, sucking all of her attention toward him.

"Hi, Trina," Jason said back, just as warmly. "How's your uncle's knee doing?"

"Oh, you know. Better? As better as can be anyway."

"I imagine he won't be ice fishing again anytime soon."

"Definitely not." She cackled, and gestured to her right. "Theater six! Last door on the left."

"Thanks!" Jason strutted forward, arms too full to hold Marybeth's hand anymore. She didn't mind though. She copied the way he was walking with a very focused look on her face, swaggering along at his side like his tiny mini-me.

"You wanna help carry something?" Jason asked her, pausing halfway down the hall. She nodded. He offered her the boxed candy, which she took with the utmost seriousness.

I shouldn't have been surprised that Jason was good with kids. Nor should I have been surprised that even the people at the theater seemed to know him. Everyone loved Jason. Everyone.

I was just late to the party, I guess.

I probably should've been more upset that I'd somehow been bamboozled into attending the movies with him. Only this time, *I* had bamboozled myself, so there was nothing to angst about.

I still didn't know what movie we were seeing. And the waste of precious time made my skin crawl as I trailed dutifully behind the two of them into the dark theater.

Things were up in the air now. I couldn't ask for the money. So, I pushed the thoughts aside and tried to focus on the present.

Going to the movies was a…friend thing to do, wasn't it?

I'd never done it.

Not with a friend, anyway. For Christmas, Mom and Dad would take us when we were kids. And a few times, as a teenager, George and Roderick had let me piggyback on one of their dates. Aside from that, though, I'd never had the balls to go to one of these on my own.

Even though I genuinely did like movies.

Jason glanced at the letters lining the aisles to locate our seats. When he'd found what he was looking for, he dipped his head up the aisle to direct us to the correct place. He glanced at me, making sure I was following along.

He was taking care of things so efficiently, my brain began to check out.

Which was not a feeling I was very familiar with.

Normally, I was hyper vigilant.

But right now…I just…weirdly enough, it felt like Jason had it handled.

"You want middle or side?" he asked Marybeth when we'd wiggled our way into the correct row. There were only a handful of other people inside the theater itself, scattered about as far from each other as possible. We probably could've spread out, but…I didn't want to.

"Side," Marybeth chirped.

"What about you?" Jason turned those all-knowing blue eyes on me. "Middle or side, Joe?"

He always said my name like that.

With purpose.

It made my skin feel hot.

"Side," I answered, voice gravelly.

"Good deal." Jason used a shrug of his shoulder to direct me to his right. Heeding the unspoken command, I took my seat in a bit of a daze. Again, I marveled at the fact that I didn't have to think.

The drinks sloshed as I moved.

Jason didn't comment.

He sat down between Marybeth and me, legs manspread in that effortlessly confident way he always had, straight out in front of him, ratty tennis shoes on display.

Humming under his breath, he began arranging the candy in his lap. Neatly too. He'd even grabbed a few extra cups so he could divvy out the candy in the most hygienic and fair way possible. It was exactly what I would've done, had I been the one to do it.

Slipping deeper into that weirdly fuzzy place in my head, I found myself settling.

He's got it, my brain provided helpfully. *Relax. You never relax anymore.*

"Do you have any allergies? Anything you don't like?" Jason asked me very seriously after he'd finished spreading the food between the three containers. He had a pack of M&M's hovering above the giant bin of popcorn, just waiting to be poured.

"No."

"Alright then." Jason dumped the M&M's into the popcorn. I frowned, baffled and mildly appalled at the sacrilege. "Don't make that face. It's good. You're going to try it, and you're going to like it," Jason told me with surety.

I didn't have it in me to argue, not when, for the first time since I'd moved away, I could feel my guard actually slipping.

Besides, I quickly discovered he was right.

I did like the snack.

Just like I was now realizing…I might like him.

It was a good movie.

And aside from bumping fingers with Jason in the popcorn bucket, the whole experience was incredibly relaxing. Jason talked a little, which was bad manners, obviously. But it was only to explain things to Marybeth that she didn't understand. As if he could read her mind, he always seemed to know exactly which bits were confusing her.

It was a kids' movie.

Home Alone.

One of the ones I'd grown up watching with my siblings during Christmas. I'd always related to the main kid. His need to prove himself. But I'd never had the guts to do what he did, nor had I ever resented my family the way he resented his.

They were loud, yes, nosy, sometimes brash—but they loved me—even if they did judge.

Jason cried during the movie. He clearly loved it. I could relate, I loved it too.

Nostalgia was the medicine I hadn't known I needed.

Scratch that—*Jason* was the medicine I hadn't known I needed.

There was nowhere for me to be.

Nothing for me to do except sit there and enjoy myself.

I hadn't realized how much I needed that or how high-strung I'd been until the movie ended. The lights came back on. The empty cartons and cups were discarded. And I felt lighter than I had in months. Light enough that I loped ahead of our little party of three to open the door for Jason.

"Thank you." He arched an expressive brow but otherwise said nothing. This time, he did hold Marybeth's hand, swinging her back and forth, and making her laugh the whole walk through the theater and back outside.

The sun had already set.

Early.

That was the worst part about fall, in my opinion.

The darkness.

I shivered as I realized I was going to head home empty-handed. I'd listen to the whistle of wind through the holes in the walls and wish I'd lingered at the theater for longer. Simply enjoying the twinkle of Marybeth's laugh and the peace of having good company.

Maybe being friends with Jason was easier than I'd thought it would be.

"Have you eaten yet?" Jason asked instead of cutting me loose.

"No," I grunted, still feeling soft around the edges.

"My treat—" Jason clapped a hand on my back. High enough that he could drag his palm up to my nape and *squeeze*. I melted. "You like Italian? Silly question. Everyone likes Italian."

"Y-yeah," I replied unnecessarily.

Jason grinned.

Dinner was delicious. Jason forced me to taste a whole variety of foods when he found out I hadn't been to Rudy's before. He told me what to try and when. Offered me a napkin when I needed it. Flagged the waiter down when my drink was empty, always smiling, always polite.

My guard stayed down.

As I ate, he and Marybeth giggled together like a gaggle of teenage girls. They swapped stories back and forth. He included me at first, but when it was clear that I preferred to stay silent, he let me be.

Marybeth's stories were mostly about the boys in her class at school and how dumb they were. What did kids that little have to complain about? A lot, apparently. Mavis had been simpler, even if she was far grumpier than Marybeth was.

Jason's stories were about the townies.

With each one Jason shared, I understood him better. Jason had his finger in every pie, so to speak. Knowing people and all their intimate details made him better equipped to care for them. A fact that was revealed when every tale he told ended in him managing to help someone or enlist help for them, in some way.

For example, the uncle he'd mentioned to the girl at the theater. Jason had heard a rumor that someone had seen him disappearing behind the grocery store after hours. He'd found it suspicious and had been immediately concerned. For a week, he'd stationed himself in a camping chair out back, waiting for the intruder to arrive.

Nothing happened.

He gave up.

Until one night, he was working late, and he heard something in the alley. Immediately, he remembered the rumor, and rather than call the cops, he went out there full of concern. Which ended up being a good thing because he'd found the girl's uncle collapsed at the bottom of the dumpster after he'd popped his knee out of place while climbing in.

Apparently, he'd been looking for expired food. Jason told me that he didn't know why the man had needed that food, and he hadn't asked. It wasn't his place to judge or know such intimate knowledge. Which was… surprisingly sweet, and not at all what I'd expected from such a well-known gossip.

The story ended when Jason called the town doctor, Ben Montgomery, for help, and sent the man home with a few gift cards and a promise. From now on, if he had anything expired worth handing out, he'd keep it in a fridge in the stock room, and he could stop by and get it—no dumpsters required.

Jason informed me that he'd told everyone—aside from me, for some ungodly reason—that the man had hurt his knee while ice fishing.

And thus—the lie was born.

Jason didn't tell the tale like he was bragging.

He simply relayed the facts.

It did make me wonder, though, if maybe he'd told me about the food in the stockroom on purpose. This was the second time that he'd rather doggedly tried to feed me after all. I may not be the sharpest tool in the shed, but I could read between the lines clearly enough.

It was a roundabout way of taking care of me, sure, but I appreciated it.

He was trying not to step on my pride.

Especially after I'd blown up at him last time.

And had yet to accept his offers.

Jason didn't realize that I didn't have that in me right now.

I still felt fuzzy around the edges. Less stressed than usual. Less panicky. With my belly full. Less lonely. Less scared. And oddly…safe with him nearby, watching over me. I didn't have to worry about a single thing.

The last thing I wanted to do was go back to my house and see the mess of projects that awaited me. At the reminder of my house and the reason I'd been out looking for Jason in the first place, I sobered.

Jason paused mid-bite, eyebrows raised in question.

Those damn eyebrows could host a whole conversation on their own.

"Jason!" an eager voice said, unknowingly saving me. "I *thought* that was you."

The newcomer was an older woman wearing one of the same "Montgomery Smut Club" shirts I'd spotted in town a few days previously. It was a weird shirt, but I wasn't judging. I'd peeked at the manga George had once— without permission—and realized how common that sorta thing truly was.

It was nice in a way, that people could flaunt what they liked.

I'd never been very good at that.

Didn't have experience in that regard.

Just thinking about sex made me shy.

Jason chatted with the woman for a solid ten minutes. Long enough that I'd finished eating, and Marybeth had grown tired. She blinked at me, a little smile on her lips. Then she brought her hand up and made a flapping motion with it like she was trying to illustrate what a "yapper" her uncle was.

I snorted.

Jason noticed immediately.

He cocked his head at me, an arm going behind my chair, hand gripping my shoulder. God, his hand was warm. Almost blisteringly so. "Have you met Joe?" he asked the woman. "He bought the orchard at the edge of town."

"Oh, really?" The woman perked up, eyes brightening. "Are you doing a U-Pick? We've missed those."

I stiffened, suddenly unsure of how to reply. "I…" My throat closed up. I didn't want to mess this up. My brain was too soft for this right now—what did I do? What did I—

"He's looking into it!" Jason said with a grin. "Though, I will say…if you want a taste, I recommend popping by the grocery store and grabbing some of his apples. They're delightful. I ate two myself the other day." Jason groaned dramatically to illustrate how good my apples apparently were.

I ducked my head, cheeks flushed.

I hadn't known he'd eaten my apples.

Had it been the two I'd knocked over?

Probably.

Marybeth helped by proudly offering the older woman the tiny apple she'd shoved in her pocket earlier. To which the lady cooed in delight.

"You can look, but it's mine," she said deliberately. "If you want your own, you need to buy it from Joe."

"Well, isn't that precious! What a good little salesperson you've got here," she winked at me.

"And!" Jason added on, giving my shoulder a little shake. "I heard a rumor he's planning to be at the Pie Festival selling his wares!"

How the hell had he known that?

I nodded because Jason was correct, and the woman grinned at me. "It's pie-baking season," she told us both. "I'll stop by. Bring the club—"

"Oh yes. He'd love that!"

"We'll buy you right out!" With that, she said her goodbyes and departed. Jason shoveled the last of his food into his mouth quickly. By that point, it was cold. He didn't complain, nor did he seem to mind. Content to have used his free time to help me. Again. His cheeks puffed up like a chipmunk as he signaled the waiter for the check.

He paid.

Just like he'd promised he would.

I was floating, and I didn't know what to do with myself. Jason's hand was on my nape as he led us out the door and into the chilly dark night. Every time he looked at me, it felt like I was on fire.

My belly was full of food he'd bought me.

And that warm, warm hand was holding me steady.

At that moment, I was pretty sure there wasn't a thing in the world that could ruin this for me.

Out on the street, the Christmas lights that ran over awnings and across trees lit the world up a hearty gold. I'd never been down here at night. Hadn't known it could be like this. That Belleville could be this welcoming.

There was something about the play of light on Jason's face that mesmerized me.

Or maybe it was how…full of *life* he seemed to be, even now. A whirlwind kinda person. A tornado. He existed, and everyone else was pulled into him, me included.

The air was crisp and I sucked in a greedy breath full, almost drugged as his hand tightened on my nape and he herded me to the parking lot where we'd parked. We'd taken separate cars here. Our trucks, faded blue and glossy green, parked right next to one another.

Marybeth was babbling, and Jason was chatting along, but I barely heard a single word, lost as I was. We'd yet to have one of the big snowstorms I'd heard warnings about, but I could sense it on the horizon. Practically taste it in the air as we paused in front of Jason's truck and he released my neck so he could unlock it.

I missed his hand the moment it was gone.

Like a brand on my skin, his touch lingered.

Blinking back to the real world, I observed Jason tucking Marybeth safely into her booster seat. He shut the door after her, then turned around to face me, all pale blue eyes and goofy grin. This was it for the night. Just goodbyes. Us alone, for the first time since he'd shown up at my house with pizza and offered me a hand up.

I sobered quickly.

Tell him what you chose.

You need to tell him.

Tell him you want to be his friend.

Tell him about the money.

Tell him.

My mouth refused to open.

Jason regarded me with quiet intensity. He'd snuck beneath the walls I'd begun to throw back up like he'd memorized where they were going. I shivered, not from the chill this time, but because even with my forts rising once more, Jason made me feel bare.

"You didn't come out for the movie," he said, voice kind, once again reading my mind. "Did you?"

My heart stuttered.

For a moment, it was hard to breathe.

Hard to admit my choice.

A big step.

A step I'd thought I was taking alone—only now…I wasn't so sure.

I shook my head, relieved I didn't have to ask. My heart was *pounding* now, and it wouldn't stop. Galloping faster than it had on my run. Making me feel sick with it. Sick with loss too, because all I wanted in that moment was Jason's hand back on my nape, grounding me.

I wanted to go back to twenty minutes ago, when the only thing I had to worry about was his smile.

But I couldn't.

I was Joe again. Not that fuzzyheaded fool. And I needed to put my "big boy" pants on and open my goddamn mouth.

Jason's eyes flashed with something protective. He'd looked at me that way before, when I'd fallen apart on him, left snot on his shoulder,and bolted because the shame and mortification of letting myself break like that had nearly torn me apart.

I didn't know what to do with that look.

"Did you think about my offer?" Jason asked.

I nodded. "I…yes."

"And you're taking it," he confirmed.

Again, I nodded.

A smile unfurled on Jason's lips.

Heart still skipping, my hands shaking, I forced my mouth to open again.

"*And* the other one," I said quietly, about ready to puke, I was so overwhelmed. "I'm accepting that one, too."

"The…other one?" Jason blinked. It took him a second, but the moment he realized what I'd been alluding to his friendship, his smile softened. Gooey. Like melted caramel. "Oh," he said simply. "I'm very, very, very happy about that."

Embarrassed, I ducked my head.

Jason's current smile was warmer than the ones he'd offered everyone else throughout the night. Smaller in a way that made it feel more genuine. "Good choice." He reached out, plucking at a lock of hair that'd fallen across my forehead. "I'll be by tomorrow with a check. That sound doable?"

I nodded a third time, throat dry, unable to look at him.

His hands rested by his thighs, still. One twitched, like he'd been about to reach out for me—but didn't.

"Goodnight, Joe." Jason waited for a beat for me to reply, and when I couldn't get my mouth to open again, his voice remained tender. "Drive safe, please."

And with that, he let me go.

Jason climbed into his truck.

The lights flicked on.

The parking lot illuminated as Jason backed up and away.

Gone.

Just like that.

With the tornado departed, I was left to stew in silence.

But it wasn't the same kinda stewing I'd done before.

This felt tender somehow.

Just like his smile had.

I went home to my cold, broken farmhouse, and a spark of something strange and new unfurled in my belly. Indigestion, maybe? I blamed the lasagna. Not Jason's smile. Or his kindness. Or the fact that we were officially, definitely friends.

Nope.

Not at all.

eight

JASON

BEFORE GOING TO THE MOVIES with Joe, I'd been feeling puzzled, to say the least. Annoyed too, because what Mary had said stuck even worse in my head than Madison's accusation about my feelings. Mary knew me better than anyone. She was my best friend.

If *she* thought I had a crush, that probably meant I did.

But I hadn't been ready to admit it.

Because I didn't know what that would mean for me.

It didn't matter if Mary said my alleged crush was "normal" or that it wasn't "inappropriate", or that "humans were ever evolving" and it wasn't "weird" to grow. Until the end of the night, when Joe had looked to me with eyes like oceans, fairy lights painting him a jolly gold, I'd been firmly in denial.

The last time I'd loved someone—Mary—I'd found out too late that the love I felt was platonic. I'd *hurt* her. Let her down. I couldn't be what she needed me to be. And a decade after the split, I still felt the pain of failing her.

I didn't want to do that to another person.

Least of all Joe.

But after spending more time with him, after seeing him *vulnerable*. Gathering "intel" the way I'd been told. Seeing him docile. *Needy*. After discovering what it felt like for him to rely on me, to need me. Just a glimpse of the man beneath the grouchy exterior—there was no denying that I'd lost that battle with myself long ago.

I had a crush.

A pretty big, massive crush.

On a pretty, big, massive man.

And I needed to accept that, especially if I was going to continue being friends with him.

It didn't have to mean anything. Didn't have to change anything. I knew that. Feelings did not equal a relationship. And besides, it wasn't like they were mutual.

I didn't even want them to be.

Just the thought made me want to run. Terrified of being put in a position to potentially disappoint someone again.

My thoughts were eating me up as I headed to the bank the next morning to pick up the check for Joe. As I drove through Belleville, waving at the friendly townies I passed by, my thoughts were far, far away.

Across town.

On that apple orchard, the white farmhouse at its border, and the man who resided inside it.

I still couldn't believe Joe had accepted my offer. Yes, it was only money.

I understood that. It wasn't like he'd invited me inside his home and made me the first to ever enter it. Wasn't like he'd allow me to actually help with what needed to be done. I wasn't naive enough to think by accepting the money he was letting me in *all* the way—but my toe was in the door now, and that was *heady*.

Joe was the most guarded person I'd ever met.

Multi-faceted.

I'd seen more sides to him now than probably anyone else who lived in Belleville. Which was most definitely stroking my ego, not going to lie. Between how gentle he was with animals, how gruff he could be with people, how shy he became when confronted with social interactions he wasn't prepared for—and that smile.

God.

That big, sunny, beautiful smile he'd given Marybeth when she'd taken his apple.

I could assume I'd been made privy to parts of Joe that he kept under lock and key.

That was a lot of pressure.

Pressure I would've buckled under if I hadn't been bound and determined not to cave. I refused to let another person I cared about down. And I *did* care about Joe. If I took romantic interest out of it, that care still remained.

The more time I spent with him, the more I wanted to make his life better. I didn't need anything from him in return. Hell, he'd already given me more than I ever would've expected, accepting my offer of friendship like that.

Eyes sparkling.

Dark with the same loneliness I felt.

Maybe caring for Joe the way he needed meant that I'd never expose my true feelings or how deep they ran. Maybe that meant I'd quietly grow to love him. Cultivate a friendship that truly blossomed without anything to complicate it.

Who cared if I'd never been more enamored with a person in my entire life? It didn't matter. It didn't fucking matter.

What *he* needed, what *he* wanted, were what was important to me. Not my own feelings regarding the matter, or my own desires.

Besides…as I pulled out of the parking lot at the bank, money secured, feeling more settled than I had since Madison had called me out, I realized Mary had been right. She often was, so this was no surprise.

Regardless of how I chose to deal with my feelings toward Joe, one thing was for certain. I couldn't let my experiences with Mary, my perceived "failures," ruin what could be a perfectly good friendship. I needed to learn to let go of the past. At least, if I wanted a chance to have a happy future.

Joe had been awake long before I arrived, despite the early hour. A fact that was made obvious by the noise that was echoing down the driveway as I drove toward the same farmhouse I'd been thinking about all morning.

Thud, thunk.

The "Santa Fund" check was sitting sentinel on the passenger seat. Dappled light bounced through the windows, painting the cushion and envelope in a colorful blur, as I dodged potholes, and gravel crunched beneath my tires.

Thud, thunk.

Thud, thunk.

The closer I came to the house, the more obvious it became what Joe was doing. There was no doubt he was chopping more firewood. I'd never done that myself, but I'd witnessed it enough times to recognize it for what it was, even before I saw him.

His truck bed was empty, the brambles I'd seen the other day missing. Unsurprising. They hadn't been there last night either, now that I thought about it.

I pulled up beside his truck and put the car in park by jamming my foot on the peddle. It wasn't a very graceful stop. Because—*woah*. Suddenly, I could see Joe, and I was just—*wow*. Heat coursed through me, settling between my legs. All I could do was take in the view.

Despite the chill in the air, Joe was shirtless.

Naked from the waist up.

Shirtless.

Naked from the—

Oh god.

Golden skin with obvious tan lines glistened with sweat as Joe hacked log after log after log. There was a rhythm to it. Like he'd done this a thousand times. A million times. The splay of his muscles danced as he moved, powerful and precise. The kind of strength that came from hard labor and repetition. Once again, I couldn't help but mentally compare him to a panther. A big *golden*, sweaty panther.

He could be dangerous if he wanted to be. And instead…he chose to be gentle.

There was so much to see.

So much to appreciate.

The glint of a gold chain around his neck.

The sweat-damp hair at his nape.

The ripple of muscle as he brought his arms over his head, his lats flexed, and the axe came right back down with a loud thud.

"I am going to Hell," I muttered as my eyes lingered on the dimples above the waistband of his jeans, and I tried not to choke on my own drool. Maybe Mary and I had that in common. Not going to Hell. I mean, the sexual…ah *appetite* when we liked someone.

I'd never felt that about her.

But I certainly felt that now.

For Joe.

For Joe and his biceps. The way he twisted when he grabbed a new log to halve. And the smattering of hair that led from his belly button all the way beneath his Levi's. For the way those big pecs almost bounced with each labored breath, pink nipples perky because of the chill.

Joe hadn't noticed me.

I got out of the truck and headed toward him.

The check crinkled a bit in my grip, and I almost laughed. The lack of control I currently had was *astounding*. It felt like the universe was playing a joke on me. I'd literally just accepted I had feelings for him, and here I was, showing up to see farm-boy-Magic-Mike.

I forced my grip to relax, keeping a respectful and safe distance as I circled around to Joe's front. The last thing I wanted to do was startle him while he was wielding a fucking axe, thank you very much.

The moment Joe saw me, he tensed.

His eyes went wide.

He slammed the axe into the empty stump he'd been using to anchor the other logs. Faster than I could blink, he had his earbuds out. He stared at me for a beat. I stared back, gauging his mood, his reaction to me, with fascination.

The guardedness was still there, of course. I hadn't expected it to go away after one spectacular holiday movie—*Home Alone* always managed to hit me right where I was weakest—and a plate of lasagna. I wasn't naive. But he was…decidedly less prickly than before.

Ah.

The power of *friendship*.

"Morning, big guy!" The term of endearment slipped out before I could stop it. Joe blinked in reaction. Otherwise, he didn't look offended or pleased. Neutral. "I have your check right here as promised." I tapped the envelope.

Joe's eyes slipped to the paper.

I held it toward him.

His lips pressed into a tight line.

Warily, like he was accepting a bag full of razors, he reached out to take the check from my hand. The bully in me wanted to keep holding on for as long as possible. Maybe give it a little tug and spook him. But I refrained.

Moving forward, and all that.

I let it go the moment Joe had it safely in his grip.

I could tell he wanted to open it. That he was curious, and maybe anxious to see if he now had enough to cover what needed to be done on the house. I hadn't actually told him how much the charity would provide, so it made sense that he'd feel that way.

Truthfully, I was pretty stoked to see his face when he opened it.

That was the nice part about being both the provider of the funds and the delivery boy.

I got the best of both worlds as both secret Santa and not-so-secret Elf.

"Open it up," I urged, eager to see the look on his face. "C'mon. I wanna see your face."

Joe's brow pinched. He was fighting with the part of himself that probably thought doing that was rude. But…I mean, if I wanted him to do it, was it rude? No.

"It's not rude," I promised. His eyes widened again, and he glanced at me sidelong. He'd been doing that more and more lately. The more time I spent with him, the better I could read him, which meant it was easy to answer even when he didn't voice his thoughts.

I had to press my lips together so I wouldn't start laughing.

God, he was cute.

Grouchy baby.

"Okay," Joe said a moment later. "I'm opening it." And then, very *carefully*, like he was disabling a bomb, he began to tear through the envelope. I had to bite my lip so I wouldn't tell him to hurry. I didn't want to rush him. I was just…excited.

When he pulled out the check and saw the numbers, he outright choked.

"Is that enough?" I hummed, practically performing victory laps in my head. "Because if you need more, I can talk to my friend—" I was the friend, obviously. "And see what I can do." I would do anything he needed me to.

"*No*," Joe bit out, voice rough. "*No*. This is…this is enough. This is more than enough."

He looked dizzy.

I fought myself for a solid two seconds before my protective instincts won and I crossed the space between us. I slung an arm over his shoulder, leading him toward the porch where he could sit down.

No passing out near sharp objects for him, no siree.

When he'd settled onto the rickety steps—after it'd made that horrible wheezing sound again—Joe looked up at me.

Up.

Which was a first.

I was practically looming over him.

A fact that made the flicker of need in my belly turn molten hot. *Fuck.* I fought a shiver as Joe's eyes turned sweet again. Needy. He was looking at me like he hoped I was going to fix everything for him and… Mmmm.

Apparently, that was my goddamn catnip.

And the final nail in the coffin.

No more denial for me.

Nope.

Because Joe and that face—those eyes—the way he regarded me like he thought I could take care of him? Was just…no. I couldn't deny how much I liked that. Not even to myself. Good thing I'd already come to terms with my feelings and formed a battle plan on the drive over, otherwise the force of desire that struck me then might've made me push him back onto the steps so I could take care of him in a very different way, inexperience with men be damned.

"If you don't use it all, keep the rest," I commanded, voice husky. "It's yours."

Joe's voice was barely more than a whisper. "But it's so much." His brow furrowed, wrinkle forming. "More than I expected. More than I need."

"Santa's decided you're on the Nice list, apparently." I rocked back on my heels, hands on my hips as I bent down close. "Besides, I won't tell if you won't." I winked.

It was the wrong thing to say. Joe's guard screeched right back up, steel walls thrown into the back of his eyes. Then he wasn't looking at me at all anymore, staring off to the side like he often did, avoiding my gaze. "I'm not going to break the rules," he bit out. "Or take advantage of this very generous perso—"

"No. No, no, no." Unable to help myself, I grabbed his face. I cupped it in both of my hands, tilting his head up so he was forced to meet my gaze. I needed those eyes on me again. Needed it like I needed air. "That was my fault. I was just kidding—I make jokes, remember? You're *supposed* to keep the money. It's *your* money. What you do with it after you cash it is entirely up to you. Hell, spend it on strippers for all I care. It's not m—the charity's anymore."

I could not believe I was getting away with this.

I mean, it wasn't like I was doing something bad?

But it still felt…quite covert.

Joe relaxed, though he gave me a perplexed look. "I thought you joked when you were uncomfortable," he said quietly.

I blinked.

My smile softened. "I joke always," I reassured.

"So, you're not…uncomfortable?"

"Right now?" I shook my head. "Nope. I'm very happy. Very pleased that my good friend, Joe, has let me put my toe in his door."

Joe grimaced. "What?"

"You know what, never mind."

It wasn't until Joe stopped panicking that I realized I was *holding* him. That his stubble was scratching my palms, and that gorgeous square jaw was cradled beneath my fingers. Cradling him the same way he'd cradled the magpie.

Like he was fragile.

Like he was beautiful.

Like he was *wondrous*.

"I joke a lot, Joe," I promised him. "You can't take me too seriously. And sometimes what I say makes little to no sense. Comes with the territory of having no brain-to-mouth filter." He nodded, a sharp little motion that was barely a movement at all. "It wasn't a very good joke if it upset you," I admitted. "I'm still learning how to communicate with you."

He didn't know what to say to that. He was quiet, staring up at me, letting me hold him—though I had no idea why. It was the kind of obedience that felt like it came naturally to him. Like simply being still because I wanted him to was the easiest decision in the world.

"Am I hard…to talk to?" Joe asked after a minute of simply staring.

"No," I said, voice rough. "You're very direct. That's a good thing. You say what you mean, I respect that. Just like I respect you."

I released him with great reluctance.

My hands tingled.

God, just *touching* him was fucking nirvana.

How long had it been since I'd felt this way?

A little voice in the back of my head whispered, *Never.*

Maybe it's time to strategically pull back.

"I know you're busy, and likely have plans. So I won't keep you. But if you have questions, come find me," I told him.

I deliberately did not give him my number.

It was better this way.

I could preserve *some* distance between us—and it also meant he'd be forced to see me in person when he needed me. Privately, I thought it was kind of nice to have someone come looking for me. I'd certainly spent an obscene amount of time hunting him down, so it was only fair.

I got a little thrill when I thought about him prowling town, searching for me like he had at the theater.

If Joe wanted my number, he'd need to ask for it.

And if he didn't? He wouldn't.

The ball was in his court.

That's where I was most comfortable.

I headed back to my truck with swagger in my steps. It was difficult not to turn around and demand Joe show me the interior of his house that instant. Even more difficult not to micromanage the entire project myself. Call in teams of people to take the weight off of him now that time was ticking even faster. Do whatever I could to make this easier on him. To give him a chance to actually enjoy the holidays with his family, the way I'd never spend them with mine.

But…again…I exercised patience.

Slow and steady wins the race, after all.

And this hare was ready to succeed.

nine

JOE

AFTER CASHING THE CHECK—HOLY-cannoli-so-many-zeroes—I was on cloud nine. I hadn't had that much money in my bank account since before I'd bought the orchard. It was nice not to feel like I was drowning anymore. And even nicer to realize I had a way up now, if I wanted one.

And a friend.

I'd never had a friend before. Not like Jason. Goofy and loud. Kind and nosy. Expressive. Abrasive. But he could be soft, too. Commanding. Reliable. Gentle in both tone and movement. Those frantic flutters of his fingers, his swagger, turned quiet and sure.

He was the kind of confident I'd always wanted to be. He knew exactly who he was, and what he was. Masculine. Warm.

He pushed when he needed to push.

And he pulled when he needed to pull.

He'd said he was still learning how to communicate with me, but privately, I felt like he'd already figured me out. He always knew exactly what to say. And though he sometimes messed up and confused me, he never left me hanging for long.

I was tethered when I was with him.

And without him…not so much.

As I walked from the bank and down the sidewalk, there was no denying how relieved I felt. My lack of funds had been weighing on me. Stalling me. Making something tender and tight seize around my heart.

Without money, I had no hope of fixing up my house.

The weight of my family's visit had hung like a noose around my neck.

And now…

That burden had lightened somewhat.

I'd always been an action-oriented person. Good with my hands. Easy to direct. Maybe not the kind of man who was great at giving orders—though I wished I was—but always eager to receive them. To accomplish what I set out to do.

Sitting, twiddling my thumbs, unsure how to move forward, had been torture.

I'm sure, if Jason hadn't come along, I would've figured things out. Would've gotten a loan, maybe. Another loan. Or…I don't know. Found another job. Sacrificed what little rest I got so that I could accomplish what I needed.

But I hadn't had to do that.

Because my Christmas Elf had come around to save the day.

And now…I was no longer in limbo. No longer distracting myself with tasks on the farm that Patrick had told me to get my "grubby mitts" off of. No longer following Jordan around to make sure he was doing what he was supposed to—even though he'd never slacked off, not a day in his life.

No longer aimless.

I was an arrow, locked and loaded, and I was ready to shoot.

I made a beeline toward the hardware store with my list in tow.

I had no idea if any of the supplies I needed would have to be special-ordered, so I figured it was better to get that done as soon as possible. I needed to measure the flooring that needed to be replaced, which I did, so I could get a quote. And the appliances I'd need were due to be delivered at the end of the week, right after Thanksgiving.

When everything had been ordered, I debated treating myself to a pastry at Baxter's bakery.

Immediately, I felt guilty—but then Jason's face popped into my head, and his words replayed. *"You're supposed to keep the money. It's your money. What you do with it after you cash it is entirely up to you."* I did have the money. He'd told me to use the money. And…privately, I guessed that Jason would be appalled if he found out I was going hungry out of a mix of guilt from not working on the house, and fear of using the money he'd secured for me.

He thought I couldn't relax.

I could relax.

I totally could.

With Jason in my head, breathing became easier.

I decided to get the pastry.

Baxter beamed at me when I opened the bakery's front door. It dinged overhead, the bright yellow walls as cheery and welcoming as usual. Just like him.

"Staying this time?" Baxter inquired in a friendly way that made it clear he wasn't judging for the way I'd bolted out the last time I'd been by. There was a knowing glint in his eyes, like he understood.

I let my guard drop a little.

"Yes," I nodded.

I placed my order with secret glee.

Since I'd moved, Baxter had delivered me sweets every so often. He was friendly. Chatting my ear off. Trying to make me feel welcome. But this was the first time I'd had money and time to stop in and buy something from him.

The card went through again, sending a fizzle of joy through me. It wasn't that I didn't trust the money. Hell, I'd used it at the hardware store just fine. It was just…nice not to worry about the financial side of life for once.

When that was done, I took a seat at the farthest booth from the door. Sitting in the back meant I could glance around. Eyeing the Bellevillians curiously. A small part of me was weighing them up and down and trying to figure out who my secret Santa sugar daddy was.

Just thinking that made me embarrassed.

Was he here?

Maybe.

He could be eating a pastry beside me at this very moment, and I'd never know. I wanted to thank him. Accepting help had been difficult. The hardest thing I'd ever done. And now that I'd done it? I wanted to… to show my gratitude.

I felt like Jason deserved the credit.

He may not have provided the money himself, but he was the reason I'd gotten it.

Which meant he was first on my list to thank.

As I settled into my seat and waited for my treat and coffee to be delivered to my table, I thought about Jason. Perplexing as he was. I got the feeling that he was hiding something. What, I didn't know. I'd never been that great at understanding people, but I'd always been able to trust my gut.

My gut said he was a good guy.

It was easier to hear that, now that the buzz of frustration was absent in my head.

He was a good guy, but he was…multi-layered. And I had a feeling I had yet to see every aspect of who he was. I mean, we'd had dinner together twice now, and Jason had never brought up anything about himself. He'd tricked a bunch of information out of me over the last few months, so maybe that was why I felt like things were skewed.

I didn't know how old he was.

Didn't know where he came from.

Was it Belleville?

Didn't know his favorite color.

Didn't know what he did in his free time, aside from hunting me down or taking his niece out.

Didn't know his favorite animal, or if he had any pets, or why he worked at the grocery store.

Hell, I didn't even know his last name.

Weren't friends supposed to know those things about each other? I felt like they were. But again, I hadn't had one before, so I wasn't really sure.

Breaking me out of my thoughts, Baxter swung by to drop off my plate a few minutes later. He asked me about my mom, how she was doing.

To which I said, "Fine."

"She's a good egg," Baxter replied.

I figured he, of all people, could tell the good eggs from bad.

His parents were what the rest of our clan had dubbed the "assholes" of the family. Horrible people. None of us associated with them. Baxter was nice though. He shared the Milton—or I guess…Baker?—blond hair. Though his eyes were green, where the rest of ours were blue.

"She is," I agreed.

Though I was anxious about her visit, now that I had the money to get the house in order, a big weight had been lifted off my shoulders. I even had room to be *excited* now. Go figure! It'd been over six months since the last time I'd felt my mom's arms around me, and I couldn't wait to hug the motherheckin bejesus outta her.

Besides…I'd never once spent Christmas without her.

If I was being totally honest, before she'd called to inform me of their plans, I'd avoided thinking about the holidays at all. Not because I didn't love them—I most definitely did, would've been impossible not to growing up in a house as jolly as ours—but the idea of being without my family for the first time ever had made me *incredibly* sad.

Now I didn't have to worry about that.

I just had to worry about renovations.

Which would be totally easy, right?

And Jason…Jason was to blame for that.

Which was why he deserved a proper thank you.

"What do you think of Jason?" I blurted out as Baxter twisted to go. He paused, turning back around, a perplexed but amused look on his face. It was a testament to Jason's presence in town that Baxter seemed to know exactly who I was talking about. Or maybe there was only one Jason?

Though, I was pretty sure the first assumption was more accurate.

"Jason is a *very* nice man," Baxter said immediately. "Chatty."

That was pretty much what I'd gathered from everyone else too. "You mean nosy?" I asked, hovering my fork over the plate of cheesecake in front of me with a grumble in my belly.

"That too." Baxter snorted, eyes crinkling at the corners. The wedding band on his hand flashed as he crossed his arms thoughtfully, head tipped to the side. "He's more than he seems," he said after a moment. "I can tell. I'm good with people."

More than he seems.

Hmm.

That was exactly what I'd just been thinking, too.

It was validating to know I wasn't the only person who'd sensed that he was hiding.

Baxter left, and I mulled over that particular tidbit of information like a horse chewing a bit. I'd misjudged him before. Thought he assumed I was an idiot. Thought he was a gossip-mongering asshole. A bit of a bully. But…while the "gossip-mongering" part was true, and the "idiot" bit was up in the air, I could now safely say that the asshole part wasn't.

Assholes didn't do what Jason did for this town.

Assholes didn't deliver checks to your house—or pizza—or buy you dinner and a movie when you really needed it.

Assholes didn't kiss their nieces on the cheek and listen very intently to every single sordid tale of elementary school drama.

Assholes didn't smile the way Jason did.

Weren't gentle the way Jason was.

Assholes didn't have eyes that stormed and stormed and stormed. All to hide the aching loneliness hidden within them.

I finished my coffee and cheesecake in record time.

There was this awful flutter in my chest I couldn't ignore as I headed up to the counter and ordered another coffee. To go. Then headed down the street toward the grocery store.

I had…a lot of feelings.

Confusing ones.

The strongest of which was a need to see Jason for myself.

Leanne was out sweeping the stoop in front of the bookshop. She waved at me, her eyes dancing. She had a back brace on, but moved like she didn't feel it at all. The Pride flag in the display window behind her caught my eye as I waved back and continued down the street.

Jason was not there when I arrived.

Which was—once again—*super* annoying.

I needed his phone number.

I was starting to think he wasn't giving it to me on purpose.

"He's at book club," Madison informed me. "They're having a luncheon and invited him to come by to grab their donations last minute."

I sighed. "Where?"

"Head down the street to the B&B, you'll find him there," Madison said, sucking on her straw in the loudest, most obnoxious way possible. There was a spark in her eyes I didn't understand. It'd been there last time too, but I'd been too distracted to see it.

Like it made her happy to see me chasing Jason down.

Weird.

"Thanks," I grunted before heading out the doors with the cooling coffee in my grip.

The walk to the B&B was nice, even if I was miffed that things had gone awry. A cool breeze rustled through the branches, sending leaves dancing across the sidewalk, crunching beneath my yellow work boots with each step.

Businesses on Main Street morphed into picturesque homes dotted between. Picket fences. Giant trees. A tire swing in one yard that reminded me of the one at the park I used to take Mavis to. Trees reminded me of my farm. And my farm reminded me of work.

I ran through the task list in my head as I walked.

We'd finished harvesting this week, and both Patrick and Jordan were manning the farm on their own. Which meant I had more free time than ever to not only do this—my errands—but also head back to the house and see what I could get done in the interim.

It was a blessing.

All hands would be on deck at the Pie Festival after Thanksgiving, but for now, I was freer than I'd been in months.

I dodged a few cracks as I moved, the old wives' tale about stepping on them breaking a mother's back coming to mind like it had ever since I was a kid.

The B&B was a cute building. I'd never really noticed it before. Only a few blocks away from the grocery store, it sat in a cluster of trees. Along the front, it had a rickety white fence. Tall and old and as friendly looking as the rest of the town, with an unkempt yard, and a somewhat freshly painted haunted house within it. The decorations themselves looked ancient, but the paint job couldn't have been more than a few years old. Halloween had been weeks ago, and yet no one had taken anything down.

I climbed the steps warily, unsure what to expect.

More skeletons, maybe?

Or worse—chatty women.

I'd met one of the ladies that frequented the book club the other night at Rudy's. She'd been nice enough. Even said she'd come to my booth at the Pie Festival—which I genuinely hoped had not been an empty promise.

Though…thinking about that brought its own layer of stress. Namely the fact I wasn't very good at talking to people and I worried I'd say the wrong thing, or give off the wrong vibe—or…

Christ.

This was why I'd been sticking to my property since I moved here.

Screw Jason for forcing me to socialize and meet the townies he obviously loved.

It was like he was doing this on purpose.

Forcing me out of my shell.

When I pushed through the front door, the sounds and smells of a party assaulted my senses. Just like I'd worried would be the case, at least a dozen older women were all congregated in the lobby. Tables covered in desserts—all clearly homemade based on the variety of Tupperware and glassware they were housed in. A giant glass pitcher was full of what looked and smelled like chilled apple cider.

The last time I'd seen a pitcher like that it'd been sitting on a log near a campfire at Roderick's wedding campout.

Despite the fact I'd just had cheesecake, my stomach gurgled.

God, I was always hungry.

TV dinners were just…not enough.

Neither was cheesecake apparently.

The entire room quieted for a moment when the door slid shut with a *thunk*. Dozens of eyes regarded me, all wearing mirrored welcoming smiles. All friendly. I felt about two inches tall all of a sudden. Desperately, my eyes skimmed the crowd, searching for Jason and his oddly calming presence. I came up short.

Only one person was familiar, the lady from the other night. She wasted no time crossing the distance between us, her gaggle of friends following right behind. They smelled like a mixture of fruit and old-lady perfume. I fought the urge to sneeze.

"It's the apple boy!" the woman I recognized said when she arrived at my side. "Remember? I told you about him. The one with the biceps. Jason's boy."

My cheeks flushed.

Jason's boy?

What did they mean by that?

"Oh! He is *just* as handsome as you said he was," another woman said, elbowing the first with a giggle. She pressed even closer, one of her hands hovering above my arm like she wanted to touch.

"Isn't he?" They tittered together for a moment. The gaggle of women had soon surrounded me. A sea of freshly curled hair, hairspray, and genuine kindness. Quite a few asked to poke my biceps. I agreed, because it felt rude not to, even though I wasn't really sure why they'd wanna do that in the first place.

I was worried my skin would start to boil, my cheeks were so hot.

"Tell me *exactly* where you're going to be selling your goods—" one woman wearing a floral dress and a tiny black hat with a rose on it said. "I mean…" she cackled, waggling her brows. "Your *apples.*" Everyone cracked up at that, maniacal laughter filling the room as my biceps were groped for what felt like the dozenth time.

"Alright, ladies," Jason's voice echoed through the room. "Let's stop terrorizing Joe, please."

They giggled, hands dropping from my biceps as Jason blissfully diverted their attention away from me. I'd never been more glad to see a person in my life. Jason was lingering in the other doorway—the one leading into what looked like a dining room—having apparently left me to my own devices.

For how long?

I had no idea.

I would've been upset if I wasn't grateful he'd stepped in to save me.

Again.

He was all casual confidence, like always. Hands in his pockets, a smile on his face, his sweater cupping his shoulders in a way that was…really distracting. No one had the right to be that effortlessly cool. The gray in his hair looked brighter today, for some reason. Maybe it was the lighting. I dunno. I liked it.

Made him look…distinguished, I guess.

"Go talk about knotting," Jason made a shooing motion with his hands.

"Knitting?" I whispered, confused.

"No, no. Knotting, dear," the floral-hat-lady said. She patted my shoulder. "That's what you call that bump at the base of a werewolf's penis."

"*What?*" I choked.

The lady grinned evilly at me. The rest of them outright cackled as they wandered back to the corners of the room where they'd been before I'd arrived.

"Someone needs to get that boy a Kindle," I heard one of them say.

The coffee in my grip was practically cold now.

Useless.

I hunched in on myself a little, frustrated with the whole situation. And also the fact that Jason was so far away. Was I supposed to move toward him? This whole thing felt like a lost cause. A failure. What the heck kinda thank you was a cold coffee?

A shit one.

"Hey," Jason's voice was honey as he strode through the room, answering my unspoken question without me having to ask. When he arrived, he didn't touch me. Not the way he had previously, palms cupping my face— or his hand at my nape, or on my shoulder.

I wished he would.

I'd feel better if he did.

"Here." I shoved the coffee at him.

Jason's eyebrows shot up as he accepted the drink. He was only a foot away, and my pulse was skittering all over the place. He had more stubble today than usual. Not that he was ever truly clean-shaven. Just…yeah.

He looked nice.

"What's this?" Jason lifted the cup to his nose, sniffing at the tiny hole a straw was supposed to fit through. If I'd thought to bring a straw. Ugh.

"Coffee," I grunted miserably.

He snorted. "Yeah, baby, I deduced that." The nickname *baby* made my skin heat even more. I was still reeling from the comment about werewolf penises. Maybe that was why I was so overwhelmed. "I meant, *why* are you giving me coffee?" His eyes were full of mischief.

Probably enjoying me squirming.

The sadist.

"Why didn't you just ask that? If that's what you meant." I shuffled a little, curling in on myself. Jason softened even more.

"You're right. Sorry." He was a lot more nuanced when it came to communication than I was. "I'll be more straightforward in the future." He eyed the cup critically, like he could see through the cardboard to what was beneath. "So? What is the *meaning* of your trip to the B&B and the coffee that you've so generously bequeathed me?"

I bit my lip, suddenly too embarrassed to look at him.

I looked at his feet instead.

At his beat-up sneakers and the way he'd pegged his jeans to show off a pair of truly heinous socks. Christmas print. Even though it was only November and we hadn't hit Thanksgiving yet.

"Joe?" Jason verbally poked.

"It's my way of saying thank you." The words were so quiet I was surprised he could hear them over the chatter of the women surrounding us. I could feel their eyes on us, observing. No doubt we'd be the subject of a rumor even without Jason's help.

I wished we were alone.

"Ah. I should've guessed. You've got a knack for gift giving." Jason's voice was sweet as pie. "You're *very* welcome, Joe. It was my pleasure, really." When I glanced back up at his face, Jason was drinking the coffee. "This is good," he hummed. "But I prefer it black." He winked. "You know, for next time you surprise me with thank-you-bean-juice."

First knotting and now bean juice?

My heart did this wobbly thing in my chest. Which was not fucking fun, not when it was paired with the squirming, the pulse racing, and the way my skin felt too hot and tight to move.

I'd said thank you. I'd delivered the coffee. And now I needed *out.*

I jerked the door open as quickly as I could, in an effort to escape those sharp blue eyes and the way Jason seemed to see beneath my skin. Outside on the stoop, my heart continued to race. The door took an extra second longer to close than it should've.

Jason was right behind me.

Of course he was.

I barely got down the walkway—far enough to see the haunted house in the backyard again—before Jason's arm slung over my shoulders, and that warm weight pulled me into his side.

"Let's walk together," he said, squeezing me tight. "Madison is probably champing at the bit to get back into the break room for a refill. I've gotta go relieve her. I'm assuming you walked? You always walk."

"How do you know that?" I asked, melting instead of fighting him off like would've been wise.

"I watch you, obviously."

A shiver coursed through me that had absolutely nothing to do with the chill in the air.

"You…*watch* me?"

"Every chance I get," Jason said chipperly, like that wasn't odd at all. Maybe I was just as insane as he was, because I was kinda…happy to hear that. Why? I had no idea. As we walked, the box in Jason's other arm rattled. Donations. Like Madison said he was grabbing.

We walked in silence for a block. The grocery store was up ahead, his end goal. I had no reason to linger, and yet I found my steps slowing down. When I glanced to the side, Jason's lips had quirked up and his eyes were dancing with mischief. Deliberately, he slowed down, too. Just to make me aware that he knew what I'd done.

"I have a question for you." Jason's words startled me. "Because we're friends now." My cheeks went hot all over again and I ducked my head, turning my attention to the ground because it was safer.

Safer to step over the cracks and dodge leaves than let Jason beneath my skin. Again, I could smell snow in the air, but the sky remained blissfully clear.

"I still don't need help," I said immediately, before he could get his hopes up.

Jason snorted. "That wasn't what I was going to ask."

My brow furrowed, and against my better judgment, I lifted my head and met his gaze once more. There was something hidden in there. Something nurturing, something strong. Lingering in the swirling pale blue like a fireplace in the center of a winter storm.

"Would you like to spend Thanksgiving with me?" Jason inquired.

"W-what?" That had not at all been what I was expecting.

"You heard me, Joe."

I paused in the middle of the sidewalk. A car drove by, the owner going so far as to roll down the windows and shout a *hello* our way. Jason waved back, grinning. I could tell his attention wasn't on them, though. Because my skin was prickling, and his eyes barely left me.

"Times ticking," Jason teased. "Thanksgiving? With me. Yes or no."

"Why?"

He had to know I had no family out here. I mean…yeah, there was Baxter. He'd made sure to invite me over to spend the holiday with him, his husband, and his two kids—but…it wasn't like it would be hard to stop by the bakery on my way to the truck and tell him I couldn't anymore.

Jason paused, staring at me for a beat. There was a war on his face, like he was debating how much to share. "Because I know what it's like to spend the holidays alone," he admitted.

My heart twinged.

"I'll come," I found myself agreeing, voice rough. Maybe then I could ask him some questions of my own. Figure out why he'd said that.

"Great!" Jason squeezed my shoulder snugly and gave me a little shake. "Meet me at the store at six."

"Six…in the evening?"

"In the morning. I have stuff to do, and you're going to help me do it." His eyes danced. "If you *want* to. If you have time to spend the day with me. I know it's early. And that's not most people's idea of a holiday. If not, I can get you the address for dinner, no biggie."

Oddly enough, I found that I didn't mind. Not the waking up early part, or the idea that I'd be spending a whole day helping Jason.

"I'm coming."

It was fine to take another day off from renovations, wasn't it? I mean…it *was* a holiday. I had some free time away from the farm…and the kitchen appliances I'd ordered wouldn't be getting here till after the Pie Festival. Besides…I was genuinely curious what a Thanksgiving with Jason would be like.

He's more than he seems.

Loud, no doubt.

Full of people.

Exhausting.

And yet…I still wanted to go.

What was wrong with me?

ten

JASON

"SO, YOU KNOW HOW I told you about my friend?" I said in greeting as I dropped Marybeth off. Mary led me through the foyer as Marybeth bounded up the stairs toward her bedroom.

Mary and Daniel had both been too busy to pick her up from school, so I'd offered. We'd had a rather lovely afternoon, and she'd been my loyal little confidant as I told her all my Joe-related woes.

"He's the big one?" Marybeth had said over her cup of cocoa. "The one you were practicing speeches for." We'd taken a detour to the park, and like usual, were enjoying the squirrels that skittered from tree to tree. I took the cap off my coffee and blew on it to attempt to cool it.

"Yep. That's him."

"He's nice," Marybeth had said wisely. "Good apples."

"I know right? You don't think that's weird?" I'd asked her, genuinely curious. "That I might…start liking someone?"

"I think it's weirder that you don't," she had replied. "Mom's married. You should be too."

She had given me the same knowing look her mom was currently leveling my way. Like they knew me better than I knew myself. Which…fair. They probably did. Also…maybe it *was* weird that we'd been separated for a decade and I'd never dated.

I shook away the memory, focusing on the current conversation at hand. Mary's eyes glinted.

"Yes, I remember. Your friend that has a crush on a man that was definitely *not* Joe?" Mary leaned against the doorway to the kitchen with a look that could've only been described as smug.

"That's the one!" My heart skipped a beat. I knew Mary wouldn't care, but she was still the second person I was officially coming out to, after Marybeth. "Well, I'm sure this is going to come as a surprise," I started, fighting back a laugh at the ridiculousness of what I was about to say.

"I'm sure it isn't."

"But that friend? It was actually me all along. And I do, in fact, like Joe. Which…as you can probably guess, is actually *terrifying*."

Mary's head dropped back, this delighted cackle escaping that sounded so much like her daughter's it made my chest squeeze. When she stopped howling, she scrubbed a hand over her face and grinned at me, amused and annoyed in equal measure.

"Not the reaction I expected," I teased. "You know. The laughter—"

"Oh, hush. You know that's not why I'm laughing."

"I know." I grinned at her, relaxing now that I'd said it out loud. It felt more real. Tangible almost. I was Jason. I was forty-three-years-old. I had more money than I could conceivably count. I worked as a grocer. And yes, I had a crush on someone. For the first time.

"So we're no longer in denial then?" Mary clarified.

"Correct. And I've invited him over for Thanksgiving dinner."

"Good. I want to meet him."

"I thought you would." I paused for a beat, wavering. "You're not offended?"

"Why would I be offended?" Mary gave me a look like she thought I was being adorably idiotic. "I'm happy for you. Truly."

There was only so long I could've pretended I didn't find Joe cute. This was just the natural way of things. Today, for example? When Joe had brought me coffee and been so embarrassed and shy and— *God*, I'd had to fight the urge to reach over and pinch his grumpy little cheeks. So adorable. It should've been illegal.

"Wine?" Mary offered, disappearing the rest of the way into the kitchen. I trailed after her, kicking my shoes off down the hallway with a grunt. Pictures lined the walls. Pictures of Marybeth, of Daniel, of Mary. A few of me, sprinkled in between.

Mary had a nice house. The kind of house that looked like it came straight out of a catalog. The kind of house she'd told me that growing up lower class in a trailer park had made feel like a dream. There were still pieces of a "home" inside it, keeping it from feeling clinical.

Marybeth's shoes randomly dotted the corners.

A few toys.

Mary's laptop was on the counter—because she was always fucking working—along with her briefcase. Yes, she was the kind of nerd who genuinely used a briefcase.

Dishes were in the sink from Daniel cooking dinner, as well as his reading glasses parked on the table beside an abandoned book.

It felt more like home than my house did, and I'd been living there for over ten years.

The only clutter at my place was my own. More derelict than a fucking crypt, even if I had the curtains and bathmats that should've made it feel well-loved. I'd never done well with silence. It reminded me too much of what the manor had been like when I was young.

Empty.

Cold.

"Boxed?" I requested. Call it protest but I preferred the cheapest shit available even after growing up with a silver spoon in my mouth.

The look Mary gave me was sour to say the least. "No."

"Ugh." I never won this fight. Ever.

After pouring us both towering glasses of the fanciest wine available in town, Mary leaned against the counter, arm crossed over her chest, legs tangled at the ankle. She had her linens on. The lightweight white fabric she wore to bed. Crisp and clean, like she never once worried about stains, even with red wine dangerously close.

"Was Joe the catalyst for the Santa Fund?" Mary asked conversationally. She'd been working on the paperwork for it, so I figured she'd have questions. Honestly, I was surprised she hadn't asked me the last time I'd seen her. Though...I suppose I had occupied her with other things.

"He was," I replied, taking a sip of my own wine with a grimace. Too fruity. Blehg.

"Why?"

"He needed help," I answered. "I provided it."

The look Mary gave me in response spoke volumes. "Does he know?"

she asked. "That you're the one offering the money?"

"No."

"Good." She took a sip of her own wine, swishing it around in her mouth for a moment just to taste. After she swallowed, she continued. "I don't want you to get taken advantage of."

The idea of Joe taking advantage of me was laughable to say the least.

"Believe me, that's not going to happen."

"Really?" She arched a brow. "Because from my perspective you're offering an awful lot to a man you hardly know. I…just—" She didn't often stumble over her words, so I knew I was talking to best-friend-Mary and not lawyer-Mary. "I worry about you," she admitted quietly as I chugged some of my own wine glass. My limbs felt a little fuzzy.

"I know you do."

"Come here." Mary opened her arms, and I crossed the distance without hesitation to sink inside them. She patted my head, hand stroking through my hair. "You have so much more to offer Joe than your wallet," she whispered quietly. "I hope you know that."

"I know." I did not know. Did I? I mean…really, truly. What could I even give him?

"Why do you like him?" Mary asked, continuing to pet me. "What is it about him…that feels so…worth all of this?"

I laughed because what I was about to say was going to either sound super stupid or very validating.

"It's a feeling," I admitted, voice hoarse. "I can't…I can't explain it. But…god. You should've *seen* him when we got out of the theater the other day; it was night and day. Prickliness gone. Joe was giving me the *sweetest* puppy eyes. God. You have no idea how good that felt. He needed me, Mary. He *needed* me."

"Gross, go on."

"I mean—I've never had someone look at me that way? You know. Just…*trusting* me to take care of everything. It was heady."

Mary shook her head, still amused. "Once again, I am reminded why you and I did not work out."

"True." I took another sip of my wine, disappointed to find it pretty much gone. "He's…" It took me a second to figure out how to explain what Joe was. "So *contrary*. So interesting. So young and yet so capable. I respect the hell out of all he's accomplished since moving here. He's got all these layers, and I never know what I'm going to get when I talk to him. He's constantly surprising me."

"And what if you stop being surprised?" Mary asked. "Are you going to lose interest in him?" It was a genuine question. A question I almost wanted to ignore, because it felt like a fucking rude thing to ask.

But…again…Mary knew me better than anyone.

And she loved me.

So I really thought about it. Thought long and hard. Thought about how I'd feel if I discovered every nook and cranny of Joe Milton. If I knew his little quirks and bad habits. If I unpicked every knot that made him up. If his yarn unspooled. If I saw him, plain as he was, all his tangles replete.

"No," I said hoarsely. "I wouldn't." The words were confident, even though nothing about this situation filled me with confidence. "What I feel for Joe isn't *just* curiosity. I'm just…I'm scared, Mary. What if it happens again? What if I don't…what if I can't—" I cut myself off.

"You won't know until you try," she said.

"I just want friendship," I lied. "That's it. That's all I'm after."

It was the wrong thing to say.

I knew that before the words even came out.

The wine made my tongue loose.

The quiet of her home didn't help either.

I was comfortable here.

Safe.

"You're practically in love with him, you set up a secret anonymous charity to pay for his home renovation, and you're *still* claiming to be only after friendship? I thought we were done with denial."

"*It's not denial.*" I blew out a breath. "I'm just…"

"Jason." Mary pushed me away so she could look at me. Her hand was tiny and soft as she cupped my cheek. "Sometimes you make me so incredibly sad. Don't write this off already."

The silence after that statement was deafening.

My heart squeezed.

Her hair was in a side braid today, long and brown and draped over her shoulder. She looked sharp. Deadly. And yet her eyes were fond.

"Oof, right for the heart," I joked. "You literally just told me to have my guard up because of the money."

"That was *before* you said what you did," Mary replied immediately. "It sounds as though Joe is special. That he needs you the way you've always wanted to be needed."

I felt sweaty all of a sudden. Lightheaded.

Mary reached out, her hand finding my shoulder. It was so small. Strange, when I'd been ogling big, suntanned man-hands all day. "I need you to hear me when I tell you that you are a *good* man, Jason." I made a sound. "For some ungodly reason, you don't see it. But even worse? You don't give people a chance."

"I gave *you* a chance," I argued.

"No, you didn't." Mary rolled her eyes. "Not really. I mean…you were always sweet. Generous. I'm pretty sure you would've given me your kidney if I'd asked. But you have layers too, Jason." Layers just like I'd said Joe had. "And until we were divorced, you never let me see that. You pretended. Hid anything you didn't think I'd like, pretended to be invulnerable. To be clear, I'm not bitter—I'm just stating a fact. You need to learn to drop your guard a bit. Maybe be wary of revealing your financial status at first—but…if you really like Joe, give him a chance to actually *see* you. Not just the parts you think are palatable. But everything." Her hand squeezed one more time before releasing me. "You're a catch, Jason. Start acting like it."

"Pshhhh," I flapped a hand. "Staawwp."

She took a step away.

"The couch is yours if you need to sleep off the wine," Mary offered.

Daniel was in the doorway to the kitchen, having witnessed most, if not the entire conversation. At least, the mortifying bits. He smiled at me, tucking his wife into his side when she crossed the last of the distance between them. He kissed her temple before he beckoned me closer.

Daniel was a hugger.

Even worse than Mary.

I sighed dramatically, feigning annoyance no one believed was real as I closed that distance myself and folded into their embrace easily.

"I already pulled out the duvet," Daniel said against my hair, rubbing my back with big, steady swipes. "Sleep it off, buddy." Rub, rub. "Mary's right, by the way."

"Not you too—" I groaned.

"It's time," Daniel said. "We all just want to see you happy."

"Your couch makes me very happy." Giving them both a parting squeeze, I released them and headed toward the guest bathroom to get ready for the night. I had a toothbrush under the sink there, as well as a bathrobe that Daniel had given me last Christmas for the nights I spent in their living room.

Sometimes my house was simply too quiet.

As I lay on the couch post robe-donning and teeth-grooming, I listened to the tick of the clock in the hall. Up the stairs, Mary and Daniel were getting ready for bed. I could hear the murmur of their voices drifting down the stairs, her laughter muffled by the distance.

I ached.

Was Mary right?

Did I have my guard up all the time?

Maybe Joe wasn't the only person with layers.

Maybe I really did need to learn to let people in.

eleven

JASON

THE REST OF THE WEEK passed by in a Joe-less blur. I'd been tempted to go over to his house on a few occasions, but I got swept up in my other obligations. I wanted to know how renovations were going. Wanted to make sure he was eating. That sort of thing. But I simply hadn't had the time.

Like every year, I was doing a lot of prep for Thanksgiving.

Madison was a menace, making comments all week. Talking about all the times Joe had come looking for me. Calling him a lost puppy. Reminding me of his eyes. Of the way he looked at me. Filling me with false hope I had to stomp out quickly for fear of the spark catching.

I drowned myself in charity work, in planning for the Pie Festival, in helping Leanne and anyone else who needed an extra boost before Thanksgiving hit. And all the while, thoughts of Joe remained.

He was with me, even when he wasn't.

A silent companion as I accomplished every task on my agenda.

Since moving to Belleville and discovering what it meant to be a part of a community, it had been my goal in life to help people wherever I could. We were all cogs in a well-oiled machine, and every single person who lived here mattered.

I truly believed that.

My childhood hadn't been like that. Just empty rooms. No one to talk to most of the time, aside from the staff I secretly thought of as family. Imagine my shock and horror when I'd discovered they were being paid to be there. Which meant…over the years, some of them left. Then most of them. Then all of them. I'd come home from boarding school after senior year concluded and realized I didn't recognize anyone anymore.

Mom's heart had broken when I told her over the phone how devastated I was. She'd offered to call them all and try to get them back, but I'd said no. I'd be going to college soon anyway. A new place. A new opportunity.

The loneliness had chased me there.

Followed me out the heavy front doors, through the gate at the end of the driveway, and all the way to freshman year.

At least…until I'd met Mary.

She was the catalyst. The person who had brought me here—to my family in Belleville. Which was why, even with my head full of Joe, and my worries regarding him and the massive project he was undertaking, I couldn't just let that go.

I had a lot of systems in place.

Systems that'd taken me years to develop and implement, especially as there were certain layers of…secrecy involved. I didn't want *anyone* to know I was behind these things, after all. Didn't want them to know who exactly donated. What mattered was that they got the help they needed, not who provided it.

Thanksgiving was the biggest food drive of all.

I'd accepted donations at the store for the last few months, stowing everything in the back till it was time to display it. Thanksgiving morning, I would spend the first five or six hours handing out everything I'd gathered.

Belleville was a small town. People were generous, but there was always room for me to supplement the donations. I figured it wasn't a bad idea, all things considered. No one ever suspected a thing when new winter coats and boots of varying sizes were available. Nor did they blink when electronics, video game consoles, a few smart phones, a couple TVs—that sorta thing— were lined up in neat little rows. I figured that come Christmas time, any of those higher ticket items would make *awesome* presents.

Not everyone had room in their budget for those things.

While I would've loved to simply hand every member of town a check, that wasn't feasible. Nor would most accept it. It was hard enough getting people down to the food drive. I'd had to market my ass off about it in the first few years. Nowadays, those who were in need heard about it through the grapevine, so I didn't have to work quite so hard.

I figured if Joe was going to make a place for himself in Belleville, he needed to start interacting more with the community. If he wanted a thriving business and to be an integral part of Belleville's ecosystem—which he totally did, even if he didn't know it—this was a good place to start.

Plus…usually I ran the drive with Mary, and she was busy this year.

We were expanding my "Santa Fund" project, and even though it was Thanksgiving, there was a lot that needed to be done if we were going to get it up and running in other towns before Christmas.

Which meant if Joe had said no, I'd be doing the food drive on my own.

It was a good thing he'd said yes.

Having Joe there to assist me would be not only fun but a genuine weight off my shoulders.

That didn't mean I wasn't fretting about him, though.

All goddamn week.

The curiosity over how he was doing was practically eating me alive by the time Joe showed up to the grocery store Thanksgiving morning. It was twenty minutes before six. He was early. And he was dressed *nice*.

Really nice.

A crisp white button-up that clung to every inch of him like a second skin. His sleeves were rolled up, ropey golden forearms on display. Veins dancing as he clenched his hands into fists, over and over, tension evident in the way he held himself, ready to bolt.

I pushed the door open, holding it with one arm and giving him space to pass through.

"Morning, Joe."

"Morning," he grunted. His fists squeezed so tight the knuckles turned white. He didn't move.

God, he was cute.

"You gonna come in?" I hummed, keeping the door open wide. Joe startled into action, even his ears pink as he ducked through the opening past my body and headed inside. Having him within the grocery store before it was open felt surreal.

Honestly, having him in my personal space at all felt surreal. An alternate reality. A couple months ago, I would've laughed at even the suggestion of this. Of Joe Milton willingly being beside me. Of my crush on him. Of him accepting my help.

"How's your house going?" I asked after closing the door and locking it behind him.

"Fine," Joe said. His eyes darted around, cataloguing everything. "What's the plan?"

Ah. A man on a mission.

"Alrighty, big guy. I'm going to give you the run-down," I hummed.

Joe nodded very seriously.

"We're hosting a charity event. For the next fifteen minutes, you're going to help me finish getting everything from the storage room to here. We're going for neat, so people can clearly see what's available. The doors officially open at seven, but we'll have visitors long before that. Some people have come to me privately with things they need, and I've made sure they are available, so they'll be here before the big crowd." I crossed my arms, tapping my bicep absentmindedly as I spoke. I leaned against the doorway, mind a million miles away—more accurately, an hour away, to the time those doors would open.

"We'll likely get cleared out by ten," I informed him. "Then we'll head on over to Rudy's for a sponsored luncheon." Sponsored by me. Again, anonymously. "It's a community thing. I like to show my face for at least a few minutes, mingle, make sure nobody got missed."

There was so much to do, and laying it out so concisely made me realize how unhinged I probably looked, choosing to do this every year without fail. Just imagine if Joe learned about the holiday-help list I created each year. Then he'd really be overwhelmed.

"After the luncheon, we'll check on the planning committee for the Pie

Festival tomorrow. Make sure that nobody needs help with anything. If all is well, around four or so we'll end up at Mary's."

"What if all isn't well?" Joe inquired.

"Then we'll do what needs to be done."

He nodded, something docile and obedient in his eyes that I didn't know how to react to. So I ignored it. For my own sanity. To his credit, Joe took everything in stride.

"Who's Mary?" he asked, brow pinched.

"My ex-wife," I explained. "Who I love very much, *platonically*. The romantic ship sailed nearly a decade ago, but we're still very close. As friends. Nothing more. Marybeth is her daughter. The little girl you met?"

"I remember Marybeth," Joe gruffed at me, still flushed.

"You'll meet Daniel, too—Mary's husband. He's a good man. Big heart. Works as a mechanic if you ever need your truck looked at."

Joe shuffled his feet a little, not making eye contact. For a moment, we stood there in silence. There wasn't a lot of time left, but I knew Joe needed that. Needed to process.

"You need to *know* people, Joe," I said softly. "Meet people. *Talk* to people. You've got a business to run and success comes from marketing. Your apples, yes. But…you're marketing yourself, too. I asked you to come today because I need your help." He straightened a little at that. "This is a lot to do on my own. And I hoped…through helping me, it might benefit you too. If there's one thing I know, it's people. And seeing you here today is going to go a long way toward getting the town to love you."

"Why?" Joe asked, still quiet.

"Why what?"

"Why are you so set on helping me?" It was a valid question. And one I didn't know how to answer. Part of me wondered if I was biased. If I was really doing this because looking at him made butterflies explode in my stomach. But, no. No. I *cared* about him.

"Because I enjoy it," I said simply. "Because we're friends." Both true. "And—" My heart skipped a beat. "Because I want you to see why this town means the world to me. I want you to be a part of it. I want to see you succeed." That was enough of an admission to get him thinking, hopefully. "What about you? What do *you* want?"

"I want…to get to know you better," Joe admitted a moment later. It looked like it pained him to get the words out. "I don't know how."

Oh.

That was…

Wow.

That was fucking adorable.

"The best way to get to know me is by meeting the rest of the town," I said honestly. "Eleven minutes," I reminded him, quickly moving on so that he wouldn't have time to stew.

"Right." Joe nodded seriously. His ears were practically glowing as I handed him the inventory list.

"I've already gone through food and clothing. The last things I need to move are the bigger items. Here, I'll show you where they're at." Joe followed me to the stockroom, and his eyebrows shot up when he saw the number of TVs that needed carrying. "I figure we can tackle them toge—oh." And there he was. Lifting up one of the massive boxes like it was nothing. Without straining even an iota, Joe marched out of the stockroom, muscles bulging.

This was going to be easier than I thought.

"You got it?" I called after him.

He ignored me, striding with purpose back to the front without bothering to reply.

"Okay." I blew out a breath.

When he returned, I offered to help, and the stink face he gave me was legendary. So, I retired to the register at the front to enjoy the show. I was content to take a break, as I'd been up for hours already doing everything else. God, my body hated this. My stomach was turning inside out from the lack of sleep, and I desperately needed a snack.

"I'm going to grab some food from the break room," I offered as Joe stalked past me with another giant TV box. "I am dying." I laid a hand over my stomach to demonstrate, but he didn't look. "You want anything? I've got donuts, orange juice, cocoa, coffee."

"Cocoa," Joe said immediately. "Please."

"Alright. One cocoa coming right up." I headed off quickly, eager to get something in my stomach so I'd feel slightly less like a zombie. When I returned, I had my handy-dandy tumbler—a gift from Marybeth last Christmas—in hand, as well as a mug of cocoa. Two donuts were balanced on top of my tumbler, wobbling with every step.

Joe twisted to look at me, all dark blue eyes, and adorable frown. He brushed his hands off, straightening from where he'd neatly stacked the last of the TVs. He was quick to reach out to help me, snagging the mug from me.

"A donut too, big guy," I urged, always eager to feed him.

His stomach growled and he scowled like it was doing it on purpose. He did grab the donut, though, and muffled a *thank you* around his first bite.

"Sure thing. Sugar probably isn't the best thing to load up on this early in the morning, but it sure as hell beats an empty stomach." I leaned against the register again, eating my food far slower than he did. God, you'd think he was raised in a pack of wolves, fighting for every scrap of food. I sipped my coffee, relaxing as the caffeine seeped into my bones.

"Ah, sweet, sweet bean juice," I sighed. "My favorite."

"Why do you call it that?" Joe asked, swallowing another bite. He took a sip of his cocoa and his eyes drifted shut. It was the packaged kind. Nothing special. Just hot water and powder. He didn't seem to mind.

"Call it what? Bean juice?"

"Yeah." He took another bite. There was icing on his lower lip, and I wanted to lick it off. I shivered at the thought. A glance at the clock showed we had less than five minutes before the first guests would arrive. He'd made record time.

"Because coffee is a bean," I retorted.

Joe stared at me like I was insane. "No."

"Yes."

"It's not a bean, Jason." Joe laughed, incredulous. I stood up a little straighter, memorizing this moment. I was pretty sure I'd never heard him laugh before. It was soft, sweet, shy almost. Raspy.

"Sure it is," I said.

"But it's *not*." There was this annoyed twitch to his brow that I fucking loved.

"Then what is it?" I was messing with him. He knew it, I knew it. But for the first time, it didn't feel mean. It just felt…fun? Joe was having fun too, if the spark in his grouchy eyes could be believed.

He enjoyed the fight.

The challenge.

Especially because he knew he was right.

"Coffee comes from a fruit. A seed from a fruit."

I knew he was right. But watching the almost befuddled expression on his face was the highlight of my day.

"That can't be right," I teased. "Then, why do they call them coffee beans?"

"Because of the shape, probably." Joe's face crinkled. "It's a fruit, Jason," he repeated, indignant. "If you don't believe me, Google it."

"I don't know how that works."

"You don't know how to *Google?*" Joe seemed to find this even more perplexing. "How can you not know how to Google?"

"Those of us from the Jurassic era got our information other ways."

"Yeah, right." Joe rolled his eyes.

"I'm serious—" I pointed out. "You were born in an age with unlimited internet. Cellphones. You don't understand what we went through."

"You're messing with me."

"About cellphones?"

"About beans," Joe shoved the last bite of donut in his mouth. "About—" His voice was muffled now, good manners thrown out the window apparently. "Google."

"You're right," I confessed, throwing a hand over my forehead for dramatic effect. "I am messing with you. He triumphantly took a sip of his cocoa to wash down the donut.

"I do know how to Google," I admitted. "But the bean thing—"

"Jesus Christ." I'd never seen him so grouchy, or so amused. He pulled his phone out after swiping a hand over the back of his mouth to clear that pesky (delicious) icing away. "I'm gonna prove you wrong right now—"

Before he could, the door swung open.

I put my coffee and donut down and twisted to greet our first guest.

Right on time.

Joe and I were spurred into action. To his credit, Joe did pretty good with the strangers. He was quiet, yes. Serious as ever. But he had this gentility about him that everyone seemed to gravitate toward. It was that same part of him that allowed wild animals to approach, I'm sure. The first customers, the shiest, the ones most in need went to him.

Like they could sense his gentle spirit.

Like he made them feel safe.

He was good with everyone of all ages too, when he wasn't overwhelmed.

Young adults, teens, children.

The fossils, like me.

When all the early guests were gone and we had a lull between then and the real start of things, I made a quick dash for more coffee. I chugged what I could on my way back and was startled, but not surprised, when Joe's hand shot in front of my face the second I was at my register.

More accurately, his phone shot in front of my face.

With an article pulled up.

About coffee beans.

I nearly spit my coffee out, and only through sheer love of the drink managed not to. I swallowed, setting my cup down with a laugh.

"Alright, alright. I concede defeat, Mr. Smarty Pants."

Joe looked triumphant. He shoved his phone back in the pocket of his tight, tight jeans. His hands went to his hips, chest puffing up as he nodded.

"This time—" I jabbed one of those delightfully bouncy pecs. Ah. Youthful testosterone. What a gift. "But, I reserve the right to continue to call it bean juice."

I'd never seen him this way, so eager and pleased. He was beaming at me, despite my words. "Okay," he said. "So long as you know you're wrong every time you do it."

You'd think no one had ever called him smart before, he looked so damn happy.

"You're such a brat," I laughed, delighted. "Never change."

Joe made trying easier than it'd ever been before.

twelve

JASON

THE REST OF THE DAY went by in a blur of activity. Joe and I accomplished everything on my agenda with no hiccups. He was a very pleasant companion, and just as capable as I'd suspected. I introduced him to every person we met, and though he was wary at first, Joe began to relax as the day wore on.

His reactions were pretty predictable. Walls up. Guarded. Slow to melt. He reminded me of frozen cookie dough. Not impossible to bake, just… less malleable. He did take my advice to heart though, and I could tell he was trying. Earnest, as always, maybe a bit awkward but eager. None of that felt all that alarming. I'd suspected he'd be that way.

I'd thought nothing of it, comforted by his predictability.

At least…until the questions started.

At lunch Joe asked me what my favorite color was. (Red.)

As well as how old I was. *Jurassic.* (Forty-three.)

Afterward in the car ride to the town hall—we'd opted to share a vehicle for practical reasons—Joe inquired if I'd been born in Belleville: to which I said, "No." After that, he barely waited a beat before asking what my "hobbies" were. I made a face, and Joe sighed and answered for me, "helping people."

"That's right," I told him, my mouth running before I could catch it. "I'm practically Santa."

That was a little too on the nose, so I quickly diverted him.

"What else?" Clearly, he was trying to get to know me in his Joe-ish way. Normally, I wouldn't invite questions, but I'd flubbed myself up there, and figured there was no better way to distract him than by doing what he wanted.

A secret part of me felt thrilled he wanted to get to know me.

How we'd gotten here, I had no idea. But I was glad.

At least now the curiosity was mutual.

Though…I wasn't sure I appreciated it being pointed my way—hypocritical as that was.

Joe got particularly excited when he asked me what my favorite animal was, and I said dog. Which just opened up a whole can of worms. Because Joe immediately had to know what breeds I liked *specifically*, and if I'd ever had one, and what if so, and what their name was. Awkwardly, I had to crush his dreams by admitting, no, I'd never had one, though I'd always wanted one.

And that already felt too close to home.

Too much information.

And we were back at square one. Me trying to dodge, and not sure how to do it.

It was getting harder and harder to dance around Joe's questions in a way that wouldn't expose my past.

"What about you?" I asked. His brow furrowed. "What's your favorite animal?"

I could not have prepared myself for Joe's reply to that.

It took him the remainder of the errands we ran—not exaggerating—to explain to me which animals were his favorites and why. He couldn't pick only one. He had a reason for everything. Practically a bulleted list of what he loved about them, why, and whether or not he'd seen one in real life.

Dude should've been a zoologist, with the way he lit up as he talked about wild animals.

Birds were at the top of Joe's list of favorites.

He thought the fact that their bones were hollow was fascinating. Loved the sounds they made. The different colors and shapes they came in. Told me one of the reasons he'd moved to Vermont was to do more birdwatching when he hiked—not that he'd had much time for that.

He admitted he missed having free time outdoors and couldn't wait till after the holidays, and his house was finished, so that he could send Roderick a hiking picture.

I thought it was cute he had a friend he communicated through photographs with. That was it. Photographs. Joe told me, and then demonstrated by pulling his phone out and swiping through their text chain.

Photo, thumbs-up emoji, photo, thumbs-up emoji.

Without meaning to, he accidentally showed me the rest of his messages too. Patrick and Jordan were at the top of his inbox. And everyone else— aside from his brother, George—hadn't spoken to him for weeks. Months, some of them.

Did Joe…still not have any friends? I know he'd said he hadn't as a kid but…God, that thought made me sad.

This was the most Joe had ever talked, and I was remiss to stop him. I found myself driving around the back roads of Belleville to stall. I just wanted to hear what he had to say next. Never wanted his quiet ramblings to end.

We drove in loops, wasting time.

Joe never commented once, even though I knew he was clever enough to have caught what I was doing.

I learned about Joe's siblings. The fact that he was the youngest. About his parents. The way he talked about them made it clear how much he loved them. I could see now, why their impending visit had left him feeling as much pressure as it had. Love could be a complicated thing, sometimes. I often felt that with my mother.

When Joe asked me about my family, I was careful with my words.

"I'm an only child and my father is dead," I explained. "It's just my mom and me now."

"Does she live around here?" he'd asked.

"A few hours north. Not far. I see her once a year around the holidays." Not because we visited each other, per se. But because we always reconnected at the Christmas gala hosted at the ski lodge every year.

Ours was a relationship that had been forged long-distance. It felt odd to change that now. We both had our rhythms. I'd long ago stopped being disappointed by her.

Joe looked completely serene as he watched the colorful trees blur by. Half the leaves had fallen now. The sky was overcast, a chill in the air that made me wish I'd thought to bring a coat. He looked gorgeous sitting in the passenger seat of my car. As though he belonged there. Settled with the seatbelt nestled between his supple pecs. Heater on full-blast.

"Are you always this…busy?" Joe inquired after a moment of silence.

"Around the holidays?"

"No…" Joe picked at his pants. There was a little hole there. No doubt he'd gotten snagged on something while wearing them. It didn't look intentional. "I mean, *normally*. You always seem to be talking to someone…or doing something."

Ah.

"Yes," I admitted.

"Why?"

He'd asked me a lot of "why's" today.

"I like it," I answered.

"*Yeah*," Joe huffed. He slumped a little in his seat. Which did nothing to make him take up less space, as he was still fucking gigantic. "But *why?*"

God, what a brat.

So cute.

"Do you want the real answer or the socially acceptable one?"

I could give him a little, couldn't I?

God, I hadn't realized till he stepped into my life how badly I wanted to be seen. Mary was right. She was always right. I'd been keeping everyone at arm's length. Joe especially. Holding on to a secret yes, but guarding who I was, too.

Keeping parts of myself under lock and key.

Never allowing anyone to detangle me.

To learn me.

Not the way I learned them.

Maybe Joe needed to be different. Even if all we ever had was friendship.

Maybe.

"The real one." Joe gave me a grouchy look that made it clear he did not appreciate me offering him any other option. He was so adorable, all broad shoulders and gold hair. And those eyes, so solemn, so eager to learn.

The tables had turned.

"My youth was very…isolated," I tried to explain. "People were all talk. No substance. And yet…the quiet was worse. Up until recently, I used to abhor silence. It reminded me of being young and powerless. Of being… alone." I tapped my fingers on the steering wheel, anxious energy making my skin buzz.

It felt so weird to admit any of this.

It really, really did.

"When I moved to Belleville…I was blown away by how different it was. Everyone opened their arms to me. Showed me that I could be part of something bigger than myself. *Showed* me, not *told* me. I grew to love them in a way I hadn't known I was capable of. And being useful is my way of proving to them that I was worth that effort. Plus…it's hard to waste away in silence, when your schedule is overbooked."

Joe processed this for a moment.

"Does that answer your question?" I asked.

Joe nodded. The understanding in his eyes was more evident now than it'd ever been.

Nerves surrounding the act of oversharing buzzed beneath my skin. I almost wanted to make a joke. Play off what I'd just said. Deflect. But I didn't. Instead, I took a deep, steadying breath. *Let him in,* I reminded myself. *Try.*

"You and I are friends," I said definitively. "Which is the only reason I admitted any of this, when normally I never would."

"If you don't normally do it, why do it now?" Joe asked.

It was a good question.

Hard to answer when what I'd just admitted was as real as I'd gotten with anyone in my life. It felt like too much, too soon to give him more. But I did anyway.

"Someone wise recently told me that I don't let people in," I said. "So I'm trying."

"For…me?" Joe looked confused, like the idea that he might be special to me was baffling. It was laughable. If there was one thing Joe was, it was special.

"For you," I agreed. "I want to be better for you." And then, because this conversation had veered way too close to uncharted territory, I did what I do best. I deflected. "Mary makes the best cherry pie in the world."

"I won't tell anyone," Joe blurted out, like he'd still been chewing through his thoughts and only now swallowed. "I'm good with secrets."

"Thank you," I said simply.

I smiled.

Joe nodded. His eyes drifted to my mouth, lingering there for a moment. Long enough, my heart began to dance. Then his gaze darted away, and his attention was back on the trees again.

I didn't push.

Sure, I'd imagined it. That Joe staring at my lips was only wishful thinking.

By the time we arrived for dinner, both Joe and I were *starving*. His stomach kept growling. If he was nervous, he didn't show it. In fact, despite how shy and quiet he seemed, he'd taken all the socializing today in stride. He'd opened up to me in a way that I hadn't known he was capable of, and in turn, I'd done the same for him.

I was *trying* to let go of the past.

Trying to let him in.

And so far…it seemed to be working. As anxious as I felt about what I'd opened up about, I did feel lighter.

Joe and I exited the vehicle and approached Mary's pretty suburban abode. There was a bicycle in the driveway, pink and red, abandoned on its side. As well as a basket of chalk. A few half-deflated soccer balls. And pumpkins on the porch, left over from Halloween.

As I took Joe home with me—to my family—I couldn't help but wonder if that saying about dogs was wrong. Maybe this pain in my chest would ease one day. Maybe an old dog *could* learn new tricks.

"So, Jason tells me you're the one that bought the apple orchard at the edge of town," Mary said, like the saint she was. She'd been keeping up conversation at the table throughout the meal. Including Joe in everything, asking him the questions I'd been dying to ask—and giving me knowing looks, like she was a mindreader and was doing it for my benefit.

Joe didn't chat as much with her as he had with me in the car.

Which was…pretty dangerous for my ego.

"I did," Joe said a moment later after liberally wiping his entire face with the cloth napkin Mary had given him. Cloth. Because she was bougie.

"How're you liking it?" she asked, taking a sip of her wine and arching a brow while she waited. To her credit, she was as patient as I was. "That must be a lot of work."

It took Joe a second to get his thoughts in order.

"It is," he said, staring down at the smashed up orange yam on his plate and the giant hunk of turkey he'd been devouring. "I don't mind. It was… my…dream."

I perked up.

"Your dream?" I said, curious.

Joe peeked at me through his lashes, his indigo eyes startled. I'd been silent for at least ten minutes, letting Mary carry the conversation. No wonder he was surprised to hear from me.

"Yeah," he agreed.

"I *love* that," I enthused.

Joe flushed.

A twenty-eight-year-old with the dream of owning an apple orchard? I loved that so much. It fit him, and certainly explained why he'd move so far away from his home. Though…hmm. Actually. I was pretty damn sure Ohio had apple orchards.

So, why move all the way to Vermont?

Away from his family?

"How's Belleville been treating you?" Mary asked, interrupting me with a sharp look. Her smile softened when she aimed it at Joe again. "That has to be hard, being so far away from home. Ohio, right?"

Bless you, Mary, you beautiful mind reader.

"Uh. Yeah. It is hard." Joe scratched the back of his neck. "But there's a lot of good parts. I like the trees. The work's satisfying, too. I'm good with my hands."

His earnestness was so goddamn endearing. I made a face. I must've, because Mary gave me her stop-being-a-shit look. I wasn't being a shit. I was just…seriously falling for the blond-bird-man.

I learned a lot about Joe via Mary.

For example, while he enjoyed cherries and cherry pie, he really truly was an apple boy. Apple pie. Apple turnovers. Apple sauce. An adorable cliché if I'd ever seen one.

Joe also hated trains, apparently. With a burning passion. He said it had something to do with Columbus and how many times he'd gotten stopped by one while living close to the city. He also hated cities in general and could never picture living in one.

That I could relate to.

Joe ate more than a small army, but none of us pointed it out. In fact, at the beginning when he'd been shy, I'd been the one to lump more food on his plate. He'd given me an affronted but grateful look, and when no one commented, later felt brave enough to add seconds and thirds without worry.

It was fun seeing him interact with my family.

It felt right.

At the end of the night, Joe insisted on doing the dishes as, and I quote, "his way to contribute." But that was only after Marybeth showed him her dog, Poncho, the decrepit chihuahua with his tongue permanently stuck out, and Joe turned into a massive puddle of goo.

He sat on the ground to murmur to Poncho and everything, stroking his ears, telling him what a good, handsome boy he was even though he had to be the ugliest (cutest) dog in the world. All patchy coated and scrawny enough a sneeze would send him to Narnia.

Joe's dinner-plate-sized hands were back to gentle again.

Poncho, who was a renowned grump—seriously he'd bite anyone, I speak from experience—crawled into Joe's lap to take a nap. And Joe had to carefully extricate him so that he could help because he felt it was the "right thing to do."

I could hear Joe splashing around in the kitchen a few minutes later as I found Mary on the couch. She had a glass of wine in her hand, one foot tucked beneath her knee, reclining as Daniel struggled to get the video game console set up for us to play.

"So?" I said quietly, sitting beside her. "He's cute, right?" I made sure to keep my words as quiet as possible lest Joe hear.

"He's very cute," she said immediately. She took a sip of her wine and twisted to look at me, lips pursed. Her swallow felt deliberately slow, like she was taking her time to measure her words. "You're cute together," she said softly. "The way you look at him. It's…different. I've never seen you like that."

My cheeks burned, and I ducked my head—the same way Joe often did. Now I was mirroring him. Even when he wasn't here. God, I really was down bad.

Madison had been right.

Joe made a sound in the kitchen, and I froze, realizing just how stupid talking about this so close to him had been.

Of course, that was when Mary decided to bring up the worst thing she possibly could.

"While I have you here, I have a question regarding the expansion for the Santa Fund." Mary's eyes gleamed the way they only did when she was thinking about work. Her laptop was open to the left. My ears were ringing, so I barely caught what she was saying, terrified as I was that Joe would overhear.

That he'd put things together.

That he'd figure out I was his secret Santa.

I made a slicing motion in front of my neck to get her to stop talking. Mary blinked, surprised. Glancing behind me, I made sure Joe wasn't around.

"Not right now," I murmured. "Later."

"Okay," Mary said, arching a brow my way, though she shut her laptop like the angel she was so Joe wouldn't see anything incriminating.

"I'm going to go help Joe with the dishes."

"You do that," Mary replied.

"If he lets me."

She arched a brow at that, but her eyes were dancing with amusement. "Good luck? I think."

"Thanks, I'll need it."

thirteen

JOE

THANKSGIVING HAD BEEN NICE. THE food had been great, and the company had been even better. I was still thinking about it days later as I got a jumpstart on peeling out the broken panels of flooring in my living room so that I could put the new floor in later. I'd had the consultation earlier that week and new vinyl panels were sitting in the back of my truck beneath a tarp to protect it from the weather, just waiting to be installed.

Snow was on the horizon. I'd heard whispers all week, the worried townies a combination of both excited and anxious for the first big storm of the year.

Renovation was going slower than I'd hoped.

It was a massive project and it didn't matter how hard, or how long I worked, it didn't feel like I was making much progress at all. One set of hands simply wasn't enough. Not when I was holding myself to impossible standards. Everything had to be done the right way. Perfect. I couldn't compromise.

That itch was back beneath my skin. Anxious energy making me nearly vibrate apart as I worked myself to the bone. Between that and work on the farm post-Pie Festival, I was running myself into the ground. I hardly slept anymore. Couldn't, even when I tried. Couldn't stop staring at the walls, imagining all the holes I hadn't touched. I saw every shadow and wondered what horrors lie within it, just waiting for me to fix them.

Thus far, I'd managed to replace the appliances in the kitchen. Things I considered to be the "easy" jobs. The dishwasher had given me some flack because of the plumbing. And also, the new one was a slightly bigger model than my previous one. Which'd had the unfortunate result of kicking up a bubble in the snap-on flooring. Something about pressure, probably. At least, if Google was to be believed.

Which meant I now had to replace that floor too.

I'd panicked, thinking the bubble was a leak at first, but quickly discovered it wasn't. Thank god.

That was the only hiccup, though. The oven went in seamlessly. As did the fridge. And luckily for me, the counters in there were…ugly but not falling apart. A quick coat of paint and they'd be passable enough for even my mom's eyes.

As I worked, I couldn't stop thinking about Jason.

About all he'd told me.

His charity projects.

But most of all, the way he'd been after dinner itself.

I'd chased him out of the kitchen on Thanksgiving for trying to usurp my dish-doing-duty, and he'd set up shop in the living room with his kinda-niece. I could hear him with her, riotous giggles filtering through the archway into the kitchen as I finished up the task at hand.

Before that, though…I'd overheard a somewhat confusing conversation about the Santa Fund. Just snippets. I'd pushed the thoughts aside till now, as I didn't have enough of the puzzle to be useful.

Once I'd finished the dishes, I lingered in the doorway, peeping on Jason and his family as covertly as I could. The same way he'd peeped on me the day I'd found the magpie. I'd thought Jason's offer to help me had been an insult then, and I was realizing…I had been a total idiot to think that. The magnificence of that moment with the bird had felt private.

Special.

Monumental.

A sign that moving here had been the right thing to do.

This felt like that too.

One of those life-defining moments. The kinda thing you think about for years afterward.

I didn't know why.

Didn't know why my heart kept fluttering, and my stomach felt funny.

Jason was dancing—if you could call what he was doing dancing—the movements were so…awkward and disjointed. He reminded me of an ostrich, all long-legged gracelessness. Hopping up and down to the beat of a game, a video game controller in his hand, his niece standing to his left. She was pretty obviously kicking his butt.

He didn't mind.

Though he did feign competitiveness.

"I'm going to trip you," Jason threatened, huffing and puffing. "I swear you're cheating."

Marybeth cackled. "I'm not!" She jerked her arms up and down, stomping her little feet. "You're just a really bad dancer."

"Mary! Your daughter is bullying me," Jason complained.

"No I'm not!"

"Kids," Mary teased from the couch. "I'm going to turn the game off if you can't behave."

Colorful buttons kept flying on the screen. Green, green, green for her. Red, red, red for him. But he appeared happy. Didn't even seem to care that he looked like an idiot. That nothing about what he was doing was even remotely cool. Which of course, made him super fucking cool.

He was confident even when being a massive dork.

On the couch, Mary was laughing at their antics. She had a laptop on the armrest beside her, probably working—if any of the comments Jason had made about her were true. Her husband was tucked into her side, fast asleep.

The worse Jason danced, the harder his little audience laughed.

I think he enjoyed it.

Liked bringing them joy. Even at his own expense.

He was free that way. The same way the magpie had been. Wings spread. Weightless enough to take flight. There was something about his smile—especially when he was looking particularly dumb—that really did me in. Like there wasn't a self-conscious bone in his body.

He was brave.

Ballsy.

Everything I'd always wanted to be. Not afraid to look silly. Not afraid to take risks. Not afraid to mess up. Not afraid to talk to people. Not afraid, not afraid, not afraid.

It was a cute picture.

All of them were cute.

But Jason?

God…

Jason really was something else.

After learning more about who he was, it was easier to appreciate him. To appreciate the choices he made to be a pillar of his community. To appreciate how he showed up for everyone in his life. So used to being lonely, but so determined not to let anyone else feel alone.

I wanted to be like him.

Wanted to…have the kinda weightlessness he did.

Wanted to fly.

The Pie Festival the next day had been much the same. At that point, I hadn't even been surprised when Jason showed up to my booth bright and early before we'd even opened.

"You helped me yesterday," he said, his hot pink tumbler in hand. "Quid pro quo."

"What?" I frowned, confused.

"That's lawyer speak for let's make it even Steven," Jason explained.

I wouldn't have turned him away, even if he hadn't been trying to trick me into accepting. Which was a thought that gave me pause as much as it felt invigorating. To know someone…that intimately. To allow them into my life like that.

Beneath my walls.

It was scary and amazing and…

Wow.

I hadn't known friendship could be so world-shattering.

Jason asked me what I needed assistance with, saluting, like a total nerd in his coffee-colored sweater. I simply told him. No fight. Nothing.

He was surprised, if his eyebrows could be believed.

But pleased.

He kept giving me these looks I had no idea how to read. Touching me. Grazing his hand over my back when he passed by to gossip with the guests that popped in—simultaneously selling bushels and bushels of apples like it was easy.

He squeezed my nape when he introduced me to literally everyone who came by. Pulling me forward and forcing me to meet people like I was a naughty puppy. It was becoming increasingly clear to me that Jason hadn't been lying when he'd said he knew everyone. He knew their names, their occupations. Knew their families and their struggles.

At one point, very memorably, he'd grabbed me by the hips and quite literally manhandled me out of his way so he could get to the register. His hands had been hot. Index fingers just barely slipping beneath the hem of my t-shirt.

I don't think my heart had ever beat so goddamn fast in my entire life.

Like I was climbing Everest, unsteady ground beneath my feet, avalanches caused in the wake of Jason and his magnetism.

And god, was he magnetic.

He pulled everyone in the world in just by existing.

Jason helped Jordan when the ice cream machine I'd rented for the apple pie sundaes broke. Not well. He was apparently shit at fixing appliances. But he tried.

He helped Patrick restock the back when we ran out halfway through the day.

He brought us all lunch, and then dinner, and at the end of the night—

when he found out I'd ridden over with Patrick and Jordan that morning—Jason offered to take me home.

Everywhere I turned, there were reminders of him.

Making my skin feel hot and my heart go fluttery.

Even my bank account practically had his fingerprints left behind.

Which meant I was juggling feelings about Jason and my first-ever real friendship with fears about not finishing my house in time for my mom to visit. A lot of feelings. Too many. My chest felt stringy as taffy stretched out one too many times. It was hard to get a breath in, I was so full of holes. So tired. Bruises beneath my eyes. My head swimming on a near constant basis.

Suffice to say, I had a lot to think about as I worked.

Nothing felt the way it had before that day in the grocery store when Jason had held me.

The silence was too loud.

I found myself turning my music up to drown it out. Tearing, repairing. And yet the house looked the fucking same. How was that possible? All that work and it felt like I hadn't done *anything*.

I hadn't seen Jason in days.

Days.

And that felt…weird. Especially after he'd been so doggedly following me around before.

I missed him.

Which, believe me, was a giant surprise.

I couldn't recall exactly when I'd stopped wanting to avoid him. When I'd stopped fearing his big mouth and what it might do to my reputation. When I'd stopped throwing my guard up whenever he was around. When

I stopped hoping for distance.

Part of me wished he'd come by. Force me to eat. Grab my nape. Take care of me the way he took care of everyone else. I didn't know how much longer I could handle this until I broke.

fourteen

JOE

SURPRISINGLY ENOUGH, AN HOUR OR so later, Jason's truck pulled up the driveway. My stomach gurgled the moment I spotted him through the window—a natural reaction to his presence. Something inside me told me I was about to be fed. When he slid out of the driver's side with a sunny grin and a pizza box in hand, I nearly laughed out loud.

I headed out the front door, feeling lighter than I had in days.

I could smell the cheese from the top of the porch.

My mouth watered.

Part of me…was wary, though. One look at me and I knew he'd see how strung thin I was. Patrick had certainly shown his concern that morning. Sent me away from the farm with the strict order to sleep it off.

I hadn't.

I'd worked on the house instead.

So now, on top of looking half dead, I was also covered in paint.

"Hey!" Jason called out as he headed my way. "How's it going, big guy?"

I grunted in response.

The sun lit him up from behind like an angel in a puffer coat and boots. The forecast had predicted snow. A lot of snow. I'd been mad-rushing to get wood chopped to sustain myself in case I got stuck indoors, so the coat made sense. Even if it was kind of jarring to see him wearing something new.

Normally, he cycled through the same three sweaters.

Speaking of the weather…fuck.

I'd totally spaced stopping by the grocery store to stock up before the storm hit.

On top of that, I couldn't remember the last time I ate. Partly because eating had begun to feel like a waste of time. And partly because my cupboards were pretty barren. Okay, very barren.

I'd been surviving on canned soup and the remainder of my TV dinners, but even those were nearly gone.

As he paused at the base of the porch steps, Jason's eyes darted around my house. Knowing him, he was cataloguing the mess of tools on the porch. He arched a brow, attention moving from my house to me, then lingering first on my face, then my chest, then lower.

My heart did this weird squirming thing.

I thwacked my chest to get it to stop.

When my hand connected with the giant smear of dried paint on my shirt I realized what he was looking at. I'd forgotten I was wearing my shitty shirt. Dubbed "shitty" because it was the one I always wore when I wanted to do something that might ruin it.

And ruin it I had.

Liberally.

With a can of blue paint this morning.

I was good with my hands most of the time, but that didn't mean I wasn't clumsy enough to spill all over myself. The spot I'd bumped was a particularly obvious smear across my pecs. Mistakes had been made when I'd forgotten that my hands were messy and scratched my chest.

I hadn't thought anything of it at the time.

That was the point of the "shitty" shirt.

But now I certainly did.

As George would say, I was a "hot mess." Bruises beneath my eyes. Covered in paint. Exhausted and two seconds from cracking right down the middle from the stress of all the projects I had looming over me.

I dropped my hands to my sides, clenching them into anxious fists to self-soothe.

The pizza was taunting me.

Like a pie in a window of a kids' cartoon.

But I didn't move down the steps. Too anxious that Jason was going to see me. Really see me. That he was going to call me out for what I'd been doing—working myself into the ground. That he was going to offer to help me again, and I'd be so weak I'd be tempted to accept.

Jason eyed my front steps like he thought the wood was going to cave the second he stepped on them. Which was fair. I had the same thought every time I did, too. It was last on my list. Simply because fixing it was the biggest fucking job I had. With the rate things were going, I wasn't going to get to it.

God, that made me feel sick.

The anxious ball of dread sat heavy in my stomach.

I'd thought the lack of money was the worst part of this endeavor. I'd been wrong. So wrong. I had no idea how I was going to accomplish this in such a short time.

Just thinking that made me seize up.

The weeks were going by so goddamn fast.

"Pizza?" Jason loped up the steps with a pinched expression—again, like he expected them to fail. They didn't.

"Uh, yeah. Thanks."

I stepped to the side, turning my head a little to try and conceal the dark circles I had. Also, maybe my expression. Because Jason was getting better and better at reading me, and I didn't know what he'd see if he looked.

"You didn't eat already, did you?" He hummed as he finally made it to the top. He stepped in close. Close enough I got a huge whiff of his cologne, something fruity and musky, as well as cheese. Molten hot. Fresh out the oven, delightful cheese.

My stomach growled again.

"No."

"Good thing I stopped by then, huh?" Jason said. "C'mon. Pizza's not getting any warmer." He shuffled the box into one arm. My eyes drifted shut as I anticipated his touch. Any second now he'd grab my nape and manhandle me into a seat on the porch. Or my hip—hell, I wasn't picky.

A shiver wracked my frame at the thought.

But…Jason didn't touch my nape, or my back, or my hips—not like usual.

Nope.

He stepped past me and yanked the screen door wide.

My eyes shot open.

"Wai—"

Jason shoved the next door open too, and then—leaned his back against it to keep them both open while he waited expectantly for me to follow. There was a challenge in his eyes. My heart was pounding, warning bells going off in my head.

"Did you think we were eating on the porch again?" Jason asked when he saw the look on my face. I opened my mouth to reply, but he cut me off. "Joe. It's seriously freezing out here." It was. It was incredibly cold. I'd been shivering since I stepped onto the porch. "Your options are house or truck. You pick."

I wavered.

Neither option sounded great. I was bound to spill if I ate inside either of our vehicles. Which was super embarrassing. But Jason inside my house? I didn't want him to see the way I'd been living. My pulse kicked up, that odd squirming in my stomach at the thought of having Jason in my personal space.

Space I'd never shared with anyone else.

Space that was ugly.

And embarrassing.

And not suited for guests.

Least of all someone like Jason—who I…who I wanted to impress.

He really is going to think you're an idiot.

"Neither." On instinct, I dove in front of him to block him from entering. When he shifted to the right, I blocked that, too. An impenetrable wall.

Jason's eyebrows were frustrated.

"*Joe.*" He'd never said my name that way. "Seriously?" His eyes were stormy for a second, regarding me with frustration before he sighed. His head dropped forward in defeat. Another new look. I didn't like it. Didn't like that I'd caused it, most of all. "Neither it is," he compromised, shifting out of the way and onto the porch again.

My heart was racing. Going so fast it was doing cartwheels.

"Here." Jason set the pizza box down on the porch. He flopped down with another sigh. So quiet I knew he wasn't doing it to shame me. Wasn't trying to make me feel bad. He was just…

Disappointed.

I wavered, hovering in front of the door, not sure what to do.

"No one's been in the house," I bit out, trying to explain myself.

"I know," Jason replied. He didn't look at me. He just sat on the top step in his big puffy coat, staring at the woods like they had the answers I didn't. "It's fine, Joe."

"It doesn't feel fine," I said, because it didn't.

He wasn't looking at me.

He *always* looked at me.

"Come eat your pizza," Jason patted the spot next to him. "It really is getting cold." Cold because he'd driven across the entire town to get to me. Taken time out of his day—again—to make sure I was fed.

Because he was a good friend.

And I couldn't…I couldn't even let him into my house. Couldn't let him see my imperfections. Couldn't let him beneath my walls.

How the hell was I supposed to prove to myself that I was brave if I couldn't even let my friend—the only friend I'd ever really had—in?

"Come inside," I said.

Jason held very, very still. He twisted to look at me. Finally. Those thunderous blue eyes were all mine. They reminded me of lake water.

Reflections. Myself mirrored back in them. "No," he responded quietly. "Not if it isn't what you actually want."

It was such a respectful thing to say it nearly broke me. I thought about his words. Thought about *him*. About how kind he'd been. Pushy yes, but kind. How he'd supported me. How he'd opened up to me, even though he said it wasn't something he normally did. How he'd offered me his help over and over and *over* again. How the only reason I'd made progress on the house at all had been because of Jason's generosity.

Because he'd seen me struggling. He'd gone out on a limb for me. Couldn't I do that for him? Especially now that we were close?

"I *want* you to come inside," I said, more firmly this time.

"Are you su—"

"I am," I cut him off.

I was.

There were some doors you couldn't close after they'd been opened. I knew that. I think he knew that, too, if the way he was regarding me meant anything. Like he knew how big this was for me. Like he respected my choice. Respected me.

And suddenly I knew, without a thread of doubt in my mind, that Jason was exactly the kind of man I wanted in my most vulnerable place. That I'd just made the correct choice. There was no reason to believe he'd judge me. No reason to think he'd find me lacking, even after he'd seen how I'd been living.

I could lean on him if I needed to because Jason made me feel safe. And nothing about that made me weak.

fifteen

JASON

JOE HAD BEEN DETERMINED AS he gave me a house tour. The pizza, pretty much forgotten by both of us, was getting cold in my hands as Joe ran through his list of projects room by room, one by one. As we worked through each space—the kitchen, the bathroom, the bedroom— he pointed everything out to me. Stuff that he'd completed, needed to start on, or was halfway through.

With each new item, he kept giving me this look.

A look akin to wonder.

The shittier the thing he highlighted, the more wonder-filled his eyes became when all I did was nod along. Taking the holes in the walls in stride. The half-torn-out floor. The half-painted cabinets. The half-completed floor in the living room.

The place was, admittedly, a wreck of epic proportions.

The only room that was even mildly alright was the bedroom. And it was in dire need of new paint and new carpet.

I wasn't shocked.

I'd read Joe's list and been mentally prepared to see something along these lines. It did make me feel alarmed to think Joe had been living here—with it like this. With it *worse* than this, more accurately. Seeing as he'd been working on it for weeks now, so it stood to reason that it had gotten better during that time.

But I knew he could handle himself.

Since the second I'd met him I'd never been more sure of anything.

Joe Milton was not the kind of man you pitied.

Which was why I so badly wanted to be the person he turned to when he needed someone.

I knew what a vulnerable thing showing me his house was. He'd told me as much when he'd reiterated that I was the only person he'd ever allowed in here. And with every one of those *wondrous* looks, that fact only felt more clear.

I wasn't going to mess that up.

Though I did worry that the only reason he'd shown me his house was because I'd reacted negatively when he'd refused the first time.

"I'm *mostly* done with the floor in here," Joe said, pulling me from my thoughts. "Next, I need to repair some of the holes in the walls, handle the mold, and take care of the nail problem." He scratched his neck, staring at where a nail was poking straight out of one of the baseboards for no fucking reason. "I don't understand why anyone would stick a nail in the baseboard like that. I mean…it just doesn't make sense."

I didn't understand why anyone would do that either.

Not that I knew much about houses, or DIY home improvement. The little I did know stemmed from the fixer-upper that Mary and I had bought in Belleville's suburbs when we'd first been married. Though… admittedly, I'd given up my home-improvement dreams fairly quickly when it became obvious I was only making things worse.

I'd hired out for the rest of the projects.

With Mary's cushy job as a lawyer, no one batted an eye at the contractors that came in and out. They simply assumed the money came from her. I was fine with that. We'd made that choice together when we'd first moved into town.

Warily, because we hadn't known anyone.

And then later, because I'd told her, in confidence, that it was nice for once in my life to be someone other than Jason Harker the Third.

Now that I'd been living on my own, I had to be even more careful.

It was a habit to be secretive.

I didn't know how to open that can of worms—even though I trusted Belleville to treat me kindly. Not after I'd lived here for twenty years and never opened my mouth.

Could I even do that?

Was I capable of being open?

Could I let people in?

History said no.

But…Mary seemed to think I could.

And I'd admitted more to Joe in the car on Thanksgiving than I'd told anyone in years. Maybe…opening up could be done glacially. One melted layer of ice at a time. Maybe Joe and I were learning that together.

Another first.

My first crush on a man.

My first time attempting to be myself. My real self. No shell allowed.

"I'm very relieved you haven't nicked yourself on the nail," I admitted honestly. "Not that you would. Fucking panther that you are."

"Panther?" he echoed.

"You know. Big. Powerful. Dangerous."

Joe laughed. It was a cute laugh. All wheezy and hoarse. The tension in his frame eased as he shook his head. "Me? Dangerous?"

"You're right," I agreed, heart fluttering, because—god, was he pretty when he laughed. "The idea of that is ridiculous."

The smile he gave me was so warm another layer of ice inside me melted away.

"Cold pizza?" I offered, waving the box at him. Joe's eyes widened. The dark circles beneath them were splotchy and unforgiving. He looked sallow. Underfed. And yet…I'd never seen a more beautiful person in all my life.

"I like cold pizza," Joe said in the cutest voice I'd ever heard.

"Good. Because that's all I've got," I hummed.

We ate in the bedroom because everywhere else was a goddamn war zone. Sitting on the single air mattress in the corner, the little space heater that whirred and whirred was surprisingly effective. It blasted at our feet as we sat side by side, munching through the food, both of us silent.

I ate one slice, as per usual, dragging it out as long as I possibly could so Joe wouldn't notice.

He was far less chatty today than the last time I'd seen him.

He was thinking about something. His eyes were far away. Chewing, but unfocused.

I figured I'd let him be, naively assumed he wasn't going to bring up whatever was bothering him. The last thing I expected—genuinely—was for Joe to finish his pizza slice and tell me what was on his mind.

"It's supposed to storm," he said, grabbing a napkin and rubbing it all over his face. "I didn't go shopping for food."

God it was cute when he did that.

"It is," I agreed. I'd been hearing about it all day. This had been my last stop before I headed home to weather it out on my lonesome. "I should probably—"

"Do you think you could..." Joe cut me off. His voice was hoarse. Weak. He grit his teeth, like forcing the words out was physically painful. I froze, staring at him. My heart skipped a beat, racing, racing. "Do you think... Maybe..." he tried again. "You could..."

Oh my god.

No way.

No way, no way, *no way.*

Was he really going to—

"Do you think you could do me a favor?"

I made a bunch of phone calls as I drove back through town and to the city center where all the stores were. The first of which was to Paxton Montgomery, the local grump—and handiest man in town (literally), the dude was a wizard with a hammer. He had a lot of experience with construction of all kinds, and as much as he liked to pretend he didn't, he had a massive heart.

There was a reason he'd swept Belleville's Baxter Baker off his feet, after all.

"I need advice," I told him. "House advice. About house things. About…building. And fixing things—and all that."

Now that Joe had opened this door—the helping him door—there was no telling whether or not he'd be opening others. I needed to be prepared. Had to be prepared. Was genuinely giddy at the prospect.

I knew this—the grocery store trip—was a test in a way.

Maybe not consciously.

But it was one that I refused to fail.

I'd prove to him what an asset I could be and that would be that.

"Do you need backstory?" I offered, though I already knew the answer.

"No." Paxton's voice was gruff and deep. "What are you fixing? Explain in the fewest words possible."

After I explained, Paxton was quiet. Then, as concisely as possible, he gave me advice. "Toilet's easy," he said last. "You can Youtube replacing the pump. Start with that."

Joe had said that was on his list.

I liked easy.

Easy was good.

"Alright. Thanks, Paxton. I really appreciate your he—"

Paxton hung up before I finished my sentence.

I grinned wryly, then jabbed my mother's contact when I was at a red light.

Not because I needed anything—or even to gossip—but because, since I'd been a young boy in a house full of endless empty rooms, whenever I felt uneasy all I wanted was to hear her voice.

She picked up on the second ring.

She was easier to get hold of nowadays.

"Jason," Mom's voice was as peppy as always. "Hi, sweet boy."

"Hi, Momma."

"Anything to report?" she asked. I was the only one out on the road, with the sun sliding low, low, low. My car idled, and I leaned back, eager to hear her voice. It was clear by her tone that she was dying to tell me something.

"Nope," I popped the P with glee, my curiosity officially piqued. "You?"

"*Wendell got engaged,*" Mom blurted out in a rush. "And the credit belongs to me!" Her laughter was truly maniacal. It belonged to a cartoon villain, not a retired socialite in her early seventies.

"No—" I gasped, eyes widening as I sat up straight. "It's only been a few weeks!"

"I know!" Mom burst into storytelling mode immediately, embellishing all the right moments as well as including the appropriate sound effects when necessary. She'd been a matchmaker for him. She claimed it was her calling in life.

I could only imagine it fed her ego the same way philanthropy always had.

Mother had a big heart, and she needed everyone to know about it.

Apparently, Wendell had softened as he'd started dating. He *smiled* now. Wendell. Who had been the grouchiest, nastiest bully I'd ever known, growing up.

Smiled.

It was difficult to picture.

The image I had of him in my head was of a snot-nosed, grubby-handed jerk.

But...I suppose I could imagine it when Mom described it. And if Wendell, of all people, could find true love maybe there was hope for the rest of us.

By the end of our phone call, I was grinning.

The tension I'd felt had eased at the reminder that people—even people who had been horrible once—could change.

Maybe that meant I could too.

I walked through the grocery store—ignoring Madison and the knowing looks she kept giving me. Slurping her coffee and wandering around behind me like her only job was questioning every purchase I made.

"TV dinners?" She hummed sarcastically, sucking on her straw. "I wonder who those are for."

"You drive me insane," I told her. "Go back to your register and stop harassing me."

"Who says I want to be by you anyway?" Madison huffed, stalking off. I barely got one thing in the cart before I tracked her down and gave her twenty bucks in apology.

"Apology accepted." She grinned evilly and shoved the money in her pocket before leaving me alone to fret in peace.

As I gathered food items—far more than was probably necessary, let's be real—I mulled over my feelings.

Everything I felt, anxiety over messing things up, the fear of letting someone in, the worry that I was all talk, and that my feelings—now that I'd come to terms with them—were only going to ruin the friendship I had with Joe. The fear that Joe would rely on me and I'd fail him.

Those worries settled inky cool on my body as my cart piled higher and higher and higher.

Joe's test was harder than I'd thought it would be.

Not impossible, though.

Because all those negative feelings, all my fears, my insecurities, were eclipsed by the overwhelming urge I felt to take care of Joe.

To protect him.

To provide for him.

To keep him safe, ease his stress, and lift at least some of the burdens he carried on his big, round shoulders.

Case in point, the way I'd pulled him into me when he'd been panicking that day in this very same grocery store, and how effortless that had felt. Like it was second nature to support him. To be there when he needed me.

And secretly…I wanted to see *that* face again.

The face he made sometimes when I got grabby. Those dark blue eyes fuzzy, normally so wary, but at those moments so overwhelmingly full of need it took my breath away.

Until Joe had walked into my life, I hadn't realized how devoid of purpose it truly was.

Sure, I kept busy. But at the end of the day, I'd still end up alone. Lying on my couch, wondering how my life had led to this. Empty rooms just like the empty rooms in my childhood. Only the echo of my breath for company.

Silence.

Loneliness.

The kind of loneliness I'd spent my life running from—filling every spare second I could with chatter just so I wouldn't have to confront it.

Mom and Dad had been busy when I was a kid.

Busy being charitable.

So busy being charitable they forgot about their only son. We communicated on the phone. Often. They were really, very loving when they remembered I existed. But I'd always been second. Second to their egos and how desperate they were to feed them.

Their kindness came with a layer of selfishness attached.

Mom loved nothing more than being told how "generous" she was.

They both wanted to save the world, and I…well. All I wanted was parents who were home.

I never got that.

When Dad died my senior year, I'd been away at boarding school.

So many people came to his funeral, it was all a blur. It would've been anyway, the day being as traumatic as it was. Heart attack. No warning. One second, he was spreading his wealth, and the next, we were spreading his ashes.

The moment it was over I ran as far away as I could get.

Mary had been different.

I'd met her when I was eighteen. We were freshmen at the same college. Hours away from my hometown and the baggage it carried. Far from the empty halls of my childhood manor. Empty still, because even after Dad's death, Mom buried herself in projects. Home felt even more like a tomb than ever with no one recognizable around.

Mary was brilliant. Top of her class. Beautiful. But most important, Mary was kind—not because it fed her ego but because that was simply who she was. She was so different from the type of people I'd interacted with previously. I'd instantly been fascinated.

She'd been fascinated right back.

It'd been a whirlwind romance.

Six months in, and I'd asked her to marry me over takeout and sitcom reruns.

She'd said yes.

It wasn't until years later that I'd realized my love for Mary had always been platonic. Born from a desire to be close to someone else, at any cost. Spawned from her kindness and my fascination with it. I loved her. But not the way I was supposed to.

I was in my forties now, for God's sake, and I still had no idea what it meant to love someone romantically.

What if I couldn't?

What if Joe decided he wanted me back—defying all odds.

What if he kissed me and it felt like it had when Mary did?

Like there was just…nothing.

No spark.

And I ruined what was a good, solid friendship by misinterpreting my own feelings.

It wasn't worth the risk.

I refused to hurt him.

Worries compounded one on top of the other. Crunched together like hard-packed snow. Building bigger and bigger the longer I was by myself. The more stuff I bought, the more my head swam. Item after item, purchased in a blur, with no regard for the kind of money I was spending, or the odd looks Madison gave me as I came up to the register to pay, all glassy-eyed mania.

Normally, I was more careful.

I didn't buy more than was believable for a man who worked as a grocer at the grocery store. But…I was too lost in my head to care. At least, until I got out to my truck and realized I had an entire bed full of things to load.

"Jesus Christ," I pinched the bridge of my nose. "You're such an idiot, Jason."

The storm clouds had rolled in, the first snowflakes fluttering down and melting on my nose. Which meant I had very little time to get to Joe's house before the worst of it hit. After panic-buying a cartload of food and nearly blowing my cover, one thing was for certain.

I needed some distance from Joe.

This crush I had on him was tearing me apart. Hell. Just one look at my grocery cart was evidence of that. I couldn't be a rational person where he was concerned. I couldn't be a good friend. Couldn't do *one simple task* without overthinking it—panicking over it—reading into it in a way that wasn't healthy for either of us.

Something needed to give.

I wasn't going to cut him off as a friend, of course not, but maybe… maybe being this close to him was a bad idea. Maybe I needed to take a chill pill and re-evaluate. No more random pizza visits. I needed to start treating him like I treated the other Bellevillians. Give him a real friendship. Nip these feelings in the bud before they could grow into something totally uncontrollable.

A landslide stopped mid-path-of-devastation.

Half destroyed was better than fully destroyed.

Yes.

That was a good plan.

The smart plan.

I'd get in, drop the food off so Joe wouldn't starve, then I'd head home to my empty house to weather the storm. And if I were lucky? By the time we met up again, I'd have gotten over my pesky crush on him entirely.

sixteen

JOE

WHILE JASON WAS GONE, I put myself back to work. The tools on the porch were placed in the basement. I still had my painting stuff out, so the kitchen was my priority. It took a surprisingly long amount of time to paint the cabinets. Because I was stubborn, and I wanted to do it right. Which had meant a lot of prep before the final coating of robin's egg blue could be added.

Maybe that was my problem.

And why I couldn't seem to get anything done.

Because I was aiming for perfection.

Maybe I needed to learn to let that go, but I genuinely didn't know how.

The pressure only continued to build the longer I worked.

When Jason returned from the grocery store, I was genuinely relieved.

I heard him before I saw him, the front door opening after a light knock that I ignored. I figured I'd finish up what I was doing so I wouldn't make a mess. Besides…I'd shown him the house already. He knew where every wayward nail was; he could handle himself.

Just thinking about the fact that he'd seen my most vulnerable space and hadn't batted an eye filled me with warmth.

Jason had proved that I could trust him.

He didn't judge or belittle me.

Simply looked at me the way he always did, with sincerity, and the need to be close. That look was growing on me, too. Just like he was. Like a fucking barnacle.

My favorite barnacle.

That wasn't a thought I'd ever expected I'd have about chatty Jason from the grocery store. Which was…surreal. But somewhere, somehow over the last few weeks, he really had become my friend. Privately, I admitted, the best friend I'd ever had.

He came in through the front door what felt like fifty times before he found me in the kitchen. When I'd hollered to ask if he needed help, he'd very firmly told me, "No. I got this."

I believed him.

Jason hovered in the doorway as I worked on painting the interior of one of the cabinet doors. It was the second coat, and things were finally starting to come together. The natural wood would've been prettier, probably, but I'd had to fill in about a thousand scratches and dings, and figured, after sanding, this was the better option.

"I'm going to squeeze by you to get some stuff in the fridge," Jason said. His coat was damp when it brushed against me.

There was something…off about him.

I frowned, turning my attention away from the brush in my hand to his face.

He wasn't looking at me.

Instead, he yanked the fridge open and began stacking food items with a vengeance. Working quickly. Efficiently. I couldn't help but admire his work ethic. Had he always been this way? And this…capable?

Had I been too blinded by how loud he was to see that?

"Thanks," I said, cheeks a little hot.

"Sure thing, big guy," Jason replied. Then he was out of the kitchen again. He returned in a blink with another armful of bags. My eyes widened a little, brush held still once more. Rinse and repeat. Jason stacked the fridge full of eggs, bacon, milk, cheese, butter. Then he was gone and back with yet another set of bags.

I hadn't expected that.

I didn't know what to do with half the stuff he'd just put in my fridge.

What the hell?

My silence must've been particularly loud because Jason finally looked at me. He had a bottle of jam in one hand. Strawberry, my favorite. His pale eyes were stormy, then soft, as a laugh bubbled out of him.

"What's that look for?" he asked, amused at my expense. "You'd think you'd never seen a full fridge before."

"I expected TV dinners," I explained. "When I asked you to go." It was what I always bought. He knew that. He always watched me.

"I got those, too," Jason smirked.

"Oh." For a second, we just stared at each other. There was something charged in the air I couldn't put a name to. This anxious sort of energy. Was it coming from me or him? I had no idea. I resumed painting, ducking my head and focusing on my task. At the same time, Jason went back to filling my fridge.

We worked in tandem.

In silence.

He was going far faster than I was. I prolonged every brush stroke because I knew it would give me an excuse to be in here while he was finishing up. And Jason…well…if I didn't know any better, I'd think he was trying to move fast so he could leave.

For the first time since we'd become friends, it felt like he wanted to get away from me. *Why?* Maybe I was overthinking things, worrying, because I was too tired to properly function.

As though he was just as uncomfortable with the silence as I was, Jason began to babble as he worked. His tone was chipper, but it felt false. Nothing about him had ever felt like that before.

"Madison says hi, by the way," Jason chattered, shoving a billion onions into the vegetable drawer in my fridge. "She helped me shop a bit. Good ole Madison."

"She has a coffee addiction," I said, surprised when the words came out. Not because they weren't true, but because I wasn't sure why I'd said them. At least…until I saw Jason's reaction.

He froze, swiveling to look at me, eyes wide.

"Oh my god." He looked hilarious with a cluster of garlic in his hand and his eyebrows climbing his face. "Did you just talk *smack*?" My cheeks flushed as a frankly *heinous* smile spread across his face. "I never thought I'd see the day. Are we gossiping? We're *totally* gossiping."

"Me neither," I replied honestly. "And no we're not."

I realized now I'd only said that to make him smile.

A real one.

The kind I'd become accustomed to having aimed my way.

"Tell me something else," Jason demanded. "Something snarky. A rumor. Anything."

"What?"

"*C'mon,* Joe." Jason's grin was wolfish. "I know you've got more. Let it rip. I am quaking in my metaphorical boots."

I sighed.

Frowning, I picked through my thoughts until I decided on another thing I thought might make him laugh.

"Mr. Peterson down at the vineyard…"

"Yessss?" Jason was practically vibrating.

"He…uh. Have you ever noticed that he always has his shirts on inside out?"

"I thought I was the only one who noticed that!" Jason outright cackled. "I had no idea you were a lil judgy judger, Joe." I wasn't going to stop flushing anytime this century, it seemed. "That's cute."

Cute?

In what universe was me judging people *cute*?

I made a sound, and Jason continued to grin. Only, his grin turned hollow a moment later. Aaaand we were back to being false again. The warmth was gone. Like before, he'd been giving me the sun, and now all I had was an LED bulb. It was still nice. But…it wasn't what it'd been.

Was he worried about the storm?

Is that what was happening?

Admittedly, I hadn't looked out the window. Maybe it was getting bad out there, and he needed to get home. The idea of him leaving so soon made me genuinely disappointed.

The truth was…I liked Jason.

There was a reason I'd *wanted* to be his friend.

There was a reason I'd spent Thanksgiving with him.

There was a reason I'd asked him questions about himself.

I was curious.

I wanted to know him better.

I wanted to let him in.

I…wanted him around.

Even when he was distracting me.

Actually…maybe especially then. His presence made it easier to let go of my need for perfection. I was more alive when he was nearby. More real. Less…terrified of messing things up. More efficient. Less stiff.

Jason disappeared into the front room again, taking his pale eyes and *confusing* energy with him. Despite that, I dipped my brush in the paint pail, relaxing only when he returned. This time, he left the fridge alone, heading toward the kitchen island—blessedly the area I'd already finished painting.

"How much food did you buy?" I asked, a little horrified by the sheer number of grocery bags he was carrying. He dumped them on the counter and began pulling the food out arranging it into neat little piles.

"A…lot," Jason's smile was bright but his eyes were dim again. "Enough to get you through the storm. Maybe the next few weeks." The next few weeks. So…that would mean I wouldn't need to go into town to see him. That should've been convenient but it left a pit in my stomach. Would that mean I wouldn't see him till after the holidays were over?

It was nice not to have to stress about this stuff myself, but I couldn't help but worry that I was missing something crucial here. I'd dodged a bullet, really, having Jason help me shop—that's what I tried to tell myself, anyway.

The grocery store had way too many choices. And though I wasn't sure what I'd do with the "ingredients" he'd left in the fridge, the boxes on the counter? Yeah. I could handle those.

Cookies, granola bars, Fruit-by-the-Foot. Gingerbread houses. Cheese crackers.

Jason had good taste in snacks.

Asking for his help hadn't cost me anything. Which…was a genuinely amazing realization to have.

"I can pay you back for the rest after I go to the bank," I said, resolutely turning away from him and to the cupboards again. *Paint, Joe. Seriously? Stop letting him distract you.* "I've only got a hundred in cash and I doubt that will cover everything. I can stop by the store and—"

"Oh, Joe," Jason said in the most patronizing voice I'd ever heard. "You're not paying me back."

"What?" Once again, I twisted to look at him. "Yes, I am."

"No. You're not." Jason set the last box down. God, there had to be at least twenty of them. They covered the entire kitchen island. Again, his smile remained, but this time there was something *hard* in his eyes. That same confidence that made me want to roll over, belly up.

I swallowed.

"So, you just…"

"It's a gift," Jason said. "I am taking care of you. As your friend. Ensuring you don't go hungry when I won't be coming out here anymore."

Was this a normal friend thing to do? To…go out and buy your buddies hundreds of dollars' worth of food? Also…what did he mean he wouldn't be coming out here anymore?

"Okay," I conceded, skin hot.

"Good." Jason's smile softened a little as he nodded. "And now, I'm going to need to head out. The snow was coming down pretty hard by the time I pulled up. If I don't leave now, chances are I won't be doing it."

Privately, I wondered if that would really be such a bad thing?

Giving up my brush for now, I covered the container with a plastic bag I was using to keep it wet, then brought it to the sink to rinse it. "I'll help you clear the snow off your truck," I said, rushing through the rinse job a little too quickly in my haste to follow Jason out so I could prolong our time together.

"No need," Jason waved me off. "I've got one of those little brush things in the back seat. I can take care of it on my way out." He turned to look at me, eyes flicking down to my bare arms for a moment. Something flashed in his gaze, that he quickly covered up.

Conflicted, I wasn't sure if I should ask him to stay when he clearly wanted to go.

"Yeah," I agreed. "See you later. Thanks for—" Again, my cheeks tingled. "Thanks for lunch. And for…you know…" I trailed off.

"I know," Jason filled in for me.

On his way past me he gave my nape a tight squeeze. So tight it hurt a little. Made pleasure zing down my spine, my lashes fluttering shut. That single touch made my skin feel the right size again. And then it was gone. Just like he was. Halfway through the kitchen doorway and out of my personal bubble.

"See you around," Jason called, as he headed through the living room toward the door with an air of finality.

See me around?

He'd never said that to me before. Like seeing me was just something that he'd leave to chance. *Had I done something wrong?* I wracked my brain to try to figure out what, but Jason was already gone.

Feeling ridiculous, I trailed after him. Lingering in the living room, I stared out the front window. Allowing myself an entire minute to watch him shovel his truck off. A shiver wracked my frame, the snow outside the glass beating against it in what had to be the freakiest snowstorm I'd ever witnessed. Wind whistled through the holes in the drywall, making the space feel drafty as hell.

I was probably reading too much into things. He'd taken my house in stride, after all. Even went out of his way to do a favor for me. That wasn't something you did for someone you disliked.

There was a storm raging outside.

He likely just wanted to get home.

It was the exhaustion talking.

Everything was fine.

I just...I wished I could've cheered him up, maybe. The way his visit had cheered me up.

As I moved toward the fireplace to get a few logs going, the pang in my chest refused to go away. And the Jason-sized hole in my life had never felt larger.

seventeen

JASON

BECAUSE NOTHING COULD EVER GO my way, apparently, I barely got a hundred yards down the road into town before I was forced to turn back. The snow was coming down so hard now that even with my windshield wipers on the fastest setting, I could hardly see a foot in front of me.

Shoveling my car off had been a nightmare. My hands were icicles. Even with the heater on full blast, there was little I could do to stave off the chill that permeated the air. My chest felt cold, even with my coat overtop it. I should've seen that as the omen it was.

But...I just...

I'd needed out.

Needed away from Joe and his puppy eyes. And the way he had clearly sensed something was amiss and was...god. He'd been trying to cheer me up, hadn't he? With his sass. Cheeks bright red like it burned him just to utter anything unkind. Not that what he'd said had been particularly mean. Both things were just observations.

He'd looked…so confused when I said goodbye, and that just…that just killed me.

Leaving had to be the hardest thing I'd ever done.

And now…I had no choice but to head back.

As reality hit, I allotted myself thirty whole seconds to panic over the fact that I would have to weather the storm with Joe—before I very carefully did a U-turn and drove down the road to Joe's farmhouse for the third time that day.

The gravel driveway spun beneath my tires, snow crunching, wheels whirring.

"Fuck, fuck," I swore as I chugged up the driveway one painful foot at a time. When I'd arrived in my usual parking spot next to Joe's truck, I could vaguely see the farmhouse through the blizzard. The lights were on and the windows glowed a hearty yellow.

Joe's farmhouse was a lighthouse in the middle of a white sea.

I'd never been more uneasy.

Unsure of myself in a way that made me feel sixteen years old and terrified of my own shadow.

I turned the ignition off. Without the engines rumble, the world was eerily quiet. It was comforting in a way it never had been before Joe. Before the magpie.

I simply let myself breathe, eyes closed, focusing on what I could control. I pretended as though things were fine. Like this wasn't the last place in the world I wanted to be. Especially when I was acting this way.

Ugly.

That's how it felt.

When I was ready, I dove out the door and bolted through nearly half a foot of snow. It packed beneath my feet, causing me to slip and slide all the way to the stairs. The front steps wheezed like they always did, creaking and groaning beneath my weight as I forced my way through the snow to the top. Once on the porch itself, I knocked once before Joe swung the inner door open.

My mouth went dry the moment I saw him.

"Oh shit," he said as I pulled the screen door wide. His eyes were on the snow behind me, blond brow pinched. He wasted no time shifting that big, gorgeous body to the side to let me in. "You better come in."

Joe's house was warmer than it'd been twenty minutes ago. Not as warm as it should've been, however, considering the fire that was currently roaring.

That didn't bode well for us. Not in a storm like this.

The forecast had predicted an entire weekend of nonstop snow. Buckets of it. The kind of storm that blocked doorways and buried cars. And here we were…trapped in a place without central heating and with holes in the fucking walls.

Christ.

Worse than that, though?

Joe was here.

Joe, who I had decided not to have feelings for anymore.

My plan to avoid him was officially going down the drain.

"You can help me paint," Joe said when I'd changed into clothes that weren't frigid and soaked. I practically drowned in the flannel he'd given me, and had to strangle my borrowed sweatpants so they wouldn't simply slip right off. I tried to ignore the little thrill I felt that I was wearing his clothes, and failed. Spectacularly.

It was a testament to how closely Joe observed me now that he'd noticed I was still off. Also, I couldn't really hide my grumbly mood. Glaring out at the storm, expression pinched.

"You're going to let me help you?" I followed after him, perplexed. "*Really*? After all that shit you gave me about not needing help?"

At that, he paused.

"Everyone needs help sometimes." The look he gave me reminded me of a naughty puppy. It took me a second to figure out why, and when I did, I had to bite back a laugh. Because in his own "Joe" way, it very quickly became clear that he was trying to cheer me up.

Seriously?

"Okay," I laughed. "Grab me a brush then."

Joe did as he was told. He handed me a brush and pail identical to the one he was using. It was a shade of pale blue that reminded me— weirdly—of my own eyes. Just a coincidence, I'm sure. I chose the cabinet on the opposite side of the kitchen.

Trying to create some distance between us while I still could.

We were at a turning point.

I knew that.

I'd realized that.

I could either stomp the sparks out before they could catch, or…they'd be blazing.

Joe was not making that easy.

When he realized how far away I was, he grabbed his own stuff and took a seat. Right. Next. To. *Me*. Jesus Christ.

"You're doing that wrong," he said, tone surprisingly gentle. I glanced down at my brush, realizing belatedly that I'd been creating drips the entire time I'd been working. "You need less paint and to—" I tuned out the rest of what he was saying, distracted by the way he leaned into my space, looming over me.

He had really long eyelashes.

Pale as wheat.

Just like his hair.

They kissed his cheeks every time he blinked.

And were those…freckles? Maybe. Faded for sure, if they were. Barely there.

"Does that make sense?" Joe finished.

"Yep." I hadn't listened to a single thing he said. I did try to be more careful, though, and he let me struggle for only a minute before he was in my personal bubble again. God, he was a fucking furnace as he leaned over me, fingers wrapping around my hand and guiding me.

Like a chick in a movie.

Ohmygod.

Whywasthishappeningtomeeeeee.

"See?" he said, releasing my hand and leaning back. "No drips."

"Yep." I stared blankly at the cupboard, pretty sure I'd blacked out the entire time I'd been painting it.

We finished in record time. To be fair, Joe had done the majority of the work before I'd ever arrived. Still, though, four hands were better than two. When the paint was finished and we waited for it to dry, I let Joe take care of the brushes, still a little dazed.

"What else?" I asked, because the idea of trying to fill the time without helping him made me feel as though my skin was on fire. "Can I help with something else?" Now that I wasn't good company, the least I could do was be useful.

Joe set the now-rinsed brushes inside the sink and nodded. I was testing my limits a bit. Seeing how far this new open-minded Joe would let me push.

He was watching me again.

Gauging my mood.

"How good are you with a hammer?"

"Terrible," I admitted.

He laughed.

Laughed!

Apparently Joe's idea of cheering me up was giving me hard labor to do. I couldn't be mad about it, though. I wanted to be occupied almost as much as I wanted to help him. He looked particularly eager when he pointed me toward the rusty nail sticking out of the baseboard and told me, with great importance, that it was, "all mine."

I was tempted to beat my head against the wall.

It was impossible not to find him adorable when he was acting like this. *Impossible.*

When it quickly became clear that I could not get the nail out of the wall on my own—I swear to god, the thing was cursed—Joe came to help with that, too. Infuriatingly patient, quiet, and sure of himself in a way I'd never really seen him be.

If I'd thought he was amazing before, it was nothing compared to how I felt about him now.

Joe was truly in his element here.

That anxious energy he'd had before was completely missing.

With a mission to accomplish, and something to do with his hands—not his mouth—he was as sure as I'd ever seen him. I couldn't help but find that…incredibly attractive. I respected it. As someone who had always been good with people and not so much…hands-on stuff, I appreciated his strength.

"There," Joe said, when the nail was out. "Now we can spackle it."

"Sure," I agreed. I only knew what "spackle" was because of my conversation with Paxton on the car ride to the grocery store. That felt like it'd happened a million years ago. Between my panic, and the storm, and now cheerful-Joe all in my business, I knew I was fighting a losing battle.

How could I possibly be distant with him when he looked at me like that?

It was like kicking a puppy.

A big, intimidating, grouchy puppy.

I gave up.

I could assert boundaries later.

For now…I wanted to enjoy this gift for what it was. Joe opening up to me. Joe…being Joe in the Joe-est way possible. Joe allowing me to exist in his bubble. Joe allowing me to be useful, even if I wasn't nearly as good at this as he was, and I knew he had high standards.

Joe cheering me up because he cared.

"You don't have to fix everything for me to want you around," Joe said quietly. We'd lapsed into comfortable silence after the nail incident. On the other side of the room he'd been working on finishing the rest of the snap-on flooring. He'd have to cut baseboards—he'd informed me—after the storm had stopped.

"What?" I asked, because what he'd just said had ricocheted through me like a stray bullet.

"I mean…" Joe said quietly. "I know you said you *enjoy* helping people." I did. "But…" he trailed off. When I looked at him, he was very pointedly not looking back. Glaring a hole into the wood panel in his hands, his head tipped down. "If you feel like you *have* to do it…I just wanted you to know you don't."

"I don't feel like I *have* to do it," I lied.

I constantly battled to prove my usefulness.

Constantly.

Maybe this was Joe's way of…not only seeing that, but acknowledging it.

My heart was pounding.

It felt like he'd pulled my ribs open and revealed my heart behind them. No one had ever looked at me so plainly. So calmly. Coaxing me forward like I was a spooked animal.

"Okay," Joe grunted. "But…I'm just…" He made a frustrated sound. "I just want you to know that. That even if the storm hadn't hit I'd want you here. Whether or not you were…you know. *Useful.*"

He'd…want me here?

Another bullet struck me right where I was weakest. He'd *want* me here. *He'd want me here.* He'd want me here even if I wasn't being useful? It felt impossible. But this was Joe…and because it was Joe I couldn't help but believe him.

"Why?" I asked, my voice hoarse.

"Because I think you're interesting," Joe said, just as quiet. He didn't look at me, staring at the floorboards as he spoke. His fist was relaxed around the hammer, despite how nervous he sounded.

"Because I think you're fun," Joe added.

I was shaking apart.

"Because…I want to be your friend." He was almost perfectly echoing the words I'd told him weeks ago, standing in his driveway, with a pizza and a dream to play Santa for the prickliest man I'd ever met.

"We are friends," I told him, heart breaking right apart. Or maybe it was mending. Maybe this was what caves felt when they collapsed on themselves, gravel, pebbles, boulders filling the gaps that'd been left behind. Falling apart only to be better formed without the holes.

"I know," Joe agreed.

God, he was a menace.

"In the light of our mutual friendship," I said, leaning against the wall, his hammer in hand. "Can I request that you continue to let me help you this weekend?" My heart was still pounding, sprinting a goddamn marathon. "Not because I feel like I *have* to be useful while I'm here. Or because I think you only want me around if I fix things. But because…I care about you, Joe. And you're struggling to do this on your own for good reason. And I know I'm shit at—" I gestured around us, in particular at the hole in the wall where the nail I hadn't pulled out had been, "—all of this, but there's nothing that would make me happier than easing some of the weight off your shoulders."

Joe lifted his head, the play of firelight on his face as disarming as it was hypnotic. He became a statue. So still, so quiet. Just like the day I'd seen him in that alley and I'd come to life again. He nodded, a short, pointed little gesture.

All my plans to put distance between us turned to smoke.

In the light of his trust, there was no point.

Because at the end of the day, no matter how uncertain I was in other regards, the desire I had to take care of Joe was stronger than my fear. I was beginning to see the tail of his yarn unravel, and I knew what that meant. Knew what it cost him.

For the first time in my life, it truly felt like I was wanted.

Not my money. Not my connections. Not what I could do for someone else—but just…just me. Just Jason Harker. Useful or not.

The spark had turned into a blaze.

eighteen

JOE

I COULD HONESTLY SAY I had never had so much fun in all my life. For three days Jason and I lived inside each other's pockets. That first day, we used our energy to repair stuff around the house. Things went much more quickly with someone there to aid me, even if Jason was, admittedly, horrible at literally everything he did at first.

At first.

Because with some solid instruction and patience, Jason proved to be a fast learner. With every project I supervised, the better he got. Sometimes he still messed up. Like with the toilet. He'd insisted that YouTube and "Paxton," some guy he kept calling on the phone, were enough to get him through replacing the pump.

He'd been wrong.

He ended up completely soaked through because he hadn't shut off the valve properly before starting. That was his only major "mess-up," if you could call it that. And it was easily fixed with a handful of towels and directions to the water valve in the basement.

Things went…a lot more smoothly with Jason nearby.

Rather than sit there stressing, I flew through the projects. He made jokes wherever he could. One in particular about "caulk" that was both raunchy and genuinely hilarious. He did exactly what he'd told me he wanted to do.

He helped me lift my burdens.

And as we finished the kitchen.

Then finished the front room.

And repaired all the holes in the walls together with no small amount of squabbling—even though Jason knew next to nothing about DIY, he still managed to argue with me over pretty much everything. I didn't mind. We both enjoyed it.

I couldn't shake the overwhelming gratitude I felt that I'd let him in. I had no regrets. With every minute that passed as the storm raged on outside, my feelings for Jason grew. Eyes lingering on his hands as he worked. Gaze snapping to his mouth when he laughed as I griped at him over how messy he was with a palette knife and a bucket of spackle.

"You're a child," I told him, and he grinned.

Sharp angles, wrinkles, and bright eyes.

The shadow he'd carried was gone.

And…something new, something bubbly simmered beneath the surface of my skin. Not like boiling water. Not violent, or harsh. Whatever it was, was soft. Soft as the blanket of snow that covered the world outside our windows. Turning everything blank and white.

A fresh start.

My eyes lingered as Jason moved.

Lingered on his expressive hands. On his eyebrows, and the conversations they held with me, no words needed. On the way his throat bobbed when he swallowed. On the bow of his legs as he walked, all effortless confidence even though he hardly knew what he was doing.

On the way my clothing hung off his frame and yet he never looked small.

It made me wonder if some people are just like that.

Larger than life.

Jason certainly felt that way to me. Bigger than this house. Than this town. Than the world I'd grown up inside of.

"I don't know if that looks straight," Jason said once, just to tease.

"It's straight." I glared at him. He was standing behind me, hands on his hips, a pinched expression on his face. His eyes danced with mischief. "Hmm. Maybe from *your* angle. But from mine?"

"Jason. I will beat you over the head with the rest of this drywall, so help me god."

"Well, that's not very nice," Jason tutted. But he was grinning.

He was back.

My Jason.

And he was warmer than ever.

As we wound down for the night after working our way through a vast majority of the projects I'd only half-finished, Jason wouldn't stop touching me. My back, my hip, my nape. Brushes of the fingers I couldn't stop staring at. Hard grips to move me out of the way, or command me to drink the water he'd grabbed from the kitchen for me.

Taking care of me.

Those first few hours taught me a lot about myself.

About Jason, too.

I enjoyed working beside him. The silence I'd found uncomfortable recently, felt easy when he was nearby. I could feel his echo even in the corners. Like he was light, bouncing off the walls. Making even the shadows brighter. Making the storm less violent. Making my world calm.

I discovered that…being vulnerable with Jason—inviting him beneath my walls—was the smartest choice I'd ever made.

The bravest, too.

I had no regrets.

That first night when we were both too exhausted to keep working, Jason and I hunted through the food he'd brought for something to eat. We had what Jason called "girl dinner," which apparently consisted of a plethora of snacks, some miscellaneous items from the fridge and freezer, and giant cups of flavored water.

We sat on the kitchen island, and Jason used my phone to help me shop for furniture.

A little thrill ran through me at the thought that his touch would be all over my home.

Maybe that should've made me realize that my feelings had changed.

But it didn't.

I'd never been very good at emotions.

After we'd brushed our teeth in tandem—again, an experience that felt incredibly intimate—and Jason changed into a pair of my pajamas, we retired to the bedroom.

"You take the bed," Jason said, hauling a blanket next to the air mattress. His back was to me, bent over. My eyes trailed over his broad shoulders. Over the way my shirt rode up his back. On the sliver of pale skin above the waistband of my sweatpants. When my eyes flitted over his ass something hot flickered low in my belly.

Shame maybe.

I squashed it quickly.

But there was no forgetting its presence.

"We should share," I found myself offering, voice hoarse.

"Can your air mattress take that?" Jason asked. It almost felt like he was running again. Maybe he was shy? Maybe he was worried it'd pop.

"Yes." My cheeks flushed as I crawled onto the queen-sized air mattress and scooted to the side to make room. "It'll be warmer." My space heater was on full blast, and in the living room, the fire was still roaring. But even with the walls patched the space felt icy.

Jason stood up tall.

He turned to look at me, his eyes dark with emotions I couldn't name. He stared at me for a moment, eyebrows neutral for the first time since I'd met him. I couldn't get a read on him, at all. My heart fluttered. It took everything I had not to squirm.

"You need a real mattress, Joe," Jason said. It wasn't admonishment so much as it was an observation.

"Maybe you can help me get one," I said, voice hoarse.

Apparently it was the right thing to say because Jason's face was on the move again. Happiness looked good on him. Made that heat simmer lower. Made the fuzziness beneath my skin spark.

"Good plan," he agreed. Jason was the one that flipped the light off, plunging us into darkness. "You need a bath mat too."

"Okay." He didn't argue as he climbed onto the mattress, though he did grimace, like he expected it to pop. It didn't. It held true. Jason made a sound as he lay to my left. He reached for his blanket, pulling it up over him. It didn't escape my notice that he was as far away from me as physically possible.

If this had been a week ago, I would've appreciated that.

But…

I wiggled across the mattress a little, heart pounding. Jason's eyebrows shot up, his head swiveling to look at me. In the dark, I could barely make out his features. A prominent nose. A cupid's bow that dipped just right. A stubborn chin. Spiky short hair.

"Jason…" I started, wanting to hear his voice again, one more time before bed.

"Yeah?" he asked, huskily.

"I'm glad you're here," I admitted. The dark made me feel bold. Bolder than I'd ever been. He made a sound. Reminded me of a wounded animal. My heart jumped again. Before I could worry, he spoke, setting my nerves to rest.

"I'm glad I'm here, too."

I relaxed. Smiling up at the ceiling. There was a foot separating our bodies. Maybe slightly less than that. I ached for him to cross the distance, but he didn't. In fact, when I'd stopped reliving how perfect today had been—I realized Jason was fast asleep.

He was turned on his side, facing me, body tucked around one of his pillows. Thank god, I'd had three. Seriously. His hand lay on the mattress, the dark, lax shape of it making something fizzle inside me. My heart squeezed and squeezed as I stared at him.

Stared at how still he was.

How quiet.

Just the steady rise and fall of his chest.

The heat between us was incubating. Keeping us pleasantly toasty, even if my nose was a little chilly. Outside the window, the snow continued to fall. And as I reached for Jason's hand, hovering mine over top it, this ache for something…more…turning me inside out, it truly felt as though we were the only two people in the world.

I didn't touch him.

Didn't know if I should.

I could feel the heat emanating from the back of his hand as I spread my fingers out, measuring the difference in our size. I wanted to trace along his knuckles. Wanted to map the veins on the back of his hands. Wanted to tangle us together till we were one.

I almost did.

Almost.

nineteen

JASON

I WOKE UP THAT FIRST morning with an armful of Joe. We'd gotten cold during the night, apparently, and had been drawn to one another. I could only assume that was what happened, anyway, as the glow of morning sun through the storm outside woke me and Joe was nestled with his back against my chest.

My face was pressed to his nape, lips skimming the fuzzy hair there. He smelled delicious. Carrying notes of the apple soap I'd found in his shower. Less like sunshine today, but still just as sweet. The underlying hint of sleep-sweat felt private. My body was more honest than would've been…appropriate.

Because my dick was throbbing where it pressed against the supple curve of his ass. Pushing at those meaty, thick cheeks. It knew exactly where it was meant to go.

For a single second, I let myself imagine it.

Let myself imagine we were together. That Joe had given me blanket permission to pull his sweats down till they settled beneath the swell of his ass. That he was still loose and wet from the last time I'd fucked him. That I could simply…press the crown of my dick against his messy hole and push inside.

God.

Yes.

What sound would he make? Waking up on my dick like that. A gasp, probably. He didn't strike me as the kind of guy to moan. Too quiet for that. Would he push back? Shift those thick legs wide open. Use his body, not his words, to beg to be bred.

God, being in Joe's bed was bad for my self-control.

I pulled back, releasing his waist and easing myself out of bed. I regretted it immediately, because our cocoon had been warm. Outside it, the world was icy. Cold. And Joe looked so…sweet with pillow creases on his cheek, his hair a golden mess, body tucked as small as he could make it. He twitched a little, and I held my breath, frightened he'd wake up to see my dick pointing right at him. His eyes didn't open, though.

Thank god.

I dragged myself into the bathroom to rinse off and take care of my little…problem.

My dick was throbbing by the time I shut the door and climbed into the shower. One benefit of Joe's place was that the water tended to run hot. Which was awesome, as the short trek through the house had been enough to turn me into a human popsicle.

Aside from my dick.

My dick that was…fuck.

Christ.

I yanked my clothes off as quickly as I could, hopping under the now hot stream of water and reaching for Joe's conditioner immediately. I squirted some onto my hand, the scent of apples permeating the air. Reminding me of the nape of his neck, all velvety against my lips. Reminding me of that big ass.

Oh fuck.

The first stroke hurt. Tight, from root to tip, easing only a little of the ache pulsating between my legs.

"Fuck," I gasped out, the second stroke harder than the last. I spread my legs a little, eyes drifting shut. Hot water pelted my back, but I barely felt it, lost in my head as I was.

I was back in bed.

Dick slipping inch by inch into Joe's tight body. Wet and messy. Slick from my own cum. Letting me ease into him as slow, as deliberate as I liked. Slow enough his hole kept fluttering, kept clutching at me, trying to beg me to go faster.

But I wouldn't.

I wouldn't.

Enamored by the way his mouth stayed parted, these broken little pants escaping with every centimeter I fed inside him. Leaning over him, drunk on his face, his reactions, the hot squelch of his hole.

He'd be needy in bed.

A pillow princess, probably.

Prince?

Either way.

Joe would want me to take care of him.

And god…

My hand sped up as my fantasy evolved. Turned from teasing him. From easing into him. To snapping my hips. To the culmination of my teasing. To his meaty leg caught in the crook of my elbow as I pounded into him from behind just so I could feel his ass bounce.

Feel my balls bump his.

God.

I could only imagine what that would feel like. Intimate in a new way. I'd grind into him, just so they would rub together. Enjoy the way his little pants turned to whimpers when I moved faster, harder.

I could tip him over. I could push him onto his chest, yank his hips up. Could fuck him from behind fast and hard—then…right when he was on the edge. Right when he started shuffling his knees. Right when his toes curled. Right when he was—there. Ready.

I'd slow down.

Movements syrupy once more.

Pull back so excruciatingly slow I could feel his hole *throb*.

Maybe I could make him cry.

Let go, the way he had at the grocery store the day I'd held him. Not because everything was too much, too hard, too heavy. But because he felt good. Because I'd made him feel good.

When I came, I had to bite my knuckles not to moan.

My dick continued to throb for several long, excruciating seconds, cum spilling down the drain along with the apple-scented water. My dick smelled like apples. The whole shower smelled like apples. God, that was so fucking cute—that Joe owned an apple orchard and bought apple-scented hygiene products.

My skin was positively buzzing from my orgasm as I washed my hair—so it'd smell like Joe—just like the rest of me. The guilt came after. Creeping up on me as I towel-dried myself—using Joe's towel—and tried not to think about the fabric touching his cock, his balls, his ass. Fuck. I wanted to wrap it around my dick and stroke, scratchy texture be damned.

"No." God, where was my self-control?

This was a problem.

A problem that I apparently shared with Joe.

Because when I headed back to the bedroom I could hear him before I saw him. Could hear his ragged breaths. Just like they'd been in my head. I paused just outside the doorway, confused. Through the crack I could see him, lying in the center of the mattress, his legs spread and up, the blanket a fort overtop them.

One of his hands flew up to his face, covering his mouth. His eyes were pinched so tightly shut it looked like it hurt. Or maybe that was the way his arm was moving, a slick *schlick-schlick* sound emitting so quietly from between his legs I wouldn't have been able to hear if the world outside hadn't been totally silent.

My cheeks went hot and I hurried away as quietly as I could to give him privacy.

In a daze, I threw together a pan of eggs on the stove, but my mind was elsewhere. Back in Joe's room. Back on his face. How flushed it'd been. That big hand strangling his mouth to keep the noises quiet as he—

"You're going to Hell," I told myself for the second time in the last few weeks. "You're going to Hell, Jason. Stop thinking about it. Stop—"

"Good morning," Joe said from the doorway. I jerked so hard I nearly burned myself. Schooling my expression, I turned around to be greeted with the single most beautiful sight in the world. Sleepy, post-orgasmic Joe Milton.

He leaned against the doorway, blinking dopily, cheeks flushed. There was this sheen to his skin that made it positively glow. His hair stuck up in messy gold tufts, and the pillow creases on his cheeks were still there.

It took every ounce of self-control I had not to cross the room and shove my tongue down his throat.

Danger, danger.

Abort, abort, abort.

"Hiii," my voice cracked maybe a little. Especially because his shirt was gone now. Like he'd taken it off. Because it'd gotten messy. And his pecs were just…ugh, fuck. Thick and bouncy, perky pink nipples poking straight out from the chill.

"I'm going to get the fire going," Joe told me, though his tits were distracting me. God. I bet anything they were big enough I could fuck them. And wasn't that a thought? Grabbing them, straddling his chest, and just…pushing my cock right between.

Hell, Jason.

Remember?

That's where you're going.

"I'm making eggs!" I announced like a total idiot. Joe, to his credit, didn't look confused or surprised. He ducked his head, cheeks pink.

"Thanks," he said sweetly, looking up at me through those pale, thick lashes like I'd just told him I was giving him my left kidney—not that I was scrambling embryos. Were eggs even embryos? I'd have to ask him to Google it.

"Uhhh no problem. Yep." My cheeks were so hot it felt like my skin was boiling.

Joe left the kitchen, and because I was a very terrible, awful, bad man, I watched him go. Watched the dimples above his ass. And then his ass. Watched the way it flexed with each step and tried not to think about fucking him.

To no avail.

After we'd had breakfast we went right back to renovation. I was better today after Joe had taken the time to walk me through some of the basics. Nothing I did looked even remotely as good as what he did, but Joe never complained. He was very forgiving for a perfectionist.

All day we worked, squabbling, but in sync.

I made a lot of trips down into the basement. Mostly because the tools were down there—having been moved off the porch in preparation for the storm. My legs were on fire by the end of the day from all the crouching, and standing, and crouching, and stairs, and standing, and crouching.

So much so that I collapsed onto the air mattress after my shower without even thinking about my lust-haze from that morning. Exhausted but pleased, because Joe had informed me that he thought we were pretty much done. Aside from a few painting things—he'd said that more eloquently—and the baseboards.

I'd spent a good hour on his phone ordering even more furniture. An actual bed frame, for one thing. A real mattress. A dining table and chairs. A couch. Hell, I even ordered him a TV. Rugs, a bath mat—because yes, he did not in fact own one.

We'd gone from not-even-close to right-on-track with one very productive weekend.

I'd done my best not to think about my own feelings about returning to the real world.

I'd very doggedly ignored my earlier panic and done my best to enjoy this for what it was. I thought I'd done pretty well, if how pleased and unconcerned Joe had been was any indication. The way he looked at me was very…different.

Fond in a way it hadn't been before.

The wariness was gone.

He smiled more.

Spoke more.

And as the day had worn on, he'd gotten closer and closer to me. Brushing against my side as he walked by. Tipping his head to invite me to grab his neck. Looking at me with these big, dark, expectant eyes every time I passed him and didn't touch him. The need in them quieted only when I did. Only when my hands were on his hips, or his shoulders.

Bliss written across his features that was not good for my ego, or my reawakened libido.

Speaking of…

When Joe walked into the bedroom after his shower, my brain just about broke.

He was glistening. Water droplets slipping down his pecs, between the dips of his abs, past his sweet little belly button. God, I wanted to lick it. Wanted to make him squirm and wiggle. Wanted to nip at the V-line that disappeared beneath his sweats. Even more than that, though, I wanted to bury my face in his crotch and inhale.

"Hi," Joe said in a way that was equal parts shy and confused. Probably because I was staring at his dick. My eyes snapped up quickly, and I surreptitiously pulled the blanket from the bed over my lap.

"Hi."

"You think the storm will let up tomorrow?" Joe asked. He flipped the light switch off. Movements deliberate as he climbed into bed beside me. There was this odd feeling in the air. Anticipation maybe.

"I'm not sure," I admitted. Truthfully, I didn't want it to. Didn't want these days to end, chilly and exhausting as they were. Didn't want to go back to worrying. To my stack of tasks that needed to be accomplished. To all my obligations and insecurities.

To empty silence.

Because the silence when Joe was around never felt that way.

"I hope it doesn't," Joe admitted, so quiet I almost didn't hear.

He was on his side a second later, facing away from me, that big back so tempting. God, this was testing my patience. I took a breath, grateful when my dick relaxed and I could get my lungs to work again. Could get my body to act like a body, not like a giant blob of need.

Joe's back moved with each breath.

He was so warm.

A furnace himself as I turned to face him, not crossing the distance, simply wanting.

Wishing.

"Do…" Joe started a few minutes later, long after I'd assumed he was asleep.

"What?" I asked, the whirr of the space heater the only thing to fill the quiet.

"Do…friends cuddle?" Joe inquired, voice low and sweet.

Ohdeargod.

"Sure they do." I couldn't tell if I was punishing myself, being an opportunist, or simply wanting to teach him what it meant to have a real friend. Someone you could trust to hold you when you needed it. If Joe was asking, it meant he wanted that.

To be cuddled.

God, I wanted that too, so badly.

Slowly, I inched across the air mattress until my chest brushed his back.

"Is this what you want?" I gave him an opportunity to speak up, my hand hovering over his blanket-covered hip. "For me to hold you?"

My heart was pounding and it refused to stop.

"Yes." Joe's voice, again, was so quiet I barely heard it.

"Over the blankets or under?" I asked, aching, aching, aching.

"Under."

I kept my movements gentle as I wiggled beneath his blanket, fingers finding his hip, squeezing it once—the way that was most familiar— before I wrapped an arm around his belly and pressed myself against his back with purpose.

I had to will my dick to behave.

"This what you wanted, baby?" I asked, the pet name slipping from my tongue without permission. It wasn't the first time. All I could do was wince.

"Yes," Joe agreed.

I felt the moment he relaxed. Sinking into me, his body dropping as a sigh escaped. He was a popped balloon. No longer rigid—bouncy, deflated, and sweet where he pushed against me. He moved a little, only to press back with more purpose.

I could feel his heartbeat.

Racing.

Just like mine.

"How about this?" I asked, hand on his lower belly, my face pressed to his nape. My lips skimmed the velvety skin there for the second time that day. Only this time, it was better. So much better. Because it wasn't circumstance that had given me this, it was Joe himself.

He'd asked for this.

He'd wanted this.

He'd wanted me.

"Mhm," Joe agreed, voice sleepy despite the way his heart danced. "S'nice."

"It is nice," I agreed, lips fluttering against his skin. It wasn't a kiss, but it was close.

Dancing along the line of what was appropriate. A line we'd both been dancing all day long.

"You feel good," Joe told me, his voice sweet. He was putty in my arms. I gave him a squeeze, and he sighed again, pleased. So, I held him tighter. Gave him something to sink into. He was a lot larger than I was, but I managed just fine.

"You feel good, too," I promised.

"You're…" Joe started after a few minutes of silence. Of me holding him. Enjoying him. Soaking up his apple-sunshine scent, and memorizing the way he breathed.

"I'm what?"

"You're the best friend I've ever had. My *only*…real friend."

My heart cracked right down the middle. First of all, because it broke me to think that he'd never had anything like this before. That someone as sweet, as wonderful as Joe could be having all these firsts when he was nearly thirty. That he could've gone decades without being adored the way he deserved.

But also because…again, I was reminded of the line between us.

The line I knew I shouldn't cross even if I wanted to.

I'd gotten good at ignoring things, though, over the last few days, so I ignored that too. Ignored that in favor of being what Joe needed. Because it made me happy to be that for him.

"You're my best friend, too," I told him, because it was true. There wasn't a single person I enjoyed spending time with more than I did with him. Not even Mary. Which was…a tall order. He just… God. This weekend in particular had made it so very evident how much I enjoyed him.

"Oh good," Joe said, sleepy and relieved. Apparently, he'd worried I wouldn't pick him back. "That's good."

"It is," I agreed, kissing the back of his neck, this time deliberately. Not because I was trying something I shouldn't but because I craved the comfort too. Joe made a happy sound in reply, and I buried my face in the hollow of his throat, simply breathing him in. Breathing in the very essence of Joe and all he was.

Maybe this was all I needed. The out I'd been looking for. Not distance, per se, but to have Joe be the one who dictated what happened between us. If I left things up to him and I found out my feelings weren't quite right, maybe he wouldn't hate me?

Which meant…

I could have this.

He was giving me this.

And this was more than enough.

I'd let Joe hold the reins.

twenty

JASON

ON THE THIRD AND FINAL day at Joe's house, the storm finally slowed. In the morning, snow had piled up against the front door, deep enough we couldn't get out, even if we'd wanted to. Taking advantage of the situation again, Joe and I spent the early hours finishing up the last of his projects. Apparently three days of construction, and a buddy, had been all he needed to get the house in working order.

There was still the matter of the porch to deal with, but I'd been dropping hints that it wouldn't be a bad idea to hire out for that.

Aside from that…he officially had a working floor, solid walls, and a kitchen that was both cute and functional. His furniture was due to arrive well before Christmas, and I was happy for him. So incredibly happy.

Happy for myself, too, because the last few days had been a dream.

I'd been trapped in a snow globe with Joe. Living in an alternate universe where I had everything—well, *almost* everything—I wanted. The snow fell and fell, and Joe and I danced around one another. Synchronized. Two people learning that they worked together, even with so much unsaid between them.

Joe was clever. Funny. *Cute.*

Capable.

Always serious.

Well, *mostly* serious.

I had cracked through his shell bit by bit as the days passed. Saw his yolk in an entirely new way. I witnessed a true laugh, for one thing. Caused by me, something I'd done wrong that he'd had to fix—head tossed back, throat bobbing. The sound of his chortling was raspy sweet. Hot honey on cornbread.

And no, that was not a crack at him being from Ohio.

Though it certainly was one about him being blond.

There was always something new to learn from Joe.

And if I ignored my lust—which was incredibly difficult come day three of my Joe-solation, I could almost convince myself that what I felt for him truly was friendship. At least, if I was blatantly lying. In denial just like I'd been for months.

Denial was a safety blanket.

One I was only sporadically allowed.

Because sometimes—when Joe smiled or laughed or breathed—it all came back in a rush. He wasn't Joe anymore. He was my Joe. And the switch in my head flipped back on.

It was stupid. I was so stupid.

I should've said something.

I knew that.

But I was…scared. Scared that I'd lose him. Scared that I wasn't capable of being what he needed. Scared of being vulnerable. Scared that the past would repeat itself. Scared that if I let him in…and he found me lacking…I'd never recover.

I kept some of my walls up as I tore his down.

And it wasn't fair.

I knew it wasn't.

But I couldn't stop protecting my own heart.

"You know, for such a careful person you are the opposite of careful," Joe said quietly. I startled out of my reverie, looking up from the absolutely horrible blob of icing I'd left on my gingerbread house. I'd bought the village set when I'd been grocery shopping. Hadn't thought about it. Hadn't expected getting to crack open the boxes and use them.

Until the afternoon on day three rolled around and we ran out of house projects to do. Joe had been the one to spot the gingerbread houses and he'd positively lit up. Begged me, "Can we make those?" Like he thought "no" was ever an option when he was staring at me with those eyes.

"Anything you want," I promised.

He'd been downright chipper as he'd set them up on the kitchen island. He'd had to move some of the food items into the now-dry cupboards, but he hadn't minded. Now, he was halfway through his third building.

They were pre-assembled, so all we were really doing was decorating. Joe was good at it. Me…not so much. My single gingerbread home—chapel? I think it was supposed to be a chapel—looked like a bird had shit all over it.

"I *am* being careful," I said with a sigh. "It just…so happens that I'm not nearly as good at this as you are."

Joe puffed up a little at that, looking proud as he bent over his project, a little smile on his lips. "I think you cut the hole in your icing bag too big," he explained, piping a perfect row of little icicles along the edge of his building.

I spied on him, and tried to copy.

Another glob came out and hit the cardboard mat the house was attached to with finality. I laughed. Couldn't help it. It was ridiculous. All of this was. This was my first time creating a gingerbread house—and I was fucking awful at it.

Privately I wondered if that was why I'd grabbed them.

Childish wishes.

Wanting to share another first with Joe.

A first that didn't feel like I was crossing lines.

Setting my icing bag down, I covered my face with one hand, snorting into it as the monstrosity I'd made loomed in my peripheral vision. God, it was ugly. So ugly.

"Here." Joe offered me his icing bag. I dropped my hand, then reached for it, heart skipping a beat at the look on his face.

His eyes said, *I don't mind that you're terrible at this.*

They said, *it's not about being perfect.*

They said, *I'm happy.*

And god.

That look tore me apart the most. It was evidence that he'd been telling the truth before. I wasn't being useful right now. Not at all. And he still wanted me around.

The icing bag helped a little.

Okay, that was a lie. I was just as terrible with his. But the bag itself was warm from his palm, and that in itself, made it feel better. Joe swapped me for my bag and began working again, in slightly less controlled lines.

When we were done, you could clearly tell who had made which buildings.

We set them along the counter between the fridge and the sink. A little village of our own.

"It looks like a five-year-old made mine," I snorted when we stood back to admire our work.

Joe shook his head.

There was something tender about his expression.

All his hard lines were gone, including the ones by his mouth. Outside, the sun was beginning to set. It'd melted a decent portion of the snow, enough that we'd be able to get out the doors if needed. The snow plow had gone by earlier, taking the worst of what decorated the road with it. We weren't trapped anymore.

But we were both pretending this didn't have to end.

"Have you never done this before?" Joe asked, still watching me with that warm, warm expression. My throat clicked when I swallowed. For a beat, I considered lying. Bullshitting about it so that I wouldn't have to be vulnerable. So I wouldn't have to admit the truth.

But…

"No," I admitted. "We hardly celebrated when I was a kid. My parents weren't really…home. Not even during the holidays."

"Oh." Joe frowned. His dark eyes were sweet. Sweet as the gravel in his voice. "I'm sorry."

He didn't need to apologize on their behalf. In fact, he couldn't. Nothing he could do would make up for the years I'd spent lonely. And yet…for some reason…it helped.

Joe didn't pity me, the same way I didn't pity him.

But he was sad for me.

Sad for the boy I'd been, and what I'd missed.

"What about you?" I asked, genuinely curious. "What was Christmas like for the Miltons?"

"Loud," Joe said. "Mom yells." He blinked, eyes going far away, transported back to his childhood. "She cooks a lot. Too much. There'd be food everywhere. Messes everywhere. Not a single place in the house would be quiet. Mom decorates the first of November so the house would be covered in tinsel and stuff with a big sparkly tree. Makes—*made*, I mean—everyone contribute. Usually I was on cookie duty."

"That sounds nice," I said wistfully. Joe nodded.

"It was," he agreed. "You know…" he cleared his throat, cheeks going pink as he stared at the dining room table. "If I'd known you then, as a kid." His words were very careful. "I would've wanted to be your friend. I would've invited you over for Christmas. So you wouldn't have to be by yourself."

My heart squeezed so tight I worried it might pop.

Joe didn't push.

I was grateful.

I was pretty sure if he said anything else I was going to cry.

"Sounds like you need a Christmas tree," I deflected, strained and shook to the very core. "Lights. If your family is coming here you're going to have to pull out all the stops to impress them."

"Yeah," Joe agreed. He was staring at the worst of the gingerbread houses I'd made, something achingly fond in his eyes. He was looking at them with a new perspective. Like they really had been made by five-year-old Jason.

It made me feel…

It made me…

"Bathroom," I blurted out. "I'll be. Back. In a—you know. Jiffy." After offering Joe what had to be the most awkward set of finger guns known to man, I darted down the hallway. Once inside the bathroom I could breathe a little easier. Emphasis on the "little" part, because—

God.

I was so in love with him it wasn't even funny.

I splashed water on my face.

I studied the haggard wrinkles around my own eyes. My laugh lines. The gray in my hair. Tried to make sense of why Joe would look at me like he did. Like I was…I was something *good.* Something worth looking at.

Like I was *his.*

"You're his best friend," I muttered to my dripping reflection. "Nothing more. Stop projecting. So what if he likes your shitty gingerbread skills. Chill."

It felt like a lie.

It totally felt like a lie.

When I exited the bathroom and looked for Joe, he was nowhere to be found. Which was, as you can probably guess, alarming. I did locate him, eventually, on the back porch. More time had passed than I'd realized.

My own fault.

As I'd been caught in another spiral.

For a moment, I debated not going out at all.

But that was idiotic.

And my drive to be beside Joe, as always, won.

So, I pushed through the back door with no small amount of struggling through the snow that populated the porch. Once outside, I took a few, deep lungfuls of fresh air and sighed. The snow was coming down again, but it was a peaceful sort of drift. The kind that made me think about holidays I wished I'd had. About manufactured Christmases and how sometimes, when I was young, I'd observe and wonder why even fake people—the ones on TV—had better lives than I did.

It was a spoiled thought. I knew that now. I'd been blessed in so many ways. But tell that to a kid whose parents sent him a postcard from whichever remote place they were visiting instead of being home with him for the holidays.

Joe shushed me without turning around to look.

He *shushed* me.

"Wh—"

"Shhh," Joe repeated. He was sitting on the back steps. There was a quarter inch of snow on his coat. Or close. He practically blended into the wild, the white had imbedded itself in every crevice of his clothing. It coated his hair, little flakes melting on his flushed red ears.

I was so confused it took me a second to realize what he was looking at.

But then I did.

And suddenly, everything stopped. The swirling thoughts in my head. The worries I held. The insecurities gone. Poof. Just like that. Like that day I'd seen him with the magpie, Joe's magnetism was something wondrous. I was present in a way I hardly ever was.

Frozen.

There was a deer in the yard.

A doe, more accurately.

She had as much snow on her back as Joe had on his. Walking slowly, each step so quiet, so careful I could hear the crunch of snow beneath her hooves. With fur that was the loveliest grayish-brown, a shaggy belly, and a tail with a bright-white underside, she had to be the prettiest thing I'd seen. Her shiny black nose twitched as she turned giant dark eyes on us. Regarding us with the same veiled curiosity we looked at her with.

Hesitantly, she took another step closer.

Then another.

Her hooves crunched through the layer on the snow that'd crystalized as the sun had melted it.

I held still, scared to even breathe for fear of frightening her off. Joe was just as still. There was something about the way he carried himself at moments like this that did me in entirely. He was sure here, in a way he hardly ever was. With an air of serene confidence. Broad shoulders still, like he was just as scared to breathe as I was.

The deer drew closer, closer, closer.

At the bottom of the porch steps, she paused. Her head tipped back as she stared up at us from a much closer vantage point. Close enough now I could see the snow in her lashes. See the flakes where they clung to her pelt, and the downy fur at the top of her head between her expressive ears.

They flicked this way and that.

She was gorgeous and she knew it.

And yet…I found my attention drifting. Found my gaze falling on Joe. On the snowflakes melting on the vulnerable skin of his nape. On his flushed pink ears. On the way he was my farm-boy statue once again.

There was no denying how much he loved this.

Seeing nature.

Breathing in the fresh air.

Like he was more meant for the wild than the people in town. At ease in the face of wilderness in the same way I found comfort in conversation. He made the silence feel…loud. Not loud in the way the world could often be, bustling, bright. But meaningful. Every second that ticked by, every breath the three of us shared meant something.

I don't know how long we remained there. Long enough my ears were frozen and my nose was running. Long enough my sleeves were half white. The snow kept coming. Chilly winds blowing flurries through the air.

When the doe eventually left, I sat down beside Joe on the steps.

My knees were weak.

Joe turned his head to look at me. There were snowflakes in his lashes, just like the doe's. His eyes lingered on my mouth the way they had for days now. Staring. Something uncertain in his gaze that I ached to soothe because it didn't feel right.

It didn't feel right for Joe to be uneasy when I was around to take care of him.

We didn't speak the rest of the night.

We didn't need to.

We fell into the rhythms that we'd set together. Brushed our teeth in tandem. Took turns in the shower. Slipped beneath the covers like it was natural. Like existing together was the easiest thing in the world.

I crowded against Joe's back and held him. Pressed my face to his nape and breathed him in. Soaked up every second because I knew the next day would bring reality with it. The sun would rise, and so would we, and there would be no more excuses not to go back to our separate lives.

Our snow globe would simply cease to be.

twenty-one

JOE

I HADN'T INTENDED TO KISS Jason. Okay, maybe that was a lie. I had intended to. Just…not when I did. The thought had occurred to me the last night Jason had stayed with me. If I was being honest, I'd been thinking about it a lot longer than that.

Maybe not outright.

Not in the way where my mind put words to the feeling.

But…there was this ache to be close. It'd started as curiosity. Confusion over why someone like him—someone who was as full of life as he was—would want to be saddled with me as a friend. And as I'd gotten to know him, as he'd answered my questions, as he'd dropped his walls bit by bit, that feeling had evolved.

Jason had been spooning me in bed the moment I realized what I wanted. His breath tickling my nape, nose nuzzling like he often did. Just feeling me, because he enjoyed it. Enjoyed how big I was, how tight he could squeeze without hurting me.

Jason was warm.

So warm.

And sure.

Sure as sunrise. Sure as the joy of a good harvest. Sure as the way Mom's cocoa always made me feel. Like my tastebuds were coming home. Something I could count on to be a bright spot of stability when everything else felt ever-changing.

The sun was peeking through the window. No clouds, no snow to obstruct it. And with it, came the promise of a new day. Our bubble breaking. The return to the lives we'd both been ignoring.

It wasn't till Jason left the bed to get ready for the day that I understood what that feeling was. That ache in my chest. The flutter in my belly. The heat I felt just looking at him. All those little moments piled up into one ginormous, overwhelming mountain.

A mountain of reasons Jason was my favorite person.

It all led to an avalanche of realization.

I wanted him.

Wanted him in every capacity there was.

Wanted him the way I'd never wanted another person. Not because he was useful. Not because he'd helped me. Not because he was firm when I needed firm, kind when I needed kind. Not because when I thought about that small, sad little boy all on his own all I wanted was to love him.

But a combination of all those things.

All those things and more.

The way he smiled.

The way he laughed.

The way he hid, and he didn't know I knew.

He was a magpie. Wild. Untamable. Wings spread at the ready to take off the moment things got too real. And yet…he was solid too. Because even though there was panic in his eyes sometimes, he stayed.

He stayed.

And that was enough.

Enough to give me courage when the time was right.

We stood on the porch steps. Jason's car was idling in the driveway, warming up after we'd quite liberally cleared it of any and all reminders of the storm we'd just left behind. He'd gone up first, to return my shovel to the spot he'd found it. And when he turned around, I was there.

On the step below his, waiting.

The stiffness in Jason's limbs disappeared, his head dipping down as he brushed our foreheads together. One of his hands found my throat, cupping me there as his pale eyes met mine. His skin was cold. Damp from shoveling snow. But welcome.

So much was unsaid at that moment. Longing palpable as my eyes drifted down to his lips. His breath hitched. I felt it. Felt the quick exhale. The way it fluttered against my own mouth. Felt it in my fucking bones.

And suddenly I knew.

I knew what I wanted.

I knew what these feelings were. These feelings that had been bubbling up inside me for weeks. Simmering, simmering like cocoa on the stove till they'd ultimately reached a roiling boil. A breaking point.

They weren't friendship feelings, even if I'd thought they were at first. They were tremulous. Wild and fluttering the way Jason felt. Scary in their newness, but exciting too.

So I kissed him. Kept it chaste because that was all I knew. Jason was still as stone at first, the hand on my throat twitching, like he didn't know what to do with it. He didn't allow me time to fret though. His mouth softened the same way his countenance had, head tipping to the side as he pressed back into me with that same solid sureness that made me feel okay to drop my guard.

I could rely on him.

He'd proven that.

Jason was the first to pull back.

His eyes were hooded, his lips chapped and chilly.

"Jesus," he murmured, thumb petting the side of my neck as we mutually processed what had just happened.

"Was it bad?" My voice wavered.

"No. It was perfect," Jason replied, hand tightening to steady me. He was my height like this. Us meeting on equal footing. Literally. That was kinda poetic, right? "Don't you worry about that for a second."

I nodded, a short jerky motion that was more twitch than motion.

And then, because I couldn't help myself, I grinned.

Jason grinned back.

He pulled back a little, staring at me for a beat, taking me in. "God, you're beautiful," he praised. My cheeks flushed. That spark I felt grew hotter. "Thank you for the gift, Joe."

"Gift?" I blinked, smile still in place.

"Gift," Jason echoed with surety. His hand slid upward, scraping along my jaw till his cold fingers dug into my cheeks. His thumb skimmed my lower lip, dragging across the chapped skin, memorizing the feel of it.

My pulse was jumping all over the place. Skipping. Lashes fluttering.

"I'm going to go now," Jason said. "Let you think about this. About if you want it again. About what it means to you." The way his thumb kept dragging across my lip was almost drugging. "From what I gather you've never kissed before?"

"No," I admitted, voice rough. "Well. Just once. But I threw up."

At that, Jason snorted out a laugh. "Sorry, sorry." He sobered. "Not laughing at you. Just…your delivery there was so deadpan it was adorable. You threw up? The first time you kissed someone?"

I nodded. Jason's thumb continued to tease. "Homecoming," I grunted, when his eyebrows questioned me. "I was…sixteen? I think."

"And you haven't wanted to try again," Jason filled in the blanks.

"Not till you." My heart continued to race.

"How long?" Jason asked. "How long have you wanted to kiss me?" I made a frustrated sound, and he laughed again, though the sound wasn't mean.

"Why are you interrogating me?" I asked, annoyed.

"Because I care about you, Joe," Jason reiterated. "And two nights ago you told me I was your best friend. Your *only* friend. And now…you're kissing me. I want to make sure this is what you want."

I gave him a look that hopefully conveyed how stupid what he'd just said was—even if it was also…kind of sensible. "I wouldn't have kissed you if I didn't want to do it," I told him.

"Alright," Jason snorted. "Fair enough. But…you have to understand why I'm hesitant."

An awful thought occurred to me. "Did you…not want it?"

"What?" Jason's eyes widened, a look of horror crossing his face that immediately made me feel very secure. "No. Of course I did. Do. I just—

there's… Gah." His thumb stopped moving and because I was apparently being courageous today, I very carefully, very shyly pressed a kiss to it. Again, Jason's eyebrows shot up. "Joe," Jason said my name like it was a full sentence, the way he always did.

"I liked kissing you," I said, cheeks hot. "I like you."

"I don't want to take advantage of you."

"Take advantage of me, how?" He wasn't making any sense.

"Because you're young, Joe. Way younger than I am. And I'm…" Everything out of his mouth sounded like an excuse. Though, I wasn't sure why he was pulling them out left and right unless there was something real behind them.

Something he wasn't saying.

Something I wasn't seeing.

At least…until I did.

"You're scared," I realized with dawning clarity.

Jason froze.

His hand twitched, like he was about to pull it away. I reached up, wrapping my fingers around his wrist to keep it firmly in place. His eyes darted everywhere, looking for escape. I was right. How…how could someone as confident as Jason be so scared? And of me of all people?

"You're scared of me," I stated, because it was true. God, how had I not seen it? "Aren't you? That's why you're making excuses."

"I'm not scared of *you*," Jason denied, eyes still darting around. "And they're not excuses." God, he was wiley as a rabbit. I couldn't believe I'd ever thought of him as a wolf before.

"You are," I frowned. I wasn't offended. Why would I be? I understood. Hell, I… "I'm scared of you, too."

At that, Jason's eyes finally snapped to mine. "What?" He looked equal parts alarmed and surprised.

"I failed before," I admitted. "When I moved away for the first time. Went crawling back home with my tail between my legs. People pitied me. They whispered behind my back. I heard it. Of course I did. I told myself I'd never do that again. That I'd prove to everyone—and myself—that I could handle things on my own. That's why I moved so far. I thought distance would help me feel more...in control." It was a vulnerable thing to admit. He seemed to realize that because his gaze never left mine. Not once. "When I moved to Belleville I was terrified of a repeat. Worried that all I'd prove was that I wasn't capable of taking care of myself, after all."

"Joe..." Jason exhaled raggedly.

"When I look at you...all I can think about is how bad I want you to make my burdens disappear. That's...that's terrifying. That I might want that. That being vulnerable might not be the bad thing I thought it was. That I might even *need* that sometimes when for so long I told myself if I did, that made me weak."

I sensed the moment Jason stopped trying to run.

Solid now.

Solid as roots buried deep in the earth.

"You got worse walls up than I ever had," I added, because he needed to listen. "I see that. I'm not blind." He inhaled sharply. "You show me what you want to show me. Never anything more, or less. You're careful. I get that."

The more I spoke the more I began to understand my own feelings.

The more sure I felt.

"I respect it," I murmured. "But...you gotta know you don't need to be scared of me. That I want to know you, the same way you so doggedly got to know me. That I get what you were trying to teach me about letting people help you when you need it. That I saw you let me in, and now I'm returning the favor."

At that, Jason's lips tipped up, like he was remembering the months he'd practically terrorized me. I thought of them fondly now, too. Perspective was funny that way. Seeing him as he was now. A lonely, generous man, desperate to put down roots.

"I don't want you to regret me," he admitted.

"Never. I couldn't. I get that you think I'm too young for you, or whatever. Or that I don't know what I want. Maybe I don't. Maybe I am. Maybe I'm still figuring things out, same as you. Or maybe..." I inhaled. "Maybe this is the first time since I moved away from home that I feel sure about something. That I'm not pretending to know, because deep down, I feel it in my goddamn bones. So, why don't you just..." My hands curled in his sweater, pulling him close. "Why don't you let me show you what you mean to me, the way you show everyone else?"

twenty-two

JASON

JOE "SHOWING" ME HIS FEELINGS had to be the single most confusing, but amazing set of experiences in my life. Starting with the fact that he found my address—the same way I'd found his. By going out of his way to *ask around town about me.*

Which he told me via text.

Because yes, we texted now.

But only after he'd shown up at my house bright and early Monday morning.

I blamed Madison. (She'd been the one to spill the beans.) Because the day after Joe and I had kissed on his porch—I still couldn't believe that was real—there he was.

Giant and golden and gorgeous.

Knocking at my front door.

I swung it open after checking through the peep hole to see who needed help before the sun had even come up. Immediately, my eyes widened. To say I'd been surprised would be an understatement. That had been my constant state of being for the last twenty-four hours, it felt. Surprise and trepidation. Fighting the fear that Joe had called me out for.

I hadn't realized Joe would be so…ah…quick about his little plan.

Or so adorable.

JesusfuckingChrist.

When I swung the door open, I was met with the completely arresting sight of Joe in a puffer coat. *A puffer coat.* He looked like a giant marshmallow, and I wanted to *bite* him. So serious, standing there, looking down at me with those big dark eyes.

Before I could open my mouth, say good morning, ask him why he was here—any of that—Joe spoke.

"Here," he said at the same time he literally shoved a cup of piping hot coffee toward me. I grabbed it before it could spill through the little hole at the top. Thank god for lids, that's all I'll say.

"No sugar. No cream," Joe recited. "Black like you said you like."

Wow.

That was just…I hardly knew what to say to that.

"Thanks, Joe—" I opened my mouth to invite him in but he was already down the steps and heading toward his truck. Inside it, Patrick from the farm sat in the driver's seat, eyeing me with obvious mirth. He waved. I waved back, still juggling my coffee.

Ah.

So, Joe had been about to run some farm-related errands and he'd *still* stopped by to give me coffee. I was half-asleep and therefore didn't appreciate the full magnitude of the gesture. Not until I'd headed back inside, drank halfway through the cup he'd brought me, the caffeine kicked in, and I realized what Joe had just unknowingly done.

He'd claimed me.

In public.

Maybe not as his boyfriend—oh god, just thinking about the future possibility of that made me want to scream—but as his something. Someone. As the person he went to before his day even began.

Belleville was going to eat that shit up.

Especially as Patrick had been Joe's witness. He was worse than I was sometimes when it came to gossip, and I had no doubt by the end of the day, everyone in town would know that Joe Milton was bringing me coffee.

I grinned, then beat my head on the table for good measure, and called my mom.

"I've created a monster," I sighed, head tipped back, coffee clutched to my chest. "An adorable, marshmallow-looking, earnest-as-fuck monster."

"Sounds like it's your own fault," she said in reply, because she clearly hadn't listened to a thing I'd just said. She was in "agenda" mode. Which meant nothing that came out of my mouth counted. "Are you coming to the gala next Friday?" Mom was *usually* better at chatting. She ate up gossip the same way I did, especially when it was pertinent to my life specifically.

I could only blame myself for her current state, however, because… I'd been dodging her texts. And her calls. Avoiding all information surrounding the yearly holiday gala. Apparently I could no longer stall.

"Yes, I'll be coming," I sighed. "I always come. You know that." I hated that party with a burning passion. Bumping elbows with the "elites." Listening to the way a lot of them talked about the "common folk," like they were royalty and not jerks with silver spoons tucked inside their assholes.

I always went, though.

"If you're still hoping to get more investors for expanding your Santa Fund project, it'll be lucrative," Mom reminded me.

"I know." I clutched my Joe-coffee close, soaking up its warmth and the reminder of the farm boy who'd given it to me. Letting him and his cornsilk hair give me strength. "It's just…since Mary stopped coming with me…"

"They look at you strangely, I know." Mom's voice turned sympathetic. "Could you not bring another date?"

"No." My immediate reaction was denial. But then— "Ah…maybe?" Because I realized…if I was going to let Joe "show me" how he felt about me, I should at least consider being honest. He was wooing only a small portion of who I was. This might be a way to test the waters before I revealed my big Santa secret.

Maybe.

It might chase him away.

Because there was no revealing the kind of money and status I came from without eventually telling him about the Santa Fund. One day he'd know what I'd done. How I'd lied and tricked him. He might not want to bring me coffee ever again.

A smaller, darker voice in my head whispered that my true worries lay in his reaction. If Joe knew I had money, would he treat me differently? My gut response was to say, no. Of course not. Joe was the kind of guy who froze his nuts off sitting in the snow just so he could watch a doe blink. He was the kinda guy who lived in a decrepit old house with holes in the fucking walls—only fixing it so that other people wouldn't judge him.

He didn't strike me as superficial.

But…I'd been burned before.

Could I tell Joe?

Did I *want* to tell Joe? To open a door I knew would never shut?

Joe brought me coffee again the next day. And the next. And the next. On the fourth day, he brought me a pastry too. Only popping by for a split second every other time, with Patrick grinning from the truck, his phone out to record us.

We were the talk of the town.

Everywhere I went, someone was making comments.

Leanne—when I was helping her restock her book store before my shift at the grocery store began—congratulated me on my requited feelings. Baxter—when I was grabbing donuts for work—gave me a wink and told me the pastries were "on the house". The Montgomery Smut Club bequeathed me with a hand-embroidered t-shirt that read, "Joeson 5ever." Which they informed me was Joe's and my "ship name." They'd made one for him too— and I'd had to convince them that it was better if I gave it to him.

I had no intention of doing that.

I didn't know how Joe would handle our…ah…pack of well-wishers.

Truthfully? Unless someone outright told him, "The entire town of Belleville thinks that you and Jason are officially dating because you keep bringing him coffee," I doubted Joe would even notice.

Joe and I had complementary strengths.

A fact that'd been made very clear to me when I'd been helping him at his house.

And while he knew his way around a hammer—*oh god, don't make that dirty, brain*—the social stuff was more my thing.

I knew how embarrassed he'd be to have so much attention on him. Even positive attention. I supposed, in a way, I was protecting him from it. Letting him live in Joe-land where everyone and their dog weren't speculating about his love life.

"I bet he's a bottom," Matilda Deed had said as I'd been on my way out of the B&B. I paused, so shocked she was speculating about my sex life— and knew what a bottom was—that I nearly walked right into the door.

"Which one?" Beatrice Montgomery, the president of the club replied. She was Ben Montgomery's mother. Who just so happened to be the person behind the werewolf smut that had inspired the club's rebranding from Belleville's Bookish Besties to what it currently was. Everyone had been surprised to discover that serious, buttoned-up Doctor Montgomery was the king of primal kink.

It'd started an epidemic.

And now, over a year later, that had only expanded.

"Joe, of course," Matilda said. "He's an omega if I ever saw one."

My cheeks were red all the way out the door.

Speculation was not the only thing I was made privy to that week.

While in line at the grocery store on day four of Joe's "wooing" phase, Marty B.—not to be confused with Marty K., who lived on Elm— informed me that he, "Hoped Joe and I lived a long and happy life together." I'd been mid-process adding him to my holiday-help list, and had been caught off guard in a way I normally wasn't by the comment.

"What?" I finished jotting down his name, address, and the task he needed assistance with. My head was still full of Christmas lights and the logistics of finding a ladder we could borrow to throw them onto his exterior. Suffice to say, I was distracted.

"I just mean, we're all glad to see you with someone," Marty said, smiling at me from behind his frankly massive mustache. The pom-pom on his hat bobbed. "Joe seems like a nice guy. I heard he let Mrs. Lancaster grope his biceps. Won points from me for sure. You get that old and it's hard to find biceps like that."

"Honestly? It's hard to find biceps like that even when you aren't old," I said, still a bit dazed by the entire conversation.

"And boobs," Madison tacked on unhelpfully from her register. She was checking out another customer, who—when I glanced up—had stopped putting items on the conveyor belt so she could listen in.

"Boobs?" Marty looked perplexed.

"Joe has the most incredible tits known to man," Madison clarified. "Also, ass."

Marty considered that, eyebrows knitting together as he pictured it.

"I can't believe I'm saying this but—can we please stop objectifying Joe?" I didn't love the idea of anyone else looking at him like that, even if his chest and ass really were legendary.

"Okay, Mr. Jealousy," Madison teased. "Don't make me get the spray bottle."

The front door swung open and speak-of-the-devil, there he was.

Joe in all his tit-ified, ass-ified glory.

He was wearing a puffer coat again though, thank god. So, even though Marty ducked his head, surreptitiously trying to ascertain if Madison had been telling the truth, he couldn't see shit.

"I can't tell," he muttered through the side of his mouth to Madison, who grinned.

Joe had a bushel of apples in his arms. Blocking the view even more than his coat did. He headed straight for me, then paused at the end of the register, obviously not sure what to do since I had company.

I still got a little thrill at the fact he was the one approaching me.

Joe's eyes darted between me, Madison, Marty, and Mrs. Beele.

"Hey—" I said, biting my tongue so I wouldn't call him baby. I wasn't sure I was ready to confirm the town's assumptions just yet. Thus far, I'd been pretty good at dodging. That felt just as momentous as bringing him with me to the gala.

The gala next week.

One week away.

God.

That was barely enough time to stress about it.

Joe grunted, not even offering a full word in response as he continued to stare nervously at the others. I saw the moment he locked-in though, standing up a little straighter, his lips set into a firm line.

"Hello," Joe said to Marty, then Madison, then Mrs. Beele. Three separate, very serious "hello's." *Ohmygodlookatmybabygo! Talking to people! Networking! Just like I'd taught him!*

Mrs. Beele tittered while Marty grinned and offered Joe his hand to shake.

"Nice to finally put a face to the name," Marty said.

Joe looked confused as he shifted his apples over to take his hand. He shook it in a macho-firm kinda way before he dropped it. No lingering. Not even a little.

"A face to the…name?" Joe echoed.

"You and Jason are the talk of the town," Marty explained. "Which I'm sure you already know."

Joe, did not, in fact, know, if his expression could be believed.

Before Marty could ask to see his tits—or outright tell Joe that everyone and their dog thought we were *together*-together—I cleared my throat.

"I can swing by after my shift tomorrow," I told Marty. "See if I can't help you get the lights up."

"Thanks, Jason," Marty replied. "The missus and I really appreciate the help. Couldn't find a friend with a ladder to save our asses, and we don't have the funds to buy one when we'll really only use it twice a year."

"I get it," I smiled. "Don't you worry. I've got you covered."

It was a solid distraction. Normally, I'd appreciate it. Normally, I filled my holiday season with as many tasks as was physically possible so by the time Christmas actually rolled around, I was too tired to feel anything but sleepy.

This year felt different, though.

Even I could tell I'd signed on for too much. Because rather than feel excited about opportunities to interact with everyone, I was beginning to feel…anxious. The list on the counter kept growing and growing.

I'd built a reputation for myself over the years. And now, even people I'd not outright offered assistance to were coming to me. A second set of hands. Errand running. Holiday traditions. You name it.

Both Marty and Mrs. Beele left. They went their separate ways, and when I turned back to Joe—and his adorable hovering—Madison twisted around to face me. I should've known she was up to no good. She had that look on her face. The mischievous one that reminded me of that time

I'd caught her shoplifting and offered her a job.

"My rates have gone up. I want thirty bucks," Madison said, right in front of Joe.

Oh Jesus. No. No.

Bad Madison.

Joe tipped his head to look at her.

I made a slicing motion at my throat so she'd stop fucking talking. But… there was no halting the train wreck coming. Not when the knowing glint in Madison's eyes made it clear she was doing this on purpose. Outing one of my many, many secrets. Making me an honest man.

"Deal," I said quickly, in vain.

"Forty," she bargained.

"Yes."

"Fifty bucks."

"Oka—"

"Fifty bucks for what?" Joe's voice was as baffled as his face.

"So that I'll leave you two alone." Her grin was positively wicked as she let the cat out of the bag like the menace she was. I groaned, scrubbing my hands over my face, too scared to look Joe in the eye after that particular pin had been dropped.

"Why do you hate me?" I lamented, still covering my face. "You're so mean. Like coffee-addicted Regina George. Only worse. Because I bought you a coffee machine. This is *bullying*."

Footsteps sounded.

I jumped when a big palm hesitantly landed on my shoulder. Dropping my hands was excruciating, but I managed. Because I knew that touch. And when Joe wanted my attention, it was impossible not to give it to him, even in these dire circumstances.

He was looking at me.

Of course he was.

Dark blue eyes, fond, gentle, the way he looked at birds and dogs and deer. Acting as though he thought I was ready to bolt. Hell, maybe I was.

Oh, how the tables had turned.

Again.

"I figured you were doing that," Joe said quietly. "Maybe not the money bit. But…it was very convenient that you were the only one here every time I came." Madison, because she was *actually* the devil, gave me a thumbs up behind Joe's back—like she'd been helping me, not hurting me. Gracefully, she took her tumbler—and mine—and headed to the break room. It didn't escape my notice that she hadn't asked for payment.

God, that was diabolical.

She was as tricky as I was.

"You wouldn't talk to me," I sighed, a fly caught in a vat of honey. Joe continued to regard me like I was something precious. He was memorizing me. I'd never had someone look at me that way. He was so fucking cute with his apple bucket tucked in one arm and his cheeks still flushed from the cold.

"I wouldn't," Joe agreed.

"I had to be…innovative."

"Mm," Joe grunted. It felt like he could see the way my heart was racing. To the way he'd wormed himself inside it, with those dinner-plate hands, and his laughter that sounded airy as smoke.

"What else have you lied about to get close to me?" Joe's words made me freeze. My whole body stiffened up, rigid as fucking fiberglass. Apparently, that was response enough, because Joe didn't poke again. He just nodded.

And then…he set the apples down on the counter.

For a second, I was genuinely confused. And then he was turning me with the hand he had on my shoulder. Delicately enough it was my choice to go or not. I went, twisting to the side as Joe slipped completely behind the register into no-man's land.

He stared at my mouth.

Ogled it, really.

The hand on my shoulder twitched. It was the same nervous tick he performed when his hands were in fists. Like he *wanted* something. Like he was overwhelmed.

"You do…a lot," Joe said quietly, eyes still trained on my lips. "For everyone…for me." His acknowledgement made warmth flood through me. More warmth, I should say. Because Joe looking at my mouth reminded me of kissing him.

Oh Jesus.

We were in public!

I'd literally just been doing my best not to broadcast our relationship to the entire town. And here he was…testing me the way I'd just debated testing him.

"Joe," his name was a warning on my tongue. It wasn't a real one though. Just a smoke screen to hide my lust. I had no self-control when it came to him. Obviously. "You need…" The list on the counter mocked me. "*Help* with something, maybe?"

His nostrils flared, and he snorted. Well, it was more an exhale than anything. Like an angry bull. But amused? Hard to describe.

Any second now, his guard would begin to drop.

All I had to do was coax a little more.

"If I didn't know any better, the way you're looking at my lips would make me think you want to be kissed," I murmured, in case I wasn't being obvious enough. My heart was skipping all over the place. "Touched, maybe," I added.

He was breaking.

His eyes took on that foggy look that made me want to crow like a goddamn rooster. Flap my wings and strut around.

"You've probably been so *lonely* all week, haven't you? Dropping coffee off for me. Setting up the furniture we bought in your fancy house. Working that cute ass off without a drop of self-care sprinkled anywhere." Joe inhaled sharply.

Bingo.

"And...I'm starting to think there's a reason for that." Again, I was bullshitting. But it was working. Joe's hand on my shoulder spasmed.

"What?" he asked, voice so quiet I barely heard it. His eyes searched mine, like he was looking for answers inside them.

"I think...you don't take care of yourself, not because you can't—" Oh dear god, please let me get this right. "But because now that you've had a taste of it...you're hoping I will."

There was a war in Joe's eyes. Sharpness fighting with the fog. Warmth and ice. His pride battling to the surface at the insinuation that he might be anything other than totally self-sufficient. But the battle was gone almost as quickly as it had come.

And I was breathless.

Because I knew what that meant.

Knew the progress we'd made.

Could see it written all over his handsome, chiseled face.

Joe nodded in agreement.

It was barely a jerk of his head, but it was there.

I hardly wanted to blink, his surrender was so goddamn beautiful.

"Is that why you came to find me?" I husked out as one of my hands curled around the back of his neck. "Because you wanted my attention?"

Again, Joe nodded.

All that ice and fire was gone now, replaced by the puppy eyes that when directed my way, made me feel like I was flying.

"Alright then." I gave his nape a squeeze. Tight the way he preferred. He melted. Literally. Turned to putty in my grip, his eyes going half mast, lips parting with a needy breath. I grinned. I couldn't help it. "You're such a good boy, Joe," the words slipped free before I could stop them. "Coming to me when you need me. Such a good, *good* boy. The best boy in the world."

Words I'd never said before.

Never even thought before.

And yet…they rang true.

He really *was* the best boy.

Multiple things happened at once. Dominos falling into place. Joe's eyes completely shut. His frame collapsed forward. He buried his face in the side of my neck, body hunched over mine, weight leaning onto me—like calling him that, calling him *the best*—had knocked him right off his feet.

I caught him, though it was a bit of a struggle to hold him up. I managed, though. Truthfully, I loved it. Loved how *big* he was. How powerful he could be. Loved the fact that his mass didn't make him scared of submitting. Loved that he was practically twice my size and still chose to let me carry his weight. Loved the way he was *leaning* on me like it never once occurred to him that I wouldn't be able to support him.

I was on top of the world when Joe chose to let me in.

It was easy.

Effortless.

It felt good.

He felt good.

And I was never more confident, or more happy than I was now—with him trusting me to carry him.

"Let's go to the back, yeah?" I murmured into his ear. "Madison won't mind if we swap. She gets paid either way."

At that, he huffed out an amused laugh. He didn't move though—just kept clinging to me.

"I gotta move, big guy," I murmured. "You don't need to let go. Just… help me a bit, okay? One foot in front of the other, baby."

Joe didn't let go, but he did lift enough of his weight that we could shift.

"Good boy."

He sighed, this airy, needy sound. I ached to pull him right back on top of me. But…privacy was a better option. As I stepped away from the counter, Joe let me go. It only took a second to figure out why. He grabbed his apple bushel, countenance docile as I led the way toward the back of the store where the break room was located.

"Won't your manager be angry if you let me in the break room during store hours?" Joe asked when we paused just outside the door. The last time we'd been next to this door together had been when this whole thing had started. When I'd held him for the first time.

It was heady how different things were now.

"I'm pretty sure he's fine with it," I grinned.

"How do you know?"

"*I'm* the manager."

"Oh." Joe blinked.

I pushed the door open, swinging around to keep it wide so Joe could come through with his apples. He'd need to restock the shelves afterward. After…what? I still wasn't sure. A cuddle for sure. Maybe more kissing?

I forced myself not to think too hard about it.

Joe entered the room with trepidation. That trepidation faded as he took in the space. I tried to look at it from his perspective. At the well-worn but cushy couch. At the giant coffee corner that Madison had covered in stickers. At all the creamers and syrups. At the pictures on the walls—of food drives, community events, Madison's graduation (which I'd obviously attended).

It looked old but well-loved.

The kind of space I'd found myself gravitating toward, especially as I got older.

If I was being honest, it felt more like home than my current house ever had.

Probably because of the memories I'd made here.

Madison was bent over the coffee station, filling her tumbler from the ridiculously expensive machine she'd blackmailed me into buying. Beside her elbow, my hot pink cup was sitting filled as well. Like she'd thought of me before she'd even thought of herself.

I softened immediately.

Was I irked she'd spilled one of my secrets to Joe? Yes. Of course I was. But…it was hard to be mad when she was so little. And young. And just a tiny-itty-bitty-baby-who-made-me-coffee-when-she-felt-bad—

"Stop looking at me like that, ew." Madison turned around to glare at me. She rose to her full height, curled around her cup like the gremlin she was.

"Boss-man says you're needed outside," I told her. "And not to come in here. For reasons."

Joe snorted. Probably because he now knew I was the boss. As we'd walked, that fogginess in his eyes had faded. I would've mourned its loss if I hadn't known I was about to put it back tenfold.

"If you two are going to make out, I don't want to know about it," Madison said, face pinched. "I don't like thinking about your mouth." She was practically green. "At all."

"No one asked you to." I pointed to the door. "Go, go. Before I stick my tongue down Joe's—"

Madison was out the door before I could finish.

I cackled gleefully.

That glee was short-lived. Shyly, deliberately, Joe locked the door behind him. My laughter died pretty damn quickly as I eyed the lock, then him, then the lock again.

"Oh," I said, surprised by how low my voice had gotten. "So *that's* what's happening, huh?"

Joe's cheeks flushed a dark, ruddy red. He ducked his head, staring at the corner of the room blindly, too embarrassed to meet my eyes.

"You said you'd…"

"That I'd what?" God, teasing him was so fun.

"Give me…" Joe squirmed.

"Attention?" I filled in for him. "Yeah. I did." My eyes dragged over his body. Across his shoulders. Over the tits I could picture behind his basket. Past his belly, to those thick thighs, down worn denim to his yellow work boots. Scuffed beyond repair. Paint splotches, now, too.

"Put your apples down, Joe-by," I commanded, heat pooling between my legs.

"Joe-by?" Joe blinked, confused.

"You know. Joe and baby. Mixed. It made sense in my head." I grinned, cocking his head to the side. "What, you don't like it? You're a classic 'baby' guy?"

I wasn't stalling, so much as I was giving him time to formulate what he wanted.

"It's not that," Joe huffed, scowling. "I just…I don't get why you're trying to call me anything but my name. You keep doing that."

"You never heard of a pet name before?" I asked, anticipation fizzling beneath the surface of my skin.

"Of course I have." Joe gave me that look. His grouchy look. My favorite. (Okay, yes, they were all my favorite.)

"Explain it to me." He gave me *another* look. Unamused. "Now, Joe." At that, Joe stood up a little taller. The flush had traveled to his ears now, down his throat, too. "And put your apples down. Don't make me ask you a third time." He put his apples down.

God, that was heady.

My dick twitched, and I had to bite back a groan.

"A pet name is…something you use when you like someone."

"Right," I agreed, intoxicated by the look Joe was giving me. Half frustration, half need. Desperate to hear what I had to say next, even if he wasn't ready to admit it. "So, when I use them it's because…"

"You like me," Joe deduced.

"Mhm." All I had to do was cock my head toward the couch, and without uttering a single word, Joe complied. He headed toward it. When he sat down, the cushions wheezed a little. It was delicious. *He* was delicious.

I rounded on him, feeling a little drunk on power. Drunk on this. On him. When he looked up at me like that, everything else in my head quieted. I was drowning in him, and I never wanted out.

Joe's lips pressed into a line as I approached, slow and deliberate, only stopping when I was standing between his spread thighs.

"I like you," I repeated, going for goofy and chipper to add some spice to the heat in the room. "You know another reason I like to use pet names for you?" Joe shivered. "Because…" I was testing the waters here. Riffing. The way I loved best. And Joe was loving it. My voice dropped low, sultry sweet. "Because you're my pet, Joe."

Oh.

Yes.

Oh fuck yes.

The thought hadn't occurred to me until now, but now that it had, I couldn't unthink it.

Joe's eyebrows furrowed, nostrils flaring as he processed this. "Your… pet?"

"That's right," I agreed. "I found you in an alley. I brought you food. I gained your trust. I *earned* your loyalty." I was both wary and excited to see what he would say in response.

"You make me sound like a lost puppy." Joe's voice cracked.

"Maybe that's what you are—were," I corrected myself. "But you're not lost anymore. I found you. And as scared as I am—I don't want to let you go."

"You don't need to be scared of me," Joe repeated his words from that day on his porch. And then, hesitantly, like he wasn't sure what he was saying was the right thing, he added, "I won't bite."

He was playing along.

I hadn't expected that.

"You biting me isn't what I'm worried about."

I cupped his face, holding him, fingers slipping behind his ears to tickle that golden, thick hair. I swear to god, I never felt more steady or sure than I did when we were like this. Like there was nothing I couldn't do. Nothing in my world was wrong or scary or dark.

I wasn't confused or lonely or scared.

"You don't know everything about me, Joe," I said. "What if you don't like what you find out?"

Joe gave me that look again. The one that told me he thought I was an idiot. "I don't know who made you think that their affection was conditional," he whispered. "But mine isn't. You earned it, remember? *You* did."

Throwing my own damn words in my face.

And then he kissed me.

Surged up to capture my lips, nearly dislodging my hands in the process. It was the second time he'd initiated things. And this time was just as clumsy and darling as the last. Joe didn't know what he was doing. He wasn't graceful or practiced. But he *was* needy enough to keep going despite this. The kind of needy that drew me in, wound me up, before it made me unravel.

I pushed him back down, hands sliding to his shoulders. Only to get him where I wanted him though, as I gave chase. Kissing him harder now than I had before, tasting him in the way I'd been dying to for months.

It didn't feel wrong. Didn't feel off. Didn't feel the way I'd felt with Mary, like I was smashing a puzzle piece into the wrong place.

Just like the first time I'd kissed Joe—hell, even more so than the first time—this felt…good.

Joe felt good.

Fire blazed beneath my skin, a sense of rightness settling over me as one of my hands tangled in the back of his hair, pulling taut to keep him in place. I didn't introduce tongue. I wasn't sure Joe was ready for that.

With every flutter of our mouths he was struggling to get the rhythm right. Clumsy earnestness that made my dick throb where it pressed into my zipper. His nose was smashed into mine, and when I twisted, he did too—maintaining the awkward angle.

Joe was the one that tried to pull back this time.

I let him, but only a little.

Both of us were panting. Breaths hot, mingling together as his thick body shuddered from just that. Just a kiss. When I glanced down, I had to fight a groan. Because Joe was hard. Rock fucking hard. We'd barely been kissing for a minute and he—

"I'm…" Joe's voice was hoarse.

"Should we stop?" I asked. Maybe he was overwhelmed. Maybe this was too much. Maybe when he'd asked for my attention this hadn't been what he meant.

"What?" Joe blinked, confused. "No. We *just* started." Again, he gave me stink-eye. "I just…" His tongue flickered out to wet his lower lip, and I groaned. "Can you show me?"

"Isn't that what I've been doing?" I teased, hand tightening on his hair. His lashes fluttered, hands spasming where they sat in fists on his spread thighs.

"No…I mean…" Joe's grumpiness faded. "Can you *teach* me?"

"As in…explain how to kiss?"

"Yeah."

"Okay." I'd never had someone ask me that before. It was funny. I knew Joe was good with his hands, and I'd always figured he was a hands-on learner. It was pretty cute to discover that instruction was the way he learned best.

Hopefully, I'd be a good teacher.

"Was this what you wanted?" I asked him, because I figured now was the time to check in before we went further. "Kissing…more than kissing?" My heart skipped a beat at the thought of getting to touch him.

I'd wanted to touch him since the day I met him—even if I hadn't understood the feelings. And I may have been surprised by my attraction to him, for a plethora of reasons. And I probably should've been nervous about getting it wrong, seeing as he was the first man I'd been with.

But I wasn't.

How could I be anything but pleased when Joe wanted me back.

I'd decided to let him call the shots, and I couldn't be happier with how he was doing it.

"More…than…" Joe croaked, obviously embarrassed to admit that was what he wanted. His face was bright red, even his ears practically glowing. "If that's what you want."

"I want what *you* want," I told him, outright groaning this time when his eyes met mine again, and that sweet, sweet look was back. No more snark for my Joe-by. No sirree. "You probably don't know the term," I added. "But I'm a bit of a service top."

I'd done my research.

Again, because I did, in fact, know how to Google.

Besides…I'd been around long enough to catch a few things even if I hadn't put them into practice till now. "Pleasure dom?" I offered. "Either or."

"And that means…"

"That means making you feel good…is what makes me feel good."

Joe took that in, eyes searching mine for a moment as he processed it. "Okay," he breathed out, the tension in his frame sagging once more. "So you'll…"

"Take very, very good care of you," Jason promised.

twenty-three

JOE

"LESSON ONE." JASON BLEW OUT a breath, the hand in my hair pulling tight for a moment before softening once more. Pleasant tingles shot down my spine, making heat pool between my legs. There was something devastatingly intimate about this.

About asking him for this.

Not even the kissing bit—though that, too.

But asking him to talk this through with me. Like communicating about something so private was normal and good—and there was no shame in my inexperience. Jason had been nothing but understanding when it came to that. Open-minded. Giving. Patient.

Leading me when I needed to be led.

Letting me have these moments of calm where I could simply be. Rather than holding the weight of the world on my shoulders, the only thing I had to worry about was him. The pressure I was under disappeared entirely.

I wasn't concerned about impressing my family, about making my farm sustainable, about proving to myself that I could be a proper functioning adult.

I could just be me.

Joe.

Warm and sweet and needy the way I'd always been scared to be.

And I wasn't ashamed.

Jason didn't make me feel ashamed.

Not for being who I was, and not for needing him.

When we kissed the first time, it'd certainly been eye opening. And since then, I'd done a lot of soul-searching. I was feeling more sure of myself now. Still inexperienced, but far less confused.

Earlier, I'd called George on the phone. Spoken to him about my feelings. Asked him questions that'd been plaguing me surrounding my sexuality— and the lack of both romantic and sexual feelings I'd felt. Been vulnerable in a way I never would've been had Jason not showed me I could.

If he'd been surprised by my admissions, he hadn't acted that way.

George had assured me that what I was feeling was normal.

He'd introduced the idea that I might be demisexual. Which was not a word I recognized, and had made me squirm when he explained. It was weird applying a label to myself when I'd never been the kind of person who'd really thought about them. George was George. Who cared if he liked men? Alex was Alex. And Roderick was Roderick. I'd never batted an eye at any of their choices in partners.

Never really applied that to myself either.

The idea that I might want a label one day was weird. That it might bring me comfort to put a word to the feelings I'd always had—the feelings I'd lacked.

It was validating too, though.

Incredibly validating.

And it was nice to understand myself better. Through that, I could be objective. I could pick apart my feelings. Could really think about what I wanted. And I had. I'd spent four days with my thoughts revolving around Jason. Chewed over George's words so much they nearly lost their flavor.

And now…here…alone with Jason again, I couldn't help but be even more sure than before that I'd made the right choice.

I'd told Jason I wanted to show him how I felt about him.

That had never been truer than now.

Sex wasn't the gift I was giving him—that was just a bonus.

The gift I was giving him was my trust.

"Joe," Jason admonished fondly. "Are you listening?"

"I am," I croaked.

"Alright." Jason's other hand cupped my cheek, gently tipping my head to the side to demonstrate how I was supposed to move. "There are a lot of ways to kiss. Different styles. Purposes. Some people prefer to be aggressive. Some people enjoy soft kisses. And some people employ a mix of the two."

I was genuinely curious which one he was. My bet was both. At least… based on the two kisses we'd shared now. Jason was too fluid of a person to be predictable.

"As for logistics…an angle will make any kiss better."

Ah. So that's why he'd moved my head.

"Why?" I asked.

"Less nose bumping."

I nodded, not enough to jostle him, but enough to show him that I was listening.

"The rest is hard to explain. It's better if I show you," Jason murmured. "Just…follow my lead, yeah? I'll demonstrate what to do. If you mimic me, rather than trying to do your own thing, you'll catch on."

Again, I nodded.

This time when his mouth brushed mine, it was better. He was right. The new angle was far more comfortable. I could really press close. Could see his eyelashes and everything.

"Close your eyes, baby," Jason murmured. "Relax." It felt weird for him to talk against my mouth like that, but I didn't mind. I enjoyed it, actually. The tickle of his breath. The vibration of his words. I closed my eyes. Jason held still, letting me get used to the feeling before his lips began to move. The moment they parted, teasing against mine, I immediately understood what he'd meant.

Before I'd just been kinda smashing our mouths together. But this?

Heat coursed through my body.

Woah.

Wow.

Kissing was—wow.

"Remember to mimic me," Jason whispered between our mouths. "You need to move, too." I grunted in reply, then did my best to do as I was told. It was still clumsy. But certainly less awkward. Warm and a little slick and—mmm.

"This is slow," Jason murmured, lips parting mine in a smooth caress. "And this…" His hand tightened again and his teeth nipped at my lip.

"This is aggressive." He took my mouth then, in a way that made me melt. Sifting like sand right through his fingers. It was almost mean, the way he devoured me, all tongue and teeth. Slipping, sliding, eating me alive.

I loved it.

With him looming over me, I felt my head slipping into that fuzzy place it often occupied when he was around. I don't know how, don't know when. But as we kissed, Jason lowered me onto the couch cushions and climbed on top of me. He was between my legs now, still looming, his arm bracketing my head as the slick sound our lips made together filled the room. His other hand was low now, hot skin bunched around my hip beneath the fabric of my coat.

It was embarrassing.

And so…so…

My hips jumped forward, pushing into Jason's of their own accord.

"You like that?" he purred between harsh kisses. "Fuck yeah, you do." Jason was confident here in a way that made me feel small and protected. I didn't have to speak at all, he just knew.

Knew me.

Knew what I wanted.

What I needed.

Knew how to take care of me.

The hand on my hip slid to my lower back, dipping beneath my shirt. Skin on skin. I shuddered, unable to help myself. No one had ever touched me like that. Spoken to me like this. Kissed me like this. Like I was delicious, delightful, addictive.

Like he didn't want anything more than to be inside me in whatever capacity he could.

Made my mind conjure up images.

Sweaty, naked, foreign images.

Ideas of other ways Jason could invade my body.

Fantasies about how I'd let him.

When I opened my eyes again—just a peek—Jason was even more gorgeous up close. Our mouths kept moving in that hypnotic, slick glide. They grew hungrier, wetter again. A loop of soft and hard and soft again that kept me guessing. At first, I tried to match him. Tried to mimic him the way I was supposed to. But…I soon found what I preferred was to simply lie back and take whatever Jason gave me.

Like he sensed I'd disobeyed, Jason's eyes opened, too.

His eyebrows twitched disapprovingly, and I quickly shut my eyes.

"Sorry," I whispered, the words achingly vulnerable. "I just…wanted to see."

Jason pulled back a little. "You can open your eyes," he promised. "Look all you want. It's okay, Joe."

I sighed, eyes fluttering open again. His eyes were even prettier this close. They had flecks in them. Gold around the pupil I'd never noticed before. It reminded me of the corn fields during autumn back home. Brittle stalks on a never-ending horizon, dappled between trees and a blue, blue sky.

"You're so pretty," Jason murmured, still meeting my gaze. "Are you nervous?" My breath hitched. My lips pressed into a thin line, words failing to escape. "You don't need to be," Jason promised. "We can stop at any time. Hell, we can—"

"No," I replied, voice gruff. "I want more."

Jason's eyebrows shot up. Then down, furrowing as he regarded me for a moment. Felt like he was digging around inside my brain. Unpicking the knots inside it. Figuring me out. Clarity made his eyes sharpen. Now it was his turn to suck in a breath.

"When you said you'd *never*…you meant…"

"Never," I swore.

It took him a second to power through that particular realization. I knew the moment he did because rather than make me feel self-conscious or like I needed to justify myself, mischief glittered in his pale gaze. I was only spared a second of gratitude before Jason was on the move again.

Tricky as he was.

Deliberately, Jason pressed upward on my lower back, urging me to grind my hips against him. My head was *swimming*.

"Is that why you can't stop peeking?" he teased.

"I like looking at you."

Jason made a sound at that. Half groan, half growl. He pressed my hips up again, this time hard enough my dick made direct contact with his. Electricity zapped through my body, making my limbs tingle, making the heat between my legs build and build and build. I was panting into his mouth now, my cock throbbing as it bumped his.

My dick is touching Jason's.

Fuck.

My dick is touching—

Wow.

My dick is—

Fuck.

I'd never been harder in all my life. Balls tingling. A heartbeat between my goddamn legs. Hole *twitching* as I felt Jason's cock—*Jason's cock*—rubbing my own. Through double layers of pants, yes. But that didn't matter. I'd never felt more naked. Or more whole.

Still panting, shaking now, I spread my legs a little wider to accommodate his hips better. I didn't dare move, worried he'd take this away.

Apparently, my face hid nothing.

"Could you come from this?" Jason asked like he was in awe. "Just from kissing? From a little—" he pressed on my lower back again, and the friction that caused made my eyes roll back. "Pressure?"

I wanted to lie.

But I'd never been good at that.

Besides…I knew Jason wasn't asking because he didn't know the answer. He was asking because he wanted me to admit it. My words were as much for him as they were for me.

"Yes," I confessed, nostrils flaring. It was hard to get a breath in. My hands clenched into fists, useless at my sides. Need burned through my body as I peered at Jason's lashes—shorter and darker than mine. At his lips—thin and slightly chapped. At the shape of his nose—angular and straight.

It shouldn't have been hot, just staring at somebody.

But it was.

It totally was.

Especially now that he'd given me permission to.

"Then do it." Jason's words were a challenge as much as they were a command.

Another squeeze on my back forced me to roll my hips against him. A circular motion that when paired with the slick glide of his lips on mine, was enough to nearly send me over the edge.

I was close.

So close.

I hadn't known sex could be like this.

My cock was *throbbing.*

This steady pulse between my legs.

"Come for me, sweetheart. C'mon, I want it. Give me your first orgasm. Make a mess for me."

That was all it took.

A little pressure, and I just—

I lost control.

Did exactly what Jason said because it felt right to do it.

I spilled with a groan, pressed right into Jason's mouth. He nipped at my bottom lip, the sting only causing my dick to spill even harder. Groaning in return, Jason's hand on my back slid lower. Low enough, he was cupping my ass. He gripped it, spreading his fingers wide so he could grab on and squeeze.

My cock spurted a little more, the sticky fabric of my boxers rubbing against the now almost sore head of my dick.

"God, you're delicious," Jason murmured. "Did you know that? Such a good, obedient boy." His kisses somehow grew hungrier. "So goddamn pretty when you're lost for me. Giving me those eyes—"

What eyes?

"Those fucking *puppy eyes*, begging me to turn you inside out and upside down. Looking at me like I'm good. Like I'm *good.* Like I'm good the way *you are.* I'm so weak for you, Joe, it's not even funny."

And then his tongue was against my lips. Flicking liquid hot and slippery at the seam begging for entrance. I didn't know what to do with it. For a moment, I clamped my mouth shut, overwhelmed by the almost tickly sensation.

"Open your mouth," Jason said sweetly. "Remember how I told you there are different styles of kissing? I'm about to teach you a new one. Spoiler alert: it's French."

My hands spasmed a little at the idea.

Even I knew what French kissing was.

"You don't have to," Jason whispered. "But…if you let me in, I promise I'll make you feel good. Didn't I just prove that I could?" I was still buzzing from my orgasm. Tingling all over. Lightheaded and yet…just as needy. Maybe even more so now that my dick had spilled.

So I did. I opened for him. And then his tongue was teasing between my lips, and I was…

"Nnnng," I gasped, chest still heaving, heart still pounding.

I'd thought kissing was amazing before. And this was leagues above that.

Jason licked deeper, sliding past my teeth, teasing along my palate and then down over my tongue. That—well. That was weird. Weird but good. When his tongue slid back around the top and he flicked deep, I knew he was making good on his promise. His tongue was wet and wiggly, and *demanding* in a way that made me immediately want to fight him.

So I did.

Not well, mind you, fucked-out as my brain already was.

Clumsy and aggressive, I rubbed my tongue along his. I attempted to chase him away, and back into his mouth. Jason laughed. Laughed! The sound vibrating between us. Apparently, he thought my little show of resistance was cute.

Apparently, he'd been gentle before, because when Jason pushed in again, ignoring my wiggling, it was downright mean. He didn't leave a single inch for me to push back. Eating me alive with a ferocity that made my cock begin to throb again.

My blood was singing.

I had no choice but to concede defeat and let him fuck-kiss me into submission. Jason practically purred the moment he figured out he'd won. My tongue turned docile, twitching beneath his, allowing him deep, deep, deep. Deep enough I was choking on him.

Full of him.

At his mercy entirely.

Couldn't breathe without smelling him, feeling him, breathing him in.

I sucked on his tongue out of sheer self-preservation.

That elicited a grunt out of him that made my spent cock continue to rise where it was trapped in my messy boxers.

When Jason pulled back, his eyes were nearly black with lust—the icy blue swallowed whole. His hand slid from my ass to my hip. Up my abs and across my pecs. He gripped one of them for a moment, the same way he'd grabbed my ass. My nipple tingled as he rubbed it through my shirt in a circular motion with his palm.

"You're so pretty, Joe," Jason whispered, his hand moving agonizingly slow. My nipple tingled, hardening beneath his palm as he moved. "So fucking pretty. I know I keep saying that, but damn. You're like the sunset. Every time I see you, I'm in awe." He squeezed my pec again. "And these fucking tits, Joe. Seriously criminal."

"Tits?" My whole mouth was tingling now, too. Just like my chest.

"*Tits*," Jason agreed. "Fun fact: I've jerked off every night since I left your house thinking about fucking them." Jason pulled his hand back a little. Only enough that he could pinch my nipple. Pleasure zinged down my spine. I jerked, surprised by how much I enjoyed the sensation.

It was almost too sensitive.

Hurt a little.

But I…

I couldn't help but push into it, silently asking for more.

Could hardly stop my mind from wandering. From thinking about Jason lying in bed, his hand on his dick, thoughts on me—on pushing between my—

"God, yes." Jason's stormy gaze moved from my chest to my face. "You know the best part?"

"What?" I croaked, so quiet it was barely a question at all.

"I pictured your expression while I did it. *Needy*. Just like you are now." He abandoned my chest, hand sliding up again. "Always looking at me, begging for more. Is that what you want, Joe? You not done yet?"

I shook my head.

No. I wasn't done.

Jason made a detour to my throat, pinching the sides of it in a way that made me hot all over, before he settled, hand cupping my jaw. Jason's thumb dropped to skim across my spit-slick lips.

He stared at my mouth.

Stared like he was memorizing everything about this moment.

Everything about me.

I never thought I'd appreciate this. Being touched by someone. Being talked to like this. Being called *needy* of all things. It should've made me balk. Should've made me angry. Should've made me so embarrassed I couldn't breathe. Should've made me shove him off and storm out the door.

But it didn't, and I couldn't.

Because he was right.

Somehow, somewhere I'd ended up needing him.

He knew it as much as I did.

And the shame I should've felt about relying on someone else was absent. There was only surety. The deep-seated knowledge that I'd banked on the right guy. Maybe it was naive of me, but I'd always been able to rely on my gut. And something told me I could trust Jason. Could give him this, and more, and he'd prove to me he deserved it.

"You did so well earlier," Jason praised, rubbing circles into my lower back as he played with my lip. "Did you know that? You were such a good boy, Joe, letting go for me like that. Sharing your release with me." Somehow he knew I needed to hear that. Needed to hear that I'd done well. That there was nothing to be embarrassed about. "You were perfect. *Wonderful.* I couldn't be more proud if I tried. I bet the mess you made was real pretty."

My breath hitched.

Okay, so maybe I could still be embarrassed.

There was this prickly feeling beneath my skin that made me feel like I was floating and falling all at once. I squirmed a little, my sticky boxers clinging to my hardening dick. The sensation was definitely not pleasant. And yet, it only amplified the rest of it. The way Jason's eyes were dark with lust.

The way my chest ached to be touched again.

This time, without the barrier of my shirt between us.

The way his arm was shaking a little from holding himself over me but he didn't seem to mind. The way he stared at me the way I looked at him. Like I was a wild, precious thing.

"Mmm," Jason said softly. His hand dragged down my body again, flicking my nipple on its way past, before settling between my legs. In a feat I definitely couldn't have pulled off, he got my button undone. "Can I see?" he asked, voice barely a whisper. "You can say no—"

The look in Jason's eyes made it clear he thought I was going to.

He didn't expect me to agree.

So I did, just to see the look of pleasure and surprise unfold in those pale eyes.

"Yes." My voice was barely more than a croak.

When Jason's hand wiggled beneath the hem of my pants, I swallowed dryly. Stomach lurching, I held perfectly still as Jason turned his palm to face my pelvis. He took his time wiggling his hand deeper, the moment so slow it only emphasized what he was doing.

What I'd told him he could do.

A war of lust and embarrassment danced inside me.

I'd never done anything like this, and here I was, letting him touch me for the first time when I'd already…fuck.

By the time Jason's fingers cupped my cock, I was panting. Everything I had was laser-focused on what his hand was doing, on what he was feeling, on…on…

Fuck.

What would he think of me? Would he like my dick? That wasn't a thought I'd ever had before, or a worry I'd carried.

The heat of his hand was so intense, the texture so foreign, my legs began to shake.

"Shhh," Jason murmured, even though I hadn't said anything. "That's it. Relax, baby. Just let me feel you." I sucked in a breath, unsurprised when Jason's eyes went straight to my chest. He licked his lips, eyes hot on my nipples before his gaze snapped up.

And still…he just kept holding me.

"You feel good," he promised, answering the question in my eyes. "Such a big dick for such a big boy, huh, Joe? Should've known you'd be proportional." I squirmed, and the wicked glint in Jason's eyes only grew brighter. "And…" He inhaled, lips curling into a smirk. "Just as messy as I'd thought you'd be," Jason husked, barely skimming my dick and balls before he curled what he could of his palm around my cock and scraped up the cum in a fluid motion. It was so tight, so abrupt, I nearly whined.

Jason's hand popped out of my pants, glistening with slick. Slippery and viscous, the cum on his skin reflected the overhead light. He held it up, eyes drifting over the creamy streaks thoughtfully. And then he made a contemplative face and brought it up to his mouth. Two fingers slid past his lips at the same time as he sucked my cum right off them.

I did whine then.

The first real sound I'd made.

Couldn't fight it back. Not when he was—when he was—

Ohgodhewaslickingmycum.

Did he think it tasted good?

Did he—

"Not bad," Jason purred when his fingers popped free. "Not bad at all. *That's* very good to know."

Thank god.

My cock pulsed, still processing the visual stimuli of Jason doing what he'd…what he'd just done. It felt cold without his hand on it. Attempting to rise to the occasion, yes, but mostly just…lonely. Because now that I knew what it felt like to have someone else's hand on it, I wanted more of that.

Right now.

I wanted his hand back inside my pants.

I wanted to rub my dick all over his fingers.

Wanted to hump and hump and hump.

God, maybe I really *was* a puppy.

I'd never felt anything like this before.

Just thinking about sex had always made me shy. I'd avoided it. Even fast-forwarded clips when I watched movies just because looking at sex made me embarrassed. Even when it was fictional.

But this?

This was nothing like watching some random stranger get naked for a camera. Being with Jason felt right. I felt safe. I was still embarrassed but…but I wanted *more* anyway. I trusted him not to judge me. Trusted him to see me at my most vulnerable.

But most of all…I trusted him to make me feel good.

"Will you touch it again?" I asked, surprised by how needy my voice sounded.

"Touch your dick?" Jason clarified. His voice was teasing. "Why?"

I glared at him.

"Did it feel good having my hand on you?" He was bullying me. It was so mean—so mean. But I still wanted it. Wanted *him*. In fact, I desired him even more because of it. He was always calling everyone else bullies but *he* was the real terror.

Taking mercy on me, Jason's hand slipped inside my pants without any further pleas. He cupped my cock again, firmer this time. "You want your cock held, is that it?" he asked. "You want it resting somewhere nice and warm?"

My dick pulsed as Jason's fingers wiggled lower, cupping my balls.

"Answer me, Joe."

"Y-yes," my voice broke, to my own humiliation. "No?" I wanted…I wanted… "M-more?"

"More it is." Again, he offered me mercy.

For a beat I wondered what he was going to do. Anticipation throbbed between my thighs, making me squirm. Was he going to rub me? Was that what he was going to do? Oh god. Oh god, yes. Maybe he'd jerk me off hard and quick, the way I touched myself. Maybe he'd—

Fantasies ran rampant, filling my head.

Reality came rushing back in soon after.

Because Jason still had not moved, despite agreeing to my pleas.

"You know," Jason said conversationally, an almost evil glint in his eyes. I couldn't believe he had his hand on my dick and he was *still talking*.

Actually, scratch that.

I totally could.

He could be such a jerk sometimes.

It was just one of the many things I appreciated about him.

"This is a first for me too. I've never touched someone else's dick before," Jason finished his thought. Finally taking mercy on me, he wiggled lower, till his fingers tapped the seam between my balls. It was a light tap. Not meant to hurt. The sensation was just—fuck. Against my will, my eyes fluttered shut. I could hardly hear over the rushing in my ears.

I pressed my hips into him, begging for more pressure.

"Pussies? Yeah," Jason continued. "But you don't have a pussy."

His fingers slid further, back past my balls. I widened my stance, feeling half-crazed with how bad I wanted him to keep touching me. I was hungry in a way I'd never been hungry before.

"You know what you do have though…? A very nice, snug little hole I'd bet. And those are my very favorite." Jason made a frustrated sound when the confines of my jeans stopped him from reaching his target. His hand was out of my pants liquid quick. He leaned back on his knees, no longer hovering, both hands going for the hem of my pants.

Fingers tangled in my belt loops, Jason paused.

"Yes or no?" he offered, staring down at me. "Keep in mind that there's no wrong answer. I won't be upset at you. You can say—"

"Yes," I cut him off. I squirmed, and Jason grinned. He was doing it on purpose. Making me reiterate my consent because it made me blush every time he did.

"You sure?"

"Stop checkin' with me every goddamn second, Jesus Christ."

Jason laughed. The sound was sweet as cider. He nodded. Just once. And all the concern in his eyes disappeared, replaced by mischief.

In one swift movement Jason jerked my pants down my hips. He didn't take my boxers off. Like he could sense I was too shy to be fully naked, even if I wanted his fingers on my…oh god.

On my most private places.

The places I'd never ventured in a sexy way.

Been too shy to want to try.

Then he was leaning over me again, that wickedly hot hand sliding beneath the hem of my boxers for a third time. Down, down it went, palm skimming the length of my cock and balls, back where it'd been before. In the secret, sweat damp crease of my ass.

"There we go," Jason purred, hand sliding further, further until—I jerked. "Mmm. That's what I wanted." Jason's middle finger tapped my asshole. I had to practically lift my leg to give him room to touch back there. The position was humiliating. Submissive. I didn't know how to feel about how much I loved it.

Sweat beaded at my temple, my head so fuzzy I wasn't certain I had a brain at all anymore.

"That's my…" I managed, though that was a miracle. "That's my—"

"Your ass?" Jason gave my hole another tap. "Mhm." My knees nearly buckled. "I was right, by the way. It's a very nice little hole. Shy but nice." Another tap. My dick was hard again. Which was a fucking miracle. I'd never gotten hard twice in a row. Ever.

"How can you tell? You can't even see it—"

"Do you *want* me to look at it?" Jason asked, voice low. "Want me to pull your boxers down, spread your legs, part those sweet cheeks, and take a peek?"

"N-no," I whined.

"I think you do." Jason gave my hole a little harder rub. "I think you're just shy. Shy, sweet, slutty baby Joe." I made an overwhelmed sound and his hand retreated as quickly as it had come. I mourned the loss of his touch the moment it was gone.

"Back—" I gasped, hands finding his wrist and shoving it back down inside my boxers. "Please. Want you to…to touch. S-sorry. Want it. Just…lots. It's—"

"God, you're perfect," Jason groaned. "Okay," he agreed. "Just so I understand, you want me to touch. But not look."

"Yeah."

"Okay. I can do that." Jason pulled his hand out of my clothes *again,* and I scowled at him. A sharp bark of laughter escaped him at the sight.

"I'm just changing angles, baby boy. One sec. Let me get a better feel of where I'm going to fuck you."

Where he was going to—

This time when his hand slipped into the back of my pants it was woah—yeah.

That was better.

Better because he had slid his hand around my back and dipped beneath my boxers and into my crease from behind. Better because he could rub, rub, rub at my hole, and I could fuck, fuck, fuck against his stomach. Better because my cock was hard again, the tip at risk of slipping through the slit in my boxers and making direct contact.

I squirmed.

My bare dick touching Jason? Pushing against his sweater. Leaving streaks of cum on the fabric. Jesus. This wasn't going to take long. Just like the first time hadn't.

Jason's fingers were sticky with my cum as he leisurely played with my hole. Stroking in circles the same way he'd toyed with my chest. In no rush. Even though we were in the break room at his work, and I was positively *leaking*.

"You know, from what I've gathered from the internet and porn—" he said, again, conversationally. "Normally we'd go for a handjob before we get to anything to do with this." He gave my hole a little tap that sent shockwaves exploding through me. "There's a natural order to things."

"I don't care," I whined.

"Really?" He grinned. "I must've pegged you wrong. I thought you were a rule-follower."

"You haven't pegged me at all." Shit. I hadn't thought that through.

Jason's eyebrows climbed up.

"That sounded like a complaint."

"It was."

"Should I contact HR?"

God, he was doing this on purpose. I couldn't stop squirming. Couldn't stop the way the need for touch, real touch, kept climbing, climbing, climbing.

"Stop fucking around and touch me," the words spilled free before I could stop them.

"Sorry." Jason didn't sound sorry at all as he slapped my hole again. "My bad." Another slap. "I didn't know you were such a needy slut that we couldn't even have a simple conversation." My hips flexed into him and he twisted his body, trying to give me a better angle to grind. Nice, even when his mouth was mean as hell.

"Jason," I pleaded.

"That's so naughty of you, Joe. Santa's gonna have to put you on the naughty list." The more he teased, the hotter I felt. My cock was throbbing. This steady heartbeat between my legs, balls drawing up tight. Just a little more teasing and I'd…and I'd…

There was something about the way he was talking that was really doing it for me. He was normally so nice that seeing this bite—this little bit of sadism was making my head turn to mush.

Jason whispered against the shell of my ear. "Bet if I wanted, I could stick my fingers inside you right now and all you'd do was gasp and say please."

The tip of his finger dipped into my hole and I just—

I lost it.

"Nng." I came for a second time with a wet whine—the loudest noise I'd ever made in bed. My heels dug into the couch cushions, and the small of his back, looking for purchase. Jason's hand was out of my boxers a moment later, sticky hand squeezing my throat, holding me steady as he drank in my expression with rapture.

I couldn't seem to get full breath in, I was so overwhelmed. Nostrils flaring. Chest heaving.

So hot.

So…so…blissed out.

He hadn't even had to touch my dick and I'd…fuck.

My head was full of clouds.

Nothing in the world could bother me now.

Nothing.

"So pretty," Jason whispered. He gave my throat another squeeze, anchoring me. Made my head stop flying enough that I could force my gaze on him. On the hunger in his eyes. On his parted lips. On the sizable bulge between his legs. A thick, long cock trapped against his thigh.

Hard.

Because of me.

Turned on.

Because of me.

"You did so well," Jason promised, leaning down to kiss me slow and sweet. "Jesus, Joe." The kiss turned hungry soon enough. Nipping. Harsh. Back and forth. Like he couldn't decide if he wanted to eat me or covet me. "Such a good boy," Jason murmured before each flutter of his lips, each stinging bite. "Two orgasms in ten minutes? God, you're a gift."

For several long glorious minutes Jason whispered sweet nothings against my mouth, against my jaw, into my ear. He stroked my chest, my hips, my shoulders. Petting me, caressing me. He turned me to putty in his grip, smooching every inch of skin he could find with butterfly kisses that only sent me flying higher, higher, higher.

Eventually I had no choice but to come down.

Reality set in.

What we'd done set in.

We were in the breakroom at his job.

Madison had been in here seconds before we'd had a quickie on the couch.

I'd lost my virginity—right? In the back of a grocery store of all places. With a coffee machine and pictures of pretty much every Bellevillian ever, staring at me while I did it. And yet…it'd been perfect. Because it had been real. And organic. And Jason had been the person I'd shared it with.

"There you are," Jason said tenderly when we made eye contact again. "How are you? That was a lot. Maybe too much. You doing okay?"

The way I was cocooned by him on the couch had made my butt go numb, but I hardly noticed. Jason's arm was shaking where it held him up, his whole body looming over mine. Keeping me safe. We hadn't done anything about his boner. Which didn't feel fair. A fact I opened my mouth to complain about—only for nothing to come out.

Words weren't possible yet, even if I was no longer flying.

I took stock of myself. Of my sticky boxers. Of the sheen of sweat on my skin.

I grinned.

"I'm guessing that sweet smile means you're okay?" Jason filled in for me. "Not ready to figure out your words yet, huh?" I nodded, baffled by his mind-reading skills once again. Either I was an open book—which I wasn't—or Jason was slowly but surely learning all my tells.

The look he gave me was so gooey-sweet it nearly sent me flying all over again.

"That's okay," he promised. "You don't need to talk. I talk enough for the both of us." He laughed at his own joke, but sobered pretty quickly. "Alright. I'm going to get off you—"

The look I gave him must've been somewhat panicked because he clucked his tongue. "Only for a second, promise. Just long enough to get a rag to clean you up." I relaxed, sinking back into the cushions, and Jason pulled away. "There's not a lot I can do about the state of your boxers. I could run into the store and grab you a new set—we've got a pretty depressing men's clothing section in the corner. But something tells me that you would rather stay sticky than have me out there buying underwear for you."

Yep. He really did know me.

"So, you'll just have to deal a little, unfortunately." Jason smirked. "Unless you want to go commando—but I'm guessing that's a no-go, too."

He slid off the couch, a bit of a wobble in his step. Didn't complain as he shook his arms out, probably to get the blood flowing again, and headed for the sink.

"We are throwing the rag away after," he reassured.

Thank god.

The idea of Madison touching anything I'd cum on was absolutely abhorrent.

"And I'll disinfect the couch," Jason added. He gave me a look that was both fond and amused as he waited for the water to run hot. He made sure to coat it liberally before ringing it out. When he brought me the warm rag, his eyes were full of affection. "You want to do it, or should I?"

he offered, hand hovering.

It was clear he wanted to do it.

Even I could see that.

"You," I managed, though it was difficult to get the word out.

"Alright," Jason agreed easily, pleased.

He settled between my legs again.

Strangely enough, having him reach inside my boxers to clean me felt even more intimate than the sex had. I liked it. Liked the way he seemed to enjoy it too, humming under his breath as he worked. Something jolly. "White Christmas," maybe?

A song that should not have been associated with cum-rags.

"There we go," Jason murmured when he pulled the rag free. "That should be good enough for you to get home without feeling uncomfortable."

I smiled at him.

For a moment, Jason studied me, cum-rag hovering, eyes drinking me in. Then his bossiness was back, that soft look on his face evolving.

"Stay put," he commanded. This time, when he rose, I snagged his sweater. He laughed, the hand not holding the soiled rag wrapping around my wrist. "Baby, I'll be right back," he swore. "I'm not going far. Just planning to grab water for you and toss this thing in the trash. You're probably thirsty, I know I am. And no, that was not a euphemism."

I didn't let go.

"God, don't give me that look. It's like kicking a puppy." Jason's fingers danced up my forearm, under my coat. The fabric crinkled a little. "How about this? If you let me go *and* you drink all your water, I'll kiss and cuddle you after? I know how much of a snuggle bug you are."

I considered it.

Having him leave had sucked but…

I supposed…as embarrassing as it was to admit, I *was* a "snuggle bug."

I nodded, releasing him. Jason wasted no time crossing the room a second time to dispose of the rag and fill up a tall glass of water from the sink along the back wall.

He didn't bring up his dick.

Even though I could see how hard it was through his pants. See the way he walked a little stiffer than usual, like the fact it kept rubbing was uncomfortable.

I didn't press, even though I wanted to. I figured we both had enough to process without me pushing for something he wasn't offering. Besides, truthfully, I was content.

When Jason returned, I drank half the water before forcing him to drink the rest.

"Stubborn as a mule," he chided, but his eyes betrayed his amusement. When he'd drunk the rest of it, he set the empty glass on the ground and made good on his promise. Pushed me into the back of the couch so I was sandwiched between it and him. Wrapped his body around me like he had those nights we'd shared on my bed. Kissed my nape over and over again.

Made me feel safe.

Made me feel wanted.

Made me feel like there was nowhere else in the world I'd rather be.

But most of all? He made me feel certain that I'd been right about him. That even though it was new—for both of us—this was the kind of thing that was good.

We were good together.

And that was just a fact.

twenty-four

JASON

IF I'D THOUGHT JOE BRINGING me coffee in the mornings was wonderful it was nothing compared to what he did next. After we'd left the break room, redressed and looking presentable, he spent his time in the back stacking up his apples on the fruit stand.

I'd told him he could head home, that I'd handle it—poor baby was…very sticky. But he'd insisted. Apparently, he trusted me to touch his dick but not to put his apples on display. Which I couldn't help but find adorable.

Peeking at him from my register—as a means to distract myself from Madison and her all-knowing eyes.

I was a little embarrassed—considering the fact I had no doubt she knew exactly what we'd been up to in there. Like I'd promised, before we left I'd disinfected the couch. Left no evidence behind. Made sure the space was as sacred and clean as we'd found it. I'd also liberally washed my hands and mouth, because as much as I liked Joe—and I did—I was still working.

Madison had yet to acknowledge me.

No customers had come in while we'd been…you know…and she was on her phone. Any second now, she'd say something biting. I just knew it. I fiddled with my holiday-help list, trying to play it cool, waiting for the emotional blow that was sure to come.

Only…it didn't.

Madison did talk.

But it wasn't to admonish me.

She set her phone down and turned to look at me. For a beat, we just stared at each other, a silent showdown.

And then she surprised me.

"I'm happy for you," she said. "Joe's…hot. Nice too. I think." She slurped at her straw, and I glanced up at her, a little shocked that she wasn't roasting me. "As long as I've known you you've never had…ah…" She glanced toward the back to where Joe was very seriously placing every single apple he'd brought the exact "right" way. "A partner, or whatever. So…you know. Congrats."

Joe walked by when I was hugging the living hell out of her. You know, after I'd leapt over the counter like a clumsy, creaky-kneed gazelle and yanked her into my embrace.

He didn't even blink.

Just ducked his head, cheeks pink, and hurried toward the door. He paused at my register for a second, but only a second, then he was on his way again.

"Get offfff—" Madison beat at me with her free hand as I picked her off the ground and gave her a shake.

"You love meeee—" I sang. "I knew it. I knew you love me."

"Stooooppp." She was giggling, but I still put her down. The moment her feet were on the ground, she scowled at me. "Why'd you stop?"

"My bad." I swept her up again, shaking her till her giggles turned to wheezes. "We need a safe word."

"Shut up."

"You say that too much for it to be effective—" I'd assumed Joe had left. He usually did. But when I turned, he was still there, hovering at the door, watching us. I beamed at him. "She loves me, Joe!" I told him as Madison made grumbly grumpy noises even though she was the one that had wanted back up.

"You're very lovable," Joe said in reply.

My whole face burned. My breath hitched. Suddenly, there was screeching in my ears—and my heart was squeezing, and I just—

Madison hugged me back. Somehow sensing my joy—like a rocket about to take off. Joy so immense it felt like distress.

Joe cleared his throat, obviously embarrassed, though he stood by what he'd said, if the way he continued to meet my gaze could be believed. He didn't regret it. Didn't regret calling me...calling me *lovable*, of all things.

"See you," Joe said, waiting a beat, his eyes still on me. "Tonight. At your house."

"Tonight at my house?" I echoed. This was the first I'd heard of that. "But I—"

Then he was out the door.

It wasn't until later that I realized my list was missing.

And by then, it was too late to stop the next chain of events.

It didn't take long to figure out that something was amiss. I'd texted Joe to ask him when he was stopping by, and he'd said nine—a bit late, but hey, that meant that I had a good few hours to kill after my shift. Hours that I'd figured I'd fill by knocking a few things off my holiday-help agenda.

It was getting long enough by that point that I figured putting in extra hours would only be beneficial.

Marty B. was the easiest, and the freshest on my mind. I already knew who I could borrow a ladder from, and I figured he wouldn't be upset if I showed up a bit earlier than I'd said I would.

Trent Montgomery was in his driveway when I pulled up. He was the slightly shorter—if you could call a mountain of a man like him, short— darker-haired, more friendly version of his brother, Paxton. Which was why I'd gone to him first. I'd been unsurprised, but pleased, when he'd answered my phone call and my request to borrow his ladder with genuine enthusiasm.

He helped me get it into the back of my truck, grinning my way.

"Can't linger, sorry," Trent apologized as we slammed the gate on the truck bed shut. "Miles made dinner. Meat loaf."

Ah, to have a husband that cooked.

Lucky fucker.

Joe and I would need to take cooking classes—*Jason. Bad Jason.*

No.

It was bad enough fantasizing about fucking him. Adding in married fantasies? Jesus. I was in way over my head.

"No worries," I waved Trent off. He flashed me a charming grin as he headed toward the front.

"Good luck!" he called.

"I'll bring it back later," I promised.

"Don't worry about it. I've got another at the farm." The way Trent was looking at me made me think he knew something I didn't. I pushed the thought aside, smiling and waving as the front door opened and Miles, Trent's even taller husband, popped his head out to check on him.

The look they gave each other was sappy as hell.

I didn't look away, even though the kiss they shared was obviously private.

It just looked so…easy.

They made it look so easy.

Trent disappeared inside, and I headed down the road to Marty B.'s place, ruminating.

Only…when I arrived, there were already lights strung across the front of his garage door, exactly where he'd been hoping. They were hanging around his windows too, and laced around the large maple tree in his front yard. Twinkling. Bright. Perfectly spaced.

I frowned, confused.

Having probably seen my headlights coming, Marty was out on the steps before I could even exit the truck. He waved at me with a big smile. There was a plate of lasagna in his arms. I could smell it as I drew closer, scenting the air like a goddamn dog.

"Thanks for your help," Marty said, offering me the plate. "The missus wanted me to make sure we got you fed in exchange."

"My…help?" Questions were spinning around inside my head.

For a moment, I worried I'd blacked out. I'd come here already—done all of this—and couldn't remember for some ungodly reason. Had I hit my head? But no. No. Because the lights were neat. *Neat.* And if I'd been the one to do it, they certainly would not have been.

"Thank you." I took the plate, stomach growling. "But…I didn't do this."

"I know," Marty grinned. "But you got it done. Same thing. Have a nice night!" And with that, he turned around and headed back up the steps. It'd been kind of an abrupt end to the conversation. Practiced almost.

I was tempted to follow him up the steps and demand answers, but I figured…I'd find out soon enough.

I was right.

When I went hunting through my pockets for my list, I couldn't find it. I panicked for all of ten seconds before I realized I'd left it on the counter at work.

Oh well.

With the lasagna sitting sentinel in the passenger seat, I went through my mental list instead. What'd been next…hm. Ah, yes. Sadie Collins. Her husband was out of town and she'd asked me to stop by to help her get rid of the boxes she had leftover from the Christmas presents she'd bought her sons.

She was pregnant again, and even though cardboard was cardboard, and she had a lot of boys to help—including her oldest, Jordan, recently back from college—I'd figured another set of hands, and a truck, would come in handy.

When I showed up, however, the boxes were gone.

They were supposed to be on the curb.

They weren't.

In their place was a plate covered in warm gingerbread cookies. So warm the plastic wrap was steaming. There was a note. It simply read, ***Thank you, Jason.***

What…the hell was going on?

I had an inkling, but…I dunno. Maybe it was that pesky denial creeping up on me again that kept me in the dark as I headed back into town to the B&B to accomplish my next task. It'd barely been half an hour and I'd done nothing, but gotten all the credit.

That and a lot of food.

When I arrived, parking in my usual spot beside the white picket fence, I gave myself a few seconds to brace for what was coming. Gift-wrapping with the Smut Club was always fun but hectic. They liked the company, even if I wasn't nearly as good at it as they were. They didn't seem to mind though.

And there were a lot of presents.

Each one of them had at least four grandkids. Which equated to a lot of fucking gifts. It usually took a solid few hours, even with all of us working together to accomplish things. I figured I wouldn't finish, just… you know…make as big of a dent as I could till I went home to await Joe's arrival.

When the B&B door swung open, I was surprised to find not only Matilda Deed, sitting behind the counter like usual, a book in hand—but a frankly massive pile of presents sitting in the corner. Wrapped.

"Hi, beautiful," I hummed, sliding up to her desk, a question perched on the tip of my tongue.

"Don't ask, Nosy Nancy." She turned a page in her book. "It isn't my place to say."

Nosy Nancy?

"Right." I blinked, swiveling to look at the pile of presents again. "Is that—"

"That's all of them. Grandkids gifts. Holi-date with a book. Secret Santa. It's all done." She turned another page. No way in hell she was reading that fast, so I could only assume she was stalling.

"The club decided to wrap without me?" I inquired, ignoring her command not to ask.

"More or less."

"With no help." I was wheedling for information and we both knew it.

"I didn't say that."

Okay.

Alright.

Laughter bubbled up inside me as things slowly started to click. It was just a wiggle of a theory but…I grinned. "You wouldn't happen to know—"

"I told you not to ask." Matilda glared at me, her bushy brows furrowed. "Now, shoo. I just got to the good part."

I grimaced, then laughed. "Alright, alright. I'll leave you to your smut."

"Would be polite, yes." Her facial expression barely shifted. Though…her lips did tip up a little. It was as close to mischief as I'd ever seen on her face.

I departed, perplexed, and…a little excited. Part of me was frustrated—because these tasks, these things were *my* things. But I was genuinely grateful for the help, too. I hadn't been lying when I'd said I'd bitten off more than I could chew.

It was practically a scavenger hunt.

Brian already had a tree from Trent's farm set up in his living room when I arrived. Someone, he wouldn't say who, had dropped it off. It was a gorgeous Douglas fir and smelled like Christmas.

The Girl Scout leader, Mrs. Pendergast, informed me that someone had already picked up the packages. Her girls had been hard at work for weeks making homemade ornaments and selling them for charity. I'd offered to take them to the post office.

That wasn't the last of it.

All over Belleville, I drove. Following leads that led to nothing. Until the clock said 8:30, and I had just enough time to head home and hop in the shower before Joe arrived. After popping the lasagna in the stove to reheat, I headed into my bathroom to perform the fastest shower known to man.

I scrubbed myself raw, you know—just in case Joe wanted me to—

Nope.

Don't think about it or you'll get hard and you don't have time for that.

When I finished, I dressed in a t-shirt and sweats and headed into the living room to wait. To say I was nervous for Joe to come over would certainly be an understatement. To be honest, before I'd left the grocery store I'd debated going home and cleaning up. I kept my house tidy. It wasn't clutter or trash that needed clearing.

More…my…murder boards?

It was hard to think of something else to call them.

Post-it notes all over the walls depicting the tasks I needed to do throughout the year. Little yarn pieces stuck between them with push-pins so I wouldn't lose track of what needed to happen when. What connected to what.

It was the easiest way to keep track of all the stuff in my head.

And normally…I didn't have guests.

So, it didn't matter that my entire living room looked like a crime scene of epic proportions. Or that my coffee table was currently occupied by a pile of thank-you letters for the donors to the Santa Fund project. We had branches now. Ten of them.

It'd…exploded somewhat.

Towns all over, with people—like me—hoping to make a difference.

The letters I did clean up, shoving them beneath a couch cushion so Joe wouldn't see something he shouldn't. I had plans to tell him. Had no choice, really. Unless I was going to break up with him—if you could call it a break up if we weren't officially together? But…when I thought about him.

When I thought about those eyes.

My resolve to let him set the parameters of our relationship only hardened.

No way in hell was I going to be the one that ruined things for us.

Joe's knock was as serious and straitlaced as he was. Just a steady beat. Three. A solid number.

I was off the couch in seconds, skidding across the floor in my socks, and yanking the door open with a goofy grin. He was as gorgeous as ever. A little sweaty. Dirt smudges on his cheeks. Pine needles in his hair.

Dressed in a new outfit—oh good, he'd gone home to change—Joe was a vision in flannel and his puffer coat.

"Hi, handsome," I gushed, unable to help myself. "How are you? You're looking lovely." I reached up and plucked the pine needle out of his hair. "Mischievous."

Joe grinned.

God, it was a nice grin.

"You think I don't know what you've been up to all day?" I teased, flicking the little green needle over his shoulder and outside. "You stole my list."

"Yeah," Joe admitted, with no remorse at all. "You're not the only one that can play elf."

He shuffled his feet, eyes flitting down to my mouth. They lingered.

"Why?" I asked.

"I wanted to help you," he said simply.

And oh.

God.

My insides turned to goo.

"Jesus Christ, you're just the sweetest little puppy, aren't you?" I sighed, reaching up to cup that heavy, handsome head. Joe leaned into the touch, blinking at me, his guard crumbling, wall by wall. He shook out of my grip a moment later, though, stepping back and out onto the porch away from me.

I only had a moment to wonder if I'd done something wrong, before my fears were dissuaded.

"Is that…" Over his shoulder, I could make out a very familiar shape in the back of his truck. "A tree?"

"Yeah." Joe loped down the steps, heading for his truck with purpose now. I was still dazed by his sweetness, so it took me a second to figure out what he was doing. And by that point, it was too late.

Like it weighed nothing at all, Joe hauled the tree over his shoulder and began trekking back up the steps toward me. I had no choice but to hold the door open for him, then do my best to get out of the way.

Needles rained down, leaving a trail behind him as he headed into my house for the first time. He didn't blink at my murder boards, just sat the tree down in an empty corner of the room with a grunt, and turned back to face me.

"I got the other stuff too," he promised.

"The…other stuff?"

"Yeah."

Joe was gone again.

I trailed after him, dazed for a new reason now. He came back with a tree stand and a tree skirt. Then—left and returned a third time with a giant bin. He set that beside the tree, and as I watched, speechless, Joe got it all set up.

"Alright." His ass flexed as he squatted down to yank the lid off the bin he'd brought in. "This part you can help with."

"What…" I stared. Stared and stared and stared as Joe pulled out ornaments and baubles and ribbon and lights. He stacked them into neat little piles, keeping everything organized. My heart was leaping. "What is going on?"

Joe paused, a fluffy white reindeer in hand. He swiveled to look at me. The look on my face must've been…illustrative, because he softened.

"I'm giving you Christmas the way you always deserved," Joe told me firmly. "And that starts with a tree."

"But *you're* the one that needs one," I echoed weakly.

"Nah," Joe said. Then, like the shit he was—obviously remembering the way I used to do the same exact thing to him—he patted the floor invitingly.

My knees were weak as I took my seat.

"Lesson one. We gotta do lights first," Joe told me, repeating what I'd said verbatim when I'd been teaching him how to kiss. "They go underneath. There's a right way to do things." I wasn't going to argue with that.

"Right." My heart had never felt bigger. "That makes sense."

"Then we do the big ornaments. Mom says that's key. Making…focal points or whatever."

"You called your mom about this?"

Joe gave me a look. "Obviously. But it's also just something we picked up from her. She likes to talk. Kinda like you. But she's more…ah…snappy."

"Oh."

"I told you Christmas was loud," Joe replied. "Alright. Grab the lights. I'm gonna show you what to do."

And then he did.

Joe and I fit four different light strings around my tree—our tree— before we even started on the ornaments. He let me place all the biggest ones. Though I did move one when he made a face—obviously not liking the placement of it. It made me laugh. Made the last dregs of tension that plagued me slip away.

Joe made this face every time I was going to place something wrong. Like he was constipated. And it was just—so cute. I did it on purpose a few times just to watch him tense, then relax when I moved the ornament back to someplace more Joe-ceptable.

"Now the little ones," Joe said, handing me the fluffy reindeer he'd been holding earlier. It didn't escape my notice that half of the ones he'd bought were animals. Little birds. Owls. Reindeer. Peacocks. Most white, but some a wild mix of vibrant colors. The cardinals were my favorite.

Two red birds sitting pretty on a fake glittery stem.

Almost looked like they were kissing.

"They're gay," Joe informed me as I placed them front and center. "What?"

"Those cardinals," he said. "They're both male, and they're *obviously* mates." He was chatty today, and I didn't want him to stop, so I stayed more quiet than usual. "They do that a lot on Christmas stuff. Cards. Decorations. Put two boy cardinals together. Makes me smile every time."

"I can see why." I let my fingers drift over their feathery little heads as I settled them into place. "It's cute."

"Yeah." Joe handed me another ornament, this time a fish that looked suspiciously like Dori from *Finding Nemo*. "That one's a regal blue tang. They're from the Indo-Pacific."

"Yeah?"

"They like coral reefs. I saw one once at my dentist office in Columbus as a kid."

"You're so fucking cute, you know that?" I couldn't help but gush. Joe blinked, surprised. His cheeks blossomed into a gorgeous, splotchy red.

"Because I know animal facts?"

"Because you're you, Joe." I held a hand out. "Now give me that fat chipmunk you've got there and tell me something cool about it."

Joe beamed.

When we finished decorating, Joe and I sat on the floor and ate plates of lasagna while we stared at the Christmas lights. In a weird way I felt like an alternate kid version of myself. Healed through Joe and his stubborn pursuit.

Staring at the lights as they flickered, red, green, yellow—over and over, I couldn't help but be overcome. My belly was full. And my eyes burned.

"This is my first tree," I told him.

"I know," he said. Even though he couldn't have possibly known that information. Couldn't have known that Mary hadn't been into Christmas until she'd married Daniel. Couldn't have known that I never pushed, never asked because I'd told myself I didn't need it.

Didn't need this.

That for the last ten years, I'd let my Christmases be just as empty as they'd been when I was a kid. Because I thought it made that absence better. Like maybe it'd been a choice all along. But it hadn't.

I knew that now.

I'd just been depriving myself.

I'd thought figuring out my orientation had been my biggest realization this holiday season. But apparently not.

"Which one's your favorite?" Joe asked me, his head tipped back as he looked up at the branches. My whole house smelled like fir. Fragrant and delicious. Better than a fucking candle. The twinkling lights danced across his skin, lighting him up in a mirage of color that made him look unreal.

And yet…here he was.

Sitting on the floor in my living room.

His own empty plate of lasagna to his left.

Realer than real.

And here for me.

"You," I breathed out.

Instead of being touched, Joe scowled at me. "Pick an ornament."

"The cardinals," I replied immediately. I didn't have to think about it. He smiled, nodding in approval. It was a small, private thing.

"Good pick." For a few more minutes, we sat there, side by side. Not moving. Not speaking. Just looking at the lights. Then…slowly…Joe shifted closer. He laid his head on my shoulder, having to hunch to do so. I kissed the top of his head.

And as the lights continued to dance, I once again wondered at the marvel that was Joe Milton.

twenty-five

JOE

I POCKETED THE FORTY BUCKS Mrs. Montgomery had given me with a quiet "thank you." She patted my cheek, her smile friendly. The basket of apples she'd called me to purchase were sitting on her dining table, ready to be made into what she'd told me was sure to be the "best damn cobbler her family had ever had."

It'd been a bit nerve-wracking transporting produce while wearing a fancy-as-fuck suit, but I'd managed.

"You off to somewhere fun?" She inquired, following me out of the house and toward my truck. Jason was in the driver's seat, waiting. And he was…god. I'd never seen someone sexier in all my life. Wearing head to toe black, with hair slicked back, and his scruff missing.

He looked ten years younger.

It was jarring, but…nice, too.

I liked seeing all the different sides he had.

Which was why I'd agreed to go out with him tonight. Despite my trepidation. I wasn't really a fancy party kind of guy. I could get clumsy, especially when there was alcohol involved. And I certainly hadn't come to Belleville with a suit.

I could still remember how Jason had made me feel when he'd invited me though, and that helped. That was before I'd driven north and discovered who exactly Santa was.

"I know it's not..." Jason blew out a breath. "I know it's weird," he admitted. "That it's probably not your thing. But I have to go—and I could use the company. Could use a friend."

"You said it's black-tie. I don't have that. A tie. Or a suit." My cheeks were hot.

"Leave that to me."

The next day, when I'd shown up to drop off his daily coffee Jason had swapped me for a bagged suit. Bagged. In one of those fancy cover things that made me sure the thing was expensive. I would've questioned where the money came from if I hadn't already figured it out.

It'd taken me longer than I cared to admit.

But I had.

In between jobs—at the farm, and trying to get things on Jason's list done before he could—I'd been on a mission to thank my secret Santa. It only felt polite when he was the reason my life was going so great. My house was fixed because of him. I'd given Jason a chance, however inadvertently, because of him.

Things were looking up.

The cashed check Jason had given me was sitting on my new dresser in a place of honor. I'd been racking my brain for days, trying to figure out who I could talk to—aside from Jason—that might know who the man was.

I was ashamed to admit how long it took me to realize his address was on the check. A quick Google search had confirmed a few things. My benefactor, whoever he was, lived only a few hours north of Belleville. It'd felt obvious then, to plan a day trip out there to meet him.

When I'd arrived at the wrought iron gate, I'd nearly turned my truck around and headed right back home, two-hour trip be damned. The manor that sat behind the fence at the end of a long, winding driveway was…for lack of a better word, spooky.

Cold and unfriendly, surrounded by a manicured yard, the brick walls and white accents did little to make the home appear anything but ornamental. It wasn't a home, so much as it was a statement. "Look at how much money I have," written by every well-placed shrub out front.

The gates were open so I continued up the driveway. A few employees were out, sweeping leaves—despite the fact that snow was sure to cover them up anyway. It felt silly. But who was I to judge?

When I parked, no one came to greet me.

I'm not sure why I expected someone would.

I just…a place like this and you'd think there was a butler or something. Or maybe that was just what movies had led me to believe. It was hard to imagine a man who donated his money to the folks in Belleville living *here*.

The front door was so large it made *me* feel small.

Which was not a feeling doors usually caused.

In fact, normally I was worried they were gonna whack my head on the way through. When the massive door swung open before I could knock, I jumped back. The man holding it open was dressed in black, his white hair as perfectly manicured as the lawn.

"H-hello," I tried, heart skipping a beat.

"Hello," he responded, detached. "Who are you?"

Was *this* him? When I'd imagined my secret Santa he'd never been so… cold. He looked as surprised to see me as I was to see him.

"I'm Joe," I said, perplexed.

"What are you doing here, Joe?" He softened a little, probably noting how uncomfortable I was. My hands clenched and unclenched, nervous energy making me feel like my very atoms were spreading thin. "The missus is on her way out the door."

"A solicitor?" A cold, feminine voice echoed from behind the door. I stepped back, confused, just in time for a woman wearing all white to sweep through the open doorway. "I told you to put a sign on the gate, Grant."

"I did, ma'am." Grant looked equal parts amused and frustrated.

Before I could process what was happening, the woman turned to look at me. Her eyes were a chilly, stormy blue. Her hair nearly the same color as the clothing she wore. Stark white, and perfectly styled. Mom would've been proud, her hair was so big. She was a hairdresser back home and had spent her life perfecting that sort of roundness.

"Can't you read?" the woman asked me, eyes sliding over my flannel and stained jeans with interest.

"Of course I can read." The words were out before I could stop them.

"Then you must not be a solicitor."

"I'm not." I stumbled over my words.

"How did you get up here?"

"The gate was open—" I tried.

"Poor timing." She turned to Grant—the man, I was now pretty sure was a real life butler— "I thought I told you not to open it until my car was right in front of it?"

"The mechanism is broken, ma'am," he replied patiently. "Remember? We've got a mechanic coming next week to look at it. Until then, someone has to go down there to open the gate for you in advance."

"Right."

She turned her attention back to me. "You're still here? Why?"

I'd never felt smaller in all my life.

"I…" I shuffled, throat closing up. I hadn't felt this wrong-footed in a long, long time. And suddenly…suddenly I wished Jason were here. If he were here he'd know exactly what to say. Hell, he'd probably make this lady his best friend somehow.

"Are you in charge of the Santa Fund?" I asked, voice small.

"No." Her brow shot up. Face expressive in a way that felt oddly familiar. In fact, everything about her did. My hopes plummeted. So…it wasn't her. "That would be my son."

Hopes soaring again, I stood up straighter. "Your son?"

"Yes."

"Can I talk to him?"

"I don't know how you got my address, but we've already given out the fund," she sighed. "I'm afraid you'll have to try again next year." She strode down the steps, and I trailed after her. The butler's hand caught the back of my coat, hauling me to a stop.

"No, that's not—" I tried again. "I'm the one…I'm the one that got the fund."

She paused at the bottom of the steps, swiveling around to look at me. Her gaze ran over my clothes again, and then my truck. "Then why are you here?"

"I wanted to thank him." My cheeks were hot. "You. Him."

Now…that I'd said that out loud my whole idea felt rather stupid.

Why would these people—with their fat wallets and their mausoleum houses—want to talk to *me*? Maybe their kindness was all a ploy? Something to make them feel better about the wealth they hoarded like dragons.

"Oh." She blinked. "Well." Suddenly the ice in her eyes was gone, replaced by what I could only describe as respect. "I'm sure he would appreciate that. He's sentimental."

"Is he home?"

"No," she said. "He hasn't been home for a long, long time."

"Do you have his number?" Grant continued to hold my shirt, keeping me from moving—even though at that point I didn't want to. There was no need to give chase now that she'd stopped long enough to talk.

"I do," she said. Then, in an act of kindness I hadn't expected, she pulled out her phone. "Let me pull it up, and I'll get you sorted."

"Thank you," the warmth in my chest came rushing back as I smiled at her.

"Yes, well." She waved off the gratitude. "I'm a very giving person."

"Generous," Grant replied from behind me.

"Always."

She relayed her son's number, and I quickly typed it into my notes so I wouldn't lose it. When she'd finished, she offered me a little smile. "Happy Holidays," she said, far friendlier than she'd been earlier.

"You too, ma'am."

Then she was off, heading toward the garage, where I had no doubt something garish and ugly sat waiting for her to drive it.

Grant released me, patting my back apologetically. "Sorry, son. You wouldn't believe the kind of things people will do when money is involved," he said. "I can never be too careful. We've seen all sorts."

It was clear he was loyal. I could respect that.

The garage opened and out came a bright red, flashy sort of sports car. The wealthy woman waved as she drove around my truck, peeling down the driveway like a bat outta hell. I watched her go, still dazed.

"Do you mind if I…" I jerked my head toward my truck. "Make a call?"

"Why don't you come inside?" Grant offered. "It's cold. You can make the call in the drawing room while I grab us some tea. My apology for grabbing you the way I did."

"Do you have cocoa?"

"I'll see what I can do."

He must've sensed my discomfort. Truthfully, I probably would've been better off alone. But it was cold. And it was a long drive back home. Maybe taking a quick break wasn't the worst idea?

Grant left me alone inside the drawing room and did as he'd said he would.

I tried not to be overwhelmed by the sheer size of the space. The ceilings were a thousand feet tall. Made me wonder how the hell someone could install windows that big. Especially as many windows as there were, baseboards to moulding, overlooking the garden.

The couch was expensive-looking but uncomfortable. Hardly any cushion.

I fiddled with my phone for a second, taking in the garish looking rugs and the massive grand piano in the corner of the room that I genuinely wondered if anyone ever used. Not to judge, but the lady I'd met didn't strike me as a very musical person.

When I'd calmed down some, I copy-pasted the number from my notes and hit dial.

It rang only once, barely giving me any time to formulate what I wanted to say, before the other end of the line picked up.

"Hi, baby," Jason's voice was as warm as ever. It rushed through me, licking at the last of the ice in my limbs, chasing it away. I glanced down at my phone, confused. Had I…had I misdialed? But no. No. I hadn't.

I knew I hadn't.

Everything came to me in a rush.

Realizations compounding on top of one another like logs in a stack. The reason Jason had been so sure that "Santa" would want me to have the money. The reason he'd stumbled over his words sometimes when talking about it. The conversation I'd overheard on Thanksgiving that I hadn't been able to make sense of at the time.

The fact that Jason was the most giving, selfless, kind-hearted man I'd ever met.

Jason was Santa.

Jason was *Santa*.

A laugh escaped me. I couldn't help it.

It felt so obvious now. Deep down, I think I knew. Of course I'd known. There was no one else in the world that was as giving as Jason was. Both Santa and Elf. It made…a wicked amount of sense.

"Joe?" Jason sounded concerned. "Are you okay?"

"Yeah," I grunted.

And I was okay.

I was more than okay.

So much was beginning to make sense. About his childhood. The things he'd admitted. About his reaction to the Christmas tree we'd put up.

"Why'd you call? Not that I'm not delighted to hear your voice. Of course I am. I just—"

"Just wanted to hear you," I said, voice soft. I leaned back into the unyielding couch cushions, looking at the room with a new perspective. "And I…had a question."

"Yeah?"

"When you were a kid did you ever play piano?"

Jason made a confused sound. "God, yes. Fucking hated that thing." It was a testament to how far we'd come that he admitted as much as he did. I could see that now. Could see the way he hid behind his lies, the same way he'd run from me. Scared that he wouldn't be accepted for who he was, as he was.

"Why?"

"It was just performative," Jason sighed. "My mom wanted to say she had a son who played, so I had to learn to play."

"Did you quit?"

"Of course."

I lay down on my back, staring up at the massive ceiling. Trying my damndest to picture what it would've been like to be a kid inside this museum. Surrounded by nothing but quiet emptiness. Only opulence for company. The answer was…lonely. It would've been lonely. As full as it was of stuff, it felt so…hollow.

Nothing about this place felt friendly or home-like. No wonder Jason had grown up as goofy and bright as he was. His personality expanded to try and fit a tomb this large. His desperation to matter seemed even more prevalent now.

How many times had he lain on this couch, staring at this ceiling, praying for someone to care?

"I thought your parents weren't around?" I said quietly.

"They weren't," Jason confirmed. Again, surprising me by how much he was opening up. A dam had apparently broken after the other night. He'd never been so candid. Something had changed. "I probably could've quit playing sooner, honestly. But I think part of me hoped that if I kept doing what they wanted me to, eventually they'd come to one of my performances."

"Did they?"

"No."

That simple, two letter word carried more weight than anything else he'd said.

"I hate your parents," I told him. Jason made a startled sound. It was half laugh, half pained.

"I did too, for a long time," he admitted. On the other end of the line it was quiet. Only the whoosh of his breath. Was he at work? Or driving? Or at home? Surrounded by his walls full of community projects. "But I don't anymore."

"Why?"

"When my dad died…" Jason paused as he gathered his thoughts. "It gave me a lot of perspective." I waited, hanging on his every word. Any second Grant might come back, cutting this short. I didn't want him to. Didn't want to miss a single thing Jason was about to say. "I realized it hurt more to hate them than to love them where they were at…if that makes sense." I wasn't sure I understood. Jason must've sensed that, somehow, even through the phone. "My mom will never be the mom that comes to my performances, checks my report card, or bakes me cookies."

My mom was all of those things.

I'd never…I'd never realized that was something I should be grateful for.

That she cared too much, maybe.

"But she picks up when I call, every time," Jason finished. "When I have a hare-brained scheme…" The Santa Fund, no doubt. "She's the one that backs me up. She wants to hear all my gossip, all the time. And she cares, in whatever way she can, even if it's not the way I always wished she would."

"You don't think she can change?" I asked, heart hurting for him.

"Maybe it's more that I don't care if she does," Jason sighed. "I'm fine with the way things are. I stopped having expectations that she'd show up for me. I have other family now. Family I chose."

So much about him was beginning to make sense.

Puzzle pieces falling into place.

Jason took care of everyone else because no one had ever taken care of him.

"I learned pretty young that family isn't blood," Jason finished. "Family are the people that show up for you when you need them."

A feminine voice sounded on the other end of the line. Madison maybe?

"I gotta go, Joe-by," Jason said softly. "Mean old Madison needs me to grab something from the top shelf—*ow*." There was a thwacking sound on the other end of the line. "Madison says hi." He laughed, and I knew— right then—exactly what he was talking about. About family being who chose to be with you.

Because Madison was there with him, right then.

Having heard this conversation, she was distracting him. Giving him something to do—because being helpful was the way Jason coped. Lighting up the secret pessimist because he needed it.

The truth was…as bright as Jason was, his light was easily dimmed. He was the kind of guy that'd gift you the shirt off his back and ask for nothing in return. Giving, and generous, the way his mother apparently wasn't. And as much as he projected optimism, this conversation had made it pretty clear how he viewed the world.

He expected to be disappointed, so that he never was.

"Oh, before I go—" Jason started. "I wanted to ask you if you'd do something for me."

"Anything." The word was out before I could overthink it.

"There's this party…I know it's not…" Jason blew out a breath. "I know it's weird," he admitted. "That it's probably not your thing. But I have to go—and I could use the company. Could use a friend."

Jason's hand squeezed the nape of my neck tight the moment I was buckled, bringing my mind back to now.

To the present.

To sitting in the passenger seat of my own beat-up pick-up truck, dressed to the nines in a suit that probably cost what the new floor in my living room had. Spending time with a man who didn't know I knew his secrets. Every last one of them.

I wasn't sure what tonight was.

If maybe he was going to tell me?

Knowing him…it could be another ploy to push me away. Assuming I'd treat him differently because I knew about his money. Thinking the worst, as always, because the worst was all he'd been shown when he was too young to process what that sorta thing did to his head.

But I was bound and determined to prove him wrong. Not just at the gala, but after, too. I wanted to show him that his one optimistic thought was right. That he had a family in Belleville. With everyone there—with me.

We were going to be the family he'd chosen.

I was going to help him, the way he helped everyone else.

Jason Harker would never be lonely again, if I had anything to say about it. And if the plan I was hatching up worked, this would be his best Christmas yet.

twenty-six

JASON

TO SAY I WAS NERVOUS about telling Joe the truth about the Santa Fund was a gross understatement. I'd made the choice to open this door. Tonight, I'd see how he reacted to the gala and through that, I'd be able to ascertain how to proceed.

I liked to think he wouldn't bat an eye at my wealth.

But it'd been proven to me time and time again when I was a kid that money changed people. That was a fact of life. I could so easily remember the first time it'd happened.

I was seven.

My nanny used to take me to the local park to play with the other kids. It was one of the few drops of normalcy I had between the functions my parents required me to attend—when they were home—and the emptiness of our home when they weren't.

It was my holy grail.

For those few short hours every day, I got to be a kid.

There was this little boy. Chauncey. He had red hair, wore ripped jeans and scuffed-up sneakers—and he'd been my best friend. Chauncey and I had been little devils. Running around the playground, hogging the slides, taking turns pushing each other on the swings higher, higher, higher.

Then one day, it changed.

Looking at it with adult eyes, I understood what had happened. The previous day, the kids had been telling me that my mom was pretty—and I'd told them she wasn't my mom. She was my nanny. And she took care of me so my mom could do more important things, like save tigers, or build cities in Antarctica—I was a very imaginative kid.

One of the parents had overheard.

Chauncey's dad.

And that had been the start of the end.

I approached Chauncey like I always did, ready to kick up dust, and cause a riot. I had a plan that we'd take turns seeing how long we could stay inside the slide before gravity forced us down. There was a stopwatch in my pocket, and a grin on my face. I'd been *dreaming* about it since the night before, lying in bed, plans compounding on top of one another.

I was practically vibrating by the time I reached him, mouth half-open, ready to speak.

But he moved away.

Headed toward the swings before I could catch up. Confused, I'd chased him down.

Maybe he just wanted to start there?

That was fine.

I was totally good with that, so long as we did my plan after.

When I got to the swings, Chauncey gave me a look. It was a weird look. Not something I'd ever seen before, and I didn't know how to interpret it. So I stood there, still ready to play, opening my mouth for a second time to speak.

"Why are you following me?" he asked, sitting on the same swing we always played on, his brow furrowed.

"Oh. I thought we could play here—" I started.

"I'm not supposed to play with you anymore," he cut me off.

I was confused to say the least.

"But—"

"My dad says that your family will sewage mine if you get hurt, and I'm the one with you," he said. "He said he can't afford any shit." I'd never heard Chauncey swear. Despite the harsh words, I almost wanted to laugh. "So I'm not supposed to play with you anymore."

"But don't you want to?" I asked, my tiny heart squeezing so tight it felt like it'd pop. "I want to play with you."

"Sure, but…" Chauncey kicked at the wood chips, sending one flying in my direction. "I guess I can't."

At the end of the day, Chauncey didn't choose me. I couldn't be angry about that. Not when he was just doing what he was supposed to. So instead…I was just…sad.

I'd been hurt and baffled as I'd gone back to my nanny. I demanded to go home—which of course, made her alarmed. I never wanted to go home early. In fact, most days I was begging to stay.

We were quiet as we drove.

"What's a sewage?" I asked her, staring out the window as we passed by the blur of houses. Houses that looked different than mine. Smaller. Warmer. I'd never noticed.

"A sewage?" she asked, sounding as confused as I was.

"Chauncey says he won't play with me anymore because my parents would sewage him."

A few minutes later she got down to the root of the issue. Explained to me what suing someone was. Tried to help me make sense of my very first friendship breakup. She softened things. Tried not to make me feel "other", but no matter what she said, I understood.

It was the money.

Chauncey's parents had been scared of our money.

And because of that, I couldn't be his friend anymore.

That's when it started. The distrust. The fear that everyone in my life would leave the moment they found out who I was. I'd carried it with me through boarding school. Carried it into college too, though there, I'd tried to reinvent myself.

Been honest, only to have my peers alienate me all over again.

Sometimes it was just a look.

This…fizzle of fear in their eyes.

Sometimes…it was manipulation.

All it'd taken was a few boys in school convincing me to buy them things before I'd realized my money was sharp on both ends.

We'd just pulled up to what had to be the most audacious lodge I'd ever seen. We'd been lucky enough to avoid another snow storm, at least for now. It was going to hit that night when we were safely nestled in our room. I'd booked us the fanciest one I could. Partly to impress Joe, but partly to…to see how he'd respond.

If he'd be uncomfortable.

If he'd treat me differently.

And depending on that…maybe I'd tell him the whole truth. About the Santa Fund. About my feelings for him. All of it.

Maybe.

Joe hadn't batted an eye at the gaudiness of the lodge, or our room. He'd been curious about the hot tub, but otherwise hadn't said or acted any differently. Just plopped his bag beside the bed we'd be sharing.

"Better than an air mattress," was all he'd said.

Which…I mean…true.

Joe turned to look at me. Gorgeous as hell in his suit. Blond hair styled. Square jaw perfectly shaved aside from a little knick at the corner that'd scabbed over since that morning. He looked like an apple pie personified. Golden and earnest. The kind of sweet seriousness that made my teeth ache.

"Thank you for coming," I said. And then, "I hate this thing."

"Of course," Joe blinked, "It's the only time you get to see your mom, right?"

God, he was smart. The fact he'd deduced that was clever as hell.

"Right."

I was nervous for them to meet. Nervous about a lot of things tonight. But…something told me Joe wouldn't let me down.

Joe was…Joe.

He wasn't like anyone I'd ever met. Wasn't like any of the people who had hurt me, changed me, molded me.

Case in point.

The fact that his expression hadn't wavered. The way he looked at me hadn't changed. Not once since we'd stepped out of the truck. He watched me the way he always did, awaiting instruction. No fancy hotel room or flighty mother was going to change that.

Gratitude welled up inside me so fiercely I nearly choked on it. On the need to be close to him. To touch him. Feel him. For him to soothe this ache in my chest.

He headed for the door, a man on a mission. Sexy as hell in his suit. It hugged his waist, making it look fucking tiny in comparison to those huge-ass shoulders and his plump ass.

I was half-tempted to fall to my knees and bite it.

Party be damned.

Hell, nothing was stopping me. Mom was always late. She wouldn't notice if I was too.

Once at the door, Joe turned around to face me. His eyes flickered over mine, and a flush traveled over his cheeks, betraying the fact he knew exactly what I'd just been thinking about.

"Don't we need to—"

"On the bed, Joe," I commanded.

Joe wavered for a moment, glancing between me and the exit. Then he shrugged, turned back around, and headed for the mattress. He sat down, bouncing to test it—like a little kid. When he caught me looking, he stopped immediately.

Ohmygodsoadorable.

"Have you ever received a blow job while wearing a suit before?" I asked, charitably not calling him cute out loud and ruining the sexy vibe we had going.

Joe blinked.

The flush on his cheeks traveled down his throat. His ears were so red they were practically fluorescent.

"You know I haven't," he husked out shyly.

"I know," I purred. "I just like to tease."

"You're a bully," he accused. His throat bobbed as he swallowed, and I tracked the movement. Tracked every inch of him. The way his hands kept bunching up on his thighs, the way they only did when he was anxious.

"We don't have to," I promised. His hands relaxed, fingers spreading across his thick, trouser-clad legs. They hugged every inch of his musculature, practically obscene. I was going to be the talk of the party tonight, with him on my arm. Whether or not I'd sucked his brain out through his cock first.

Joe gave me my favorite look.

I grinned.

"Are you going to get mad at me for asking for consent again?" I inquired as I crossed the distance between us. Every time I took a step, Joe's nostrils flared. Tense, but eager. He shifted a little, legs widening, aaaand there it was.

His dick.

Already hard, and trapped against his inner thigh.

He was so much fun.

"Yeah, 'cause you ask every five seconds," Joe huffed.

"Sounds to me like we need a safe word."

"What's that?" He blinked up at me when I came to a stop between his spread legs. I kicked one of them gently, and he spread wider, without even having to think. He looked up at me, big blue eyes swimming with curiosity and trust.

Trust that I had him.

That I'd take care of him.

And god, was that heady.

"A safe word is something we can use in place of 'no' or 'stop.' That way, you can say those things without me—"

"Stopping," Joe finished for me. He contemplated this. "And if we had one…you wouldn't keep checking in?" He looked hopeful.

"I still would," I said. "I know you don't like it, but it makes me feel safe when I don't know for sure that what I'm doing is something you want."

"Oh." Joe obviously hadn't thought about it that way.

"You hold the power, not me," I explained. "But that means I need reassurance, too. In my case—when I check in, and you say yes, or you nod—it gives me the confidence to keep going."

"So, it's for you…"

"For both of us. Imagine if there was something you didn't want?" I cupped his cheek, unable to resist the urge to touch him when he was this close. "And you didn't know how to tell me. I don't ever want to put you in that position."

Joe tipped his head into my palm, blinking up at me, his eyes swimming with emotion as he thought through what I'd just said. He was a thinker, my Joe.

"We both need to feel safe for it to feel good," Joe said.

"Yes."

"I don't hate the check-ins anymore," he promised, just as quietly. "You can keep doing them."

"Okay. Good." I pressed a kiss to his forehead, lingering there for a moment. This…this was just as intimate as touching his dick. Open communication. The respect and desire we obviously shared for one another.

"I can compromise though," I told him, still kissing his forehead. "How about I give us a safe word, and if I can trust you to use it when you need it, I can check in maybe a *little* less."

Joe made an affirmative sound.

"What about rutabaga?" I offered. "That's not a word I imagine either of us would ever use, especially in bed."

"I dunno…" Joe frowned. "What about…Arkansas."

"Like the state?" I asked, amused.

"Yeah."

"That's fine. I'm just curious why not rutabaga." I kissed his cheek, and Joe made a little sound.

"I'm a farmer. What if I accidentally talk to someone about rutabaga and you hear?" I didn't have the heart to point out that we were talking about sex situations, and I seriously doubted he'd be talking about produce with another farmer while we had sex.

I just liked that he wanted to contribute.

That we were both equally invested in this.

"Arkansas it is," I agreed.

"Cool." Joe smiled at me shyly.

Outside the window, the stars were peeping through the clouds. It'd been overcast earlier, so I was surprised to see them at all. They framed Joe's head, making him look even more angelic than usual.

Then slowly, surely, I sank to my knees between his legs.

I rubbed my hands up his calves, partially to get him used to being touched—and partially to get myself ready, too. I'd never done this. He knew that. I knew that. I didn't want to get it wrong. Though, truthfully? I doubted Joe would care.

Based on how enthusiastically he'd enjoyed my shitty not-hand-job the other day, I didn't think he was all that picky.

"Are you gonna touch my butt again?" Joe asked. He stumbled over the word "butt" like he hadn't been sure if that was the right word to use.

"Your hole?" I offered. He nodded, a sharp little up and down.

"Do you want me—"

"I brought lube."

Oh dear god, he was going to kill me.

"You brought lube?" My heart skipped a beat.

"Condoms, too," Joe admitted. He wouldn't look at me, staring somewhere along the back wall. The picture of perfection with his legs spread and his hard dick throbbing between them. "In case you wanted…I mean—earlier…you said…" I was quiet, letting him piece together his thoughts. "Before you said that you were touching me…where you were gonna fuck me. So I just—is that…what you want?"

I opened my mouth to speak, but Joe surprised me by cutting me off again.

"I know you said you want what I want. I looked up those terms. Pleasure dom. Or um. Service top. I get what they mean now. And I like that you're that way. I think it's…" His throat bobbed. Poor baby would need a glass of water, he was talking so much. "I think it's good you're that way. Compatible with me. 'Cause I'd rather, usually, not do anything at all. And the idea of being the one to fuck you freaks me out. I'd rather…you do all that. And I just…" God, he was so cute. "That's embarrassing, right?"

"You think being a pillow princess is embarrassing?" I tried not to be amused and failed.

"Yes." Joe squirmed. "I mean…isn't it?" Apparently, he knew what *that* meant, too.

I didn't want to dismiss his feelings. "No." I shook my head. "You're allowed to enjoy and desire whatever you want, Joe. And feeling embarrassed, or nervous, is natural. Sex is sticky. It's vulnerable. That's normal. I know I was nervous the other day, worried I'd be touching you wrong—since I'd never done it."

"You were nervous?" Joe gawped at me. "But you were all…all *dirty-talking-me*." The last three words were said so quickly they meshed together.

I grinned. "It turns me on when you squirm," I admitted. "And talking is easy for me. It's one of my strengths. It was the other stuff I didn't know how to do. I wanted it to be good for you."

"It was." Joe stared at me, baffled. "It was so good. Why do you think I brought condoms? I want more."

I laughed. I couldn't help it. I buried my face against his inner knee and giggled. He was so cute. So fucking cute. As earnest as ever, even in bed.

"I've been practicing," Joe soldiered on, pretending I wasn't giggling between his legs. "So you could…*you know*…if you wanted. Google said I needed to stretch."

My laughter died immediately.

Suddenly, that day I'd caught Joe masturbating came back to mind. Only the memory shifted. This time, it was Joe on his back, no blanket, those thick fingers wiggling around inside his tight little hole. Probably huffing, whimpering. Because he couldn't get the angle right. Couldn't fuck himself the way he wanted. Couldn't get deep enough.

"Oh fuck," I groaned, biting his inner thigh, pleased when he yelped. No more games. "Okay. Yes. I want to fuck you." I dragged my nose up his inseam. "I want to fuck you so fucking bad, Joe." I bit the meaty part right next to where his cock lay. "*Jesus.*"

"G-good." Joe's voice was hoarse. He wasn't super vocal during sex. At least…not at first. I'd gotten him whining by the end of last time, and had every intention of doing that again.

"For now, though? Before the gala? I'm going to suck you. Maybe eat you out a bit. Test to see if you've been practicing the way you should." I'd done some research of my own. "And after…well…depending on how it goes—"

Joe reached for his belt without letting me finish. He had it unbuckled and his zipper down in seconds, wiggling out of his pants till they got in my way, forcing me out of his crotch. I helped him yank them down to his ankles, amused and delighted when I saw the boxers he'd picked were covered in magpies.

"One sec," Joe yanked his button-up up to his arm pits, thick tits on display. "For the mess," he explained.

Jesus.

The crown of his cock was poking out of the leg of his underwear, flushed bright red and leaking. It twitched as I hungered after it, and Joe stared down at me like I was fucking God. I wanted to see the rest of it. Wanted to show him Heaven, in every way I could.

"Boxers off?" I asked, trembling with anticipation.

My own dick was pulling, but I ignored it. Ignored the heat in my balls, and the way I had the ungodly desire to climb on top of him and fuck him right the fuck now—everything else be damned.

Joe nodded, a short jerk off his head.

I pulled them off quick as a Band-Aid. Didn't want him to get stressed out. And as much as I adored teasing him, I knew some situations were better for that. Right now, I just needed my mouth on him. Needed to taste him. Try my hand at a blow job and hopefully blow his mind.

Get it? Blow his— *Anyway.*

I dove in, lips first. Kissed his sac, and studied his cock from the best seat in the house. It was just as big bare as it'd been covered. A fat vein on the underside that begged to be licked. Thick and long, with a crown that was slightly smaller than the rest so it gave it an almost tapered appearance.

Just looking at it made me feel like I was burning up.

Joe made a sound, his hands clenching tightly into fists where they lay on his thighs by my head. I kissed his sac again, and he gasped. When I looked up at him—god, it was hard to look away from a dick like that—he appeared dazed.

He was so responsive and I'd hardly done anything.

His dick flexed, begging me to touch it again, so I did.

I'd intended to take things slow for the both of us. To learn him. Figure out my own limits. See how it felt to have a dick in my mouth. But…I'd never been good at slow when I wanted something. Nor had I ever been able to stop myself from pushing. So, fast was how I went. Sucking at the vein, growling when Joe's head fell back. He was trembling as I worried my teeth against the skin.

"Teeth good or?" I offered.

"Good." Joe's voice was so hoarse I barely heard it. Couldn't see his face anymore, either, because his head was so far back.

"Lie down," I commanded. I wanted to see his face, yes, but he was going to give himself a neck-ache if he kept that up.

Joe lay down. He spread his legs even wider, and I grabbed his hips, yanking them off the bed. In this position, I could see his balls and cock in their entirety. Could see his hole, too. Which I didn't hesitate to tell him, just to watch his fists spasm again, betraying his arousal.

His cock was slightly salty when I got to the crown, lapping at it, testing the smooth, hard texture. I'd had a dick my whole life—and I'd never really thought about that before. A dicks texture. How it was both soft and hard at once.

When I sucked, Joe exhaled harshly through his nose. Loud enough I could hear him.

That was it. The last of my patience gone.

I went to town with fervor. Licking, worrying it with my teeth—because he'd said he liked it—digging my tongue into his slit curiously to see if he'd leak more. He did. I sucked on his balls too, enjoyed how soft they were. Pulled them up with my hand and dove lower, lapping along his perineum.

I probably should've been more nervous about rimming him. According to the internet, that too was kinda a…further along step.

But…

It wasn't that different from eating out a cunt.

"Leg on my shoulder," I told him, helping him so that he could get his knee up. When he was settled, half his weight on me, I lapped down his perineum again. "You want your hole licked?" I offered, cheating maybe, because my breath skimmed the fluttery little entrance to entice him.

"Y-yes," Joe gasped out after a moment of embarrassed silence.

"Good. Because I want to," I told him. "I want to lick your little boy cunt till it's sloppy. Just like I licked your cock. Do you want that, Joe? Do you want me to make your pussy nice and wet?"

Joe made a garbled sound. His hips flexed toward my face, heel digging into my back. "That's what I thought."

The first swipe of my tongue against his hole was illuminating. I didn't think I'd been harder in my entire life. It fluttered, just as shy as Joe was. He made another sound, louder than the last. Apparently, Joe was quiet until his hole got touched.

Which was just…really good to know.

I flattened my tongue, rubbing it back and forth for a few delightful seconds, fingers biting into his hips to keep him still. They kept jumping up, like he wasn't sure if he was pushing into my mouth or away from it.

Either way.

He had the tools to get me to stop, I'd checked in. And he was…god. So enthusiastic. Even if he was embarrassed.

"You know what I bet?" I said, the moment a thought occurred to me. My tongue slid away, leaving his hole twitching. "I bet you've never even seen your pussy, have you?" Joe shuddered. "That makes me the first." I laved another long lick over it. "Unless I'm wrong." I was taunting him, I couldn't help it. "And my sweet little Joe has gotten his legs spread in front of a mirror, and bent over so he could see his own little fuck-hole."

Joe whimpered.

"Is that it? When you practiced?" I grinned, then licked him again. "You had to see, huh?"

Joe's leg jerked, and I squeezed his hips even harder.

"Stop teasing," he snarled.

"You love it," I hummed. He didn't deny it because we both knew it was true. To reward him for his honesty, I dove in again, lapping at his hole with more confidence now. This time, I kept the pressure light. Flicking in circles around the little ring. Every time I did, it'd clench down, like it was trying to invite me inside it.

I alternated for a few minutes, spit running down my chin, flicking his hole, then sucking on it, then laving it with fat licks that made my baby Joe sing. By the time I pushed inside it, just the tip of my tongue, he was outright sobbing.

I'd never heard him so loud.

It was gratifying to say the least.

"J-Ja-Jason," Joe whimpered, pushing his hips against my mouth, trying to force more inside him. "J-J-Ja-son." Hearing my name on his tongue, so sweetly uttered, a plea as much as it was a complaint made me feel ten feet tall.

God, how could I ever have thought Joe would treat me differently? I was such an idiot.

I pushed deeper, deeper, until I couldn't push anymore. All that wet, tight heat, spasming around me. Making my dick pulse as I imagined replacing my tongue with my cock. Pounding him into the mattress till he was crying because I was so far inside him he didn't think I'd ever come out again.

All it took was one brush of my hand along Joe's hard cock for him to spill.

That was it.

Just one.

And he spread milky cum all over his abs, his chest, a few drops landing dangerously close to those hard, perky nipples.

It was a good thing he'd pushed his shirt up.

A very good thing.

When I pulled my tongue out, Joe sobbed again. His back arched off the bed, heel kicking against my back like he was trying to haul me in. It was such a sweet wordless plea, I couldn't help but comply. Stuck my tongue right back where he wanted it so he had something to squeeze around.

I'd never been a guy who thought about sex toys.

Not until that moment.

And suddenly…I desperately wished I had a plug to put inside him in place of my tongue. Something small. Just to give him something to squeeze around when my tongue couldn't be inside him.

I fucked him a few more times, let his body acclimate to the idea of being empty, before I pulled out. He didn't move. Didn't even twitch as I kissed his now-spent balls and cleaned his cock up with my tongue.

The flavor was better this time. Maybe because it was my second time tasting it. Oddly…pineapple-y. I sucked every stray bit of cum from the golden curls at the base of Joe's dick, then dragged my tongue up his lower belly, lapping the rest of it away. I had to put his leg down to get to the cum on his chest.

He didn't protest.

Didn't do anything but pant, glassy-eyed as I licked away. Then I grabbed his tits and smashed them together as best as I could. It wasn't a perfect tunnel. Good enough, though. Keeping the muscle as smashed together as I could, I worried his nipples with my teeth.

Maybe a little mean, considering how overstimulated he was. I really was a bully.

His hand found my hair, grabbing on to it as he forced me from one side of his chest to the other, then back again. I debated with myself for a moment—before deciding…fuck it. I climbed on top of him, straddling his ribs, my hard cock pointing right at his pecs.

"Do you—" I started.

"Do it," Joe rasped. His face was flushed, tears and spit slick down his cheeks like he'd been drooling and crying as I'd eaten him out. "Do it," he said again, this time as a challenge.

"Unbutton your shirt and pull your tie off," I instructed him as I reached for my belt buckle.

He did as he was told, but his eyes never left my hands. They traced over them hungrily, along my fingers, along the veins, across the Rolex I only wore when I was going to the gala to keep up appearances for my mom.

With his shirt peeled to the sides and his tie gone, there was nothing stopping me from doing what I'd been wanting to do.

"Hold your tits together," I commanded softly. "Can you do that for me, baby? Can you hold those pretty pecs?"

Joe didn't blink at the terms. He hadn't reacted to me calling his hole a cunt either. I supposed, at the end of the day, it didn't matter what I called them, he liked it either way.

His hands went to his chest, cupping each thick pec as he forced them together as far as they could go. They were made of solid muscle. They didn't move like real breasts did. A fact that genuinely only made it hotter as I pulled my dick out and aimed the crown at the crevice he'd created.

It was more a valley than a crevice but…it was good enough.

Joe held still, breathing harshly. He kept glancing down his nose, straining to see my dick, even though he couldn't from this angle. Struggling to keep his chest where it needed to be for me to fuck it, Joe painted a pretty fucking picture splayed out on white sheets.

Taking pity on him, I pinched my crown and brought my cock straight up so he could see.

"What do you think?" I asked, cock twitching. "How does your first dick look?" My cock twitched. It was shorter than Joe's, leaner too. Not by much, though. I'd always been complimented on my cock size. Wasn't my fault Joe was a giant. The skin was a slightly darker shade than his was. Cooler toned. More veiny too.

"My only dick," Joe corrected so quietly I almost thought I'd hallucinated it.

"Your only dick," I agreed, a possessive sort of pleasure burning through me. "How does your *only* dick look?" I asked again, the correct way this time.

"Good." Joe licked his lips.

"It's not as big as yours," I mused, tilting my hips so he could see my balls too. "But it'll still fill you up nice and full. I promise."

Joe whimpered.

Whimpered.

I lost the war with my patience pretty quickly after that. Pressed my cock back in the channel he'd made and ground my hips forward. And the whole time, Joe stared up at me, enraptured. His lips were parted, his eyes half-lidded as I pounded his pecs and my head swam.

It was so good.

So fucking good.

Tense, thick muscle. Soft skin. I rubbed my crown on his nipples a few times each just to leave them wet. Then snapped forward again. The sound was filthy, especially as my precum began to leave a sticky mess behind.

Joe's throat bobbed every time he swallowed. Eyes glassy. His chest shuddering with each breath. And I felt them all. Every last one.

When I came it was with a growl, all over that tan, sweaty skin. Streaking his tits pointedly, back and forth, leaving little droplets on the backs of his hands. Then up his throat, marking him the way he was meant to be marked.

Joe was such a good boy when I cleaned him up. Scrubbed him till he was pink and didn't smell like cum anymore. He held perfectly still and docile, blinking dollishly up at me as he listened to the praise I doled out, and soaked up every kind word.

"You're so perfect," I promised him as I swiped the last of the cum from his throat. "My sweet baby boy, aren't you?" Joe blinked, lips curled into a little smile. "Thank you, honey." I kissed his cheek, then his chin, then his other cheek. "That's just what I needed."

He looked very pleased.

Sweet thing.

I got us both redressed.

Before we headed down, I cuddled Joe for a solid twenty minutes. Didn't care that we were late. Not when he was curled into me, puffing breaths against my throat as he came down from wherever he'd been flying.

When we did eventually leave the room, Joe looked downright peppy.

Once again, a good orgasm had given him energy.

Whereas with me…god. I'd love nothing more than to curl up and nap.

Still though, I couldn't leave my mom hanging. My plan to test Joe felt stupid now. God, I was an idiot. I should've known he was an A-plus student.

Joe let me lead the way from the elevators to the ballroom. That was the only way to describe it. Huge with massive glass walls that overlooked the night sky. Somewhere between sex and now, the clouds had come back. Snow was falling, wispy and sweet as it batted at the windows.

The room was crowded, like always. The titter of laughter could be heard even from the corner as I took Joe straight to the dessert table so he could pile up.

Baby needed calories.

Joe didn't ask me why we were here. Didn't ask me about the suits. Didn't ask me a single thing—aside from where the bathroom was in case he needed it. And for the next few hours, he ate snacks and stayed by my side. He wandered around behind me while I schmoozed the people my mother wanted me to schmooze.

I hadn't seen her yet.

Which was unsurprising.

When she did eventually show up, Joe stiffened a little at my side. He didn't say anything, though, just stared at her as he shoved a handful of olives in his mouth. Olives he'd been collecting from the drinks he'd had. It'd been a while since his last one, however, and I could tell he wasn't even close to drunk.

I kind of wanted to see drunk Joe.

I bet he was clingy as hell.

Probably a happy drunk.

"Hi, sweet boy," Mom said as she approached. She was dressed to the nines in some sort of silk and chiffon get-up that made her look half swan. When she coaxed me into a hug, I grinned, squeezing her tight.

"Hi, Mom," I said into her perfect hair. When I shifted back, she was beaming.

"Who's your friend?" she asked. Her eyes flitted over Joe, widening a little. "He's handsome."

"He's the one I told you about," I explained. "Remember?"

"The marshmallow?"

Joe's face was bright red. He had so many olives in his mouth he resembled a chipmunk. I had a newfound appreciation for the animal, because Joe had fed me animal facts about them on the car ride over.

"That's him," I answered, amused but a little annoyed that she really hadn't been listening.

"Have we met?" Mom asked Joe, curious. "You look familiar."

Joe glanced at me for help.

"I probably showed you a picture."

"Oh." She nodded. "Maybe." Her smile softened. "Did you talk to the Petersons?"

"I did." I sighed. I'd talked to everyone she wanted me to. No doubt, by the end of the night, the donation pool would be twice as large after all the kissing-ass I'd done. She'd feel good giving that away. Could lord that win over her friends for the rest of the year.

"You know…" Mom turned back to Joe. "It's *bothering* me."

Joe swallowed his olives, red face now positively green. Mom squinted, trying to figure it out.

"I meet a lot of people," she informed him with an air of importance. "And I *never* forget a face."

Joe nodded slowly.

"Ah! I've got it." She snapped her fingers. They were as glittery as her dress. "This may be a long shot, but do you know Alex James?"

Joe sighed. "I do."

"*That's* what it was." She grinned wolfishly. "You were at his wedding. I saw you in the photos." Joe nodded. "Good family, the Jameses. They've got a lot of money in real estate. Did you know that, Jason?" Mom turned to me. "That your new friend had connections to the Jameses?"

"I did not." I shook my head. Glancing sidelong at Joe, I tried to convey how sorry I was.

"My brother is Alex's husband," Joe piped up, putting in effort where he really didn't have to. It was cute, though. Him trying. For me. He was relaxing by the minute now that Mom was no longer scrutinizing him.

"Ah!" Mom perked up even more. "Is he? Yes. I think I've seen a few things on Netbook about that. I like to keep up," she explained. "Their father is one of my favorite donors. Very nice man. Big pockets. New money, but you'd never know it with how graceful he can be."

Ugh.

"He is nice," Joe agreed. He was being so patient with her. So… devastatingly patient. I couldn't help but melt. "He's been real good to my brother. They have Sunday dinner together."

"How cute!" Mom smiled. "Do you, by chance, have their numbers?" she asked. For some reason, that made Joe flinch a little, his guard going back up.

"Ah…Alex's dad?" he clarified. "Or Alex?"

"Yes. Or Juniper, the sister. I'm not picky."

"Yeah, sure." Joe pulled his phone out. He was stiff as a board as he gave Mom the information she wanted. When she'd finished interrogating him, she turned to me. "To your left!" she said, high-pitched and eager. "Wendell. With his fiancé." I twisted a little to see what she was talking about. "Oh, aren't they cute?"

"They are." Wendell looked happier than I'd ever seen him.

"They owe me a bouquet or something," Mom gushed. "An acknowledgment? At their wedding maybe. A toast!" she tittered.

"Maybe you should go tell them that," I laughed.

"Good idea!" She beamed at me. "Always such a pleasure, darling." I bent down, and she kissed my cheeks. "I'll see you next year?"

"Yep. As always."

That was it.

Then she was gone. Flouncing away to mingle with the rest of the guests. I sighed, turning back to Joe to do some damage control. When he pushed a champagne flute in my hand, I blinked.

"You need a break?" Joe offered as I sipped the drink gratefully. "I saw a corner in the back with less people. You have to be here the whole night, right? For your mom?"

I nodded.

She wasn't likely to talk to me again. But she still wanted me present. Till the very end.

Joe didn't leave my side once. He used his bulk to block me from the rest of the room when we were in the corner. Gave me a chance to get my head screwed on straight. And best of all…he didn't comment about my mom.

Didn't ask me why I came here, when I was mostly a means to an end.

Didn't complain about the way she'd treated him.

Just…accepted me.

Accepted her.

Accepted this room and its people for what they were.

The way I'd never thought someone else would.

twenty-seven

JOE

"I HAVEN'T SEEN YOU AROUND before," a friendly, very male voice drawled from my left. I startled, the champagne flutes I'd chased down sloshing. Some splashed on my shirt, and I had to bite back a groan. I'd gone almost the whole night without spilling.

"Yeah," I swiveled around, still clutching the drinks. Jason was… somewhere. We'd been together up until five minutes ago. He'd told me he had to run and talk to someone, and I'd offered to get us drinks.

The man who'd spoken was dressed the same as everyone else—including me. Black and white. Not a hair out of place. He was shorter than me. But…most people were, so that wasn't necessarily alarming.

"This is my first time," I admitted.

"That's what I figured." His grin was wolfish. I couldn't tell if it was… genuine or not. If he was like Jason's mom, trying to figure out if I had money. Or…god. I dunno. This stuff was where I struggled.

Be nice, don't embarrass Jason.

"Well, nice to meet you," I said, still holding my flutes.

"It *really* is," he purred. His eyes dragged over my shoulders, then down my body. I wouldn't have recognized the look for what it was, if I hadn't seen Jason give me a similar perusal. I stiffened, eyes widening.

Was he…

Was he *hitting on me?*

"If you don't mind me saying so, you're gorgeous," he flirted. I did, in fact, mind. "A pretty guy like you shouldn't be left alone." He was definitely hitting on me. "I'm going to dance with you," he told me.

My hackles raised.

"Ah—" I didn't know how to say *Hell No* in a way that wouldn't get me thrown out. "I—"

"He's not interested." Jason's voice snapped from behind me. Rather than jumping—because he was the second person to sneak up on me—I relaxed. I'd never heard Jason sound that way. Authoritative and cold. Not soft and sweet like he was with me. No. This Jason was downright *icy*.

I…was embarrassed to admit my dick outright twitched.

"Jason Harker," the man said, eyes widening. "He's *yours*? I didn't know."

"He's mine," Jason agreed. He stepped in front of me, crossing his arms. "Which I know you know. You've been eyeing us all night." He had? "And Joe is clearly holding two champagne flutes. What did you think you were doing here? Hitting on my date?" He laughed without humor, and again, my dick twitched.

"He's mine" kept replaying on repeat in my head.

It was…god.

No one had ever claimed me before.

Seeing this hard edge to Jason was really just…wow. I licked my lips, suddenly grateful that we were about done with the party for the night. I wasn't sure how much longer I could take this without begging him to shove his tongue down my throat and embarrassing the both of us.

"You know what they call that?"

"I…" the guy stumbled.

"*Tacky*, Maurice." Jason's words were like a whip crack. I stared at the back of his head, at the slightly thinner fluff on top, still perfectly styled. At the mole on the back of his neck. I nearly spilled the flutes again, he was so overwhelmingly hot.

"*Tacky*?" Maurice echoed, looking so offended you'd think Jason just told him he'd eaten the last slice of pumpkin pie on Thanksgiving. "You—"

"Good*bye*, Maurice." Jason cut off his spluttering, turning around to face me. His nostrils flared, lips pressed into a thin line. His eyes were dark, possessive. I'd never seen him so…so…

I shivered.

The ice in Jason's eyes melted away as he studied me.

Maurice left, dismissed with no small amount of shame.

"You okay?" Jason asked tenderly. "I'm sorry he bothered you. Maurice is a major pain in the ass. He used to do that to Mary, too."

"Did you tell him she was yours, too?" I asked, a roaring in my ears that I could barely hear through. Jason blinked. For a moment, he didn't speak. His eyes searched mine. One of his hands came up, maneuvering around the champagne flutes so he wouldn't knock one free as he cupped my cheek.

"No." He said that simply, but god, that word carried a weight I couldn't name.

"So, I'm the…the…"

"The only person I've ever been possessive over? Yes." Jason's thumb slipped down to stroke my lower lip. "Does that bother you? I can turn it off—"

"No." I shook my head. "I want to be yours."

Jason groaned. His thumb pulled my lip down, releasing it with a thwap. "Keep talking like that, and I'm not going to take you dancing before we head upstairs."

"Do we have to dance?" I asked. "I don't…I don't know how. Maybe upstairs is better—"

"You don't know how to dance?" Jason looked surprised. "What about homecoming? I thought you said you went."

"Yeah, but I didn't dance." I squirmed at the reminder.

"Do you want to learn?" Suddenly, Jason looked eager. I nodded. "Buckle up, buttercup. You're in for a treat."

Forty minutes later, Jason and I were spinning around the dance floor. It'd taken me a while to get the feet right. I'd stomped on his a few times, but I'd always been a fast learner. Jason was patient, too. He knew just how to talk, slow and sweet, demonstrating with his body and his words so I could follow his lead.

The crowd thinned as the night wore on so we had more room to move. The donation pool had already been announced, and Mrs. Harker was gone. So this…this was just for us.

Leisurely spinning around the dance floor.

In front of everyone.

Staring at the way the spiky locks of gray-brown hair on Jason's head were escaping their gel as he sweated. It was a reminder. A reminder of the man I'd fallen for back in Belleville. The same man who was holding me here, surrounded by opulence, but rejecting it because it'd been a cage rather than a home.

"That's it, Joe-by," Jason murmured as we swung round and round and round. "You're a natural, baby. Good with your hands and your feet, huh, sweetheart?"

I ducked my head, pleased.

"Sweet thing," Jason purred. "Look at that flush. You like that? That I know how clever and good you are? That I'm proud of you?"

My insides squirmed.

"I'm going to spin you now. Ready?"

"Ready." The spins were my favorite part. Jason didn't know how to do anything but lead. And even though I felt kinda silly because I was…way bigger than he was—and we were both dudes—and he was throwing me around like I was a chick at prom, I loved it.

I *loved* it.

The only other time I'd been to a dance had been homecoming. We'd sat on the bleachers the whole time because I hadn't known how to dance and she hadn't really wanted to be there in the first place. When she kissed me, I'd been so full of spiked punch I'd thrown up.

This wasn't anything like that.

Wasn't awkward or weird or uncomfortable.

It was fun.

Jason spun me in circles. I grinned when we came back together. He was breathless. Sweat at his temples. So goddamn handsome. His eyes. His crows feet. The little lines that were permanently etched into his cheeks from all his smiling.

Just looking at him made me melt.

"Again?" I requested.

Jason laughed. His head fell back, throat bared, laughter escaping. "Again?" he said, when he'd gotten ahold of himself. "Anything you want." He spun me out a second time. Then back in. Then out again. Over and over as giggles escaped me.

I tried not to be loud.

But the harder I laughed, the brighter Jason smiled.

Spinning me so much I got dizzy from it. When we came back together, I let him hold some of my weight, head swimming.

"You're precious," Jason said, swaying us back and forth, his arms looping around my waist. "You know that? So goddamn precious, Joe."

I could hardly get a full breath in. My cheeks hurt from smiling. "So are you," I echoed. I recalled the way he'd danced horribly with Marybeth and couldn't help but wonder if he'd been pretending to be awful, just to make her laugh.

Probably.

Always looking out for everyone else.

"Lovable," Jason replied. "That's what you called me the other day."

"Cause you are," I flushed. "Really…really lovable."

His eyes looked wet all of a sudden, this sheen to them that made me worry he was about to cry. "You mean that," he said softly. "I can tell."

"'Course I mean it." I frowned, confused. Jason hugged me tighter.

"You said you would've been my friend if we were kids," he added. There was something fragile in his eyes now. Brittle as paper-thin glass. "After seeing this…is that still true? Would you have been my friend, Joe?" He was careful with his words. Careful to look for reassurance.

Testing me, the way I'd thought he was.

"Yes," I said with no hesitation.

Jason made a sound like he'd been shot. He dropped his head down, hiding it in my chest. Hiding from me. And I let him. Because…I loved him too much to force him to perform. And for some reason, he was bound and determined to keep his vulnerability from me.

He squeezed me, our feet stilling. Around us, the dregs of the rest of the couples kept spinning, but we held still.

Still.

Still as that day I'd held the magpie.

Still as the day I'd seen the deer in my yard.

Still as nature, and time, and all the things that kept going long after we were gone.

Jason held me for a long time. So tight I worried my bones might crack. I didn't complain. Just buried my head in his hair and let him have what he needed. When one of his hands slid down to grope my ass, I knew he was feeling better.

His head tipped back, a smile on his lips.

Pushing my ass back into his hand, I studied him, heart skipping a beat.

Like magic, we were on the same page.

"Can we go back now?" I asked, voice husky.

"We can."

Jason and I didn't pretend to be anything but eager as we practically sprinted out of the ballroom, our hands laced together as we raced through the lodge, dodging opening doors and lingering people chatting in the hallways. It felt like we shared a smile then. A heartbeat. Every breath.

On the elevator ride up, we kept beaming at each other, fingers interlocked, suits askew.

Then down the hallway we went again, sprinting to get the keycard out. Falling through the doorway with a flurry of laughter. We kissed all the way to the bed. Jason's hands yanked my shirt out of the hem of my pants, and I went for the buttons on his shirt.

Laughter was scattered between kisses as we fought to get each other undressed, leaving a discarded pile of fabric-wealth on the floor.

Being bare with Jason was a religious experience.

He climbed on top of me, all that warm, delicious skin pressed to mine. My hands didn't know where to touch first. The fur between his pecs? As peppered gray as his scruff. The slight squish at his hips. Between his legs…where his cock stood proud in a nest of brown-gray curls.

He was pretty lean for a dude who ate donuts daily and didn't exercise.

Though…I supposed some of the errands he ran helping other people— playing Santa—were pretty physical.

"Why'd you go straight for my stomach?" Jason laughed, batting at my hands with one of his, obviously a little insecure. "Jesus—"

"I like it." I ran my fingers over it, sighing happily. "So much."

"Oh." Jason's eyebrows shot up as he leaned over me, watching my expression. "You never cease to amaze me." He ceased trying to get me to stop touching him then. His hands went back to bracketing my head as he kissed me, long and slow.

The kind of kiss that made my toes curl.

Made my head swim.

Spinning, the way it'd spun on the dance floor.

Only it wasn't a lack of equilibrium that made me feel like I was dancing. It was Jason. Jason…who made my world feel lively and safe. Jason who was teaching me what it meant to build a home, a family, out of nothing.

I wanted to tell him how I felt about him.

I did.

I'd hinted at it.

Toed the line.

But…I had a feeling showing him, still, was the better plan. Words he could pass off as empty. But if I…if I gave him everything I had. If I let myself be his, the way he'd said I was, maybe then he'd see.

Nothing about how I felt was empty.

"Where are the condoms and lube?" Jason rasped, kisses sliding along my jaw to my ear. His breath tickled, made my cock perk up, poking right at him. He was panting. Cock bobbing. "I need to be inside you."

It was the first time he'd told me he needed something sex-related.

I couldn't help but feel elated.

"Front pocket in my duffel bag," I gasped.

"Alright." Jason gave the shell of my ear a pointed lick, and I groaned. He sucked on the lobe, worrying it with his teeth a moment later, probably feeling the way it made me shake. My dick was so hard it fucking hurt.

Leaking.

My hips kept pushing up, trying to hump whatever part of him I could reach. Fuck, I really was his puppy.

Jason released my ear with a breathy growl. "I'll be right back," he promised. He was off of me a moment later, walking butt-naked across the room and crouching over my bag. It should've been funny to see him like that. Bare. When I'd never seen him anything but fully clothed.

But it didn't.

It felt intimate.

Jason was trusting me.

Giving me more pieces of himself.

Pieces he kept closely guarded.

I knew what a gift that was.

When he returned, he was grinning. Strutting across the room—prowling? Like a predator.

"Up the bed," Jason murmured. "Spread your legs." I shuffled back to give him room, sliding till my head nearly hung off the other end. Jason grabbed one of my ankles before I could spread, and forced my legs open on his own. "Let me get a pillow under you."

The moment a pillow was beneath my hips, he climbed between my legs again. I felt exposed in more ways than one. I was sure my adoration was written all over my face. I couldn't hide it, even if I wanted to.

"God, you're a vision," Jason said, kissing the inside of my knee as his other hand pulled the cap on the lube open. "You really are," he added. "Prettiest fucking thing in the world."

I couldn't hide from him, not when he was looking at me like that—even if I was embarrassed to be so thoroughly complimented.

That fuzzy feeling was back. Fizzing through my limbs, making me feel relaxed and easy. Ready to do and be whatever Jason wanted. It was freeing, this level of trust. To just…allow myself to be.

"You said you've been practicing," Jason said conversationally against the inside of my knee as he warmed the slick between his fingers. "Did you do any stretching today?"

"Yes." My face felt so hot it might as well have been on fire.

"Fuck." Jason's hips flexed a little, his hard cock pointing right at me. "That is so goddamn sexy." His dick was just as flushed as mine was.

When I glanced at it, hunger filled me so viscerally I nearly choked on it. I wanted that inside me so badly. So fucking badly.

It was a weird feeling.

Not one I'd thought I'd have.

And yet…nothing had ever felt more right.

Jason rubbed his fingers around my hole for a minute, relaxing the muscle. "Relax." He kissed my knee again. "And bear down when I start to push, okay?" I nodded, nostrils flaring as I tried to get in a few, solid breaths. He looked gorgeous above me. His hair was spiky. Somewhere between our dancing and the sprint through the lodge, it'd gone back to its usual mess.

I loved it so much.

Loved everything about him.

Loved *him*.

"First one," Jason warned. "You ready?"

I nodded, heart pounding. The first push was as uncomfortable as always. I bore down as instructed, sucking in a breath and trying to relax—though I wasn't sure I succeeded. I was anxious to get more of him inside me as quickly as possible.

I wanted to get this right.

To be good for him.

Jason only got the tip of his finger in before I tensed up again.

"Hey," Jason said, kissing my inner knee again. He rubbed his cheek against the skin. "Joe."

I blinked, confused by the conversational tone he'd just taken. My gaze moved from his forearm, from the veins that danced up it, from the coating of soft hair.

"W-what?"

"I'm inside you," Jason said. "Did you know that?"

It was such a ridiculous thing to say that I laughed. I couldn't help it. My hole squeezed around his finger as I did, then relaxed, and suddenly—just like that—it slid all the way in.

"There we go," Jason purred, nipping my knee before beaming at me. "That wasn't so hard, now was it?" He flexed his hips forward. "Not hard like I am, anyway."

"That joke's not even close to as good," I snorted, but I felt myself relaxing again despite this. No longer clamped like a vice around him, he was able to move, wiggling his finger a little before he pulled it out and pushed it back in.

"Got you to laugh again, didn't I?" Jason purred. "So it had to be at least a *little* funny."

I shook my head, but found myself smiling again.

"You doing okay?" he asked, checking in. Now that I knew it was as much for him as it was for me, it felt easier to answer. I was simply completing my half of an important mission.

"Yeah." I shifted my hips a little, breathing through the in-and-out of his pointer finger. "Just…want to be good for you."

"Is that why you're so tense?" Jason asked, blue eyes full of understanding. "Because you're trying to be good?"

I nodded sharply.

"Oh, Joe," Jason said. Those two words were laced with so much affection I melted.

His eyes said, *there isn't a universe where you're anything but good.*

"There isn't a universe where you're anything but good," Jason echoed. Proving once again how expressive his face was. Even more than that—it proved how well I'd gotten to know him. Just like he'd gotten to know me.

A mutual sort of understanding.

The sort of understanding I'd only ever felt with animals. When I looked in their eyes, and they looked in mine, and we just…knew.

Bone deep.

That neither of us was ever going to hurt the other.

I hadn't known I could feel that way about a person. Hadn't known it was possible to adore someone so much they superseded all my insecurities, my faults, my flaws. That they could change me. Help me grow.

Fertilize me.

In more than one way.

A muffled sound escaped me. Half-whine, half-laugh. Jason beamed. "You're safe," he said softly. "You know that right? That there isn't a single thing you could say or do that would make me want you less."

"I know," I replied. And I did know.

Somehow I did.

"There's no failing at this," Jason reassured. "Not with me."

Jason's expression was downright adoring. Then, like the shit he was, he pulled his finger out. I mourned its loss. But then two replaced one, rubbing at my hole, asking for permission to let them in.

So I did.

This time, when I bore down, it was with purpose. And I didn't tense up after. His fingers slid in, easy as butter. Going far deeper than my own had ever really managed. My head fell back, a gasp escaping as Jason spread his fingers a little, testing my walls, before pulling out and pushing right back in before my hole could close.

"It's the same," I managed somehow, despite the fact my hole was burning in the most…pleasant, wonderful way possible. "It's the same for me."

"What is?"

"You can't fail," I whispered, shifting my hips and pushing back against him, begging for more.

"Thank you, baby." Jason's fingers picked up the pace. A steady push pull that made my head fill with cotton. My mouth was dry as I melted into it, letting him stretch me. Letting him prep me. Because soon…soon it would be his cock in place of his fingers.

Jason's cock.

Inside me.

Because he needed me.

Just as badly as I needed him.

"Bear with me," Jason said. His tongue poked out of the corner of his mouth as he focused on what he was doing. "I'm trying to find…" his fingers curled, wiggling around for a moment before they—oh fuck. My legs jerked, a little howl escaping. "Oh, there we go."

"Ohmyfuck," the words were out before I could stop them.

"Oh my fuck is right, huh, baby?" Jason tapped my prostate again, and I whined. It was impossible to bite back the sounds. Impossible not to shove back against his hand, begging for more. "That feel good?"

I nodded. Didn't overthink it. Just tried to get more—more of that.

"God, this is gonna be fun." Jason gave it a pointed rub, memorizing where it was, and I…well…I made noises like I was dying. Stars danced in my head. An explosion of pleasure making me feel stupid because of it.

In and out now, Jason added a third finger. I barely noticed, despite the burn. Because now on every thrust in, he gave my prostate a deliberate rub, and I just… God. There was no stopping the way I thrashed and kicked.

Fingers bunching in the comforter, hips fucking back against his hand.

"So fucking slutty," Jason purred. "You love being fucked, don't you? I worried, you know, that you wouldn't. I shouldn't have." Jason fucked his hand forward again, and I howled. My eyes were open but I wasn't seeing anything. Every ounce of my attention was on his fingers—and when they'd next touch where I needed him most.

"Of course you like to be fucked," Jason continued, pulling his fingers out slow and mean before jabbing them back in. I thrashed. "You're made for this."

I didn't know how long he was going to torture me.

Truthfully, I didn't care.

My dick had already made a puddle on my belly. Thin liquid, sticky and rub-rubbing every time my cock bumped into it. I was drooling too, somehow. Defying fucking gravity. And I knew I looked stupid as hell, mouth open, seeing nothing—my dick just fucking bouncing with every slap of Jason's wrist.

But I didn't care.

I just wanted more.

"M-more," I whimpered. "Please. Please. Want it. Want you. Need— need—" The words spilled free and they just kept coming. "Need fucked. Need it. Need your dick. Jason, please." He growled. His fingers pulled out with a slick, naughty sound.

"Fuckfuck," he hissed. Dazed, I glanced down. He was strangling the base of his cock. It took me a second to figure out why. Figure out that me begging him had nearly sent him over the edge. "Fuck." His dick was practically purple, it was so engorged. Angry, needy.

Just like mine.

I bunched my fingers behind my knee, pulling my leg up. "Please," I begged, hole winking pink and slick and open, probably. It wouldn't close. Even when I clenched. Loose and glistening with the lube he'd fucked inside me. "Please."

"Fuck." Jason groaned, eyes on my hole. Staring at it like it was nirvana. He squeezed his dick tighter, so hard his knuckles went white. "Now who's the bully?" He laughed.

"Not a bully," I shook my head.

He softened.

"You're right. You're not a bully." Jason licked his lips, gaze dragging over my body. It didn't feel the way it had when Maurice had ogled me earlier. This made me feel good. Gorgeous. Something worth looking at. "You're my sweet, sweet puppy."

He reached for the condom, releasing his dick.

I sighed, excited because I knew what that meant.

Knew I'd be getting what I wanted soon enough.

Jason bit through the wrapper with a clumsy movement. He rolled the condom down his cock, wasting no time. Not lingering. Not even when he smeared a liberal amount of lube all over it. And then he was pushing forward, pressing the crown of his dick against my hole.

"You want this?" he murmured. "You want—"

"Want you," I said. "Need you. *Need you, Jason.*"

"That's not fair," Jason whispered. "Goddamn." And then he was pushing forward. Slow and easy. Inch by inch. I didn't need to be told to bear down. Did what I was supposed to, eager to feel him, split wide—so wide I couldn't breathe.

Full of him.

Getting fuller.

I was burning from the inside out. On fire. All of my sinapses bursting at the thought that Jason was finally, blissfully inside me. That he was making room for himself in my body the same way he'd made room for himself in my life. Fucking me open. Something primal, yet human all the same.

With every inch that pushed inside me, I grew more eager. Thrashing a little, shoving my hips against him, trying to take more. Trying to feel that burn longer. To feel him, as close as two people could get.

It felt so good. So fucking good. My inner walls clinging to him, sucking around his dick. I was dazed and panting, wild, as I grit my teeth and stared up at him with raw need.

"I'll give you what you want," Jason husked out, as affected as I was. His face was flushed, his chest heaving, too. Like it took everything he had to be as still, as patient as always. His eyes were hungry, black pools. Staring down at me like he wanted to eat me. Like he was two seconds from pushing my legs up to my ears and pounding me like I wanted. I kept pushing back, little swivels, and Jason groaned. His lips twitched into a pleased little smirk. "Tell me how it feels," he demanded when he was halfway inside.

"So…so…" I growled, hole clenching down as I tried to force him deeper. Jason pulled back a little, just to spite me. "So full. So big." My lashes fluttered. He only kept pushing when I'd stopped trying to force him. "Good." "Yeah?" Jason pressed forward another half inch. "You love your little cunt getting split open, huh? God, yes. You're shaking, Joe. Did you know that? You like being fucked so much you're *shaking*." There was something akin to wonder in his voice. "I like you," I replied. "Like… like that it's…that it's…yours. Your…cock…in me." He made a sound at that, hips pressing forward more insistently now. Those words had broken through the last of his resolve. And apparently, it'd only been hanging by a thread. He was still careful though, if eager. But there was no more pausing, no more taunting. No more questions.

Just Jason rearranging me from the inside out as my hole pulsed around him, and his cock split me open.

It took a century before he'd settled, hips flush with mine. His dick twitched inside me. I squeezed it in answer, and Jason growled. He flexed forward, trying to fuck deeper even though it wasn't physically possible.

"You're Heaven," Jason told me, hands bracketing my head again. "You know that? You're my Heaven, Joe." His forehead was pressed to mine, our breath mingling. I kissed him. Kissed him because I didn't know what to say to that. It was poetry. And I'd never been good with words.

Jason kissed me back.

Poured everything he had into the brush of our lips, licking into my mouth, giving me something to suck on as he began to move. Cautious wiggles at first, letting me get used to the sensation. Until I relaxed again. My legs tangled around his body, pulling him in close. Jason enjoyed that, if the muffled moan against my lips was any indicator.

He varied the rhythm.

Building confidence.

Sometimes faster, then slow. Driving me crazy. Bringing me to the brink before tearing it away. One of his hands slid to my throat, cupping it as he pounded into me. He was grunting into my mouth, these needy little sounds that reminded me of a dog in heat.

It was primal and delicious.

Human in others.

Because the look in Jason's eyes was anything but simple. It was months of feelings, of need. Years of longing for this. For this feeling of being seen. Understood. And wanted.

"That's it," Jason murmured against my lips when I got close again. "That's it, baby. Give me it. I wanna feel you come on my dick." He slammed into me, his cock stretching me wide. He was so big he was pushing into my guts. My hole was so wet the sounds it made every time he thrust deep were obscene. Wet and messy.

He was slow now.

Syrupy.

Pulling out and guiding himself back in. Savoring the way my head fell back, my throat bobbing beneath his hand. Stars burst behind my lids as his fat cock head struck my prostate, rub, rubbing against it.

"So good," I gasped. "Just a little—"

"Anything for you," Jason promised, kissing me again. He pulled out, then rutted right back in. Another sticky slap. My hole clenched, and he groaned. More fireworks exploded.

My mouth parted, my panting growing louder. I really was shaking. I was losing my goddamn mind, I wanted him so bad.

"Just a…little. Just—faster. I need—Jason, Jason—"

Another pull and push. More stars. Apparently, I hadn't actually needed him to go faster, because I came before I could even recognize what was happening. After one, deliberate grind-thrust. I spilled between us with a sob that Jason tasted with gusto. His hips flexed, riding me through the orgasm at that same, controlled pace.

How he had that much self-control, I had no idea. If it'd been up to me, I'd be fucking bouncing on his dick.

When I'd come down from my high, still dazed, but more myself, I shoved my ass back against him pointedly, urging him to continue. "C'mon," I groaned. "Fuck me like you mean it."

"You sure?" he asked against my lips.

"Yes."

"Alright."

Jason didn't need any more encouragement. With a brutal snap of his hips that made me fucking howl, he pounded into me with the energy of an animal. There was something *greedy* about the way he fucked me then. Riding my ass with brutal smacks of our hips. Snapping into me over and over, making me whine and shake as he chased his orgasm.

As he took me the way he wanted to.

He was gorgeous above me. Sweat dripping down his forehead, his eyes wild. His mouth posed in a snarl as he used his grip on my knee to spread me till it burned. The wet squelch of his cock smacking my ass was obscene. I stretched wider, shaking anew, whimpering when Jason's eyes drank in the expression on my face, then down my body, eyes settling on where his cock speared the hot-pink of my hole.

"Goddamn," he hissed through his teeth. "Look at you take it." He snapped again, and I sobbed. "Can't believe that tiny hole can fit me. Can take a fucking like this. And you…you love it, don't you?" His eyes were back on my face now, memorizing me, black with lust and the need to have me under him where I belonged.

"L-love it," I gasped.

When he came, he bit my lip, growling into my mouth and rutting till every last drop filled the condom he wore. Then he just sort of…collapsed onto me. Didn't pull out. Let me throb and clench around him as my useless hands released the comforter and came up to stroke through his sweaty, half-gelled hair.

Jason kissed me again.

Slow and sweet.

And I melted beneath him, full in a way I'd never been full before.

More sure than ever that Jason was the home I'd been searching for.

twenty-eight

JASON

THE WEEK FOLLOWING THE GALA was the best of my life. Joe showed up for me every day. He brought me coffee in the mornings, and after work, he'd pull up to my house in his faded blue pickup truck to help me with some of the tasks on my list. He kept giving me these hungry looks, eyes catching between my legs. I swear to god, I'd never strutted so goddamn much in my life, knowing Joe was thinking about me and my dick and what it felt like to sit on it.

He never got tired of me, and I? Well, I never got tired of him.

It was the little things, too. The kinds of things that matter most of all. The way he'd text me a picture of his work. The empty storage room, all the apples from the harvest sold. A cardinal in a tree in his yard. A warning that he'd be busy Friday and Saturday, picking his family up from the airport—then showing them around town.

A promise to try and pick up when I called.

That he'd see me soon.

He kept me in his life in every way he could.

Made me feel…made me feel… God.

So many things.

Normally I'd be in a dark pit around this time of year, with Christmas Eve the next day. Dreading loneliness. Mary always invited me over, but I always refused. It felt like…crossing a line somehow. Not for her, but for me. Thanksgiving was one thing, but Christmas?

Which was why I always went out with her the day before.

But this year…this year I was all smiles—even if Joe's promise of "soon" wouldn't be till after Christmas was over, no doubt. I'd be alone this year, just like I was every year. No family, and nothing to do, and yet I couldn't bring myself to be sad like usual. (Okay, yes, I was still sad, but not drown-myself-in-boxed-wine sad.)

I had his memory to keep me company.

I'd never forget the way Joe had opened up to me the night of the gala. Those dark eyes on mine, his body parting to let me deeper than anyone had ever gone. Nowadays, I hardly ever stopped smiling. And that was… terrifying.

"You know what I think?" Mary said, over coffee and pastries. She was in full-on winter gear now to combat the chill. We'd opted to eat inside, a flurry of snow spinning outside the window.

"What?" I'd just finished explaining—probably badly—the last few weeks to her. How they made me feel. How Joe made me feel. How confused and uneasy I was because I was just waiting for the other shoe to drop.

"I think you've spent so long pretending to be happy, you don't recognize when you actually are." Mary took a sip of her coffee like she hadn't just dropped a fucking bomb on my head.

"W-what?" My head spun. Visions of Joe and all the ways he made my life better swam to the surface. His smile. His laughter. The way he'd wanted to be spun, and spun, and spun when we danced. The ease in which he'd taught me how to fix things at his house. Sitting by him as we both stared up at the Christmas tree. His gentle hands. Magpies. Deer. Puppies.

"You let him in a little," Mary said. "I'm proud of you."

"I…" I closed my eyes, trying to breathe. "Why? Why…could I do that for him, and I couldn't for you?" It was the last piece of the puzzle. The missing slot.

"Because I'm not your person," Mary said simply. "He is. So, now it's time to stop performing, don't you think?" Her eyes crinkled, so full of affection it made me breathless. "It's time to stop expecting the worst and just…"

"Just…"

"Accept that you're happy."

Mary's words stalked me. They were a noose around my neck as I finished the last of my Christmas tasks and headed home. My house was full. A Christmas tree. Garlands up the railings. A plate full of cookies on the table that Joe had dropped off—from god knows where, considering the fact I knew he didn't cook. His touch was everywhere. The Christmas he'd told me he'd give me glaring at me from every nook and cranny in the room.

The gingerbread houses we'd made sat on the coffee table beside the letters I'd finally completed for the Santa Fund program.

I sat on the couch.

Sat there for hours.

Processing what Mary had said.

Trying to…understand it.

What being *happy* might mean for me. Real happiness. What—and who—I might be if I stopped pretending.

It was dark before I finally had my epiphany. Finally realized that Mary was right. Somewhere along the way I'd gotten so caught up in my own lies I'd stopped being able to recognize what was right in front of my face.

I didn't have to figure out what being happy was like.

Because I already knew.

And that…god.

The moment I realized that—for the first time in my life—I could breathe.

There was still the weight of my secrets there. But…Joe had taught me not to expect the worst when it came to him. I could tell him about the Santa Fund. He'd taken my money in stride. Accepted me, for who I was, not who he wished I was.

But could he really forgive me for this big of a lie?

Could I be what he needed?

I'd once thought that what *Joe* needed, what *Joe* wanted, were the only things that were important to me. Not my own feelings, or my own desires. But as I sat there, forced to confront my own feelings I realized how unfair that'd been to him. If I wanted to be a real part of his life I needed to start being an active participant.

It was time.

Time to put everything on the line and do what Mary had told me to do. I think, deep down, I'd known this was the end of my mirage, too.

It'd just taken hearing it out loud from someone I loved for it to truly hit.

I should've felt anxious.

Should've felt like running.

But for once, the idea of telling the truth—of being vulnerable—didn't feel scary.

Life was about choices, and I was choosing to come clean.

What I lacked was opportunity.

It was hard to get a hold of Joe—even if I hadn't been wary of interrupting his time with his family—for the first time since we'd started this. Every time he picked up the phone, he was breathless, his family's voices on the other end of the line. The chatter of people was so loud it was hard to hear him.

On Christmas Eve, I called, that ache between my ribs impossible to ignore.

"Sorry," he said. "Mom's been hovering so much it's been hard to call—"

"Is that your boyfriend?!" a loud, feminine voice sounded. "Put him on the line."

"Ma, no." There was the sound of a scuffle.

I couldn't believe that Joe was telling people I was his boyfriend. That's what that meant, didn't it? That he was telling his family about us.

"I understand that you're the reason Joe has a bath mat," the feminine voice said. Joe's mom, I imagined. I sat up a little taller, even though she couldn't see me. "And curtains." Her voice was dancing with mirth. "And a real bed."

"Yes ma'am."

"Thank god." She laughed. "Good work."

"Ah. Thank you."

"Give me my phone back," Joe sounded grouchier than I'd ever heard him.

"No. I'm talking to Jason. Don't be rude."

"You're the one who stole my phone!"

I covered my mouth so they wouldn't hear me laughing. I...was beginning to understand what Joe meant about his Christmases being loud. I ached. Dreading the silence that would greet me as soon as the line went dead.

The echo of Joe's presence in my house helped but...I just...I wanted him.

Didn't want to spend another Christmas alone.

Hadn't realized how badly I'd miss him, until he was gone.

I had all these feelings...all these things I wanted to say.

And I couldn't.

I didn't want to ruin this time Joe had with his mom after all he'd done to make it run smoothly.

"Joe tells me you're a silver fox," Mrs. Milton said. It was a gentle poke. A way of acknowledging that she knew about our age gap and was fine with it. I sagged, breathing a sigh of relief. That had been certainly weighing on me. As much as Mary had said it was normal, I'd still...well.

"Unfortunately."

"If you ever want to dye the grays you just let me know. I've got a salon back home and I can—"

"No!" Joe outright yelled. "Don't you *dare* touch his hair."

"I was just—"

"Mom!"

The line went quiet.

A few seconds later, it rang again. When I picked up, I assumed I'd be hearing Joe's voice. Assumed he'd have won the battle with his mom.

But it wasn't Joe on the other end of the line.

"Hi," an unfamiliar voice said. "Jason, right?"

"Uh…yes." I felt like an idiot, talking to Joe's family while sitting alone at my dining room table. "Who is this?"

"This is Alex."

"Oh." Alex. Joe's brother George's husband.

"They're still fighting. Just figured I'd let you know that your boy's probably going to lose. Nobody wins against Mama Milton." Alex's voice was as full of mirth as Mrs. Milton's had been.

"Thanks for the heads up."

"No problem. Us Milton-lovers gotta stick together, right?"

"Right."

"When you come for dinner, bring wine," Alex instructed. He had a nice voice, melodic and easy to listen to. "That'll get you on Mama Milton's good side. If you have weed, bring that too—Mr. Milton likes to smoke for his back. At least, that's what he says. We all know he just likes getting high with his wife and eating snacks. Packaged cookies are the best. Don't wear white. Dark colors help when Joe's been drinking— he has a tendency to spill." I'd noticed that. "George will judge you if you match brown with black, so don't. If you're offered something, eat it. Doesn't matter what it is. I'm guessing you want to make a good first impression?"

I hadn't known I was coming for dinner.

So I was…

Confused.

"Yes," I said immediately.

"George is like a bloodhound. He'll sniff out what kind of cologne you have. So wear something fancy. Lacey's even worse."

"Lacey?"

"Joe's older sister. She's judgier than anyone else. Has a soft spot for her daughter, though, so if you're good with kids you've got an in there."

"Why are you telling me all of this?" I asked, flabbergasted.

"I told you," Alex's laugh was warm. "We gotta stick together. I gotta go. But just remember what I told you, and you'll be fine."

The line went quiet for a second time.

I stared at it, heart pounding.

Joe was going to invite me to Christmas Eve dinner with his family?

It felt too good to be true. But...I tried not to question it. Leaping into action, I ran around my house getting ready. I heeded all of Alex's advice—hoping that he had good intentions, and hadn't been messing with me.

When I was dressed in a black sweater and jeans, I waited impatiently for my phone to ring.

Like he'd sensed I was ready, Joe called me right then.

The phone buzzed, and I snatched it up, answering it on the first ring.

"Hey, baby."

"Good evening, Jason." Yet another unfamiliar voice spoke. This one was deeper than Alex's, and clipped. "This is George."

Oh.

"Hi, George! It's nice to meet you. Joe's spoken highly of you—"

"Likewise. And I'm sure he has. I'm calling because Joe would like to formally invite you to spend Christmas Eve with us, but as he is currently occupied—he's tasked *me* with calling you." No doubt, Joe was incredibly busy if he hadn't been the one to ask.

"Thank you," I said, nervous. "When do I—"

"Right now."

"Oh." Good thing Alex had warned me, Jesus. "I'll be over in fifteen."

"See you soon."

I stopped by Mary's house on the way to grab a bottle of fancy wine.

Fifteen minutes later, I was driving up Joe's driveway. It was the same as always. Surrounded by trees. Snow. Gravel crunching beneath the whirr of my wheels. And yet…everything felt different. *I* felt different. I was ready to put everything I had on the table. That was…freeing.

When I parked next to his truck, I noticed several rental cars beside it. Two of them were garishly expensive. No doubt Alex's and Juniper's, if they were both here.

It was dark out.

The sky was clear, so the stars were drenching the sky with pinpricks of light. I paused, breath fogging out in front of me, head tipped back to drink them in as I prepared myself to turn on the charm. My wine bottle was tucked under my arm, and I was…nervous.

I'd already sweated through the t-shirt I had beneath my sweater.

I wanted to make a good impression.

And then…when Joe and I had a minute—when there was some quiet.

Maybe not tonight.

But later.

I'd tell him how I felt.

Tell him the truth.

The front door opened before I could step foot on the rickety front stairs. Golden light spilled across the wood, creeping down each step until it reached me. I felt better immediately. Laughter and voices echoed through the night, filling the quiet with noise.

The kind of noise I'd always craved during Christmas.

The man in the doorway was…George, I guessed.

Because he looked like an alternate universe of Joe. If he was a twink. And wore suits. He stared at me, hand on the door, brow arched as he waited for me to climb up the steps. Once on the landing, I paused, letting his gaze flicker over me.

He nodded once, with approval, probably noting the lack of black and brown. Or maybe it was because he smelled my cologne. I sent a silent thank you to Alex—wherever he was—as George stepped to the side to let me in.

"Joe's in the kitchen with Mom," he told me. "I'm George."

"Nice to meet you." I'd said that on the phone too, but I was pretty sure he'd been too distracted by what was going on around him to notice. When the door swung shut behind us he offered me his hand.

"The pleasure's mine." I took his hand and gave it a firm shake. "Joe told me you're the reason he's come out of his shell."

"He did?" I blinked. The family room was totally full of people. Half of them were blond. The same shade George and Joe shared. A tiny little girl was climbing all over the laps of the people on the couch that Joe had bought. She had a toy in her hands—a unicorn—wearing a Santa hat.

None of them had stopped playing whatever game was on the TV to acknowledge us.

Hovering behind George's shoulder was a tan, dark-haired man with pale blue eyes. He was as muscular as Joe was, though shorter. Alex, my mind supplied. Probably. He grinned and gave me a thumbs-up.

"He also told me that you're good to him," George said. "His friend. Respectful. Helpful. A bit pushy, but in the right ways."

"Yes." My cheeks felt hot.

This felt like a shovel talk. But it didn't sound like a shovel talk.

"I hope, for both our sakes, you keep that up."

Aaaand there it was.

I couldn't help but laugh a little. Which made Alex snicker. George twisted around to glare at him.

"You're not helping."

"Was I supposed to threaten him too?" Alex asked, eyes dancing with mischief.

"Well, no but—"

"Jason," Alex slung an arm over George's shoulder. He leaned on him, though his eyes were on me. "Hurt Joe and I'll kill you." He was joking. Right? I hoped.

"Ohmygod." George elbowed him. Hard.

"I didn't hear that!" a woman's voice called from the couch. Joe's sister, Lacey, probably.

"She's a lawyer," George supplied helpfully. "Likes to call herself an 'officer of the court.' Thinks it's her job to uphold justice."

"Because I am." Lacey flipped him off without turning around. "And I never said that."

"So, you're just nosy then."

"Oh fuck off."

The little girl sitting on Lacey's lap perked up. "Fuck off!" She cackled. The whole room collectively groaned.

It was warm.

So warm in here.

Yes, the temperature—because that was a shit ton of people to fit into a small place. I counted…at least seven. Yeah. Seven. And no Joe or Mrs. Milton in sight. But mostly the vibes. As much as they squabbled, I could tell everyone here loved each other.

And…they'd clearly been hard at work, if the way it looked like Christmas had thrown up all over Joe's house was an indicator.

A giant garish tree was in the corner, covered in ornaments that appeared decades old. I could only guess that Mrs. Milton had either brought them with her, or shipped them here in advance.

Lights had been tacked around the walls, casting the room in a jolly, colorful glow.

The fireplace was roaring.

And the beep-beep of a video game was echoing behind the chatter.

I had never been more glad in all my life to receive a Christmas invite.

Alex and George herded me around the room, introducing me to everyone. I kept my wine clutched close so I could give it to Mrs. Milton. Mr. Milton was a quiet man. Didn't offer me a single word, just a nod of his head and a handshake.

If he thought it was weird I was so much older than his son, he didn't show it.

Just scooted over to give me somewhere to sit, squished between him and his grandbaby.

Mavis, because the little girl's name was Mavis—took a liking to me immediately. She climbed onto my lap, showing me her unicorn and telling me all about the magical country it came from. She'd come up with a whole story behind it. A caste system. It was genuinely amazing.

"Luuuucky," Alex groaned. He leaned over the back of the couch. "She hates me."

Mavis stuck her tongue out at him, proving his point.

"One of these days, someone else is going to pop out a baby who loves me," he sighed wistfully. I followed where his eyes went, surprised to note they were on George. What? I was missing something, obviously.

"I can't get pregnant," George huffed. He was in the corner, organizing a stack of gifts by the person that they were dedicated to. Each stack had little name labels, all matching. I was surprised to note…there were a few for me.

More than a few.

At least six.

I'd never…

I didn't know what to do with that.

"We should keep trying, you know, just in case," Alex hummed. Mr. Milton didn't react. At all. He just continued to play his game, fingers fiddling with the controller.

"Motherfu-dger," Juniper, Alex's sister said from two cushions over. She was the one playing with Mr. Milton, and was clearly losing. Alex's smaller, more feminine counterpart was very obviously frustrated. She was wearing a dress that emulated wrapping paper more than fabric. "I swear he cheats."

"No," the whole room said. "He's just better than you."

This was clearly an argument that'd happened more than once.

Her husband was sitting on the ground between her legs.

Roderick.

Joe had told me about him. That he was the one who shared hiking pictures with him.

I liked him immediately. He was a very normal-looking guy. Warm eyes. Dark hair. Not scarily handsome the way Alex was—or pretty in the way every Milton seemed to be. He smiled at me, holding a cup of cocoa between his legs, careful not to spill.

I wanted to find Joe.

But…I didn't want to be rude.

"You want a turn?" Alex offered. "June's gonna start throwing hands if she keeps up this losing streak for any longer."

"I'm good," I promised.

And I was.

So good.

There wasn't space for sadness or loneliness in this room. Packed as it was, full of people. Sleeping bags lined the floor. A few air mattresses beside them. Making it clear that the family was staying here to be close to Joe, rather than at the B&B.

I was melting.

Sinking into a headspace that felt…comfortable.

"Do you want a cracker?" Mavis offered me a moment later. I remembered Alex's advice, so I said yes. She handed me a soggy, sweaty animal cracker. I smiled at her.

"Thank you."

When she wasn't looking, Alex offered me his hand. I gave him the cracker and he surreptitiously tossed it in the trash. After giving me another thumbs-up, he headed toward where George was sitting and plopped down behind him. Wrapped around him like a human-blanket as George fussed over the presents and their organization.

Apparently, Joe wasn't the only Milton who needed things to be done a certain way.

After a few more minutes of peace, relaxing into the chatter, content to listen and not participate—I figured it was time to go find Joe. It wasn't rude now. Peeling myself out of the puppy pile on the couch was difficult, but I managed.

My wine was tepid as I made my way toward the kitchen, following the sound of voices.

"Mom—"

"Finish frosting."

"But Jason's—"

"Your boyfriend can wait until you finish the frosting."

I'd never heard Joe be so petulant. It was so cute. Jesus. I paused in the doorway, taking in the scene, my heart squeezing. Tray after tray of cookies were covering half the counters. Most of them were already frosted, artfully—because Joe had been the one to do it.

The stove had several huge pots on top of it, including one that made the whole room smell like chocolate. Marshmallows were scattered on the counters, as was cocoa dust. Confusing my nose, the scent of roast turkey filled the air from inside the oven. There were mashed potatoes on the stove too, and Mrs. Milton was beating them into submission.

She was a small, round woman with even rounder hair. Her dress was covered in holly leaves and berries. Garish and gorgeous. There was an apron around her waist that I had no doubt she'd brought with her.

Joe—was in the corner, his back to me. There were a few icing smears on his back. Looked like they were left by tiny hands—probably Mavis. His white t-shirt hugged every curve of his body. Jeans practically painted on his ass, though loose by his legs.

Just looking at him made my knees weak.

It felt like it'd been a lifetime since the last time I'd seen him.

Touched him.

Mrs. Milton noticed me before Joe did.

"You must be Jason," she said in greeting. I turned to face her, though my eyes stayed on Joe. It was worth any accidental rudeness to see the way he snapped to attention. He spun around, the biggest, brightest grin on his face the moment he spotted me.

I nearly dropped the wine bottle, he was so pretty.

"Jason!" Joe said my name with obvious enthusiasm. "You're here!"

"I'm here," I said, my heart in my throat.

"Mom!" Joe set his icing bag down and skidded across the room on socked feet. He was in my space quicker than I could blink. High on excitement, Joe was like a giant puppy as he looped his arms around me, picked me off the ground, and gave me a shake. "This is him!"

"I can see that," she laughed.

My lungs wheezed and I fought for my life not to drop the wine as Joe squeezed the hell out of me. He set me back down, beaming at me. "I'm frosting cookies."

"I bet you're a pro," I said, remembering how good he'd been at making gingerbread houses.

"Hi." Joe kept smiling. His skin was flushed. I cocked my head to the side, amused and curious.

"Are you drunk?"

"What?" Joe blinked owlishly. "No!"

"He's had three cups of eggnog," Mrs. Milton laughed. "And yet…still the best froster I have."

"I love your eyes," Joe told me. "And your hair. My mom said she'd dye it. Don't dye it, Jason." Joe frowned. "Don't do it. Promise you won't? Promise you—"

"I won't let your mom dye it," I laughed.

Joe sagged, relieved. "Oh good. I love your hair. Did you know that?"

"I do now."

He was totally a happy drunk.

"Can I kiss you?" Joe's words caught me off guard, especially with his mom literally right there.

"Of course."

"Oh good."

Then he kissed me. Practically swept me off my feet again. Hands cupping my face, smearing frosting on my cheekbones and jaw. I didn't even care. Soaking him up. Tasting the eggnog and chocolate on his lips. It shouldn't have been a good combination but it was.

When we parted, Joe looked dazed.

He glanced down my body, hungry eyes catching between my legs.

"It's been too long," he sighed.

"Oh, believe me, I know," I replied.

"Should we…"

"Hell no." I kissed him again, just to soothe. "Not with your family five feet away." I kept my words quiet enough I hoped Mrs. Milton wouldn't hear. My efforts were in vain.

"They can go," Joe wheedled. "For just…twenty minutes. They can go."

"Disloyal," Mrs. Milton laughed. "You'd send us out into the snow just so you could get some nookie?"

Joe's face scrunched up with horror.

"I think she heard me," he told me.

"Yeah," I agreed. "I think she did."

He smiled. "Later?"

"Good plan."

He kissed me again, then pulled back. "You have frosting on your face."

"It's okay," I promised him.

"Oh good."

Jesus. He was so cute. I wanted to bite him.

"How good are you at icing?" Mrs. Milton asked. "He's gotten slower and I've still got twenty cookies that need done so we can get them out of the way."

"Oh, he's terrible," Joe said. I laughed.

"I'm terrible," I agreed. "But—willing?"

"I'll take it."

Christmas Eve dinner was just as chaotic as the lead up had been. There wasn't room for everyone in the kitchen so we all spread out. I ended up sitting in a corner, with Joe on my lap, munching through a giant plate full of turkey and mashed potatoes.

He was sobering up now.

Which was probably good.

I could tell because he kept squirming on my legs, like he was worried he was crushing me. He and George were having a conversation about Joe's website. Apparently George was a graphic designer and had offered to make one for him for free.

They squabbled over pricing.

But George ultimately won that particular fight.

I didn't want to be an ass for rooting against Joe, but…I was glad. Glad to see Joe accepting help now, without pushing back.

He'd changed.

Hell, so had I.

I was dreading going back home.

And as the night wound down, and I lost to Mr. Milton at *Mario Kart* three consecutive times, that dread only grew. It was nearly two in the morning before the adults decided it was time to retire. Mrs. Milton had drunk the entire bottle of wine I'd given her.

I stayed while they took turns brushing their teeth in the single bathroom.

Jesus. That many people sharing a bathroom?

Nightmare.

I lingered till after everyone had laid down in their respective spots. Joe was the last in the bathroom. I'd said goodnight to him already. Kissed his shoulders, his neck.

When I headed into the hallway, then the living room, I quietly stepped over the sleeping bags. I was heading for the door, when Joe's voice stopped me.

"Where are you going?" he asked, muffled around toothpaste.

I paused, then turned around.

"Home?" My heart skipped a beat.

"No, you're not," he said. The foamy tooth brush was still in his hand, some of that white fluff smudged around his lips. "Get your ass in the bathroom and brush your teeth."

He'd never talked to me like that.

It made me laugh.

But I did as I was told.

Joe had given his bed to his parents. Which meant that we were squashed onto the same air mattress we'd shared when we'd been snowed in. He turned his back to me. When I didn't snuggle up to him quick enough, he patted his own shoulder pointedly.

So, I settled against him, pressed my face to his nape, and breathed him in.

"I told you I'd give you the Christmas you deserve," Joe murmured sleepily when I was bundled around him like I was supposed to be.

He was out like a light a moment later.

But I stayed up long after.

Listening to the symphony of breaths that echoed through the room. Listening to the beat of his heart. Staring up at the play of lights on the ceiling. At the Christmas tree. At the family I'd somehow been invited inside.

When I fell asleep, it was with a smile on my lips.

And the certainty that I was in the right place.

I was happy.

twenty-nine

JOE

I'D BEEN HARD AT WORK the last week. Not just with my family but with my overall Christmas plans. I'd had this…idea in my head. A plan to show Jason that he didn't have to spend Christmas alone, ever again. Inviting him to spend the night with my family was only step one in my master plan.

All week, I'd been spreading the word.

Talking to every person on Jason's list that we'd helped, and asking them to assist me. It would take a village to pull together the kind of party I wanted to throw for Jason. I figured…there was no better way to spend Christmas than with family. A *Home Alone* style reunion.

And Belleville was his.

Talking to people had never been my strength. It was difficult. I stumbled over my words. Got things wrong, and had to fix it. But somehow, I managed. Struggling through my weaknesses because Jason was worth being uncomfortable.

Mary had been the biggest help.

When I'd told her my plan, she'd been downright ecstatic. Baxter and his husband, Paxton, had been a big help, too. Pulling together, grudgingly on Paxton's end, their network to spread the word.

And by the time Christmas morning rolled around, everything had fallen into place.

I woke up in Jason's arms. Surrounded by my favorite people in the world. Content and warm and—

Oh shit.

I needed to get ready.

He didn't want to let go of me. When I tried to get out of bed, he grumbled, squeezing me tight. So I succumbed to a few more minutes of cuddling, plans be damned. Eventually, Jason let me free. I climbed off the mattress, dodging bodies and heading into the kitchen to help Mom.

Breakfast would come first.

Then presents.

Then…

The *surprise*.

Jason had no idea what was in store for him.

The thought made me giddy.

Mom instructed me as to what she wanted me to do. As I whisked up Christmas pancakes, we murmured quietly back and forth. Not once had she shown disdain for my house, or made me feel small. In fact…the longer she stayed, the more I realized how unfair to her I'd been.

Demonizing her.

Because, at the end of the day, I had the kind of mom who baked cookies. The kind of mom who read my report cards. The kind of mom who loved me when I failed. The kind of mom who flew across the country so I wouldn't have to be alone.

"I love you," I told her, still whisking. My cheeks were hot.

"I love you, too." She looked surprised when I glanced up, but her smile was kind. "What brought that on?"

"I was just…I dunno. I'm just glad you're here."

Mom melted.

She reached up to pat my cheek, eyes crinkling at the corners. "You're my baby, of course I'm here."

"Not all moms are like that," I said. "Not all moms do what you do."

"No," she agreed. "And that's a damn shame."

My eyes burned a little. I nodded. She gave my cheek another pat before releasing it. "For the record," she added. "I'm proud of you."

"For my house?" My brow furrowed.

I'd worked so damn hard on it. Wanted nothing more than to prove to her that there was a reason she could be proud of me. To prove that I was capable.

"For your capability to love," Mom said. "Your big heart. Your softness. I used to worry a lot about you. Lonely as you seemed." I'd seemed…lonely? "Stressing yourself out, trying to impress me when you never needed to."

"W-what?"

"I may be hard on you sometimes, but I will never cease to be impressed by all that you've accomplished," Mom said.

I couldn't believe this.

That all along she'd been…she'd been thinking about me this way.

It struck me then, the reason I'd been able to offer Jason love that was unconditional. The reason I'd known it existed. My mom had been the one to teach me that. And I…suddenly I could see with clarity how silly, how immature I'd been.

How wrong.

To think she'd come here and judge me.

Mom was here because she loved me.

It wasn't a test.

It had never been a test.

I'd misjudged her the same way I'd misjudged Jason.

"You don't worry about me anymore?" I asked, my thoughts whirring from the realization.

"Of course I do." Mom gave me a look. "But…less now. You spread your wings. It was hard to see you go, but I'm glad you did. I'm glad you finally proved to yourself that you could." She cracked another egg into the giant bowl she was prepping for scrambled eggs. "Of all my kids, you're the most independent."

"I…am?"

That was news to me.

My heart fluttered.

"There's nothing you can't do," Mom said. "Just look at this…this place. This *home* you've made for yourself. The friends you've found. The world you've made your own. This—party you've planned is a perfect example. When you get an idea in your head there's nothing you can't do."

Mom and I worked together to finish up breakfast before the others woke up. And the whole time, her words were spinning around inside my head. Settling a part of me that'd been ruffled my whole life.

Jason was groggy as hell when I woke him up with a plate of pancakes and a glass of orange juice. We ate on our air mattress, quiet. Listening to everyone else chatter. I didn't spill my juice. Which was genuinely a miracle.

A Christmas miracle.

One of many.

We opened presents, working from oldest to youngest. Jason was super embarrassed but adorable when he realized he was third in line after my parents. His whole face was red. Nobody commented though. I kissed his shoulder as he unwrapped the present I'd gotten him—the first in his pile.

A sweater, just like the ones he always wore.

This one was blue.

"It's the same color as your eyes," I told him, pleased with myself.

"It matches your cabinets," Mom said, amused. I blinked, confused as Jason held up the fabric, smiling at it.

"No it doesn't," I replied.

"Yes it does," George piped in. "Practically a perfect match."

"Does it?" I turned to Lacey, looking for support.

"Yep."

"Oh." Now it was my turn to blush as I looked at Jason for help. He just kissed my cheek. "Did you know that?"

"That you painted your cabinets the same color as my eyes? I mean…" he shrugged. The whole room erupted into laughter. I didn't mind being the center of it. Not when Jason looked so pleased.

"I didn't bring gifts," he admitted to me as we moved down the line. "Just the wine. I…"

"Your presence is the gift," I told him.

"No, but—"

"Jason," I said quietly. "The only thing we want from you is this." I tangled his hand with mine, heart thumping when the look he gave me was equal parts baffled and sappy.

"Just this," he echoed, squeezing my hand.

"Yep."

Someone bought me a dildo. The gift was unmarked. The moment I opened the package, I choked and shut the lid before Mavis could see.

"Y'all are going to Hell," I told the whole room. The few that'd seen the gift cackled.

"What?" Mom asked. Her eyes were twinkling though. And I had the sneaking suspicion—in the most horrible, embarrassing way possible—that she knew all about it. Jason wouldn't stop laughing. Choking on it. Burying his face in my shoulder as he snorted over and over. Wheezing.

The rest of our gifts were nice things.

A new planer for me, so I could do more wood working.

A parka for Jason that matched the one I always wore, that Mom had given me.

Christmas pajamas—matching—for the both of us.

Mugs with gay cardinals on them, 'cause Mom knew how much I liked them.

I was buzzing with anticipation the whole time, eyes on the clock, just… waiting.

Waiting for it to happen.

For my surprise to come together.

To give Jason the best Christmas he'd ever had.

Around three things began to wind down. It was time. Everyone was privy to my secret, and not a single person spilled the beans. Not as Jason and I dressed in our matchy coats. Not as we said our goodbyes, and I headed out the door with him.

"You're coming home with me?" he'd asked.

"Yep."

He hadn't argued, even if he was confused. I think he was just relieved to not be alone. Which again, made my heart hurt so fucking bad.

He climbed into the driver's side after opening my door for me like a total gentleman. My cheeks were hot as I hopped inside. The doors shut. The heater kicked on.

And suddenly, just like that, we were alone.

Jason noticed, too.

He turned to look at me, heat and affection burning in his gaze as his lips curled up.

"This has been the best Christmas I've ever had," he admitted quietly. "Thank you."

He had no idea what was coming next.

And yet…already he was saying it was the best.

"I should be the one thanking you," I told him. I'd never been good at words, but I tried now. Because Jason needed to hear this.

"For what?" His brow furrowed.

"For *everything*, Jason. For showing me what Belleville could be. For being here for me. For being my friend. For changing my perspective."

"Oh." He flushed, ducking his head. "I don't…I mean. I don't think I deserve credit for all that."

"I do." I buckled up, then reached for his hand. Held it between mine.

It was cold. Clammy. Like he was nervous.

"I've been…" Jason exhaled. "I've been wanting to talk to you."

Wanting to talk to me?

About what?

Jason closed his eyes, head falling against the seat rest. He gathered strength. I frowned, confused. "I…you know how I said there was stuff I was keeping from you?"

"Yes."

"Well…" When Jason looked at me, there was no fear in his eyes. Not the way there'd used to be. Somehow, somewhere he'd stopped being scared of me. "I think I'm ready to tell you. All of it."

Across town, my surprise was waiting for him.

And yet, I didn't hesitate to nod. Everyone but him could wait.

"There's no easy way to say this," Jason started. His lip wobbled. "But I—"

"You're Santa." I put him out of his misery.

"I—what?" Jason's eyebrows shot up. His jaw fell open, shock warring across his features. "What? How did you—"

"I went to your mom's house. She gave me her son, *the benefactor's*, number. I called. You picked up."

"Oh," he breathed out. "That's why you asked me about the piano."

"Yes."

"But…" Jason shook his head, eyes storming with emotion. "Shouldn't you be angry with me? I lied. I…I lied. I tricked you. I promised you no more tricks and I still—"

"You know what I thought? When I was sitting in that big ole house, and you picked up the phone?"

"What?" Jason hung on my every word.

"I thought… Thank god. Thank god it was you. Thank god I can understand you better now. Thank god I finally get to see all of you."

"All of me…?"

"All of you." I took a breath to gather strength. "I see how you're the most giving person in the world. See *why* you're a secret pessimist. See the reason you don't understand how great you are, even though you should. I've seen the mausoleum you grew up inside and I get it now."

It was the most eloquent I'd probably ever been.

But I'd been reciting this.

Picking through it.

Sometimes even writing it down—just so I could really figure out what I wanted to say when the time finally came for Jason's lies to come to light.

"I understood why you lied," I told him. "The second I saw that place. Understood why you are the way you are. Why you became…this." My heart tripped over itself. "Guarded."

"I don't know what to say." Jason's voice was hoarse.

"Was that it?" I asked. "Your secret."

He wavered.

Now it was my turn to be surprised.

There was more?

How could there be…

"You know…the first time I saw you, it felt like I woke up," Jason admitted. "I didn't realize what it was then—that feeling I felt when I saw you. Not till later. Till I had time to pick it apart and run from it."

My brow furrowed in confusion, my heart skipping a beat.

"I told myself you couldn't want me. Not really. I mean…look at me.

Even if you forget the lies, and the fact I'm an imposter." Jason gestured toward himself. "I'm old. I've got gray in my hair. Eye bags. Pudge on my belly that I never used to have. Hair where it didn't grow before." He laughed. "I'm not...I mean..."

When I opened my mouth to speak, Jason squeezed my hand, silencing me.

"It was easy to hide behind insecurity," Jason admitted. "Easier than admitting the truth."

"The truth?"

"That I'm pretty sure we're soulmates," Jason whispered. "As silly as that sounds—someone like me, a 'closet pessimist' believing in soulmates." He laughed at himself dryly. "But I...god. Joe. I've been in love with you since the moment I set eyes on you."

My head spun in circles.

Over and over, like the day we'd danced and danced and danced till we were dizzy.

"You..."

So everything he'd done.

He'd done it while he—

"I wasn't trying to trick you," Jason whispered. "Wasn't trying to manipulate you. I just...I just...even though I didn't understand my feelings—was insecure and...and...sure I didn't stand a chance, didn't deserve you—I just wanted to help you."

He shook his head, almost angrily.

"No. No. That's...that's, I mean, not a lie. But...not the full truth either. You wanted the truth?"

"Yes."

"The truth is I would've done anything just for you to look at me. As awful as that sounds." He laughed again, but this laugh was even more sad than the last. "I'm a bad person, probably. I don't know if I'm capable of loving you the right way."

The idea that Jason thought he was a bad person made me laugh.

He startled, eyes snapping to my face, to my mouth, and the smile there. His brows knit together. "What—"

"You're *not* a bad person," I said immediately.

"But I—"

"And if you were? So what?" I twisted to look at him. "*So what?*" That was clearly not the response he'd been expecting. "You're still the person who shows up for people when they need it. The person who holds me when I need him to. Who challenges my perspective. Who listens to me. Pushes me to grow. Who showed me—despite all his own misgivings— that it was okay to rely on other people."

Tears swam in Jason's eyes.

One dashed down his cheek.

I squeezed his hand tight, and his lips tipped up.

He didn't reach up to touch the tear, though he did clutch my hand back just as tight. He was staring at me like I was the most beautiful thing he'd ever seen. He'd given me that look before. More times than I could count.

"I fell in love with you—*all* of you." Just getting those words out made me feel free in a way I never had. "You don't get to pick what parts of you I like. And what you think of yourself, doesn't change the way I think of you."

"But—"

"I *like* that you're tricky like a fox. I like your pushiness. Your goofiness. I like your gray hair. I like your wrinkles. Your eye bags. The pudge at your belly. When you're with me…life just feels…it feels *good*. I feel safe. Appreciated. You make me feel like I can let go. Loving you is *easy*."

"Easy?" Jason echoed.

My heart wobbled. I nodded. "And…I don't know why you think you're not capable of loving me like I need. Not when that's what you've already been doing the whole damn time."

Jason stared at me, something devastatingly fragile in his eyes. He closed them for a moment, savoring the words. Outside, the world was devastatingly quiet. When he opened his eyes again, the storm within them had settled.

"You said life is about choices. You said family can be chosen. *You* taught me that. And Jason…I'm choosing you," I whispered. "I choose *you*."

For a moment we sat in silence. The enormity of what we'd both just admitted settled between us. The heater continued to blast. The windows in my house had filled with silhouettes. My family being nosy, watching us, because we hadn't left when we were supposed to.

I ignored them.

I unbuckled all the way and leaned over the console to meet Jason's gaze.

"Do you choose me, too?" I asked.

Jason didn't hesitate. "Yes." He closed the distance between us. Didn't kiss me. Rubbed our noses together, breath mingling, hearts beating as one. "I don't want to fail you," he said. "So I won't."

There was a surety to his words that I'd never heard before.

"I want to keep loving you, so I will," he added. "I want to take care of you, so I'm going to."

Jason was making his choice.

Just like I had.

And it was…god.

It was beautiful.

The most beautiful thing in the world.

Prettier than sunsets, than lost magpies, than the flutter of cardinal wings. Prettier than snow so tall it blocked doorways. Than snow globes, and Christmas lights.

I think…Jason had been waiting, all this time, to realize he wasn't lost too. That he had control over his own fate. That it was okay to be uncertain. And that happiness was a choice one could make, no matter how late in life they took to make it.

thirty

JASON

MY HEAD WAS STILL SWIMMING from my confession as Joe and I got on the road. We were both aching to be alone together. To…to express the enormity of what we'd just decided physically. My skin was buzzing, my heart ten sizes too big for my chest as we drove past his orchard, past the other farm houses, and into town.

I couldn't wait to get home.

To hold him the way we both needed.

Joe was practically vibrating in his seat beside me.

Excited.

And he wasn't even drunk.

He wasn't talking, so much as he was *buzzing*. Staring out the windows, then at me, then out the windows again. He reminded me of a dog. I almost wanted to offer to roll the window down for him so he could stick his head out.

But…I wasn't in the mood to tease right now.

So instead, I brought his hand to my lips and kissed the back of it.

Joe looked at me again, his smile soft.

He really did look at ease.

And now that I knew I was the cause of that, I just…god. Again, my heart was too fucking big right now. I was pretty sure I was going to explode if he kept looking at me like that.

His eyes said, *I'm glad you see me.*

They said, *you're not alone anymore.*

They said, *I'm not scared of this.*

The funny thing? I wasn't either.

Not anymore.

I was so distracted by Joe, it took me an embarrassing amount of time to realize something was amiss. Namely, the sheer amount of cars parked on the road leading to my house. At first, I just assumed it was people gathering for Christmas. But…even then, that was a stretch.

I saw people crossing the street, and I slowed down to let them pass, perplexed.

Joe continued to vibrate.

"Was that Patrick?" I muttered, confused. "He doesn't live even close to here—" We'd passed his house on our way here. "Leanne?" I frowned. "What the…"

We kept driving.

When we rounded the corner and my house came into view, I nearly choked.

Dozens—and I mean *dozens*—of people were on the road. My baffled gaze followed the line of Bellevillians, like ants, with arms full of Tupperware. All of them…*all of them* seemed to be heading to the same destination.

My house.

What the hell?

My front yard was completely full. I swear to god, it looked like the entire population of Belleville was packed into my cul-de-sac. My heart was pounding as I gawped, open-mouthed, parked mid-road because I didn't know what to do—where to go.

"What the—"

Joe leapt out of the car without a word.

"You—" Apparently he was tired of waiting for me to find a proper parking place. Hell. Whatever. I put the car in park, yanking my keys out of the ignition. My door was pulled open a moment later, and there Joe was, cheeks flushed, eyes bright.

"Did you do this?" I asked him, sliding out of the vehicle and staring up at him perplexed. "Did you…"

"C'mon," he urged, fingers lacing with mine as he tugged me toward the crowd.

I yanked him to a stop, and he paused, those dark eyes on mine, a smile on his lips.

"Joe," I could hardly get a breath in. "What *is* this?"

"You've spent enough Christmases without family," Joe stated, using his words to emotionally eviscerate me in only the way he could. "I wasn't going to let it happen again."

For a moment, I didn't know what to say. I didn't know what to do. Didn't know how to exist in a world where someone as good, as kind, as wonderful as Joe Milton loved me. He'd told me he was good with secrets, and that had never been more apparent than it was now, staring at what had to be the most beautiful Christmas gift I'd ever received.

The truth was, I didn't know if I deserved it. I wasn't sure if I'd ever know. If it'd ever simply click.

But something told me it might.

That all I had to do was try, really *try*.

I could deserve this the same way I could choose to accept happiness. I didn't have to bend over backwards to be loved. Could exist in Joe's orbit. Could let him change me, because he already had. With every wall he eradicated so that he could be a part of my life he had shown me the way to this moment.

Shown me the way he'd promised he would.

That I was lovable.

That I was loved.

He let me see this gift for what it was.

These people, who had been my family, for who *they* were.

All my life, I'd been searching for this. The moment I understood I mattered. That I was *worthy* of the kind of love I'd seen others receive, no-strings-attached. That people would show up for me the way I showed up for them.

That I didn't have to be useful to be loved.

I'd desperately tried to prove to everyone around me that my love wasn't performative. That I wasn't like my parents. That I didn't do what I did, because I wanted accolades.

I thought I'd been unpicking their knots, learning them, figuring out where I fit.

As I stood there, staring at the friendly faces that awaited me, Joe's warmth at my side, the truth finally settled into place. They were the ones that had been unpicking me. And I was the biggest tangle of all.

With my knots undone, my yarn unraveled, suddenly, I knew.

I'd never had to prove myself to be worthy of Belleville's love.

Because some loves were unconditional.

All along, my fears had been unfounded.

Mary was at the front of the mass of people. Marybeth stood between her and Daniel, a big smile on her face. She was wearing a dress that resembled a Christmas tree, and Poncho was in her arms, ugly-beautiful as ever. Beside them, Madison was standing, a grouchy expression on her face. She hated crowds. I knew that. So it meant even more that she was here.

That she'd heeded Joe's plea.

That she'd wanted to show me that I mattered.

Madison's mother was behind her, chatting away, though it didn't appear that Madison was listening. She was too absorbed in her phone. Like usual.

The closer we came, the more people I recognized. Marty B. And his wife and kids. Sadie Collins and her army of sons. Baxter Baker, his grouchy mountain of a husband, Paxton. Both their kids. Miles and Trent were there too, as was Ben and his partner, Robin—and their kids. Mrs. Montgomery. Matilda Deed. Every single person I'd talked to at the Thanksgiving food drive this year.

And more.

Practically the whole town was there, standing on my lawn. Someone had thrown up a buffet table on my porch and it was entirely covered in snacks. Beneath it, piles and piles of presents glinted, red and green and white. So many different kinds of wrapping paper it looked like Christmas confetti. Beside the presents was a basket.

A massive basket.

Full of letters.

Hundreds of them.

"What—"

Joe tugged me toward Mary's family. The moment we were within hugging distance, Daniel yanked me in. He smushed me, and Mary crowded in beside him, patting my back. All while Joe watched.

"He's a good egg," she whispered in my ear.

"He's—"

"And so are you." She kissed my cheek, pushing me back a little so she could see my face. "Your presents from us are in the pile."

"It's a huge pile," Marybeth said, obviously jealous.

"Is it…"

"For you?" Joe's voice said from behind me. "Yeah, Jason. It is."

"All of it?"

"All of it," he confirmed.

"Miss Marybeth," I turned to her. She saluted. "I have an important mission for you."

Marybeth grinned.

I lost count of how many hugs I'd received by the end of the day. Hundreds probably, more hugs than letters. It was a whirlwind of love I never could've anticipated. Every person I'd met, every person I'd befriended over my twenty years in Belleville, all having shown up because Joe had asked.

Joe.

Who hated talking to people.

Who I'd had to coach through the necessities of marketing. Joe, who would've gladly lived the rest of his life alone in his little farmhouse with only woodland creatures for company. Joe, who got shy and awkward and—he'd…

He'd done this.

Talked to dozens and *dozens* of people he didn't know.

Because he'd wanted to *show* me.

Show me what I meant, not just to him, but to the family I'd chosen. Because he'd wanted to give me the Christmas he said I'd always deserved. Which…wasn't that just…swoony as hell? Jesus Christ.

By the time everyone left, the sun had well and truly gone down. The Miltons plus Jameses had shown up at some point, partaking in the festivities. And that had been…interesting. Not because they weren't welcome, but because I'd caught something—a whispered conversation that made things come crashing down, only to rebuild all over again.

"We're just glad we can cheer him up," Beatrice Montgomery said to Mama Milton. I was behind them. They hadn't seen me. Still teary-eyed and embarrassed by the way that I'd freaked out over the thank-you letters I'd just had the blessing of opening.

I paused.

This weird feeling in my chest that I needed to hear what came next.

"Cheer him up?" Mrs. Milton said, confused. "Why would he need cheering up?"

"He's always sad after he goes to that fancy party," Beatrice said. "Visits his mom. Sees all the other fancy-pants-rich people, then comes back to us a husk of himself for a week or two.”

“I’m not sure I follow. Other rich people?”

“Oh. You didn’t know? I just assumed, given your son is his life-partner.” Beatrice laughed. “Jason’s net worth is in the millions.”

My ears were ringing as I stared at the two of them.

“Ah.” Mrs. Milton nodded. And then. “Who made the yam casserole? It’s delightful, and I need the recipe.” I suppose it made sense she didn’t bat an eye. Her son-in-law was Alex James, after all. And his family was as prominent—maybe more prominent—than mine.

Still though.

I was in a daze as I headed toward Joe. He was easy to spot, towering over most of the crowd, his ears flushed from the chill. Half the party had moved indoors, but he hadn’t. He’d stuck by me as much as he could. But we’d gotten separated at some point between the letters and now, and as I approached I could see why.

Joe was with Patrick and Jordan.

No doubt, talking about the farm.

“I was thinking—” Patrick said. “It wouldn’t be a bad idea to—” I didn’t catch the next part, my head still spinning from what I’d just overheard. If Beatrice Montgomery knew about my financial status, did that mean… did that mean everyone did?

How?

When?

How had I not known?

The answer came to me as I reached Joe.

Because…it hadn’t mattered. I hadn’t known because it hadn’t mattered. It didn’t matter when they learned or how—because at the end of the day, no one had ever treated me any differently. Where I came from didn't impact how they viewed me.

I was still Jason.

And Belleville was still Belleville.

"Hey," I said, curling an arm around Joe's waist the moment I saw him. He twisted, raising his arm so I could settle into his side. He smiled at me, all soft-eyes and warmth. I felt better immediately, all my realizations falling to the wayside as I became drunk on the way Joe looked at me.

"Having fun?" he asked me quietly.

"Yes," I said immediately. "Best Christmas I've ever had. And I'm not just saying that."

Patrick and Jordan excused themselves with a smile, leaving Joe and I alone—but not, because we were still surrounded.

"Did I—" Joe started.

"Show me? Yeah, baby. You did."

He melted, twisting so we were chest to chest. He looked happy. Tired. No doubt, he was peopled out. He hadn't complained. Not once. Joe had to be uncomfortable. Overwhelmed. And yet…he'd pulled all of this together despite that.

For me.

God, he really did love me, didn't he?

"Thank you," I said, cupping his face in both my hands. He sagged, letting the weight of his head rest in my hands. His eyes drooped, the long day catching up to him. "Thank you, Joe."

Joe's smile was soft.

"You don't need to thank me," he said quietly.

"I'm thanking you anyway."

Joe huffed at that, but he looked pleased.

More hugs were handed out. I was practically bruised from all the love I'd received by the time the yard was empty, and the house even emptier. There were plates of treats and food populating nearly every surface in my home.

Marybeth helped me unwrap my presents, and those had places now, too. Doilies on the counter. Hand-knit sweaters on my bed. Matching ceramic cups for Joe and me that said "Joeson5ever" on them to mimic the shirt I'd yet to give him. A kindle for Joe and I to share.

The echo of my family was everywhere.

Joe followed me through the house, silent as a statue, letting me take it all in.

It felt different without bodies and voices filling every nook and cranny. And yet…

It didn't feel lonely.

"Aren't you going to head home?" I asked him. "Not that I want you to. But your family is here."

"I already told them I'm spending the night with you," Joe told me. He hadn't said a word in nearly an hour. Worded-out, I was sure.

"Good." I pulled him into the bathroom. Undressed him piece by piece, taking my time to thumb over his nipples. Kissing his belly button when I yanked his pants and boxers off. When I rose back up, he was hard, his cock poking against my belly as I worked at my own clothing.

"It's been a big day," I murmured, yanking my blue sweater over my head.

Joe nodded. He stared at my mussed hair, something tender in his eyes. The need to be taken care of rising up, even as he fought it down. Sweet baby had spent the entire holiday making sure that I felt loved. It was my turn to take care of him.

I couldn't wait.

"You know what you need?" I murmured as I yanked my pants and underwear off. Joe waited patiently for me to finish without interrupting. His eyes slid down my body though, trained on my cock. He licked his lips. "You need a nice, hot shower."

Joe's cock was hard between his legs, flushed and flexing toward me. The tip was leaking. It twitched, and I had to fight the knee-jerk reaction to reach out and stroke. I'd never get over the way he collapsed into me when I did. The way he was so eager for it. Pathetic in the hottest, most lovable way possible.

"You need pampering by your boyfriend—who loves you very much." God, just saying that out loud made me feel weightless. Admitting it. Everything out in the open. "And you need to rest."

Joe frowned at me. I had to bite back a laugh. "What?" I asked, mock concerned. "Was there something I'm missing in my plan? Something else you need?"

Joe's frown turned into a glare.

I grinned.

"Oh," I said, snapping my fingers. "Water. You probably want water. You've had to talk a lot. Is that it?"

"*Jason.*" That was a complaint if I'd ever heard one.

"Cocoa then, because it's Christmas."

"*Jason,*" Joe outright whined.

I turned the water on, waiting a beat for it to heat up as I turned back to Joe.

"*Joe,*" I chided, amusement laced in my tone. "If you want something you're going to have to ask."

He didn't appreciate that. His nostrils flared, and he grumbled at me. He obeyed though, using his body to beg, instead of his mouth. Joe stepped forward, his cock bumping against my abs, leaving a hot streak of precum in its wake.

"Oh," I said, adopting a look of mock-surprise. "Was that what's bothering you?" He nodded, hips jumping forward to outright rut. "Does my puppy need his big cock touched?"

Joe nodded rapidly.

"Or…" My hand slid around his back, feeling the muscle. "Does my puppy want…" I moved down, cupping his ass. Squeezing that thick, bouncy muscle. He whimpered. "Does my puppy need attention here?" I corrected myself as my fingers slipped inside his crease. I tapped his hole, just a reminder.

"Both," Joe whispered.

"*Both?*" I gave his hole another rub, and his knees nearly buckled. I had to grab him so he wouldn't go right to the floor. "That's a little greedy, don't you think?"

"It's Christmas," Joe complained.

"You're right," I purred, the tip of my finger tucking inside. I didn't want to hurt him. Dry was not the way to go. But this—this was just enough to show him what we both wanted. "I should be charitable, huh? Give you a present, after you gave me so many."

Joe nodded. He was outright panting now, lips parted, that glassy look in his eyes.

"Get in the shower," I commanded. "Face the wall."

He did as he was told.

The water pelted his back as I climbed in beside him—after grabbing the lube, of course. His skin was flushed from the heat. Or maybe that was from the situation itself. I wasted no time pressing against his back, kissing at the hollow of his spine as I set the lube to the side and grabbed the soap instead.

Joe flinched when my soapy hands worked over his skin. He relaxed soon enough, though. Turned to putty as his head dropped forward into the spray, and I spread suds down his arms, over his back, down his legs.

I cleaned his cock, his balls.

Soaped up his crease and kissed the skin at the top of his tailbone as I worked lower. He had to lean on the wall when I got to his feet, but didn't complain. Not once. I soaped them up too, rubbing his insoles, between his toes, and up his calves.

The muscle there was hard as a rock, covered in golden hair so see-through I felt it more than saw it. Felt the way it clung to my fingers as I ran my hands across his legs, up the sensitive skin at the inside of his knees, then his thighs.

With the soap rinsed, I parted his ass cheeks, groaning at the sight that met my eyes. Joe's hole was just as pink, just as twitchy as I remembered. It winked at me, small and shy. Eager. I bent forward, sucking a kiss around the little ring of muscle, tongue rubbing it till it kissed me back.

Joe was silent.

His legs spread a little wider, hands braced on the wall. I pulled back a second later, just to watch it twitch. God, it really was pretty. Amazing too, that something so small could fit my dick inside it.

I could still remember the last time I'd split it open. Flushed. Sloppy. Stretched wide and clinging as I pressed in, in, in. Giving in to me. *Submitting* to me.

I dropped one of his ass cheeks so I could pet over the sweet little hole in thanks. "Can't believe this tight little thing can fit me," I murmured, stroking along the golden hair that surrounded it. "So fucking cute, Joe. Such a good cunt. The best." Then I kissed it again, licked around and in till Joe pushed up onto his toes and sobbed.

He was loudest when there was something inside him.

I knew that.

But I also knew I didn't want him braining himself on the tiles or falling down. So…eating him out here wasn't going to be an option. I rose, groaning a little as my knees ached. Tile was such a bitch that way. Worth it, though. So worth it.

When I grabbed the shampoo and conditioner, Joe barely moved. Just twitched at the sound of the cap. Pavlov's dog. Thinking I was opening lube to fuck him, he spread even wider. Wide enough his legs bumped the walls.

"I'm washing your hair, sweet thing," I told him, so he wouldn't be disappointed. "First," I added. "Then I'll touch your hole. I promise." Joe nodded. Didn't fight me at all as I turned him around. I let him lean against the tile, reaching for his hair and carding my fingers through it, soaping it up.

He stared down at me, eyes blown black with lust, that dazed expression on his face that was my favorite. My favorite because it was mine, and mine alone. It meant I was doing well. Giving him someone to trust, to lean on.

Joe's eyes drifted shut, lips parted, these slow syrupy breaths escaping as I turned his hair into a foamy mess so I could prolong scratching his scalp. He loved that. Practically putty in my hands as I rubbed across his temples, behind his ears, up to the top of his head.

This was a first for him.

Just like it was a first for me.

"Forward, sweetheart," I murmured. "Eyes closed. We're going to rinse."

He did as instructed, stepping forward, his head dipping down into the spray. Suds rained down his body, over his face. I brought my hands up to protect his eyes. Joe smiled. It was a small, private thing. So small I wasn't sure it was even meant for me.

It was Joe's.

Joe's happiness.

"Conditioner," I murmured, just loud enough to be heard over the pour of the shower head. "Then I'm going to take you to bed."

"Okay," Joe breathed.

I massaged his scalp again when I conditioned it. Took my time. Enjoyed every hitch of his breath, every flutter of his lashes. Every single second. My skin felt the right size again as I cared for him. And I…

God.

I'd never loved anyone like this before.

With my whole being.

Because I *did* love him.

Loved every single little thing about him. Everything. Loved how grouchy he could be—how soft. Loved that he'd taught me not to be scared of the quiet the way I'd been before. Loved that Joe was Joe—in the Joe-est way possible.

I hurried through washing myself.

Joe didn't complain, just watched me through damp lashes as I worked suds over my own body. He'd tried to help, but I'd grabbed his wrists, squeezed them and put his hands on his thighs.

"No," I said softly. "You just relax."

So he had.

When we were both clean, I towel-dried him. Scrubbed every inch of his body, from head to toe. Kissed his hands, his feet, his knees. Kissed his hipbones, his tummy, and each delightful pec. Kissed his throat, and then his mouth, too—because how could I not? When he was swaying toward me, begging for it.

Silently.

Dark eyes trained on mine.

When I made love to him, it was slow. The kind of slow that felt like forever. Joe's knees were bunched over my elbows, his head tossed back. The wet squelch of my cock pushing inside him was as filthy as ever. Hole giving beneath every pointed thrust.

Clinging to me.

Clinging the same way his hands did. Digging into my shoulders, kneading like a cat, his head tossed back as he took every thrust because he was made to take them. Because he was made for me.

In a way, it made me sure that what I'd told him about us being soulmates was true.

Maybe sometimes it was possible to find someone who just *fit*. The kind of person who was just as interesting unraveled as they were tangled in knots. Someone who accepted you—not because of what you could do for them—but because sometimes love was just a feeling.

A feeling of ease.

Rightness.

Comfort.

Confidence.

Joe was the stability I'd always craved. Apples and sunshine. A promise that life could be good. He was the home I'd never had. The family I'd always wanted. The person who needed me just as fiercely as I needed him.

We fit.

Two mirrors reflecting each other back. Growing together. Tangling roots.

When we came, it was in tandem. Joe clenched around me, and I lost myself. Painted him inside as my head tossed back and everything I felt exploded. Only it wasn't a supernova. Wasn't violent. Wasn't scary.

Every atom in my body had been replaced. The Jason I had become was the same shape yes, but surer. Calmer. The ache of loneliness was gone.

"I love you," I told Joe as I took his mouth with my own. "I love you, Joe."

"Love you," Joe replied back, hoarse and sweet.

His hands moved then. Cupping my face. *Cradling*, not holding. Hands the size of dinner plates cupped so still, so calmly, he might as well have been a statue. Eyes regarding me with warmth I never knew could be aimed my way.

They mirrored me.

And because of that, I couldn't help but reflect.

My dad had taught me that my worth was determined by how much I gave. My mom had taught me to stop expecting people to love me the way I needed. Chauncey had taught me that my money would always affect my relationships with people. And Joe?

Well…

Joe had taught me the greatest lesson of all.

That all of those other lessons were bullshit.

That love wasn't something that had to be earned, nor could it be measured. Sometimes it was a feeling, something too strong to be put into words. Something easy. Something soft. Love could be compromise. Could be vulnerable. Could mean letting my walls down. Letting someone in and trusting them to keep my secrets safe.

Love was made up of a thousand tiny choices.

Love was finding peace in silence when you were with the right person.

Love was growing with them. Mirrored effort.

Learning that I could try.

That I could be happy.

That flaws and all, I could love and be loved, the way I'd always wanted.

And sometimes…only sometimes…love was standing inside a grocery store alley mid-June, peeping at a man cradling a magpie, and letting him change me irrevocably.

epilogue

JOE

One Year Later

"ARE YOU SURE YOU'VE GOT everything packed?" I worried, eyeing the suitcases.

"Yeah, baby." Jason was as patient as ever. "Do you want me to check again?" He had the packing list that we'd made together lying on the bed, each item crossed off.

We'd be flying to Ohio tomorrow to visit my family for Christmas. Until then, I was working through my other list—tasks I had at the farm. Stuff around the house to prepare it for us being gone for over a week.

Jason had taken over half the tasks—packing included.

He would've taken over everything, but I'd told him I could handle it.

I was…starting to think…I'd been wrong.

Over the last year it'd become more and more clear to me that he was an incredible partner. He carried me when I needed to be carried. Told me I needed to breathe when I was getting too worked up. Held me when things got to be too much.

Taught me that relying on someone else wasn't weak.

Showed me by example, every time he opened his walls, and let me in even deeper.

When I was with Jason, I didn't feel ashamed, or unsure.

He took my burdens—when I let him—and made my world a better, brighter place.

And in turn, he let me carry him when he needed to be carried.

He was my person.

"No," I shook my head. "I trust you. I'm just…"

"Anxious, I know." Jason took my head in his hands, holding me still, eyes on mine. "You know what I think you need?"

"What?"

"A night to relax."

"I can't, there's—" Jason's brow arched, and I quieted.

"I am going to take care of everything that needs to be done, like I wanted to in the first place. No arguing—" he cut me off. "Patrick knows what he's doing. Jordan told us he can handle your tasks while we're away. Mary's got all of our animals handled. Everything else is my domain, anyway."

"But what about—"

"I've got it," Jason said. "Deal?"

I sagged, nodding.

"Good boy." He kissed me softly. "Now…" Jason pulled me into the bathroom. I blinked, surprised to note the tub was already totally full. The air was steamy, bubbles piled high. "You're going to take a bath. And when you're done, you're going to come find me, and I'm going to give you something to do to occupy your mind while I finish checking us in for our flights."

I nodded.

It was so easy to melt into this. Into him. To do what he wanted me to, because I trusted he always had my best interests in mind.

Jason helped me undress, touching me more than was necessary. Enough my cock perked up. But he ignored it. Instead, he offered me his arm as I climbed into the bath. The moment my legs were enveloped in the hot liquid, I began to relax.

"There we go." Jason helped me sit down—not that I needed help—he just enjoyed when I let him take care of me. I sagged, head falling back. "Better?" He hummed, scratching through my hair.

"Yeah."

"Good." He kissed my forehead. "Now, stay there. Leave it all to me."

An hour later, when I came out, flushed from my bath, and back in that fuzzy headspace that felt like home, I found Jason sitting on the couch. He had his laptop out. The light illuminated his face as he perched it on his leg.

"Over here," he said without looking up.

I followed his command.

Before I'd come out I'd discovered that he'd laid out a pair of sweats and a t-shirt for me on our bed. My plug had been there, too. It'd been a gift on our anniversary—the day we'd met. I squirmed, just looking at it. Knowing what it meant. What he wanted.

It was stiff and unyielding, but just what I needed as I stretched myself with fingers first, then slid the tapered toy snug inside. Once full, I felt better.

More settled.

Jason had taken care of everything, just like he'd promised.

Which meant I was fully dressed and comfortable as my eyes immediately slid to the cushion he had on the floor at his feet. I shifted from foot to foot, shuddering as the plug jostled inside me, pushing right where I needed it. In the spot that made me want to fall to my knees and beg.

I was still…soft-minded as I slid to my knees on the cushion Jason had provided without a second thought, or a moment's hesitation. Jason's legs shifted wider to accommodate me, and I sighed, licking my lips as my eyes drifted to his cock.

We'd done this before.

Over a dozen times.

Other stuff, too.

There was a pretty large drawer in the closet dedicated to the toys, bondage, and puppy gear we'd gathered over the last year. Always experimenting. Always having fun. I'd enjoyed everything. Especially being tied up, forced to hold still. Forced to let Jason do whatever he wanted, as long as he wanted.

But this…

This was my favorite.

And Jason knew it.

"Good," Jason purred. "Such a good boy, baby. You look better. Do you feel better?" In contrast to his sweet words, the actions of his hands were positively filthy.

I nodded.

He shifted the laptop to the arm rest, already reaching for his belt buckle. I knew what we were about to do, this fizzle of pleasure zinging down between my legs. More than that though, I felt myself falling even deeper.

Deeper into that fuzzy-white in my head.

Jason's cock was only half hard.

Which was fine.

I'd done this before when he was fully soft and enjoyed it just as much.

"Open," he murmured, aiming his cock at my lips. I opened, shifting between his legs to take his dick inside my mouth, my throat. It was thick, hot. Pleasant as always as I gave it a needy suck and my eyes drifted shut. "Stay there," Jason commanded, one hand in my hair. "Keep it nice and warm for me, please, while I finish this."

I didn't need to reply.

So I didn't.

Instead, I let his cock thicken on my tongue, let myself drift, anchored only by his hand in my hair and the dick I held. Jason's hand carded through my hair as he worked. I could hear the tap, tap of the keys distantly.

It didn't take long for him to complete what he'd been doing.

When he did, he shifted a little, setting his laptop on the coffee table, one hand on my head to keep me still. We'd transported the table from his old house to mine when he'd moved in a few months after we'd started dating. The couch, too. His had been more comfortable than mine. We'd donated the furniture we didn't need duplicates of.

It'd been tricky, deciding whose house we were going to keep. Ultimately, we'd chosen mine. It was smaller than his had been, but closer to the orchard. And Jason had made it his mission to go on hikes in the woods with me. The hikes I'd wanted to go on when I moved here, but never managed because I was too busy.

He always got excited when we saw animals. Not the way I did—

because his attention would move to me immediately. Like he was more excited to see my reaction to them than the creature itself. He was also a horrible hiker. He hated it. I could tell. But he still bought us the fanciest hiking gear money could buy, and never complained once.

In fact, he was pretty doggedly enthusiastic about everything I liked.

Because he wanted to see me happy.

Jason didn't make me stop sucking him, even though he was done.

Instead, he picked up the TV remote and put on a show. Something mind-numbing that neither of us were paying attention to. It was just to fill the silence. So I wouldn't be embarrassed by the slurping sounds I made.

By the end of the first episode I could tell he was nearing the end of his patience. His dick was *throbbing*. Every time I swallowed, a fresh spurt of precum spilled on my tongue.

Thus far, all I'd done was hold it.

But I…

Well.

I sucked pointedly, tongue rubbing along the underside. I didn't open my eyes. Wasn't sure I was ready to be anything but Jason's cock sleeve yet. He made a sound, half growl, half whimper. His hips flexed up.

"Joe," he warned. "You were only supposed to hold it."

I sucked again, pulling off until the tip was the only thing kept between my lips. I opened my eyes, looking up at him. His cheeks were flushed bright red. The first two buttons on his shirt were undone, gray chest fur showing. Jason's nostrils flared, his hand in my hair pulling tight.

Tight enough all I could do was moan.

"Okay," he conceded. "Did you—"

I shifted my legs, pressing my ass back to jostle the plug inside me. I moaned when it moved, nudging where I needed it most.

"Oh fuck. God. Yes." Jason's hand pushed me down, forcing his hard dick into my mouth, my throat. For a second he held me there, not budging. And I watched him. Watched the way his head fell back, throat bobbing. His chest shuddered, then his head dropped down, a dopey, goofy look on his face.

Like staring at me choking on his dick was making him emotional.

I swallowed and the look bled into something far darker, more hungry. More mean.

"Off." Jason pulled my head off his dick, using my hair as a handle. The moment my mouth was empty, I missed him. He knew, somehow. Two fingers slid inside my mouth, teasing along my palate, giving me something to suck. He hooked them, using them to guide me up off my knees and on top of him.

"Hands on the back of the couch," Jason instructed, the hand in my hair gone now, sliding around my back to my ass. Through the fabric of my sweatpants he groped the shape of me. The touch pushed the plug against my prostate, and I sobbed. "Jesus, Joe. You're perfect."

He yanked my sweats down as I slurped on his fingers. His hands found the plug immediately. After giving it a few taps that made me see stars, Jason was efficient as he pulled it out, slow and easy. My hole fluttered, clenching around nothing—empty.

But not empty for long.

Because Jason notched his bare cock against my hole and used his grip on my hip to push me down. My eyes rolled back as I sank onto him, stuffed full, throbbing. I squirmed the moment his balls tapped mine. The soft skin rubbing.

"Need more lube," Jason whispered against my ear. "You're wet but not wet enough for how hard I want to fuck you." Oh god.

He dropped my hip, fumbling in the couch for the bottle of lube we kept there. His hand came back slick as I rose up, only the tip of his cock staying inside me as Jason liberally coated his dick. So much that the next slide down was so loud it made my face burn.

"There we go," he purred, petting my palate again.

I swallowed around his fingers, drool slipping down my chin as I stared at him.

"I love when you look at me like that," he growled as his hips snapped into me. "Like I'm your god. I'll never get over it." His movements were brutal. Cockhead slamming right against the spot that sent stars exploding behind my lids.

I moaned, and Jason's grin turned from sappy to sadistic.

"That feel good, baby?" he said, snapping into me again. "Fuck." Again and again. The harder he fucked me, the more sound I made. Muffled around his fingers, but still loud. Embarrassingly loud. It'd been a year of this.

A year of him playing me like a fiddle.

And I'd still never get over it.

Never stop being embarrassed by the sounds he was able to pull out of me.

Jason sank deeper into the cushions, rutting into me. My hole clenched around him, hot and wet, clinging to the shape of him as his crown popped through over and over again. He loved to do that. Pull all the way out. Just to watch my face pinch as he pushed back in.

My dick was heavy between my legs, sticking straight at him, leaving a mess on his sweater as he fucked me with a brutality that made all the anxiety in my head disappear entirely.

"I know you can come from this," Jason groaned, biting my shoulder. "I know you can—c'mon, baby. Come on my cock. Come on Daddy's—"

I came.

Made a mess of him.

Streaking his sweater, his chin. Eyes falling shut again as I howled around his fingers.

Jason came right after, filling me up. We'd discovered we preferred that. No condoms. I enjoyed the evidence of him left behind. It made my skin get hot and tight when I couldn't move without a little of his cum dribbling out.

Nothing felt like it.

Jason held me afterward. Held me till I came down from my high, my head against his chest, his fingers still inside my mouth, giving me something to do—something to hold.

"Better?" he asked, his other hand rubbing up and down my back.

I made an affirmative sound, full of him.

Full.

Content.

When he pulled his fingers free, then his cock, I scowled at him. Jason laughed. He wasted no time grabbing my discarded plug and gently fitting it against my hole till I bore down and took it inside me.

"I took care of everything," he promised me, pulling me back against his chest. He grabbed the comforter to our left, bundling it around me as I smashed him into the cushions. He didn't complain about my weight. He never did. "We're good to go tomorrow."

"Okay," I sighed, kissing his pulse point. Enjoying the prickle of his stubble. It was longer than usual. He'd told me he was debating growing a beard for the winter, and I hadn't complained. He looked sexy no matter what he did.

Jason fucked me one more time—me bent over the arm rest, him pounding into me from behind as I saw stars—before we found ourselves upstairs.

He fell asleep before I did, tuckered out by how thoroughly he'd fucked my brains out.

For a moment, I drank him in.

Ogling the way he sprawled out, drooling, still dressed in his cum-streaked sweater like he was proud of the mess he'd made me make, and I counted my lucky stars that we'd met. Quietly, sneakily, I crept into the closet. Behind my underwear, I'd stashed the ring I was planning on giving him during our time away from home.

The velvet box was familiar to the touch as I pulled it out, flipped it open, and inspected the ring like I had a hundred times since I'd bought it.

Jason's snoring stopped.

"Joe?" His voice was sleepy and confused. "Where're you?"

I fumbled with the box, trying to get it back in the drawer. I dropped it. The damn thing rolled out of the closet and into the bedroom. Fuck. Hopefully he hadn't—

"What?" Jason's voice was louder now.

I turned around slowly, cheeks flushed, shoulders up to my ears. He was out of bed. Bent over, hands picking the damn thing up. It took him a second to figure out what he was holding. When he did, he simply stared at it.

Ogled it like he'd never seen a ring before.

Then his head snapped around and his eyes were on mine.

There wasn't even a lick of the sleepy guy left. Jason was wide-fucking-awake. His eyes were alert, lips parted.

"Joe…"

"Damn it." I sighed, strolling across the carpet. I took the ring from him. "It was supposed to be more romantic than this."

"What…what was?" When I fell to my knees, Jason started hyperventilating. "What—"

"Jason." I opened the box, turning it around so he could see the simple silver band inside.

"Ohmygod." Jason's jaw fell open. "Ohmygod." Tears swam in his eyes, spilling down his cheeks. "Ohmygod."

"I was hoping you could help me with something," I said, stumbling over the proposal I'd had planned. It was supposed to be more suave than this, damn it. I'd had…god. I'd made George help me draft it up. Romantic. It was *supposed* to be romantic.

"Help you with…" Jason covered his mouth. He sobbed.

"I've been wanting to…to…" I stumbled. "I've been wanting to ask my boyfriend if he wanted to—"

"Yes." He dropped his hand. "Yes."

"You didn't let me finish."

"Joe—" Jason started. "Joe—" he tried again.

"Jason," I couldn't help but laugh. "You gotta let me finish."

"But Joe—"

"I have the whole thing planned," I complained. He tried to sober up. Tried to act serious, but he was smiling so big it took up ninety percent of his face.

"Okay, sorry. I'll let you do your thing," he promised. He mimed zipping his lips.

"Thanks." I took a steadying breath. It took the pressure off, knowing he'd already said yes. But I was determined to get this right. "Okay." I took another breath.

"You're so cute and I hope you know that," Jason gushed.

I glared at him. "Shut up."

"Shutting up!"

"Jason…" I tried again. "When we met, you were hellbound on helping me. Doggedly…uh…"

Goddammit, now I was forgetting my lines. "Doggedly pursuing me. And um. I said no a lot when you offered. So I just thought…" Now my brain was blank. "I thought maybe it would be romantic to…to ask you for help with this."

"Full circle," Jason acknowledged, voice hoarse.

"Yeah," I agreed. "Full circle."

He was smiling still. Tenderly. The affection he felt for me was so evident I'd never once doubted it. Not since we started this. He was steady. Comforting. The only thing I could truly count on. Things changed. They got hard. They evolved. But my love for Jason felt steady.

It never wavered.

"I'm…" I swallowed, my throat clicking. "This whole third-person thing George helped me write is confusing me." I shook my head. "So just…so just. Will you let me spend the rest of our lives showing you what you mean to me? Will you? Will you…be my person? Will you choose me again?"

"Yes."

Jason let me put the ring on. Let me have my moment. Let me feel as though I'd succeeded, because I had. When he pulled me into a kiss, my heart skipped and skipped and skipped. His hands curled in the back of my hair.

He held me.

Held me the way I'd held that magpie all those months ago.

And I knew, with surety, that I'd made the right choice choosing him then—choosing him now. Because Jason Harker was a good man. A good partner. Everything I'd never known I needed. He was the brightest light I'd ever encountered. I trusted him. Trusted him with every fiber of my being.

He made me unashamed to be who I was.

My perfect, wonderful tornado.

And loving him was the easiest thing I'd ever done.

The End

Jason's

Holiday-Help List

-~~Marty B. (help with lights on~~
exterior of his house)
-Mrs. Beele. help with bringing
deliveries in
-Sadie Collins (cardboard?)
-Gift-wrapping with the Smut
Club (holidate with a book and
grandkids? I think)
-Drop off packages for the Girl
Scout Group

thank you!

THANK YOU SO MUCH for reading and happy holidays to all of you! This project was genuinely such a joy to create. It was so much fun to return to Belleville and revisit a lot of our old friends, as well as bring some new ones into the mix. Joe and Jason were hard to pin down at first, but I could not be happier with who they ended up becoming at the end of the final draft.

This book taught me a lot about my own perseverance. For that, I will always be grateful. I swear I started over four different times because I knew, deep down, I needed to do these two justice and I wasn't sure who they were yet.

I know a lot of you adored the Christmas Daddies series, and I truly hope that **SNOWY SKIES** *and* *Puppy Eyes* made you smile just as much as spending time with the Montgomery brothers did. Queer joy is the best kind, especially around the holidays.

Thank you so much for all your comments, messages, and motivation. It has meant the world to me as I was creating this book to know how many of you were excited to read Jason and Joe's story.

Special thanks to Molly for making my books look like magic. To DL and

Gena for listening to all my stressed-out ramblings. To all my wonderful beta readers for keeping me sane and motivated as I wrote! I love you all to bits.

Thank you to everyone who contributed their time, energy, and love to this project; you are all my dear friends. And most of all, thank you to the reader, because without you, the creation of this story would have been meaningless. I write the words, but you are the ones who bring the story to life. Each and every one of you is priceless. Thank you for falling in love with these characters alongside me. I love all of you so much.

If you'd like to keep in touch with me and get access to exclusive mini-fics, character art, author updates, and more, you can sign up for my newsletter at **faelovesart.com/newsletter**. Or join my Facebook group, **Fae's Faves**! You can also find me on Instagram **@fae.loves.art** and on Patreon.

All shares, comments, reviews, and discussion of **SNOWY SKIES** *and* *Puppy Eyes* are encouraged and appreciated!

Happy Holidays! I'll see you in 2026.

about fae

FAE IS OBSESSED with anything romance. From a young age she realized she had a passion for falling in love over and over again. She loves to tell stories through both her art and writing. With a passion for classical monsters, meet-cutes, and contemporary romance, you can often find her with her nose stuck in a book and her pet corgi, Champa, on her lap.

She currently resides in Utah with her amazing husband and her collection of squishmallows. When you read one of her books you can expect to find love stories between humans, monsters, and loveable assholes that will make you laugh (and cry) as you get lost in their worlds for just a little. Every story comes with a happy ever after guarantee.

Find her online at:
WWW.FAELOVESART.COM